WHEN NORSE WINDS BLOW

M.R PICKBOURNE

Copyright © 2012 Margaret Rose Pickbourne. All rights reserved.
This work is registered with the UK Copyright Service
Registration No: 284660006
ISBN: 9781790338931

DEDICATION

To my dear father,
Patrick Mundie
&
Son-In-Law
Julian C. F. Hobday
"Forever in Our Thoughts"

CONTENTS

Chapter One	9
Chapter Two	43
Chapter Three	77
Chapter Four	104
Chapter Five	126
Chapter Six	158
Chapter Seven	191
Chapter Eight	216
Chapter Nine	238
Chapter Ten	272
Chapter Eleven	294

PREFACE

When my Husband and I were renovating our cottage in the Shetland Isles, to our surprise, we unearthed a large stone slab with strange markings. We were busy at the time, so we set it aside in a corner of the garden. Over the following year I found I was strangely drawn to the stone, and would feel compelled to touch it. I wondered who had carved the markings so many years before, and the reason as to why. In the months following, I began, at night, to dream of Vikings, of tragic events that had happened in their lives, of many battle scenes and raids. These dreams were so vivid I began to write them down. Having never at any time in my life ever dreamt of Vikings, I found these dreams strange, because although there is a strong element of Viking tradition on the Islands, their way of life was not something that had even passed through my waking mind.

As time went by these scraps of paper containing my dreams began to mount. One day I sat down to read what I had written, at this point I realised it was an ongoing story. I began to do some research on Vikings and was surprised to find that some of the named characters in my writings had actually existed.

One of the characters I dreamt about puzzled me. He was a dark, silent foreigner who lived with the Vikings, and I would question myself as to why such a person would be living among them. That was until we took visiting friends down to see "Jarlshof", which is the largest Viking settlement on the Islands. While strolling through the small museum on the site I happened to glance over and see a new pamphlet that had just arrived. It depicted the face of a dark foreigner. The pamphlet stated an artifact had been found on the settlement, with the portrait scribed upon it. It was not known who this person was, but it was deemed he must have been an important man to have his portrait scribed in such a way.

At that moment I felt very strange. Do stones retain memories of the past? Could it be that Vikings were much maligned and somehow their version of events had to be told? Who knows? All I know is had I consciously thought about writing a book I would have probably picked another subject, but in this instance the subject chose me, and for that there must be a reason. I finished "book one," but shortly after the dreams began again, as if to say my work was not done. The story did not end there, and will continue in "book two."

This large 6th Century stone slab is the only one known to exist with these particular markings. It now stands in the Lerwick museum encased in glass. Preserved for mankind, for eons to come.

CHAPTER ONE

Many years ago in the land of the Norsemen the harshness of winter had finally passed. In its wake came stillness, heralding the start of a newly burgeoning spring. Dawn broke, and the first whisper of light revealed a dense shroud of mist hanging low over the sea, but with the rising of the sun it slowly dispersed leaving the morning bright and clear.

Leif, deep in thought, strode purposefully in the direction of the waiting ships. The scattered drifts of grounded seaweed, blown ashore in the winter storms, crunched beneath his feet as he walked briskly along the length of the shore. Raising his head, he inhaled deeply, savouring the tangy freshness of the crisp, clean air. His spirits were lifting now they were ready to sail, and taking time to glance around his stride shortened and his steps slowed as he looked at the shimmering water quietly lapping towards the shore.

He smiled, his eyes narrowing as he scanned the vast expanse of the calm blue sea. "Yes", he murmured with a nod of satisfaction, this was a good day for what would be the start of their journey. Turning, he continued walking towards the dock and he could feel the faint warmth from the spring sun on his head as he watched his men go back and forth loading last minute supplies onto the knorr ships before they set sail.

He was aware that an air of melancholy still lingered within the settlement because his people were somewhat subdued. Like him, they had welcomed the activity in these first few weeks of spring. The winter had been hard, he thought with a sigh of resignation, it was not only he who had found the dark nights long and filled with loneliness. Everyone missed the companionship of their loved ones lost, two years past.

With these thoughts Leif's steps faltered, and once again he came to a halt. Standing there alone, on the shore, he gazed out at the softly rippling water, and he found his eyes unwittingly drawn to the array of hypnotic glints that were twinkling reflections from the bright rays of the rising sun. Slowly, in the quietness of his mind, recollection of those tragic events gradually surfaced and the noise from the bustling settlement faded as his thoughts began to drift. He frowned, and a feeling of sadness rose up from deep within, making him despair, because it seemed like only yesterday when he had stood on this same shore with the laughter of his father and the men ringing in his ears as they set sail leaving him behind.

He could remember the start of what had looked to be a promising year, and the day when he had cause to curse his unfortunate injury. An injury serious enough he knew to result in him being left behind. The debilitating ankle wound had been caused by timber dislodging and rolling as they were loading the large knorr ships with goods for trading. He had been unhappy, and more than a little angry at that time, knowing this would mean he would be forced to stay at home. Trade in those first weeks of the year was vital, and he had to resign himself to the fact they could not postpone sailing for the weeks it would take for his ankle to heal.

Their land was favoured by the Gods, providing many goods that could be used for trade. They had trees which grew in abundance, giving them a constant supply of timber needed for the construction of boats and dwellings. It was widely known their various animals produced thick fur pelts, and they were sought after for the warmth they could provide in the cold of the long winter months. These were but a few of the goods they used for barter when trading. In the summer months, when the weather was calm, their ships made many voyages in order to trade their wares. Up until those fateful events of two years ago they had sailed mainly to the countries that lay to the south. Their relationship before then with the people of those lands had been one of trade. Now, however, he grimaced as his sadness turned to anger, it was one of war.

Leif sighed, his thoughts now dwelling on that time two springs ago when he had watched the fully laden ships cast off. At the prow of one had been his father, a giant of a man, a great warrior, and a leader much loved by all who knew him. By his side had stood Jon, the eldest son of Ragnar, who was a lifelong friend and a much-valued advisor to Leif's father. The two sons, Jon and Leif, had grown up together, and had been close friends since childhood. They would normally be inseparable, as they spent most of their time in each other's company, but on this occasion Jon had opted to take Leif's place, which would have been at his father's side on that last fateful voyage.

Leif remembered how he had watched with envy as they slowly set sail. His father's ship had been in front, with Ragnar's boat following close behind. Leif had laughed at their good-humoured taunts shouted back as they sailed out to sea. He smiled to himself now, the vision was still clear in his head.

He recalled missing the camaraderie of his friends, and remembered how quickly he had become bored in their absence. Restricted in movement with his injured ankle he had spent the following weeks working on his favourite pastime, carving a new figurehead for one of the longships. Early in his childhood his father had presented him with the gift of a knife, and thus began his fascination with wood. He found he had a natural aptitude for carving shapes in discarded pieces of timber, and as he had grown his skill had quickly developed until it was matched by no other. His finely carved figureheads were much prized, and they adorned many of the longships used for war.

Working on the figurehead had helped keep his arms strong and his muscles taut, but still, with the absence of his father and Jon, and most of the men, to him the hours had been slow in passing. Nevertheless his feeling of unease had not surfaced until the warmth from the summer sun was strong, because by that time, the boats should have returned.

He had constantly watched the water for any sign of the returning ships, but their continued absence in the ever lengthening days only gave cause for his unease to increase. Finally, deciding to wait no longer, he had called together the men who, like him, had stayed behind to prepare and load more goods to use for trade.

Hurriedly rigging one of the longships, they almost had it ready to sail when they spotted one of the knorrs on the horizon. Their relief at seeing the ship, Leif remembered sadly, had been short lived. When Ragnar's boat entered the bay Leif had known immediately something was badly wrong. His heart had plummeted, and he could recall the feeling now, when he saw the body wrapped and held in Ragnar's arms. Everyone on the shore had stood frozen in shock, while looking in disbelief at the slowly approaching ship which had bodies strewn about in any space that was available.

Leif sighed deeply. That was a time of great sadness, when he had watched his people sink into despair. The women were understandably inconsolable, and some were so deep in shock they refused to accept or believe in the loss of so many of their men. His own feelings of despair however quickly turned to rage, an overwhelming helpless rage, which erupted when Ragnar told of the events leading up to the death of the men.

This was one tale that would be forever etched in the memory of his people. Ragnar and his crew had watched his father's ship sail into the port where it normally traded before their own ship carried on to a place further down the coast. Ragnar's cargo had sold to merchants the very day he had docked at the new port, and pleased at having completed his business sooner than they thought, he then sailed back to help his friend sell his.

It was not long before they were sailing into the port where Leif's father's ship should have offloaded, but it puzzled them when they could see no sign of the ship. Ragnar had decided to berth at the dock, and leaving some of the men onboard, he and the others had quickly gone ashore in search of information. They found workers who remembered seeing Leif's father and crew disembark, early on the previous day, and they pointed in the direction they had gone. These workers had stated they did not see them return to the ship, but went on to say when they arrived at work that morning, the boat had gone, and so it must have set sail in the darkness, sometime through the night.

Ragnar said on hearing this news he had become increasingly anxious, and knowing then that something was definitely amiss, he and the men had immediately set off in the direction inshore to follow the path they now knew the others had taken. They had walked for some miles and were about to give up their search, when suddenly, and inadvertently, they stumbled upon the massacred bodies of their people.

Leif remembered the tears in Ragnar's eyes as he had struggled to continue. The sight of all the dead bodies had thrown Ragnar and the men into a frenzy of despair. Leif's father lay butchered, with Jon's dead body lying close to his side, and they must have fought fiercely, for their very lives, Ragnar said almost choking with grief and anger, because bodies of men, who wore clothes adorned with a cross, were strewn all around.

He and the crew had begun to search for any survivors, and hearing a faint sound they found one of the men, barely alive, and seriously wounded, who tried, before he died, to give some account of what had happened. A messenger it seemed, Ragnar said, had appeared at the ship with an invite for everyone to attend a feast. He said his master wanted to talk of trade. Vikings, who were known for their hospitality, would at this point have had no reason to be suspicious. The dying mans words were faint, but Ragnar had understood they unknowingly, and trustingly, followed this treacherous messenger only to be led right into an ambush. They had been caught unawares, suddenly surrounded and overcome by a large band of heavily armed men.

The Vikings were hardy warriors themselves, but, as Ragnar said, being greatly outnumbered they would have had no chance without their swords and shields. Nevertheless, as far as Ragnar and the men could see, they had fought bravely with their knives and hands before succumbing, as the number of enemy bodies all around had indicated.

Ragnar told them he had pulled from the neck of one, this cross they all seemed to carry, and he had held it high for everyone to see. These barbaric cowards, who attacked and killed unarmed men, he said, had also it appeared, commandeered Leif's father's ship and all the cargo still within her.

Ragnar went on to explain how he and his crew had tried to carry back to their own ship as many of the bodies that they could. The others they regrettably had to bury, but being in a state of deep despair, and aware of the unknown dangers that could surround them, they were forced to dig quickly, and because of this, only managed to place the remaining bodies in shallow makeshift graves.

Leif could remember the feelings of overwhelming rage that had swamped his body. The gut wrenching anguish he had felt at not being at the side of his father and Jon in their hour of need was, to this day, still fresh in his mind. He had been consumed with the need to wreak revenge against those who had committed this murderous act, and word had soon spread throughout the land to all his people. Being as deeply angered as he at the deaths, they had travelled to the settlement to come to his aid. They came together, united in their grief, and while some worked at preparations for the burials, others prepared for sail his ships of war.

Leif rubbed his hand over his face when he remembered how hard it had been to bury so many from his community. A strong and deftly decorated ship was used as a burial ship for his father, to carry his body on the voyage of afterlife, where he would join with the gods in Asgard. The figurehead that Leif had worked on was attached to the head of the ship, before it was positioned facing into the sun.

His father's body had been ceremoniously carried on board, and placed carefully at the centre on top of what was the finest of furs. His magnificent sword, won in battle, and his axe with its finely decorated blade, was placed in his hands. His shield fixed on his arm. Leif, being overcome with grief, had cut off a lock of his own hair to place in his father's decaying hand, so part of him would accompany his father in the long journey that lay ahead. He could still recall the emptiness and pain when he had said his goodbyes, and the many tears which had spilled, unbidden, from his eyes. He remembered also the rage and anger which overwhelmed him, and filled his very heart, at the loss of the two men who had been the centre of his world for as long as he could remember.

Eager for revenge, they had quickly filled the ship with goods and treasures his father would need in the afterlife to come. They ensured he had a fast steed and hunting hounds, with accompanying bows and arrows, so he could continue to participate in the sport he had always loved. There was food in plenty, fine wine, and placed on a table was his favourite game with which he could pass away his time. The pieces had been carved in horn by Leif. It was a gift his father had treasured. Finally, a wooden tent was placed over the body, for shelter, and only then did the men begin to dig. They had worked in silence, continuing to dig steadfastly until the whole of the ship had been covered and interred by a large mound of earth. Leif looked over at the small hill that was now an Island of rest for his father's earthly body, but he knew his father's spirit had long since left to travel on. The hill was a monument in itself, Leif thought, to forever mark the passing of a great and much loved man.

Leif was saddened when his thoughts turned to Jon, recalling how painful it had been to say goodbye to the friend who had parted from him forever in this life. He remembered he had wanted to roar with rage, to drag Jon's dead body and somehow shake the life back into it. He had wanted Jon to smile, to speak, but it was all to no avail. He was gone, and it angered Leif to know his existence had been extinguished in such a cruel and needless way.

When all the burials and ceremonies of the dead had been completed the ships of war set sail. The women were left behind to grieve, while the men's mourning had, by necessity, been set-aside in their need for revenge. With sails hoisted high, the wind carried the boats swiftly to the lands of the south. They had gone in under cover of darkness, to search out places with the symbol of the cross, and they struck swiftly and viciously before searching for any sign of involvement in the killing of their people.

Leif and his men had shown no mercy to those who were now the enemy, and their Viking skills as warriors soon became widely known. Their belief in their own strength and ability ensured they always fought hard, and they never showed fear to any who dared stand in their path.

Their grief, at the time, had been their driving force, and they searched and carried out raids the length of the coast for what remained of that summer. Eventually however, Leif remembered the downturn in the weather had forced them to reluctantly set sail for home. Their continuous search for the boat and the barbarians who had taken it, had been fruitless; the missing ship was still to this day, nowhere to be seen.

That first winter, with the loss of so many loved ones, everyone's grief felt overwhelming and insurmountable and the whole of the settlement mourned. Memorial stones, for the warriors Ragnar had not been able to bring back, were carefully carved. These were placed next to the other graves, in order to be of some comfort to the families who had been left with no bodies to bury. To occupy everyone's mind the work was then diverted to preparing weapons, in readiness to strike at the enemy at the first break of spring.

The year now past, Leif recalled, they had set out to sea while the weather was still rough. The need for vengeance still gnawed at their innards, making them impatient to be off. Skilled sailors, their boats built to sit atop the waves, the rough weather had bothered them none, and they had made good progress. They took the enemy by surprise yet again. That year they pillaged, taking goods his people were short of because of the time they had spent at sea. They took captives to use as slaves, to do the work normally done by themselves and by the men who had died. Provisions of food and drink was also taken, to allow them to carry on raiding, instead of returning home to restock.

One of the ships they had filled with grain, animals, ale, captives and other goods. It sailed home to unload, then returned, and they refilled it each time with the pillaged goods his people would need. They spent all summer and autumn travelling the coasts. The element of surprise was maintained by moving quickly across water whilst under the cloak of darkness, and by leaving one area and going to another to attack any place marked by a cross.

His father's ship was not to be seen however, and no evidence of the goods within her was ever discovered. Leif remembered the deep resentment and dissatisfaction everyone felt at not having wreaked their revenge on those responsible for the cruel and murderous acts. However, winter weather had again set in, forcing them to sail, without delay, back to their home.

The touch on his arm brought Leif back, with a jolt, to the present. He looked with surprise down into the bright and shining eyes of Vaila. Being deep in thought he had been unaware of her approach. She smiled up at him as she swept back her fiery copper hair. "Your thoughts were miles away" she said laughingly, while holding out the box of food she had prepared for his journey. He smiled back at her fondly. "Just thinking what a good day it is for the start of our voyage," he lied, not wanting her to know of the memories that still returned to haunt him. He swept the hair gently from her face, then kissed her forehead as he took the box from her hands.

For as far back as he could remember, in the years of their youth, Vaila and he had always been friends. His love for her was a familiar love, based on the closeness of the friendship they both shared. The care and compassion she had bestowed on him since the loss of his father and Jon had brought them emotionally closer together, but recently he had become aware that, for her, friendship alone was not enough and she now wanted more. However, although he looked upon her with great affection, he had made no commitment, being more than content to let things drift in a friendship that to him was good.

He joked with her, making her laugh, and turning, they began walking together towards the berthed ships where his men, now aboard, were ready and waiting to go. He bent over to kiss Vaila's cheek, and he said his goodbyes before quickly jumping onboard to take his place at the prow of his ship. Glancing round to check everything was in order, he then looked over to Ragnar and gave a nod for the men to cast off. Leif's muscles stood out as he stretched to gather up the rope, and the sight of him made Vaila's heart ache. She watched the oarsmen start to row and the boats slowly pull away. Leif stood at the stern, his long blonde hair stirring in the breeze, and his laughing eyes seemed to shine, she thought, as he turned to her to smile and wave. As the ships drew out of the bay, Leif looked back to see Kelda, standing alone, on the hill. That was where she now seemed to spend most of her time, continuously watching and waiting. She waved, a bit crazily, at the departing ships, and Leif lifted his arm to wave back.

Kelda was to Leif's people, a seer, and her powers of healing had until recently been renowned. Her husband and two youthful sons had been part of the crew on his father's ship and their sudden loss had left her alone in her solitude, where the suffering of such sadness and overwhelming grief, had all but destroyed her. When Leif thought about Kelda's twin sons, who mirrored each other, with their golden hair and laughing smiles, his heart was heavy and he knew her pain.

Kelda, Leif thought sadly, was now going through a period of denial. She had become somewhat deranged. Not having had the twin's bodies brought back for burial, she now refused to believe her sons were dead. She had taken to watching every boat come and go, and insisted repeatedly, that his father's ship would return once more with her sons on board.

Even with these convictions, she still, nevertheless, continued to blame herself for the loss of all the men in the tragic events of that year. The fact she had not taken time to look to the oracle to foresee any possible signs of danger was, to her, unforgivable. There had seemed no need as it had only been a trading voyage, with nothing untoward expected to happen, but she now doubted her powers and felt in herself she should have been given some sign, to warn of the dangers facing the ships ahead.

No one lay blame at her door, but to this day, she had proved to be inconsolable. When she eventually came to terms with the reality of all her skills of seeing and healing being of no use to her husband and sons, her mind had slowly become confused. This had caused her to gradually withdraw into a private world of her own, a world no one else knew how to reach. She could quite often be heard chuntering away to herself as she drifted aimlessly around the settlement. At other times, she would remain silent for many a long hour, sitting hunched up, staring vacantly into the flickering flames of the glowing fire.

Leif himself however had to admit, that at certain times he was also overwhelmed with feelings that were strange. What manner of fate had deemed he would not be at his father's side, on that day of all days, he questioned of himself? Had the Gods already decided, before that time, on what his destiny was to be? He often wondered if, had he been present at the time of the attack, would it have made any difference at all, or would he too have departed this earth and journeyed with his father to Asgard? Only time would tell, he thought sighing and stretching, what the fates now had in store for him.

It was after midday when the boats finally reached the wide expanse of the deep blue sea. The ships they used for carrying cargo were large, but their square shaped sails were strengthened with reinforcing strips of cloth, to ensure when the wind was behind them they made steady progress. This was a fine day to be at sea, Leif thought, as he watched the bow cut through the water with ease, allowing the ship to gather speed. Looking round at the faces of his men, a feeling of contentment settled over him. He was pleased to see them smile once more. It was only now, he knew for certain, the decision he had taken had in fact been the right one.

Two weeks hence a messenger had arrived at the settlement, carrying a request for trade. He had come from Islands which were ruled by a Jarl called Olaf. Leif had heard his father speak of this man when relating adventures of his youth. Olaf, Leif knew, was known to travel far, to many distant lands, and it was said his trips were successful and lucrative. He had sent word that he had not long returned from one such venture and had fine wines, silks, herbs and silver to trade, in exchange for wood, furs and livestock. Some of the men however were reluctant to spend time trading. They still felt dissatisfied with the outcome of the past two years and had voiced the need to set out again with the ships of war.

Leif had thought about what they should do. They had wood and furs in plenty, and many animals they had taken in the raids that last year. A trading mission to acquire spices and silks, among other things, he thought, would not take up too much of their time. It would please the women to have these goods, and might help in some way to lift their spirits from the sadness of the past two years.

He had gathered the men around, then told them his decision was to make their first trip one of trade. It was important to keep their avenues of trade open, and this they had neglected to do over the past two years. There would be time enough in the months ahead, he had explained, to continue their raids and to search the coasts in order to recover their ship.

Leif sent the messenger back to Olaf with word of the agreement to trade. His men, with the winter now being over, were eager to be at sea, whatever the reason, so had given way and willingly set to work loading the ships with the cargo they would need for their first voyage of the year.

Over the course of the following days, the two ships continued to sail abreast of each other, and blessed with good weather, Leif watched the men begin to relax. It was clear they were enjoying the journey. Even Ragnar, Leif thought fondly, was seen to smile.

The anguish and grief Ragnar had suffered had been matched by Leif's. They both found it hard to accept the devastating loss of two men they cared so deeply about. Leif missed the close companionship of his father and also that of his lifelong friend Jon. He knew Ragnar missed them too. Leif sighed deeply; he still found it hard to believe they would never again stand by his side. All the memories of the past years, when they had played laughed and drank together, now began to cloud his brain. This pain when he reminisced was too much to bear, so he dismissed these thoughts from his head, and tried instead to concentrate on the course they would now have to follow.

He knew of these Islands belonging to Olaf. A number of times, when on trips with his father, they had glimpsed them on the horizon. However, they never had cause to visit at that time and had always passed at a distance. He would have sight of them now, he thought sadly, but unfortunately it would be in the absence of his father. Leif ran his fingers through his hair, and with a dismissive shrug he rose to his feet, shouting an order for the men to turn the sails into the wind. He could see from their position that in a few hours they should soon have sight of land.

With the wind behind the sails the boats picked up speed, swiftly travelling across the wide expanse of deep water. Within hours they were drawing close to the Islands, and as the unfamiliar land became clearly visible, Olaf's need of trade for the wood Leif's boats carried, became obvious to all.

They steered the ships towards magnificent tall, sheer, cliffs, which jutted dramatically out of the sea, and their eyes could see large numbers of gulls and various other sea birds, nestling high up on the cliff edges. These birds were soon disturbed by the approach of the boats and they flew off their perches, screeching loudly. The men looked up and watched with awe, the spectacle of birds as they circled and flocked together before swooping to dive from their great heights at the crest of the cliffs.

As they sailed closer, Leif could see clouds of drifting vapour from spray thrown up by waves that pounded and smashed continuously against jutting outcrops of rocks. He called for the men to quickly lower the ships sails, and others to hastily take to the oars. The men were glad of Leif's foresight, because all too soon they became aware of many places surrounding the cliffs where the current flowed strong, and they had to pull hard against the oars to carefully steer the boats away from the turmoil of swirling pools that could easily suck their ships into the depths.

There was a definite chill in the air surrounding these Islands. The men shivered while looking up at landscape that appeared windswept, colourless and bleak. For as far as the eye could see, large expanses of the land appeared to be barren, lacking any of the trees that grew so abundantly in their own country.

The men were unaware that, having been informed of the ships approaching, Olaf already stood on the shore watching, awaiting their arrival. His thoughts were of Leif, whose reputation did precede him. It had reached Olaf's ears, from others he had met on his travels, that Leif was truly his father's son. A good man it was said, who was as skilled a warrior as his father had been. Leif's men, unlike some, Olaf thought wryly, were known to be fiercely loyal to their leader. They would, it was said, always stand fast at their leader's side. Leif had great wealth and his practice of generosity towards his people was much discussed. Olaf had known Leif's father many years ago, and it would now be of some interest to meet the son. Raising his head he looked up to see the ships, their sails lowered and tightly furled, slowly round the steep cliffs as they entered into the shelter of the large bay.

The men continued to row, steering the large boats towards a short wooden pier, where they could see people awaiting their arrival. Some of Leif's men stood up, in readiness to cast the ropes, but their smiles were quick to fade when their eyes were suddenly caught, and held by, what was to them, a strange and unfathomable sight. It was a sight like no other, and they instantly became still.

No one noticed Olaf, a powerful figure of a man himself, who stood smiling in welcome, because all eyes were drawn to the dark apparition standing close by his side.

This image of blackness was as strange a sight as Leif and his men had ever seen. The ships drew into berth and no one spoke. Their reaction was unanimous. Both crews were immediately on their guard as their brains struggled to make sense of this strange manifestation before their eyes.

Was it real, or was it a demon, each of them puzzled? They all stared in silence at this large unmoving figure, whose skin was dark, like the very blackness of night. The hair, they could see, was shiny and thick, and it was fashioned to rise like a horse's tail, straight up from the centre of the head. The face was grim and unsmiling and the breadth, height, and stature of his form stood them in awe. He wore large pendants and arm rings of strange design, one piece shaped like the quarter moon, was strung through, and hung from a dusky ear. All eyes looked down at the extraordinary ornate swords, which were shaped in an unfamiliar curve and crossed at his waist. They took in the long, woven cloak, draped casually across the broad shoulders. The cloak, its colour being unusual with its yellow hue, looked somewhat stark against the darkness of the shadowy skin.

They all continued to watch in silence, and Olaf, concerned at the visitors' reaction, stepped forwards himself, smiling all the while, in an effort to greet and reassure them. The unsmiling demon figure however, never moved. Leif, being as mesmerised as his men at the strangeness of this sight before him, struggled to tear his eyes away, as he hesitatingly returned Olaf's greeting. The sound of Leif's voice brought the men out of shock and they shuffled to gather round him, hands on the hilts of their knives, ready to defend him if the need arose. Leif had to push his way through those who barred his way, in a move to step ashore, and the men keeping close, all tried to disembark together.

They formed a semi circle around Leif, while never for a moment taking their eyes from this strange, but unmoving, apparition. Olaf, seeing the men's reaction, took Leif by the arm and began walking with him away from the ships, towards buildings that were set well back from the shore. The men began to follow, then they saw the demon move. The men stopped, startled, their hands never leaving the hilts of their weapons. The demon stopped, staring, waiting for them to proceed. Olaf glanced back, shouting to the men to, "Come, keep up." Looking round at their leader, the men realised he was now some way in front. This prompted them to move and they began to walk quickly in order to catch up. Some of the men walked sideways, keeping a wary eye on the dark figure, now following closely behind.

Ragnar and his men however, their mood having quickly changed, kept to the rear. They were a swarthy band of seasoned warriors, ever watchful, and they now looked carefully around as they strode purposely along. The unexpected sight, of this resident demon, had left them feeling distrustful of this place and unknowing of its threats. Ragnar found, as he followed in the path of the men, he now trusted no one. They had all learned well about treachery from those fateful events of two years past. It had taught him to remain alert and on his guard. Those tragic events, from that time and on, would he knew, be forever etched in their memory.

However, Ragnar's doubts were, in this case, unfounded. Olaf led them all directly to a dwelling where, on entering, they could see long tables laid with much food and ale, in what could only be in preparation for their arrival. In the centre of the long room a glowing fire burned bright, and it cast a welcome warmth, dispelling the chill of the cold spring air. Looking round the large room they could see immediately that the people, who busied themselves here, were undisturbed by the strange demon who walked among them. Their manner towards him, the men noticed, was one of respect.

Leif and his men were directed to benches and asked if they would care to sit. Chairs were brought forward for Olaf, and for the dark figure Olaf called "Toork." Once seated, they were immediately served with a selection of fish, bread and cheeses, with milk and ale to wash them down. While they ate, Olaf calmly discussed what the weather had been like on the voyage, and he questioned how many days the journey had taken. He spoke of Leif's father, because the tale of his untimely death had been related to them by previous visitors. Olaf offered his condolences, and told them about his sadness, on hearing the news of the death of such a good man.

Toork, who was aware he was being watched by the visiting men, remained silent, as he sat at Olaf's side. Leif found his curiosity increasing in regards to this dark figure who sat in their midst. He studied him, wondering because of the creature's lack of words, if this strange apparition could indeed understand their tongue?

The men, meantime, were glad of some respite, and of the chance to satisfy their hunger, before unloading the cargo from the berthed ships. Olaf waited until they were relaxed and enjoying their food, then jovially informed them he had ordered a feast to be prepared in their honour. On hearing this news, Leif's men looked to each other and smiled. They nodded; a feast they would welcome after the boredom of being cooped up for long winter months. Olaf went on to tell them all hands had been instructed to assist in the unloading of their cargo, so the task be finished by evening. Then the feasting would begin. Leif and his men could, he went on to say, choose their goods of trade in the days that followed. "There will be time enough to reload your ships after you have enjoyed the entertainment we will provide in celebration of your visit!" he bellowed out with a grin. This was an agenda, the men, as they smiled back, were all heartily agreed on.

Some time later, rested and with hunger sated, Leif's men stood up, ready now to start work. Olaf spoke casually to Leif, "You my friend can remain here with me, and with Toork," he said with a wide grin, clapping the dark shadow on the back, "while the men work at offloading the ships." Leif smiled and turned to look at his men, but, by the expressions on their faces this was one invitation they were not comfortable with. He sensed their reluctance to leave him unprotected, in what to them, was still a strange and unknown place. He saw his men look to each other, and a few moved their shoulders and bent their heads to look at the floor. Leif glanced over to Ragnar, who stood looking back, his face grim and unsmiling. Leif hesitated momentarily, then heeding the wishes of his men, he graciously declined Olaf's offer, making some excuse of the need to oversee the unloading of the two ships himself. Leif's men knew they were perfectly capable of carrying out what was required, but in any strange place, until they were sure of its safety, they liked to keep their leader within their sight.

Leif and Ragnar stood on the short pier watching the men work at unloading the boats. The two men began to discuss the strange appearance of the dark skinned entity that Olaf called Toork. The sight of him had shocked all the men, having never before set eyes on anyone who had skin of that colour. "How did it get to be like that," questioned Ragnar? Leif shrugged his shoulders and slowly shook his head, having no answer. Ragnar knew their own skin darkened, some, when the summer sun was strong and they were out at sea. So believing the cause to be the sun Ragnar said, "In the land from where this Toork originated the sun must be strong indeed to turn skin to the colour of night. How could any being stand that amount of heat?" he remarked, in puzzlement. Leif knew no answer to that either and he said to Ragnar, "His attire is strange, along with his manner, and he seems to voice no opinion. I wonder if there are others like him, in some far off land, and if so why is he not there with his people? Why is he here with Olaf?" Both men slowly shook their heads, and their thoughts turned to that strange and distant land, whose shores they had never visited.

Later that day, when the last of the cargo had been carried ashore, the men, now sweaty from their labours, were led through the settlement to a large dwelling. It was explained this would be for their personal use for the duration of their stay. The men were pleased to see wooden beds lining the walls of the long narrow room, because this was where they would later sleep. By the sides of the beds stood urns filled with water, and cloths were provided to refresh and make good their appearance. Impressed at the extent of the hospitality on offer, they found their spirits beginning to lift. They heard the faint strains of music and a sudden burst of laughter coming from the direction of the longhouse, at the same moment, a tantalizing aroma of roasting meats wafted in on the breeze, bringing their hunger to the fore. Realizing the feasting had already begun, eager to eat and make merry, with much jostling they hurried to make themselves presentable. Before long, led by Leif and Ragnar, they were strolling towards the building where all the noise of a celebration could be heard drifting through wide open doors. They entered and found the room already partially filled, and they could see Olaf was jesting with the dark figure, who sat like a shadow close by his side. On looking up and seeing his visitors had arrived, Olaf grinned, and he bellowed out, "Welcome!" He stood, beckoning to them, calling out for them to come and sit and to partake in the feasting.

Leif walked over and found he was to be seated across from Olaf. Before he was even settled on the bench a large curved horn, filled with as fine a wine as he had tasted, was jovially shoved in his hand. A plate was placed before him, piled high, and his men, being hungry, did not stand on ceremony but also started to eat. Smiling widely, they helped themselves from the array of food spread out on the laden tables.

Leif, as he supped, suddenly became aware that the eyes of the dark and mysterious Toork, were focused solely upon him. It seemed, he thought wryly with an inward smile, that the tables had been somewhat turned. Toork had chosen to sit back, and he was now the one silently observing Leif.

However, the night progressed without incident, and with much ale and wine continuing to flow everyone relaxed. Olaf, a great storyteller, began to tell tales of happenings on his last venture. He had travelled far, to distant lands, where people had customs and a way of life, his visitors soon learned, that were strangely odd and very different from their own. Leif and his men, who always loved a good tale, listened intently. Olaf was in the middle of relating a particularly amusing incident, when Leif's head went back in laughter. This action widened his vision, and without warning he was unexpectedly distracted. His eyes were captured, and held, by the sight of a woman of such beauty that his breath caught and the laughter died in his throat.

She stood at the entrance, framed in the doorway, with one large hound at either side. Leif, not having seen her throughout the day, was surprised at her appearance, and he stared, wondering who she could be. His eyes remained fixed, his thoughts centered solely on this vision of beauty centred in the doorway.

She walked forward, entering the room, and Leif, unthinking of his actions, found himself standing. Her long flowing hair, from a middle parting, fell like a curtain of black silk reaching down to her waist. It drifted in wisps around her, and the breeze from the open door made it touch against the pale delicate skin of her lovely face. The eyes looking directly into his, were doe shaped, like deep brown pools he thought, into which a man could drown. His eyes swept slowly down her length, taking in the gentle curves of a body clothed in a finely woven red woollen tunic. The tunic was held up by two large circles of intricately worked silver, and the gleaming brooches were joined together by a central curving chain. She halted for a moment, and stood as still as he, her eyes returning his look, slowly taking in the stature of this tall, blonde, warrior at her father's table.

She suppressed a smile at the boldness of his probing blue eyes, but his look was also causing a flutter of feelings deep inside, so, with the slightest of shrugs, she pulled herself together and continued walking towards the table, struggling all the while to control her senses, which were reacting in this unfamiliar way.

Olaf appeared, and walking between them, he broke the spell. Leif had been so distracted he had been unaware of him leaving his seat. Olaf put his arm lovingly around his daughter's shoulders, and brought her forward to be introduced. Leif's stomach lurched. He felt a stirring when, for the first time, Fraida's hand touched his. Her voice in greeting was soft, like a gentle breeze he thought, and he could not tear his eyes away from her beautiful, now smiling, face. He held onto her hand longer than was acceptable, and Fraida herself made no attempt to remove it, which resulted in a faltering silence spreading throughout the crowded room. Ragnar glanced over at the now stern faces of the men before him, and feeling uneasy he sat forward. Coughing low in his throat, at the same time he gave Leif a slight nudge. It was enough to bring Leif back to the present, and to remind him of where he was. Leif quickly released Fraida's hand, and she moved away, to take her seat beside her father. This strange entity called Toork, Ragnar thought when sitting back to observe those around him, seemed to be very protective of this young beauty. Ragnar also noticed, and did not like, that Toork had looked solemnly at Leif, before placing himself firmly at Fraida's other side.

Normal talk resumed, and Ragnar began to relax, but throughout the course of the conversation he observed the mood of these people closely. One thing he did notice, was that Fraida's inquisitive eyes strayed often to Leif's, to be held there, until this Toork purposely obscured their view by leaning forward to pick up food from the middle of the table.

The feasting and merriment continued without incident, and carried on well into the night. The men began to talk of weaponry, and at this point Olaf proudly brought forth his sword. They all gathered round taking time to examine it in turn, and everyone agreed, enviously, this was a weapon supreme in its perfection. The honed blade was sleek and sharp, of a metal which shone like the hue of a new August moon. A fine crystalline pattern ran down the centre of the glistening blade, which was topped by an intricate hilt, finely decorated with gold wire. This very finest of swords was deeply inscribed, but the symbols were strange and not familiar to Leif and his men. However, the meaning of the signs was soon explained by Olaf. With pride in his voice, he stated these signs meant the Gods would protect the user. The maker of this fine sword, to the men's surprise, was Toork. This dark, silent, stranger, they could see by the exquisite workmanship, was clearly a master in the art of metalwork. Toork's own magnificent swords were strange in shape, but when offered to the men for examination, they gave further proof of the skilled workmanship. His work in the most precious of metals, showed the same perfection. The arm rings he wore, the jewellery about his person, and Fraida's tunic brooches, were all apparently fashioned by him.

Olaf's constant praise for Toork made it obvious to everyone, that he held him in high esteem. Leif began to sense a deep friendship was shared by the two men. They clearly held respect for each other, Leif thought fleetingly, but, he was puzzled, because as far as he could see, this Toork did not seem to have need of the spoken word.

Leaf's thoughts however were soon otherwise occupied, just as they had been throughout the course of the night, often distracted from the conversation because his eyes, almost of their own volition, continued to stray to Fraida. When she spoke, he found himself watching her lips, lips that he had the strongest urge to cover with his own. His immediate attraction to her was at odds with anything he had experienced before, but there was no denying, when his gaze settled upon her, unfamiliar feelings stirred within him. Her beauty was captivating, and glancing once more over her way, he found these feelings increasingly harder to ignore.

Olaf, her father, who sat across the table from Leif, was also distracted, lost in thoughts of his own. He had observed his daughter's unexpected reaction to this man sitting opposite, and it had come as somewhat of a surprise. Olaf was puzzled, because these were reactions she had never before shown to any other. He had allowed his daughter a free hand to choose whomsoever she willed, and many had asked for her hand. Some were suitable, and some were not, he thought wryly, but she had shown no interest in any. He studied Leif somewhat surreptitiously, and thoughts began to form in his head. Could this be a man most worthy of his treasured daughter, he wondered? He knew in himself, that he, and almost certainly Toork, would be loath to part with Fraida, but she was a free woman, who definitely, he thought fondly with an inward smile, had a mind and will of her own.

Olaf found himself quickly surfacing from his reflections, as the subject of his thoughts stood up to take her leave. The two large hounds immediately stirred, and arching their backs, they stretched their long legs, before lopping over to stand at Fraida's side. Toork rose from his seat, and he stood for a second looking directly at Leif, before turning to escort Fraida from the longhouse. Toork had not uttered a single word, but the intense look left Leif with a feeling that he had just been warned off. However before Leif could digest this further, Olaf, who had been waiting his chance, lent forward. He held back until the couple had made their departure, then hurriedly told Leif and his men to gather round; telling them if they were quick, he would at last begin to satisfy their curiosity by quickly relating the story of how this dark stranger came to be living with Olaf and his people, here, in a land that was so different from his own.

Without hesitation, Olaf began. On one of his ventures a number of years ago Olaf said hurriedly, and in almost a whisper, as Leif and the men eagerly crouched forward. In a far off dust riven land, he had learned of the existence of a nomadic tribe, who were, at certain times, willing to do trade. A barbaric and untrustworthy lot, they were rumoured to be, he said, somewhat menacingly, but he knew they had many treasures worth having. He was told they were in the area and open to trade. Nevertheless, he said, to a now captive audience, he had at that time travelled with most of his well-armed men, as protection against these unknown, and very unpredictable, ill bred people, he stressed, raising his voice.

Olaf paused, then continued. After what turned out to be a relatively short, but uneventful journey, they eventually reached this outlying camp. However, once there, much to their disgust, he said with a grimace, just as he and his men began negotiating trade they suddenly became aware of a dark figure, restrained and imprisoned, in a roughly built wooden cage. A strange noise seemed to be emitting from this pitiful creature, and his low moans of pain had somewhat curdled the stomachs of himself and that of his men. Half alive, and covered in sores and blood, the figure, they could see, seemed to drift in and out of consciousness. What manner of people could treat a fellow human like this? Olaf, as he shook his head, asked of his audience.

Leif's men looked at each other and shrugged, and Olaf continued. However, worse was to come, he carried on to say, because one of the barbarians then showed them the tongue of the ill-fated creature, which he had hung round his neck like a trophy! Leif's men grimaced, and Olaf slowly nodded, then he said, it was at this point that he and his men, being horrified, had suddenly been overcome with pity for the creature. They found themselves unable to walk away from the inhumane sight before their eyes. By the look of him, they thought, death would not have been long in coming. Better he died in peace with them, his men had whispered to him; than leave him to the mercy of these unfeeling animals. So Olaf, who had agreed, had bought him, much to the amusement and laughter from these tribesmen, who themselves were convinced that the creature was indeed, nearing death.

The last laugh however proved to be that of Olaf's, he said sitting back with a smug smile. As they themselves could plainly see, he said, spreading his arms in an encompassing gesture, Toork, with his inner strength, had not in fact died, but survived, and was now Olaf's much treasured friend and protector! Olaf laughed and raised his voice as he stated, he now blessed the day fate led him to that camp, as the destiny of Toork, from that time and beyond, proved to be, till this day, entwined with that of his own.

The men grew quiet, now understanding the awful cause of the silence from the mysterious Toork, and when the subject of the conversation again appeared, Leif watched him as he strode across the room. This man must be strong indeed to survive such unbelievable horrors, Leif thought to himself. Toork and Olaf together, he was beginning to think, as he studied both men, were a powerful force no man would be wise to challenge.

Later, after excusing himself as being tired, Leif left the longhouse. He lay down on the bed that had been provided, but he could not stop his thoughts from straying to Fraida. For him, the light had gone out of the evening when she had excused herself and left their company. What had come over him he wondered? He felt a slight twinge of guilt when he thought of Vaila, and he questioned of himself, if this could be why he had held back from taking their relationship a step further.

When his eyes had first settled upon Fraida, her beauty had overwhelmed him. Those almost instantaneous feelings were unlike anything he had ever experienced before. He was captivated by her smile, and he could not help himself as he was drawn, without resistance, under her spell. He began to question, as he lay there, if fate, like with Olaf and Toork, could have had a hand in this? The gods must surely have steered his course this day, on this voyage of destiny, he thought yawning tiredly. He wondered was it to be that the fates of himself and Fraida were to be forever, he hoped with a smile, lovingly entwined? With these thoughts in mind, he rolled over, and pulling the furs over his body, he closed his eyes to give way to sleep.

The next morning, Leif and Ragnar went for a stroll, to stretch their legs before rejoining the others, who had stayed at the feast throughout the night. Ragnar wanted to use the walk to advise Leif to reign in his youthful exuberance; so he began by saying casually as they strolled along" I want you to be careful". Leif, in puzzlement, turned his head to look questioningly at Ragnar. Ragnar continued "Remember it is not just some wench who smiles at you, but that, it is in fact, Olaf's daughter." Leif's steps faltered, and coming to a halt he said to Ragnar with a grin, "You noticed?" Ragnar raised his eyebrows and retorted somewhat wryly in reply "Everyone noticed". Leif smiled "She is a true beauty though Ragnar, even you must agree," then laughing at the expression on Ragnar's face, he said slowly, "and had I known of her existence I might have made some excuse to visit these Islands before now." Ragnar gave a loud exasperated sigh, and said, as they carried on walking," Just as well you didn't know then, because many have tried for her hand, this I know, but none have been deemed suitable. When it comes to his daughter, Olaf can be highly unpredictable," he said ruefully, shaking his head. "And that's not all, I have noticed the dark warrior guards her possessively, at all times.""Mm... that I did notice," said Leif thoughtfully with a nod, "and that could be a problem." Ragnar stopped. He looked at Leif with an expression of astonishment on his face, before sternly saying, "Have you been listening to a word that I have said?" Then, as Leif just stood there grinning, Ragnar said urgently to him, "Don't start anything you can't finish Leif, and remember where you are." "Oh, I know exactly where I am," said Leif, still grinning. "You know me, I never start anything that I can't finish." Ragnar, further exasperated, threw his hands up frustratingly, and he said, "That's exactly what I am afraid of!" but before he could voice more of his opinion, the subject of their conversation suddenly came into view.

At his second sight of her, Leif could see she was even more beautiful in the light of day. The two hounds walked one at each side, and with their long legs they reached almost to her waist. She looked around, searching for him, and a small smile appeared on her lips as her eyes found his. Leif felt that lurch in his innards again, and he watched her closely, as she turned to make her way over to where they stood. Today, she wore a decorative band around her forehead, of a colour that matched with her cloak. Her various armbands of silver, which differed in design, glistened in the sun as she casually walked towards them.

To Leif's frustration, before Fraida had a chance to reach them Olaf came into view, with his shadow Toork, following close behind. Fraida stopped and waited until the two men joined her. Ragnar and Leif continued strolling towards them and greetings were exchanged. Olaf smiled and asked if they were well rested after the feasting of the night before. Leif remained silent and let Ragnar answer. He, in himself, did not feel well rested. His night had been full of dreams of the woman who now stood by their side.

Olaf hooked his arm round his daughter and beckoned for them to follow, leading the way to the longhouse, where the feasting still continued. Leif positioned himself as near as he could across from Fraida, and took every opportunity to glance, somewhat casually, over at her face. On several occasions she raised her eyebrows slightly and gave a small smile, but he could also see the twinkle as she teased him with her lovely eyes. He struggled hard not to grin, and kept his face impassive; being well aware the eyes of Toork were often upon him. Fraida also knew Leif faced both her father and Toork, and her expressions became bolder, in an effort to make him react. This intimate game continued throughout the day, and Leif heard little of the stories, told for entertainment. He pretended he was listening by the odd mutter and grin, and Fraida did the same, but their emotions were totally wrapped up in the actions of the other.

It was late afternoon when Fraida stood up to leave. While she was gone all Leif could think about was where she might be, and would she rejoin their company. His thoughts drifted until she returned, and then, for the first time, he smiled at her fully, before casually glancing away. Entertainment began, but for Leif and Fraida the night continued as the day. All Leif could think of was a way in which he could get her alone.

Fraida stayed in the company for as long as she could, but there came a time when she knew she had to leave. She stood up, reluctantly, to say goodnight. As ever the two hounds stirred and Toork rose to accompany her. She gave the slightest of shrugs to Leif, before taking her leave. Leif stayed on, but he found any enjoyment gained from the evening, ended when Fraida left. He participated in the conversation for a few hours more, for appearances only, then, he too left to retire.

Leif lay on his bed and sleep evaded him. He thought of this woman, who he had only just met, but already he knew he wanted her. He also knew, he didn't just want her for a night, or for a day, but that he wanted to own her, to possess her; for her to walk by his side as his wife. He knew they could only stay another day, two at the most, before they had to set sail for home. She lived too far away for any normal courtship, and his time would be taken up sailing south, to recover his father's ship. How would Olaf react, if he asked for her hand in marriage, this soon after meeting her? Eventually, he found himself giving into sleep, because he could find no answer.

The following morning Leif, Ragnar and the men gathered together. They sat down to eat and soon began to discuss what the day would hold. It was not long before it was decided, and agreed, they would complete their trading first, then reload their ships, before returning to carry on with the feasting. That would ensure they were ready to sail on the early morning tide of the following day. Leif kept silent. He yawned and stretched. He was still tired from his lack of sleep the night before. He knew he wanted to stay on this Island for a few days more, but he could find no excuse to give to the men. He had spent a restless night and his dreams had all been of Fraida. He needed more time to spend in her company. He wanted her, of that he was sure; but he needed time to plan what he should do, in order to achieve his aim. Leif heard Ragnar call out a greeting, and he looked up to see the woman who filled his thoughts ,walking towards them, but she was accompanied by Olaf and Toork. He waited until Olaf and Toork's attention was taken up by Ragnar, then slowly, and sensually, he looked down the length of Fraida; playing her at her own game. When his eyes returned to her face, she was blushing. Raising his eyebrows he smiled wryly, before turning his attention to the group of men who now stood at his side.

On hearing the men's request, Olaf jovially led them to a large goods shed at the centre of the settlement. When the doors were opened, they could see it was packed full of many exotic wares. Leif and his men looked up in appreciation at barrels of fine wine, stacked roof high. Next to these barrels, they could see many boxes containing different kinds of spices. As they looked further, they saw rolls of silk lining another wall, of such unusual but beautiful colours, they looked like they must have been plucked from the very rainbows that arched gracefully across a grey and misty sky. Much prized blocks of silver and gold, which could be used to make some fine jewellery, were stacked in a corner. Fraida, knowing some of what womenfolk would use, drew the men's attention to various plants and herbs. She urged them to take these for the women. The names of madder, woad, and weld, were strange to their ears, but she explained how they could be used to produce the bright colours of the woven cloaks and tunics they now saw around them. She herself, had learned of their use from Toork, and she passed her time weaving the splendid cloaks they now wore.

The men took time to look closely at the many wares being offered as trade, and they spent some hours carefully choosing the goods and gifts they thought their people would most like to acquire. Fraida used this opportunity to brush against Leif, and this she did on a number of occasions. Leif felt like his insides were on fire, and he knew that had it been any other woman; he would have thrown caution to the wind and trapped her in his arms. Fraida could sense the effect she was having on him, and Leif looked her over, slowly, when he heard her giggle quietly to herself.

Eventually, each of the men having had an input as to what was chosen, they sat back, taking stock, pleased and satisfied with all the exotic merchandise they now had to take back to the women. Olaf smiled as he looked at the traders. He was glad to see everyone was happy. He explained that, although they possessed an abundance of these fine wares, their settlement suffered because of the lack of trees on their land, and it made their basic need for wood an urgent one. As he stood there, he then thought to himself this was a fine time to request further trade; so turning, he asked Leif if he would be prepared to trade another few shiploads of the sturdy timber. Leif, who was at that moment distracted because his thoughts were on Fraida, inadvertently said out loud, the thought that was in his head. His eyes never strayed from Fraida as he said, "I will exchange boatloads, and more, for the hand of your Daughter." Leif heard Fraida give a small gasp and he smiled to himself as her eyes widened, ever so slightly.

Everyone was stunned at this unexpected statement. After a few seconds, when it had sunk in what Leif had just said, the smile slowly left Olaf's face. He looked over at Leif in surprise, and the sudden silence that ensued, became somewhat ominous. Leif's own men, in shock, turned to stare at him. The look on their startled faces questioning, had he gone mad? Toork stood up and his face was like thunder. He moved his hand to his sword, but Fraida stopped him by putting her hand over his. No one uttered a word and the air quickly filled with tension. Olaf looked at his daughter and something passed between them, then he laughed out loud as he said to Leif, "You've got courage, I'll give you that." Leif's men however, thought differently. They thought he'd lost his mind! They looked at him in shock, wondering at his behavior. After the passing of what seemed like minutes, everyone found themselves sighing with relief when Olaf again laughed and said, "but my daughter is not for sale, she does as she will."

Toork however, was not so forgiving, and by the look on his face he was, unlike Olaf, definitely not amused. He glared defiantly at Leif, before possessively taking Fraida firmly by the hand. With one last look at Leif, he swirled angrily, and pulling Fraida behind him, he quickly lead her away. She did, however, turn her head once to look back at Leif, and raising her eyebrows she gave him a small smile. Ragnar, who stood by Leif's side, found himself greatly relieved things had not got out of hand. At the first opportunity he dug Leif in the ribs, whispering fiercely to him, "In Odin's name what possesses you?" "She does," replied Leif quietly, and as Ragnar looked at him in dismay, Leif said determinedly," I mean to have her."

Trading over, the men worked steadily at storing the cargo aboard the ships. All the while, they kept glancing over at their leader, wondering what he was about. Leif kept silent, choosing not to speak his thoughts at that time. He waited with his men until the ships had been made ready to sail on the early morning tide of the following day; then they returned to the feasting. They found Fraida herself was already present, this time placed on a seat between her father and Toork. She was now in a position to watch Leif as he walked through the door. She smiled to herself, recalling what was said earlier in the day. Strange feelings stirred within her when she looked at him. His strong face and laughing eyes teased at her senses. When they had been introduced two days before, she had experienced a strange urge to step into his arms. No one had affected her like this before. The need to know more about him was uppermost in her mind. Her father had already informed her about Leif's reputation as a warrior, but what she really wanted to know was, what he was like as a man?

The feasting, once again, carried on late into the night. Leif sat as close as he could get to Fraida, but it wasn't close enough. Toork, now being aware of Leif's interest, continually tried throughout the night to intimidate him with the fiercest of looks and expressions. Leif was unaffected. The more annoyed this Toork became, the nearer to Fraida Leif would go. Leif feared no man. He thought if his skill as a warrior could not win the hand of this vision of beauty, then he would not be worthy of it.

Fraida watched, with concern, the effect the two men had on each other. It had not gone beyond the notice of Leif's men either. They were now beginning to feel tense and uncomfortable. Knowing Leif would not back down, they were on edge ready to defend their leader if the need arose. Fraida knew she had to do something before the situation got out of hand. The next time Leif looked in her direction, her eyes caught his. She then moved her head very slightly to the right. He slowly turned to look, then brought his eyes back to her. She gave a slight nod, then moving her eyes and head to the right again, she saw by his look that he now understood. Leif waited. He remained seated until some minutes had passed, then rose to his feet. Muttering something under his breath, he began walking innocently away from the tables, making it seem his departure was solely for the reason of going outside to relieve himself. He went beyond the central circle of light, just far enough into the darkness to where he knew he could not be seen, and that was where he waited.

Fraida sat on, and then excused herself as being tired. She stood up, as if to go, and the dogs, never far from her side, stirred, in order to accompany her. Toork was not easily fooled. He stood up just as Fraida started to walk away from the table. Olaf, however, quickly grasped him by the arm and bade him sit. The events of the evening had not passed over his head. "His brazenness," he whispered to Toork, "shows he has courage. He is a true warrior, and he has wealth, so he could be worthy of her hand. Let us wait and see what Fraida makes of him."

The grim look on Toork's face showed he was not pleased, but minutes later his expression changed and he folded his arms and sat back. The beginnings of a faint smile crept over his face. The dogs accompanied Fraida, Toork thought, somewhat relieved; so he knew for certain no man would touch her this night.

Fraida, on leaving the longhouse, knowing she was still in sight of the others, had set off walking in the direction of her home. She walked deeper into the darkness, and at a point where she knew she could no longer be seen, she doubled back to meet up with Leif. When she found him, he eagerly reached over to take her hand. Dalgar, however, Fraida's male hound, emitted a long low growl, from deep in his throat. Fraida, in her sternest voice, whispered to the dog to be silent, and Leif quickly leaned over to try again. This time Dalgar stepped forward menacingly, and baring his teeth, he snarled at this stranger who tried to touch his mistress. Leif, although he was annoyed, stepped back, because he knew the noise from the dog could easily give them away. Leif looked over at

Fraida, but she just shrugged her shoulders and shook her head, because she was unable to keep the guarding dog quiet. Turning, they began to walk further away from the dwellings to go deeper into the darkness.

At first, they kept slightly apart, to ensure the dogs following in their path would remain silent. Leif, then made a few moves in an effort to get closer to Fraida, but Dalgar would always bark, which frustrated Leif, forcing him to keep his distance. They carried on walking, and eventually, Fraida led them to a place where large stones lay scattered in a small field. Fraida sat down on one of the sprawling rocks and Leif quickly joined her. Dalgar immediately bared his teeth, and barking ferociously he forced Leif to move. Fraida, to her consternation, found nothing she said or did would control the dog. The only way to keep him from barking was, apparently, for them to remain at arms length.

Leif was frustrated at this situation, but Fraida just laughed. She felt a little shy of Leif, unsure of how to act, because this situation was new to her. She was content to just sit and talk. Knowing they did not have much time, she wanted to learn as much as she could about him before they had to part. Fraida's curiosity led her to ask about Leif's people. How they lived, and if their customs were similar to her own. Talk between them began to flow and they found they conversed with ease in the absence of others.

Leif watched Fraida, enjoying the fact he could at least listen to her speak. He relished every word that passed her lips. Lips, that if it wasn't for these damn dogs, he thought in frustration, he would now be covering with his own. Lost as they were in each other, time flew by. All too soon daylight crept in with the dawn. Fraida said she really had to go. Leif knew that he would also have to make a move, as very shortly his men would be ready to set sail. They lingered, both feeling reluctant to part. They stood up. Leif began to assure Fraida he would soon return, to bring more of the wood her father had requested. They stood facing each other in silence, and Leif's thoughts raced. He felt he could not leave when matters had not been settled. Deciding to throw caution to the wind, he told Fraida what he had in mind, with regards to her, eager to see if she felt the same.

Leif spoke softly as he said, "You do know the amount of cargo your father has requested is more than enough to ensure a number of trips?" Fraida smiled and nodded. Then, after hesitating for a few seconds more, Leif said brazenly and with a smile, "In the space of that time, I hope to persuade Olaf, your father, to allow our marriage to take place."

Confused and a little embarrassed at his boldness, Fraida burst into laughter. Then, still smiling widely, she raised her eyebrows. Looking directly at him she said "The decision is not my father's alone," and with a twinkle in her eye continued, "so, we will see what the future brings." Leif laughed at this coyness. Irrespective of the dogs, he again tried to attempt a quick kiss before parting. This time Dalgar flew at him, and taking him off guard the large hound managed to knock him over.

Fraida could not help but laugh at the sight of Leif sprawled on the ground. Trying to control the laughter in her voice, she called the dog sharply to heel. It was growing ever lighter and she knew she really had to go. Still smiling at the sight of Leif on the ground, she turned, and with a fleeting wave hastily set off in the direction of her home. Leif watched her departure with some regret. He watched her run, her long hair and cloak billowed out behind her in the wind, and the two hounds, Dalgar and Volga, gracefully bounded along at her side.

The silence of early morning was only broken by the noise of the men calling to each other as they cast off. Ragnar looked pointedly over at Leif. They had all noted his absence in the hours before dawn. Leif, who had a heavy head through lack of sleep, ignored Ragnar's unspoken question. The oarsmen smiled at each other, then began to row. As the boats drew out of the bay Leif heard a bark. He looked up, and there on the headland stood Fraida. She was wrapped in her cloak, both dogs at her side. She waved. He made his way to the stern of the ship and stood watching until she faded from view. Damn those dogs, he thought some time later, and pulling at a blanket he settled himself down to sleep.

Leif slept away the first day at sea. But come evening, he was awake. As he hungrily ate his supper the men began to laugh and taunt him about the new love in his life. "There are some at home who will not be pleased with this news," they said jokingly. Leif began to smile. "I am my own man," he said continuing to chew on his bread; but they all knew of whom they spoke. Leif had made no promise or commitment, but he was well aware of Vaila's hopes, and did not relish the thought of hurting her. She was a friend who he had a deep fondness for, but Fraida he would die for. He was himself surprised at the depth of feeling he now had for this woman, who, until a few days ago, he was not even aware existed. This turn of events would indeed, he thought, be hard to explain to Vaila.

On the return journey the wind was up, the ships, with their large sails billowing, skimmed quickly across the water, making good speed. Being relieved of their heavy load made the ships lighter, this shortened considerably the length of time taken on the voyage home.

As the boats sailed closer to land and the shoreline was within sight, the men were surprised to see the longships they used for war, prepared for sail and berthed at the pier. They could also, because of her agitated actions, not help but see Kelda, who by now was a familiar sight up on the hill, as she watched for the ships return. The men waved to her and she jumped and waved excitedly, if not a bit crazily, back. Making everything seem normal, Leif thought, by her abnormal state!

Reaching the docks, they rowed alongside, and some of the men waiting on shore quickly grabbed the ropes as they were thrown from the ships, and fastened them tight to the pier. The gangplanks were put across and a couple of the men boarded to speak with Leif. Ragnar jumped over onto Leif's ship to join them.

"Word has come of a sighting of your father's ship," one of the men said quietly but urgently to Leif. "It was seen sailing near the coast of the lands to the south." Just hearing this news was enough to set off the anger within Leif, and raising his eyebrows he looked over at Ragnar. The men explained they had kept it quiet, not wanting the women to hear of it in case it brought their grief to the fore. However, they said, still talking in a low voice, in Leif's absence a unanimous decision had been taken. They had prepared the longships ready for departure, for when he and the men returned. Leif praised the men for their quick thinking. "You have done well," he said, clapping one on the back. "Time, we all know, is an important factor. With the ships almost ready we will need but a couple of days to get our personal belongings together, and to allow for rest, then we will be ready to set sail again." Ragnar's face was grim, but he nodded and agreed.

By the time they stepped ashore Kelda was down from the hill. She darted between the men, still looking and hoping for sight of her two golden haired sons. Leif approached her. On gaining her attention, he managed to keep her still for the time it took to enable him to place a fine woven cloak around her shoulders. Then he put a soft woven blanket in her arms. These were some of the gifts he had chosen with her in mind.

Fate had, unfortunately, dealt Kelda such a blow that Leif knew she had little, or no, pleasure left in life. She looked up at Leif and suddenly gave him one of her rare smiles. For an instant her mind seemed to clear, but it hurt Leif to see the haunting look of pain in her tired and weary eyes. Leif put his arms around her and managed to give her a small hug of comfort before she shrugged and moved away. He stood watching with some concern as, muttering dolefully, she hurried off to make her way back to her dwelling up on the hill.

All the men helped to offload the ships. The cargo was carted up to the central storehouse where the women had, in anticipation, quickly gathered. They were now huddled together happily examining all the fine wares. Many exclaimed in delight at these new silks with their beautiful and unusual colours. Vaila however, remained silent. She stood apart from the group of chattering women. Her mind was elsewhere, lost in deep thoughts of her own.

For her, some of the delight had been taken out of the joy at seeing Leif return. Earlier she had stood alongside the people who were patiently waiting for the men to come ashore. At any other time Leif's eyes would seek her out, acknowledging her with a wave and a smile. But this time, he had stepped onto the dock, and no matter how she tried she had been unable to catch his eye. She was beginning to feel he was avoiding looking her way.

Eventually though, he had finally approached her. She had been happy to see he had brought her a beautiful cloak, like Kelda's, but as he placed it around her shoulders, she noticed she received no hug. He had smiled, but knowing him as she did, she saw immediately that the smile did not reach his eyes. She had felt uneasy, sensing as only a woman can, that something had inexplicably changed. Nevertheless, she had stretched up to kiss him, but he had held back, then joked with her as she questioned it. He had shrugged and walked away from her laughing, calling as he did for wine to be drunk that night, in celebration of their return. Something was wrong, Vaila thought worriedly, but no matter how she tried, she could not think of what it might be.

That evening, Vaila watched Leif as he sat feasting with the men. She began to feel anxious, as again, she sensed he seemed to be avoiding her. However, her fears were soon dampened when later into the night, after much drinking; Leif came to seek her out. He smiled as he put his arm around her, drawing her away from the crowd. He walked with her outside, to a place where they could be alone.

Vaila stood before Leif with a feeling of rising excitement. She watched as he took from his pouch a beautiful arm ring, made of shining gold. Its design was of two horse's heads, their noses touching where it closed on the wrist. The horse's deep inset eyes were glittering gems of green. A colour that matched well with her own. Her heart lifted, thinking her feelings for once had been so wrong. However, that lasted only for the few seconds it took to look up into his blank expressionless face.

The pained look in his unsmiling eyes caused her heart to drop, it seemed, into the very pit of her stomach, and her grateful smile faltered and froze on her lips. Leif began to speak, and with his words her face slowly crumpled. Although she bit her lip and struggled hard, it did not stop her eyes from filling, or the tears from spilling down her ashen face.

She listened, unwillingly, to words that she did not want to hear. All the time keeping her head bent, unable to trust herself to reply. His words caused her heart to scream out in pain, and anger, but the only sound Leif could hear, was the sobs she tried so hard to stifle. Leif, not liking to see her pain, tried to explain to her, in as gentle a way as he could, what changes there now had to be in their situation. For him, it was a difficult task. But eventually, when he thought she understood where his feelings now lay, his words trailed off and he became quiet.

Leif waited for Vaila's reaction, but she did not move. So putting his arms around her, he hugged her close. Kissing her softly on her forehead, he gently placed his gift of friendship into her cold, trembling, hand. Only then, did Vaila raise her head and look him squarely in the face. Her lovely green eyes were still awash with unshed tears, and she found, as the sobs welled up in her throat, that she could not speak. Instead, she instinctively lifted her hand and drawing it back, she hurled the gift as far as she could, out into the dark beyond. She said nothing, but let her actions speak for her. Turning her back on him, she left him standing watching, as head held high, she proudly walked away.

Two days later Vaila stood quietly, behind the people, watching the warships make ready to sail. It was a sight impressive to behold. Large wooden shields, their rivets gleaming in the sunlight, ran the full length, both sides, of the longships. The ornately carved dragon heads stood erect at the prows, like fierce sea serpents rising from the waves to strike at their enemy's ships. The men's thick leather helmets, were in part, overlaid and gilded with shining silver; reflecting the bright rays of the rising sun. Wrought silver eye pieces lay flat against the sides of Leif's helmet. In battle they swung round to meet the attached leather nosepiece, which was pointed like an arrow and studded with silver. This gave him a slight advantage in battle, when sunlight was reflected into his enemy's eyes.

Vaila's heart was heavy. Her eyes misted over as she watched this man she had loved for so long. His broad, trusty sword, was slung from a deftly patterned leather baldric, which carried over the left shoulder, crossing to the scabbard at his opposite hip. The axe, positioned at his waist, was impressive in its decoration, and was gleaming and sharp. Hanging from his tanned and muscular neck, was a much-treasured gift from his father. A large silver pendant in the shape of the hammer of Thor. This pendant had been designed to be worn in battle. The magic properties were known to always give the wearer protection of the gods. Vaila watched Leif move to board the boat. The strong muscles of his tanned legs showed above the straps of his knee length fur boots, as he quickly stepped aboard.

Vaila found she could no longer stop the tears from welling in her eyes, and they spilled over, to roll silently down her soft cheeks. She watched, with sadness, the united movement of the oars as the boats gradually drew away. The men slowly unfurled the sails, and she whispered a plea to the Gods, to keep Leif safe. The unfurled sails revealed long, bold stripes, broken only by a large circle. Within the circle was a hovering falcon, the hammer of Thor held tight in its claws. These symbols they used had magical powers. With these signs came protection, in the form of Thor, their God of war.

The boats sailed off into the distance, and people slowly began to disperse. Turning away from the sight of the departing ships, Vaila clutched to her breast, what was possibly the last gift she would ever receive from Leif. Finding on that previous night, that she had been kept awake with crying, she had decided to rise and go outside to face the silence of the early dawn. No one stirred, and she had quietly searched until she found her beautiful arm ring. Clasping it to her, she had returned to her dwelling. However, later in the light of day, she found her tears of pain turning to ones of anger. That afternoon she had gone to seek out Leif. When she found him, she had exploded in fury. She questioned his sanity. Asked how he could make such an important decision in such a short time? But nothing she said, no amount of arguing, or reasoning, could make him see sense. His mind, she could see, was set. Her heart had felt like it was breaking in two, when it became clear she had lost him. Because he apparently, in such a short time, had found, that he now loved another."

CHAPTER TWO

Having left the shelter of the bay, Leif maneuvered the steering oar to set the ships on course. The men worked to reposition the large sails, and capturing the wind they began to stretch and billow. They looked back to see the land now receding into the distance, as the ships sailed swiftly on, into the vastness of the open sea.

The men chatted among themselves as they settled down, and Leif, draping his arm casually over the steering oar, relaxed. He was glad their journey was at last underway, because now he had time to sit back and think of Fraida. There had been few quiet times in the last couple of days and his thoughts of her had been fleeting. He could picture her now, in his mind's eye, with the dogs standing close by her side. She would, in all probability, he thought, with some regret, be eagerly awaiting his return.

Because of his change of plan, he had instructed the men who stayed behind to fill the knorrs with the first shipload of wood, furs, and various other goods requested by Olaf. They would sail to the Islands to deliver them, and while there, would explain the cause of his absence.

He had filled a small wooden box with consolatory gifts and trinkets, which, he told the men, to hand to Fraida. The contents consisted of an assortment of pins, carved in the shape of various animal heads, and there was a comb, intricately worked in walrus ivory, for her long, flowing hair. He had also chosen a necklace of small delicate beads of glowing amber, which were strung on fine threads of silver. With these, he had enclosed a message saying, "Until we can be together."

However, Leif thought, with an inward shrug, unfortunately, to avenge his father's death, was, at this time, his main priority in life. So as they sailed out into the open sea, he sighed, and stretched, and put Fraida from his thoughts. He needed to concentrate fully on the task ahead.

Leif began by trying to calculate how far their missing ship could have travelled, in the time since it was last seen. He was aware this would depend on the experience of the crew who now sailed her. He tried to work out if his ships could head the boat off, in order trap her. He then thought of what his father would do in the same situation. But these thoughts set off an uncontrollable anger which threatened to overwhelm him, and he bit his lip to dampen it down. Haunting memories of his father and Jon began to surface. He thought of the many happy voyages they had travelled together. These were memories that would remain with him forever, he thought with a sigh. Once captured, he swore to himself, he would show these cowards no mercy. They would rue the day they chose to attack unarmed Vikings, to commit their villainous and murderous act. He vowed then, in his anger, that he himself, if need be; would launch all those who were involved, into the very darkness of eternity.

The weather, this voyage, remained in their favour, and the longships with the wind in their sails, soon covered the vast distance on their journey south. Land lay once more in sight, but here, at this particular point and place, they kept well out at sea and out of sight of anyone who happened to be on shore. They continued on their voyage, and keeping the boats on a steady course, they headed for a destination further down the coast.

The outline of this long stretch of coastal area was very familiar to Leif and his men, having sailed these waters many times in previous years. Being skilled men of the sea, they travelled quickly over great distances, and they could navigate in any weather. Their enemies were always unaware of their presence, and they achieved this by using various ploys whenever they were on the move. When setting out on a raid, they would use water to their advantage and row up shallow rivers into estuaries, keeping the masts lowered and the sails furled so the boats could remain hidden in the long reeds and grasses lining the banks. The darkness of the night and the morning mist cloaked their movements when searching for places to raid. They were always on the lookout for any sign of their missing ship.

The plan, however, on this trip, was for the boats to split up and go their separate ways; this would enable them to cover a greater distance in a shorter time. The men had worked out a route before setting off, to ensure they would have some idea where each boat would be at any given time. They would remain silent and listen out for any faint sound of the horn, which would be the signal that the missing ship had been spotted. This being so they would all come together for battle, to recover their stolen ship.

When darkness had fallen, the ships made for shore. They berthed for the night at an inlet at the mouth of a small estuary. From here, at first light, they could split up and quickly go their separate ways. Leif had worked out this would be the best place to start their search, but he knew they did not have much time, because their food stocks were depleting with every day that passed.

They gathered together to eat, and quietly went over their sailing routes. They would cover as much of this area as they could on the following day, then meet up and berth for the night, further down the coast. There was a feeling of excitement and expectation among the men, knowing they may have a chance to wreak revenge on those they had long searched for. Leif could only hope his workings of the area proved right. That the ship was still somewhere in this vicinity, and could soon be found.

Having gone over their movements the night before, the men were up and ready before first light. Dawn broke, and the boats, one by one, set sail into the greyness of the early morning mist. The drifting mist was patchy, but some areas were clear of it, and here their vision of the coast was good. Where the fog proved to be thickest, they hugged the coast, sailing close to land. Everyone kept a keen eye out for any sign of the missing ship.

Ragnar's ship had gone but a few miles, when, on emerging from the mist, they spotted a large boat, at anchor, some way further up the coast. The men immediately left their oars to rush excitedly to the prow of the ship. Ragnar stood straining his eyes, trying to identify the make of it. Sweyn, Ragnar's second son, climbed the bulkhead in order to have a clearer view. After a few minutes, he cried out excitedly, "It's her alright, it's our ship. I can just about make out the figurehead!"

The men cheered, and Ragnar could not believe their luck, but, although he was excited himself, he immediately bellowed for them to be silent! "Noise carries in the silence of early morn," he stated sternly, as he looked at the men, "and we don't want her to be warned of our presence."

Ragnar placed his hand on his chin and stood for a moment to think. He knew if he blew the horn, their ships would still be within distance to hear. But the ship anchored further up the coast would also be alerted. He would have a better chance of catching her, given the element of surprise, if he went after her himself. But this, he thought wryly, would not please Leif. Turning, he quickly gathered the men around. " I want the sails up, and everyone ready at the oars, before I blow the horn," he said urgently, "because when I do, they," he said pointing, "will become aware of our presence." Ragnar stretched and rubbed his hand around the back of his neck. He said, "We will have to give chase ourselves, and hope the others soon catch up, because we cannot lose sight of her now!" Ragnar cast his eyes around his men and he said quietly, but menacingly, "Whatever happens, I want that ship," then, after a pause, he said angrily, "and more so the men who sail in her!" His men all smiled at each other, feeling the same, and they quickly turned to raise the sails.

The sails were up and the men ready at their oars. Ragnar and one of the others stood to blow the horns. They let out one long blast, which echoed loudly in the stillness of early morn. They lowered their horns and everyone waited in silence until there was a faint echo in reply. Without hesitation, Ragnar bellowed "Row!" and soon the ship was gathering speed, with the men pulling hard as they could on the oars.

Ragnar stood at the helm. He cursed as he saw the ship in the distance start to move off. They had heard them without a doubt, he thought angrily, and they knew only too well what was coming. However, at this point, Ragnar was not so concerned. He knew the longship was faster than the knorr, and they would soon catch up. Turning he continued to urge the men to row, and they began to gain ground. He could now see the ship clearly.

Ragnar gritted his teeth because a great heaviness tugged at his heart. A vision of when he last had sight of the ship came into his head. When his friend, and his son Jon, still alive, stood waving goodbye. These men would pay dearly, he vowed angrily to himself, for depriving him of those he had loved.

Ragnar continued to periodically blow his horn, so the ships following would be aware of his course. He knew they were closing in because their returning signal could now be clearly heard. The sun had risen, but it was with some consternation that Ragnar saw the heat was causing more mist to rise from the water. Ragnar looked ahead, and he cursed when he saw the thick bank of fog that was rolling ever closer. The men could see it too. They rowed with all their might, knowing they could lose the ship now within their sight, if it entered into the cloaking mist.

Ragnar swung round. He cursed and banged his fist off the bulkhead as the ship in front disappeared into the mist. They had been close enough for him to almost see the faces of those who were onboard. He bellowed out in anger for the men to stop rowing, knowing they could not enter the mist without the other two ships at their side.

They did not have long to wait before the two ships came into view. As Leif's ship drew near, Ragnar threw up his arms in anger. "We were this close!" he yelled to Leif, shaking his head in rage. Leif shouted back, "All is not yet lost Ragnar," but he was angry himself because they had not been quick enough to even glimpse the ship. When the signal of the second ship had reached their ears, they had been the furthest away. Although they had turned immediately and rowed for all they were worth; they had been too late to see the ship, before it sailed into the mist.

Leif instructed the third boat to position itself at Ragnar's port side, then, throwing ropes across, they joined the ships to each other. They began to spread out, putting some distance between each ship, until the lines were taught. They would enter the mist together, keeping in line. This would ensure the fleeing ship could not double back in an effort to evade them. If it tried to slip past between them, it would pull the ropes, which were loosely fastened, and that would then alert them to its position.

Leif raised his arm then let it fall. All three ships began to row in unison into the cloaking mist. They continued to row quickly and silently; all the while listening for any sound of the evasive ship. They rowed for some time, until they emerged into the sunlight again. To their consternation there was no sign of the fleeing ship. Leif called a halt. There was anger and disappointment on all their faces. They could see clearly some distance ahead, and they knew the knorr ship could not have outrun them. She had obviously sailed up some river or estuary to escape their reach.

They regrouped and sailed slowly back the way they had come, this time staying close to land. They discovered a number of river mouths and estuary's the knorr could have slipped into; but at this moment there was no knowing which one. Leif knew that being aware of their presence, the knorr would not surface again that day. So the three ships sailed back to where they had berthed the night before.

The inlet was familiar to them, having used it before on previous raids. The men quickly furled the sails and lowered the masts. They rowed the boats further upstream, to where the dense growth of tall reeds and grasses on either side ensured they remained well hidden. To Leif, his men's frustration, like his own, was plain to see. Therefore, he did not waste any time when they berthed. Gathering them together he began to tell them about a plan that had been formulating in his mind.

"Once again, my father's ship has evaded us," said Leif, addressing his despondent men. "Those murdering marauders who took it, must have sailed her further inland. It probably lies now, at this very minute, up river in one of the ports. But we lack the information as to where." Leif paused for a moment to rub his hand over his face, then he continued. "To advance at this time, would, we know, remove any advantage we have of a surprise attack. Our food and ale is running low, but our position is; if we raid to replenish stocks, our presence will be revealed to the people in this area. Word will soon spread and we ourselves, will be open to attack. A murmur came from all the men as they nodded their heads in agreement. We could however, I have been thinking," Leif stated angrily, "still avenge ourselves against those who struck the first blow. They made us their enemies, and that is something they will live to regret." The men looked at each other and nodded and called out in agreement.

They all listened intently as Leif continued. "Tonight, when darkness has fallen, we will sail back down river, and each boat will anchor at a different entrance; in case the ship tries to slip away in the night. However, if she does not make an appearance by late morning, we will have to take it that she is long gone." A disgruntled murmur went up from the men and Leif raised his voice and stated, "It would be pointless to waste time sailing up each river, because it places us open to attack. They could, by now, be gathering a force to meet us head on," he argued," and I don't intend to lose more ships and men to these people. That would be defeating the very reason we are here. Besides," he went on to say, "even if this is not the case, while we are searching the length of one river; she could be sailing down another, to make her escape." The men now began to understand his reasoning and they nodded despondently. "Nevertheless," Leif went on to say, "I have been working on a plan that will bring some satisfaction in our need for revenge." The men looked up with interest. "If there is no sign of our missing ship," Leif stated, "then we will attack those who choose to hide her." The men murmured in agreement, then looked back expectantly at Leif.

"Normally, when we attack," he said firmly, "we carry out only one raid in each area; in and out quickly, and that is what our enemy now expects." The men nodded. "This time, however, we will deviate," Leif said, "and do the unexpected. Let the wrath of Odin fall upon these people! Early, at first light," he continued, "we could strike a blow at one of these places displaying this sign of a cross. We could carry out the first raid quickly, then travel up river, and before anyone has time to raise the alarm, we could strike again. We could follow this up by sailing some further distance up the coast, where we could strike once more, at sunset, after which, we would then set sail for home."

The men, on listening to the plan, began to nod. With the prospect of retaking the missing ship now being faint, they thought well of this concept and immediately began to discuss what would be their best strategy. On the first raid, some said, there would be no burning, as that would alert those who lived in the surrounding area. Others then stated, they could leave some men on board the ships, so the boats were prepared and ready to move as soon as they returned from each raid. This would enable them to go swiftly to the next place of attack. Several other suggestions were thrown into the ring, and now eager for battle, they continued to discuss their strategy for some time before they were satisfied with what would be their plan of attack.

Buildings that used the symbol of the cross were, from the water, easily seen. Normally larger than other dwellings, and with the cross reaching up to the sky, they stood out on the horizon. While travelling down the coast on their continuing search for the missing ship, Leif had taken mental notes of such areas. Mapping the distance between them in his head, a plan, one that he thought could just possibly work, had formed in his mind. He was now glad that it had. It would be bad enough having to return home without having retrieved the ship, but carrying out these raids, he hoped, would in part, appease his people's growing need for revenge.

The men sat together talking quietly, while eating what remained of the food. The plan was now set. So at the onset of dusk, they moved from their position and rowed downriver, to moor at the mouths of the estuaries. Each ship posted guards; who worked in shifts throughout the night. Dawn broke and still they waited with hope, but there was no sign of the missing ship. By mid morning, they realized all hope was gone. Despondently, they had to resign themselves to the fact, that the recapture of their ship would not take place on this trip.

The three ships regrouped and Leif led them to a place near to the first area of attack. They rowed up a narrow estuary, which had steep banks and dense growth along the top edge. Lines had been cast over the side as they sailed, to catch fish, and as they berthed, some of the men jumped ashore to start small fires.

They rested, and ate their fill. Then as darkness closed in a check began of their weapons. Each man would ensure he was personally prepared for the battles ahead. Leif's attention was caught by a grunt from Hakon, who was staunchly holding out the thick, leather tunic Leif was supposed to wear in battle. Leif took it, dropping it by his side. He, himself, preferred to leave it behind; finding at times, in certain situations, it restricted his movement. Ragnar however, always insisted he wore it. Just as he insisted Hakon should remain at Leif's side whenever they entered into battle.

Hakon's looks were not at all pleasing to the eye, Leif thought wryly, but he was, he reluctantly admitted to himself, a good man to have at your side in battle. He was a giant, whose strength was such, that he could fell a tree in minutes. Leif, however, found his manner to be sullen and dull. Hakon lacked humour, he thought, and Leif missed, badly, the good humour and light-heartedness of Jon. Jon had been the one who, in previous battles of the past, had always opted to stand by Leif's side. However, Leif now sadly admitted to himself, Jon was no longer here and no one would ever, in his eyes, be able to replace him.

Shrugging off his despondent thoughts, Leif looked round to check everything was in order. He quietly watched as the men settled themselves down to sleep. They would all need an early night, he thought, as he began settling himself down, in preparation for the early rise and the battles to come the following day.

Leif awoke to the new day with a start. He found himself staring straight into the snake like eyes of Hakon. Hakon's face was only inches from Leif's as he peered at him, while trying to shake him awake. Leif shuddered, and gagged at the rancid smell from Hakon's breath. Hakon was breathing heavily and directly into Leif's face. Leif pushed at him, and Hakon, satisfied that Leif was now awake, straightened up and moved away. Leif expelled his breath, gulping, as he quickly drew into his lungs some fresh, cold, morning air. Rising, he yawned, and slowly stretched, in a bid to shake off the residue of sleep.

Hakon, who had laid out Leif's weapons, now turned. He stood holding out the leather tunic in a stance that brooked no argument. Leif glanced across to where Ragnar and Sweyn stood. They were watching, he knew, but they both turned away when they saw Leif look over towards them. Their shoulders were shaking and Leif just knew they were laughing! He looked at the grim, sullen face of Hakon, and suddenly, he was able to see the humour in the situation himself. So trying to hide his smile, he reluctantly gave in and put on the offending tunic.

They started the day running in unison, keeping to a steady pace. Helmets on and weapons tucked in their belts, their heavy wooden shields they carried almost effortlessly; on arms made strong and powerful from constant rowing. They covered the distance quickly and quietly, and crouching, they managed to remain unseen in the dim half-light of dawn.

It was not long before the outline of the first place of attack was hazily visible to their straining eyes. The men came to a halt. The sound of voices chanting in unison, drifted out in the stillness of early morning. The men altered their pace and proceeded with stealth. However, when they approached the building, they found the way forward was clear. There seemed to be no one about at this early hour. They crept round to the back of the dwelling and found a large wooden door, through which they quietly entered.

This door led them into a spacious room, and they were surprised to see it held an abundance of food. These people ate well, the men thought, looking around in amazement!

Large hams hung suspended from hooks screwed into the beams of the ceiling. Cooked joints of beef and plump chickens lay next to each other, on the many broad shelves lining the square room. Bread and large cheeses, lay along the sides of the tables, and placed in the centre, were jugs filled with creamy milk. The men looked at each other and smiled in silence. Without hesitation, they quickly helped themselves. Having had no food left to eat that morning, they gratefully crammed the bread and cheese into their hungry mouths. Lifting the jugs, they passed them to each other, washing the food down with the fresh, creamy milk. Wiping their mouths, they then took time to look around.

They spotted, in the corner, a barrel of apples. By its side lay empty sacks. The men moved quickly, and lifting the sacks, they filled them with all the food they would hold. Ragnar then silently instructed a few of the men to immediately set off back to the boats, with the now fully laden sacks.

Leif signalled to the rest of the men to follow. He led them towards the sound of the chanting. As they moved stealthily down a wide corridor, the singing suddenly stopped, Leif, who was walking in front, halted the men who followed behind. They listened for a moment, before again creeping forward. They found they were just in time to see a departing procession of figures, all dressed in long flowing robes. The robed figures, they quietly observed, were, at that moment, being led through another door at the opposite end of the facing room.

Leif and the men watched and waited until the robed figures disappeared down, what looked to them to be, a long narrow corridor. Leif raised his brows as he turned to look at his men, then quietly, together, they entered the room that had just been vacated.

They looked silently about. At one end of the room was a recess, which had within it a large stone altar. Standing on the altar were cups and chalices of gold and silver. Placed at the back, was a large, gold cross. Leif signalled to the men to take it all. They carried on moving silently down the aisle. Leif signalled to the others to remove the fine tapestries from where they lined the thick walls. They crept through yet another door. To their surprise, they now found themselves to be back outside; but this time at the front of the building!

They all looked at each other in astonishment. They stood still, not moving, until realisation of what had just happened began to dawn. They had, somehow, unbelievably, managed to raid a building without having to strike a blow! They stood trying to stifle their laughter, but in the light of what had occurred, Ragnar and Leif decided to leave these people and to conserve their energy for the battles ahead. On this day, fate had smiled upon the people of this place. They were fortunate to escape with their lives.

Leif pointed in the direction of the ships, and they all began to make their way back amidst much joviality and humour. They laughed all the way when thinking about the faces of these people, when they discovered they had, somewhat mysteriously, just been deprived of all their much-valued food and possessions.

On reaching the waiting ships, Leif and the men, still laughing, jumped agilely on board. They quickly dropped the loot into large wooden chests kept at the prow of the ship. The men already on board shoved off quickly, by using the oars as levers, to push them away from the banks. Those who had been left behind, on questioning why the raid had taken so little time, all laughed heartily when told of what had just transpired. However, they rowed quickly on. Taking turns at the oars they ate on the move, in order that no time was wasted. Bread and cheese washed down with milk was sufficient. They would feast later in the day, when all the planned raids were behind them.

One hour later, they stepped off the boats. The plan was the same as before; with some of the younger crew left onboard to be ready to push off as soon as the others returned. This time, the men ran quickly across the fields, their way now being clear in the new light of day. The two robed figures, digging up some vegetables in the silence of early morning, were unaware of the invaders closing in behind. A noise, however, caused them to turn. They leapt up in fright at the sight of the advancing warriors. Terror showed clearly on both their faces as they looked from the advancing men over to each other. Shock momentarily inhibited any movement and held them motionless. Finally, they managed to propel themselves forward in a run. By this time it was too late. Ragnar, his sword held out from his side, struck one down without even altering his stride. As he ran on, Hakon took down the other.

There was no creeping up in silence this time. Leif and his men roared loudly, bursting through the large wooden doors. The sudden noise and rush of men, brought great confusion to those within. The people inside immediately jumped up in shock. In the ensuing chaos, they bumped haphazardly into each other in their haste to escape. Some were braver than others and they decided to stand and fight; but the rest took to their heels, eager to flee from these devils who sought them out. Leif and his men showed no mercy. Their hearts had long since been hardened by the loss of their own. They struck down all who stood in their path, and as they advanced they searched the place from room to room.

In one of the side rooms, two of the men came across some thick fur skins, half strewn across a large bed. On closer examination, there became no doubt at all of their origin. Looking at the markings on the backs, the men realised these were the first goods to be discovered that originated from Leif's fathers ship. They quickly called the rest to come and see. The men, as they stared down at the furs, all became quiet. Sobered by the grief that surfaced to remind them of all those they had lost. Anger then erupted and Leif and his men began to rage through the rest of the building. Without pity, they mercilessly struck down all those who tried to hide. Then they looted. They took out all they could carry, and set fire to the rest. There was no laughter this time as they hastened to return to the ships. Leaving a large fire raging, each man walked away in silence, their thoughts being of their own loved ones, who had been slain and left to die in the same cruel and ruthless way.

The ships skimmed over the water, anger now driving the men on. They drew into shore for the third raid of that day. This time, everyone wanted to take part in the battle, and only a couple of the younger men were left on board to watch over the ships. They would not have the advantage of surprise now, as it was later in the day. However, the mood of the men had changed. All were eager for whatever battle that now lay ahead.

They did not have far to go before they struck. The noise and sight of the invaders placed fear into the very hearts of those who were being attacked. The sun now reflected off Leif's helmet and the silver visors covering his eyes; and with his long blonde hair splaying out from beneath, he looked, to these terrified people, like a descending avenging angel. He struck out wildly, letting loose his intense rage; in a bid to try to rid himself of this great emptiness gnawing at his insides. He was driven on by the knowledge that, never again, would his father or Jon stand by his side. It felt in that moment, that the burden of this grief would consume his very soul.

This time, they did not kill everyone. They allowed some to live. These people were quickly rounded up and taken prisoner, to be put to good use as slaves. Farm carts, with horses to pull them, were taken, and loaded with all manner of goods to be transported back to the ships. Leif had ordered the men to take some fine oak benches that were deeply carved and ornate, along with two matching large oak chairs. These chairs, he thought, would suit Olaf. They would make a fine gift on his next visit when he would, he had decided, because he was unwilling to wait any longer; ask for Fraida's hand.

The men themselves, now tired, but at the same time somewhat satisfied, happily returned laden to the ships. Again they left nothing behind but a large raging fire. This time, they ensured no building would remain standing. All that would be left for anyone to find, would be large mounds of black, smouldering ash.

Out at sea once more, the mood of the men again changed. Pleased to be on their homeward journey, they now relaxed. They began to eat well of the food taken on the first raid of the day. They jested with Leif, as he sat like a king on one of the oak chairs at the prow of the ship. He laughed, then bending over he joined them in the feast; satisfying his hunger with the bounty of rich, tasty food.

After a while, feeling full, his hunger now abated, Leif sat back in comfort. Swinging his legs up, he raised his head to look at the clear night sky. The weather should be fair on their return trip, he thought, but he knew the return journey would take longer with laden ships. His thoughts then turned to Fraida. He suddenly began to feel impatient, wishing that matters regarding her, had already been settled. He rubbed his hand roughly over his face and thought of how weary he now was of being alone. What he wanted when he returned from future trips, was for her to be there; smiling, as she waited to greet him. He wanted the cares of a wife and a family. Not for him to return, as usual, to an empty home and an even emptier bed. He sighed deeply. He would use the time they had in the sailing days ahead, he decided with a shrug; to plan what his next move would be.

The return trip was uneventful, but they made good time. The men, being bored, were eager to reach home; so to pass the time, everyone took turns at the oars to speed the boats on. The men all smiled as the ships neared land. They waved at Kelda, who was up on the hill frantically jumping and waving and trying to get their attention.

People soon began to appear on the shore, pleased their boats had safely returned. As soon as the ships had been sighted, far out at sea, an air of excitement had swept through the settlement. The men rushed to build up the fires, over which carcasses of meat were put on spits to roast. The womenfolk prepared vegetables for the pots. With preparations all in hand, they made their way to the dock to help berth and unload the ships. Everyone was eager to see for themselves what goods had been taken in the raids.

Leif stepped ashore. He spotted Kelda in the midst of the people excitedly rummaging through the offloading cargo. He laughed as she promptly sat down on one of the oak chairs, and clinging on tightly, she steadfastly refused to move. Leif watched as two of the men tried, but were unable, to remove her.

He strolled over, and smiling he took hold of her hand as he said, "This one is not for you Kelda." He looked up, still smiling, to see Vaila watching from some way back. The smile that stayed on his face however, was not returned. Vaila's face remained impassive. Her eyes travelled over him as if to reassure herself that he was unhurt, then turning her back, she walked away. Leif, in that moment, felt a twinge of hurt and guilt; but after a pause, he shrugged his shoulders and turned his attention back to Kelda. He took her by the hand and led her away to find something to replace the chair. He hid his feelings from Kelda, but deep inside, he already missed the close friendship he had always shared with Vaila. At that moment, he wondered if it would ever be possible to regain the relationship of easy companionship they both had always enjoyed.

The following weeks were quick to pass, and at the height of summer Leif, for the first time since his father's death, felt relaxed and content sitting astride his tall and trusty black stallion. Today, both the horse and rider, were enjoying the warmth of the midsummer sun, while managing to maintain a slow, steady pace, through the bustle of the growing settlement.

The loud bark of a dog suddenly unnerved the horse. Snorting softly, it began lazily flicking its tail, and pulling at the reigns, it jerked its head as it shook its long silky mane. Leif's hand went up, and patting it gently on the side of the neck, he bent over to talk soothingly in its ear. The horse calmed down, and as Leif straightened, he swept back his own lengthy blonde hair; which, at that moment, was drifting about like the whisper of a caress, in the soft gusts of the warm summer breeze.

The horse, having settled, now continued obediently on its way. It ambled along until they reached the crest of the gently sloping hill, overlooking the thriving settlement. On reaching the top Leif began to slowly tighten the reigns, gradually drawing the horse to a halt. Sitting upright he scanned the scene before him.

He smiled to himself as he looked down on his people, who were busily, but happily, going about their work. He glanced around, and his eyes were drawn to the many furs and hides that had been cleaned, worked, and stretched tight across wooden frames. The frames had been carried out and laid in rows, so the skins could dry in the heat of the midsummer sun. Some of these hides and furs, he knew, would be kept by themselves as material to replace any worn out shoes and boots. Others, they would keep to use for warmth on the cold winter nights. The rest would be put aside and stored ready for use in next year's trading.

Leif put his head back, and drawing in air through his nose he could smell the familiar tang coming from the salted fish and meat, which hung about the dwellings, in long regular lines. When dry, these would be stored, ready for use in the winter ahead. He then glanced down at the women, standing huddled together in small groups in front of their urns. They chatted and laughed among themselves as they stirred and pounded the cream from the milk. Their constant churning, gradually turning the thick creamy mixture, into tasty fresh butter and cheese. Looking over, he could see in the distance, cattle being herded out to further pastures. His eyes swung round to scan the fields of tall grain, not yet ripe enough for harvest. His land was indeed rich, Leif thought with satisfaction. It produced, in abundance, more than enough to provide for the needs of his people.

Leif then watched the slaves being supervised and instructed as they carried and stockpiled the wood the settlement would need for the fires, in the long winter months that lay ahead. This thought then drew his eyes to the distant palisade, where some of the ships were moored; sheltered from any sudden change in the weather. Further inshore, he looked to where his knorr ships were berthed. He watched his men go back and forth, busily storing on board the cargo destined for Olaf.

He began to feel restless; his thoughts now turned to Fraida. The men reported they had been well received by Olaf, when they had gone to the islands to deliver his goods. Fraida's disappointment at his absence, they said jokingly, had been plain to see, but she had been much pleasured by the gifts he had sent. Leif himself was now eager to see Fraida face to face, but he had to wait until the ships were fully loaded before they could sail.

The time it was taking to load the ships, seemed to him, to be too long. He wanted things settled before the approach of winter. Time was now becoming an important factor. He was beginning to feel impatient, more than ready to be off on the start of their journey. Drawing the horse round, he decided to ride down through the settlement to go in search of Ragnar.

Ragnar and some of the men happily accompanied Leif as he rode out to where the trees were now being felled. Their forests stretched for miles, but each generation followed a careful plan when harvesting the wood. A different location was chosen each year. When they removed the mature trees, the young trees and saplings were left standing. The area cleared was then left untouched for a period of years, to allow time for the young trees and saplings to grow and mature. This way, their forests continued to thrive and produce many tall trees, giving them their constant supply of the much sought after timber.

It was only a short ride away, and before long, Leif and the men reached the felling area. They emerged from the cool shade of the forest into a large clearing, where the sun beat down on the workers within. There, in the heat of the sun, Leif spotted a sweaty Hakon, who was expertly overseeing, what looked to be, the heaviest of the work.

Wooden horse drawn carts were, at that very moment, being loaded with large trunks of the felled trees requested by Olaf. Seeing the men arrive, Hakon slowly strolled over, in his own lumbering way. He assured Leif this was the final load and they could now prepare to sail as soon as it was aboard the ship. Pleased with this news, the men, smiling at each other, turned the horses round, and they quickly rode back, to start preparing for their forthcoming journey.

Leif himself supervised the loading of the finely carved oak chairs, which would be his gift to Olaf, before asking for the hand of Fraida. Ragnar, after the last trip, had suggested to Leif that he wait awhile; to give the matter further thought. The woman was striking in her beauty, of that there was no doubt, Ragnar had said; but Leif had only just met her and it was not like him to act so hastily. It was a big step to take, he had stated, and Leif needed time to deliberate. Leif could not find the words to explain to Ragnar why he felt destiny had deemed Fraida was meant only for him. He told Ragnar there was no need for further thought. He was never more sure of anything in his life. He then asked Ragnar to trust him, as he would be proved right. He knew instinctively that his feelings were true.

Leif felt the time for him to take a wife was now, and he believed the Gods had steered him towards Fraida. He had grown tired of being alone. Losing the companionship of his father and Jon had made the winters seem long and dark. His spirits this last winter had remained low, and he had not been able to rid himself of an infernal restlessness, leaving him impatient for the first signs of spring. The laughter had gone out of his life and he wanted it back. He wanted someone he cared about to be with him in the winter that lay ahead, and family that he could call his own. Jon, who he sorely missed, had gone on to Valhalla; of that he was sure, but he had left behind his son Eric, who was now 6 years old. Leif himself, on reflection, thought if he was suddenly and unexpectedly called by the gods; then he too wanted to be sure some part of him would be left behind to walk this earth.

Leif banished these cheerless thoughts from his head when he and the men came together, to talk about the forthcoming journey. After some discussion, it was decided Ragnar would accompany Leif and his crew on the longship. They had other men, more than capable, it was decided, who could crew the knorrs, which would follow with the cargo close behind. On this trip, Leif wanted to impress Olaf and Fraida. So his orders had ensured his best longship was pristine. With all the shields lining the sides, it now looked magnificent.

Later that day, the men, their weapons and helmets glinting in the shining sun, looked as good as the ship. With the cargo now on board, both ships were ready. Stored aboard was a wooden chest filled with, what Leif hoped, would be tempting gifts for Fraida. Leif had chosen fur boots that had been made from the finest skins, and a polished metal disc set in wood that could reflect her beauty. An assortment of wooden cups and bowls, carved by him, helped to fill the chest. Combs made from antlers of the deer, and cloak pins carved in walrus ivory. Amber beads, that Leif could visualise sitting upon the pale skin of her lovely throat, were among some of the fine jewellery he had picked to ensure the chest was full.

On board there was also a second casket, filled with gold and silver. This was the bride price. It was now common knowledge throughout the settlement that Leif hoped to return with the woman he wanted as his wife. The people were happy and pleased Leif had at last chosen someone who would sit by his side. However, there was one who felt no happiness at all, only despair; and that was Vaila.

The boats were finally underway, and Leif looked back to see the knorr ships being moved into berths vacated by their departure. Work carried on, supervised by Hakon. Advantage had to be taken of the good weather in the summer months, and in their absence, some of the ships would sail to his township filled with cargo for trading. This would ensure the settlement had all that was needed for the winter ahead. He began to smile to himself at the sight of Kelda, who was still, he could see, jumping and waving from her position up on the hill. He waved back, although he was not at all sure if he would be seen, because they themselves were now some distance from the land; but by now it had become a habit.

The journey to the Islands was uneventful. With fair weather they were all in good spirits, and this ensured they made good time. Leif's attempt to impress was not to be in vain. Their ship had been spotted on the distant horizon and a welcoming party had gathered on the islands short pier to await its arrival. Some of Olaf's people stood along the shoreline and they watched the boat as it gradually approached. All those who watched agreed that it was, indeed, a magnificent sight. The shields lining the sides of the longship glistened, the men's helmets and weapons flashed, mirroring the bright reflections of the shining sun. Leif's men continued to pull at the oars, and synchronised as always they rowed in perfect unison. Leif himself stood proudly at the helm. The whole scene stood out, silhouetted like a picture against the golden glow of the summer sun. If only Leif but knew, that the reflected aura surrounding this spectacle in the water, created the illusion that his ship had been sent by the very Gods themselves; straight from the halls of Valhalla.

Excitement began to build within Leif, at the sight of Fraida, who smiled, as she patiently awaited his arrival. His feelings for her had not diminished in any way, he thought achingly. Gazing upon her he now realised they had in fact increased.

Fraida stood with the dogs at her side, next to her father and Toork. She watched Leif as he at last returned to her. The sight of him, this magnificent figure standing at the mast, set her heart racing. The weeks since his leaving had passed slowly, and he had been constantly in her thoughts. Her patience had slowly dwindled because of the length of time spent waiting for his return. So, unwilling to waste any more precious time, she had taken matters into her own hands and approached her father. She informed him of Leif's intentions and was decisive on what her decision would be.

Her intentions were already clear to Olaf. He had watched her as she constantly gazed out to sea, willing this boat to return. Olaf could only hope that Leif did indeed feel the same. There would be no peace in living with his daughter if he did not.

In the previous weeks, with Leif's continued absence; Fraida had become bored with moping about. Finding the time too slow in passing, she set herself a task to make the days go quicker. She had decided to weave the finest of cloaks for Leif. The colour she chose was of a purple hue, to set off the fairness of his hair. This kept her busy and she worked steadfastly away, eager to have it finished before he returned. However, much to her disappointment, when the cloak was finished he still had not returned. Undaunted, she then began to weave a tunic to match with the cloak. Now her waiting was thankfully over, and he was here before her; being warmly welcomed by her smiling father.

Fraida held the dogs close to her side when Leif stepped ashore to be greeted by Olaf. Toork, as always, stood back. He remained, as ever, silent and still. Olaf had watched the ship approach, and he had to admit to himself he could not help but admire all that was before him. The sight of this ship in all its splendour, was strengthening his approval of what was surely to come. However, although he would not speak of it at this time, he knew in himself, that he would not be rushed into handing his daughter over so easily. For his own peace of mind and even that of Toork, Olaf knew, they themselves, would need to have sight of this land where his daughter would be expected to live, for what was to be the rest of her life.

Leif turned from Olaf and smiled as he looked into Fraida's radiant and happy face. Her beauty took his breath away. Her lovely hair was pulled back, so that it was cooler in the heat of the sun. It lay in a long, thick, pleat, stretching way down her back. The style exposed the full beauty of her features. Leif gazed at her lovingly and she came forward to place her hands in his. Both tightened their grip, loath, after all this time, to break apart. Leif spoke quietly, and he said, "It's been too long." The expression in her eyes told him she felt the same. Dalgar, who was standing with his head low and ears down, began to emit a long, low growl. Laughing at the dog's antics, they reluctantly released each other and stepped back.

In Viking tradition, good hospitality was always a high priority and any excuse was used to lay on a feast for visiting guests. It was a means of showing off their wealth. In this, Olaf was no exception. The Island had been prepared for the boats arrival, and the men could see long tables, with seating benches at their sides; placed outdoors so they could enjoy the warmth from the midday sun. People were basting large carcasses of meat, which roasted on spits, over big open fires. The men grinned, their hunger sharpened by all before them, as they walked towards the now familiar settlement.

Everyone began to mingle and chat. There was a growing excitement in the air at the thought of the feasting and celebrations to come. Leif's men removed their helmets when reaching the tables and Olaf laughed, as he bellowed out, "Please, don't stand on ceremony, help yourselves to whatever you choose!" The men smiled, and quickly lifted their drinking horns, which were eagerly filled from the jugs of ale held by the waiting women. They drank thirstily, then turned to the array of food which was more than plentiful. Being hungry, because they rationed their food at sea, they happily sat down to eat their fill from the laden tables before them.

It was a relaxed atmosphere in which they all sat; basking in the warmth of the high summer sun. Leif, as he looked across at Fraida, could not remember the last time he had felt this happy. Fraida, who sat opposite, was content to let her eyes feast on this man she herself had waited for, it seemed, so long.

There was much laughter as people related tales from the past. It whiled away the time on the warm afternoon, but Leif and Fraida hardly listened. They only had eyes for each other. They waited patiently. Then after judging the time to be right, they eventually stood, leaving the tables together. Fraida's faithful dogs, as always, followed close behind.

Everyone watched as they strolled on the beach; but aware of so many eyes upon them, Fraida felt slightly uncomfortable and their talk became stilted. Leif, feeling impatient, bent down to pick up some stones. He tossed them casually in his hand for a few moments, testing their weight, then drawing back his arm, he threw them as far ahead as he possibly could. When the dogs chased after them, he took his chance, and grabbing Fraida by the hand, he drew her down and told her to pretend to look for shells. Out of sight of the others, he held onto her hand. He looked directly into her eyes and said, "I love you, and I can't wait for the time when you will be mine." Fraida's heart jolted at his words. She felt herself begin to blush. She smiled widely, and only had time to place her other hand over his, when Dalgar suddenly appeared back on the scene, and he barked loudly at Leif. Leif looked sideways at the dog, and slowly shook his head. Then grinning wryly, he pulled Fraida to her feet. Turning, they gave up on any chance of privacy and strolled slowly back to the tables, to join with the laughter and joviality; which everyone intended, would carry on well into the warm, summer night.

The light of day was beginning to fade, only to be replaced by the shadows of dusk. People left their seats in order to mingle. The noise and laughter coming from everyone, meant it was easier for Leif and Fraida to slip away, unnoticed. Fraida motioned to Leif, as she led the dogs away from the circle of light cast from the newly lit torches. Leif, seeing her beckon, followed. They only walked a short distance, before Fraida tricked the dogs, by getting them to enter into an empty dwelling. She then quickly closed the door to trap them inside. Turning she smiled at Leif, and he smiled back, then they stepped eagerly into each other's arms. Their lips met, and the anticipation leading up to this moment, left them drowning in an explosion of feelings, of the like that neither had experienced before.

Leif's strong hands began to press their bodies closer together, and he skilfully deepened their first, long awaited kiss. Fraida's body arched to meet his. Her hands clasped at his head, her fingers pushing fervently through his long, blonde hair. Their kisses began to lengthen. They clung desperately to each other. But kissing alone was not enough. It just added to their frustration, leaving them unsatisfied and wanting more. Leif's hand moved up towards Fraida's breast, at the same time his strong, muscular, thigh, pushed at her legs, forcing them to part. Fraida gasped and drew in breath as a wave of emotion explode inside her; but, at the same time, the loud barking and whining of the trapped dogs, now began to penetrate both their consciousness. Leif raised his head and cursed quietly under his breath. They stood looking into each other's eyes for a moment, while trying to gather their senses. Fraida said, somewhat breathlessly, "The dogs are making too much noise, and Toork will come," so reluctantly, they broke apart. The dogs were now barking loudly and frantically scratching at the barrier of the closed door. Fraida reluctantly opened the door to release the overexcited animals. What neither needed at that moment in time, was for Toork to make his way towards them, to investigate the reason for the dogs commotion.

However, on walking back, they found themselves relieved the dogs had indeed disturbed them, because they had returned just in time. Leif's knorr ships had been spotted in the bay and were making their way to land. Some people now carried torches to light the path and everyone was following in the direction of the pier, to welcome the visiting crews ashore.

The next few days, although constantly in each other's company, the times Leif and Fraida actually managed to be alone, was really few and far between. It frustrated them to be watched so closely by so many. Nevertheless they, along with everyone else, were happy to continue with the festivities.

Leif sat back, and he casually looked around while waiting for Fraida to arrive for that night's ongoing entertainment. His eyes swung round the room and his glance came to rest on Toork. He stood in the corner like a large dark shadow, and at that moment he was alone. His eyes, which normally absorbed all going on around him, were for once cast down. He seemed to be lost in his own thoughts. Leif watched him for a moment and felt a twinge of pity for this strong silent man. Because, whatever his thoughts may be at that time, they would, unfortunately, be forever hidden in the silence that had been forced upon him.

Unknown to Leif, Toork's thoughts, as he listened to the laughter around him, had been of Olaf and Fraida; and of the bond they would share for as long as he breathed life. This gathering of people, and what it might mean, had triggered memories he had long since locked away in the dark recesses of his mind. Having these moments alone had allowed his thoughts to drift back, somewhat reluctantly, many years, to a day when fate had struck him a terrible blow.

That fateful day, which he tried not to dwell on, had started like any other he thought, with an inward sigh; but he now knew to his cost, that it would end with his way of life being changed forever.

The start of that day would always remain clear in his memory. It was the last time he had looked upon his wife and children, as they lay peacefully asleep. Toork rubbed his hand wearily over his face. Had he but known then he thought, with a sigh of regret, that he would never return.

He had left his home in the early hours of the morning, to travel to the dessert for a day of sport. Accompanying him had been some of his best men. Their destination was to be a lush oasis, where they could test in flight some new, young falcons, which were a gift from his gentle and loving wife.

He remembered the day had been bright and warm. Enjoying the freedom of the ride, they had all ridden for some considerable distance, before reaching their destination. He could still picture the oasis; where they eagerly removed the hoods from the new birds in order to release them into flight. The eyes of himself and his men, he remembered, had all been focused on the hovering birds, high up in the sky; when, their ears picked up this strange, unfamiliar sound. They had been given no time for thought however, because suddenly, from out of nowhere, there came many men on horseback. They had found themselves quickly surrounded and ambushed by a tribe of lowly, screeching marauders.

Although heavily outnumbered, he and his men had immediately started to fight. They fought long and fiercely, for their very lives. But, unfortunately, he remembered sadly, it was to be to no avail. Although they took many of the enemy with them, all his good men had eventually been slain. He himself was overcome and taken into captivity.

As a Prince, and head of his region; his capture had held much esteem and glory for those murdering marauders. He soon found he was not to be immediately killed, but to be humiliated, and over the following days he was dragged around and paraded in front of jeering crowds as these infidels wallowed in their pathetic victory. In the weeks that followed, to prolong his suffering, they were not content to see him die. So he had endured, in that time, torture, the like of which he could describe to no man. His body shuddered involuntary, even at the thought of it now.

Eventually though, they had tired of their cruel game. He found himself being sold on, time and time again. Each tribe was worse than the last. Every one having only one intent, to add to his humiliation and suffering. These nomads had taken him further and yet further from his home; till he knew not where he fell. For him, it ended when his tongue was removed. Cut out by a group of unclean, hysterical, infidels. This was to prevent him from speaking about what he had endured. Leaving him unable to tell anyone of the land from where he had originated.

Because of the hopelessness of his situation, he had prayed for death many times over the months. But at the time of his capture he was young, his body strong and extremely fit, and it refused to give in. However, he thought wryly, even the fittest of bodies cannot endure endless abuse. He remembered when, at last, the day had come when he knew that his time was near. He had welcomed it, as it meant he would finally be free from the nightmare of pain in which he existed.

That very day, while lying in his cage, waiting for the finality of death; he remembered slowly drifting in and out of consciousness. He had emerged from the darkness at one point, and had become, somewhat aware, of a group of men. His eyes had tried to focus on this large and powerful figure, who spoke in a strange tongue, and for a short while, till the darkness had once more descended, he watched as goods were bartered and exchanged between these men and his enslavers.

The next time he surfaced to consciousness, all eyes were upon him. His enslavers had roughly removed him from his cage. He had understood nothing at the time, but feared the worst. He had been hauled to his feet, and the pain had overwhelmed him, dragging him down into the very depth of darkness, which thankfully, once again, freed his mind from further thought. He then knew no more until sometime later, when he opened his eyes, only to find he was laid on a bed, aboard a boat. He remembered struggling hard to organise his thoughts, but his mind had been unable to grasp his situation and blackness had once again closed off all consciousness. The coldness of the air had next woke him. Toork smiled to himself as he remembered how his mind had puzzled at the strangeness of his breath turning to clouds as it left his body. A face had appeared before him and a warm drink had been held to his lips. He was at the time, aware of some weight on his tortured body. When he managed to look down, he saw a blanket, with furs on top, covering him and keeping him warm. This small movement however, had caused the pain to overwhelm him again. From that time on, he could remember nothing of what turned out to be, a long and arduous journey.

He had been taken to Olaf's Islands and strange as they were; he found the cold was the biggest shock. It took the passing of many moons, before he began to return to the land of the living. Many times, in the horror of his nightmares, he was pulled back from the blackness, soothed by the sweet singing of a young child. She sang softly, as she gently rubbed ointments and lotions onto the sores and wounds that covered his body. Toork knew, she alone, had been the one to drag him from the very borders of death, back to the light of life. Over the years that followed, her love and gentleness had helped heal his scars, both inside and out. That child, who he had grown to love and adore as if she was his own, was Fraida.

Fraida's reaction, when Olaf returned with Toork, had been one of horror. As a young girl, she could not stand to see anything in pain; be it man or animal. She had demanded her father give an order that Toork be taken to a building where she and some of the women would look to his wounds. Olaf, surprised that Toork was still alive, had not held much hope of the poor creature's survival, so, he had willingly given in to his daughter's whim.

Fraida, over the following weeks, had found herself becoming fascinated by the strangeness of this large, dark figure. She felt pity for the pain he must be suffering. Judging from the many wounds and sores he had about his body. She sat with him for hours, willing him to live, while watching with patience, his continuous struggle to survive. She wondered where he had come from? Who had done these awful things to him? The women tended to his needs, and washed and cleaned his wounds, and she learned from them what she must do.

Fraida was determined he would not die. She was convinced, in her childlike innocence, that she alone could save him. She gathered the herbs and flowers known to have healing powers, and worked with the older women to grind them down and boil them; making them into potions and lotions. She forced him to drink, at every given opportunity, wine for his blood, honey with milk, soups and potions that were known to heal. He remained asleep though, for what seemed to her, to be a really long time.

Often he would moan in his sleep, and twist and toss. At these times she would speak and sing softly in a soothing voice, trying in the way of a child, to give him comfort. Her patience in caring for him over the weeks however, had been rewarded. No one was more pleased than she, when Toork won his fight to stop himself from entering through the doors of eternal darkness; which would have ensured his time on this earth would most definitely have been at an end. When he at last opened his eyes to the light, the first thing he saw was this earnest child, bending over him, concentrating hard, as she held a cup to his mouth, while trying to force him to drink.

It had taken the passing of time before Toork, once again, came to be the figure of a man that had made him a leader in his previous life. A man who, indeed had strength, a strength that his enemies had once learned to fear. Over that time, his bond with Olaf had become very strong. They had entered into many battles, standing together, and learning much from each other in the different ways they fought. Toork had gradually grasped the meanings of their unfamiliar language, even though the words of which, he would never be able to utter.

It had been the first winter after his recovery, when Toork had decided to show them his superior skill in the making of weapons. First, he had forged his own swords, which at that time, they had thought to be strange in shape. He had then used his skills to make, with gratitude, the magnificent sword for Olaf. The very sword that Olaf still treasured today. In the years that followed, he cast and formed jewellery for himself, and for Fraida; in designs they had never before seen. He had taken delight in Fraida's exclamations of pleasure at every piece he had made. When Fraida had grown older he had made her a sword of a weight that she could handle, then he taught her how to use it. He was now more than confidant that she could always defend herself, if ever the need arose. This, Leif would learn to his cost, he thought, smiling to himself; if he ever crossed her.

Feeling a touch on his arm, Toork surfaced from his reverie and smiled as he turned to look down into the face of Fraida, who had only just arrived. Of one thing he was more than certain, he thought, as he fondly kissed her forehead. He had sworn in his heart to be her protector for as long as he breathed life, and in that, nothing had changed.

The early evening's entertainment began in earnest with the arrival of Fraida and Olaf, and when everyone had their fill of jugglers and acrobats, the people went back to chatting and drinking. Leif now deemed the time was right, and leaning over, he whispered inconspicuously in Ragnar's ear. He asked him to instruct the men to fetch from the ship the chairs they had brought as a gift for Olaf. He also requested at the same time, they bring the wooden casket which held the bride price.

Leif lifted his drink, sat back and watched as some of his men casually rose from their seats. He watched them slip away, unnoticed, from the room. It did not take long for them to complete their task. They soon returned with the chairs. Carrying them in, they set them down in front of a questioning Olaf. Leif stood up, and going over, he presented the chairs to Olaf as a gift from himself.

It was immediately clear that Olaf was more than pleased, as smiling broadly, he himself also stood and walked round the table to join with Leif. Olaf, intrigued with these gifts, quickly bent down to inspect the large wooden chairs, close at hand. Marveling at the intricate carving of the sturdy oak, Olaf turned and promptly presented one to Toork, whose surprised face, for once, showed some expression of pleasure. He too approached to examine the fine workmanship in the carvings of the dense wood. Olaf then ordered the chairs be taken from the longhouse. They were to be placed in the dwellings of both men, and kept there for their own personal use.

Olaf, after they had all returned to their seats, leaned over the table to heartily shake Leif's hand and he thanked him profusely for the fine gifts. Leif sat back and let things return to normal. He waited, until everyone was relaxed and chatting, then he stood up and again approached Olaf. Placing down the wooden casket, and in front of all the people, he proudly asked for the hand of Fraida.

The room went quiet. Leif opened the casket and gasps, followed by murmurs, came from the direction of the watching crowd. Fraida herself gasped at the amount of gold and silver Leif offered for her hand.

Olaf looked down at the brimming casket set before him and he began to smile. He respected Leif for the value he set on Fraida, a value that, indeed, matched well with his own. These riches were not for the benefit of Olaf, but for Fraida, because if Olaf did agree to the marriage, as father of the bride, he would keep the laden casket only until the wedding took place. It would then, in turn, be given to Fraida on the day of her wedding, along with her dowry, and then all of the riches would belong to her alone.

However, Olaf was still concerned at the speed at which events were taking place. When Leif first appeared, it brought forth a reaction from Fraida that had never before been shown. From the first time their eyes met, it had been easy to observe they were drawn to each other. Any concern expressed by Olaf at Leif's ways, as yet, being unknown to them, were immediately dismissed by Fraida, who was herself open and trusting.

Everyone sat quietly, eyes focused on Olaf, as they awaited his reply. When it came, Leif was not surprised. He had in fact suspected they would not hand Fraida over so easily. Olaf sat in silence looking over at Toork's emotionless face, then he smiled and said to Leif, "To say that your offer is generous would be an understatement," and he laughed heartily. After a pause he then looked up, "and yes," he said, nodding as he continued, "I do think you a man most worthy of my daughter." He slowly stood up to continue. "However, on this day I will only shake hands on an agreement to the betrothal. My full agreement on the marriage itself, I'm afraid, must be conditional." Leif raised his eyebrows and looked at Olaf in question. "The only way I could be sure in myself that everything was satisfactory for my daughters well being and happiness," he continued, "is for me to view your lands and your people; given, that this would be where my daughter would be expected to live for the rest of her life."

Fraida jumped up in shock and exclaimed "Father!" After having taken the time to speak to her father, to relate to him what her wishes would be, Fraida was more than annoyed at Olaf's statement. She did not, in any way, expect any conditions that would hold back the union of herself and Leif. Forgetting where she was, she began to voice her objections. She told her father he knew she did not want any delay of her marriage! These weeks of waiting she had found too long in passing. When the time came for Leif to go, she wanted to be with him, she stated forcefully. Olaf, grim faced, looked back at his daughter. But he was resolute, and he stood firm in the face of her objections. He held his hand, palm facing out towards her, telling her he would not be swayed in any way by her pleas. This would be his final word, on what had long since been decided.

Fraida looked over at Leif, who had remained silent, and she pleaded with her eyes for him to do something. Leif began to think. The usual custom was for any marriage to take place at the bride's family home. These journeys back and forth could end up with them having to wait many months. This was time Leif was not prepared to wait. If truth be told, he didn't want to wait another night, let alone another few months.

Thinking fast, he said to Olaf, "I have a proposition to put to you." He began by telling Olaf, somewhat proudly, that he himself knew his own worth. "Because of this, I am sure there will be no obstacles in the way to allow you to feel you would withhold your final consent." Leif held his head high as he continued. "This being so, would you give your consent for the marriage to take place at my home? Preparations could be made to coincide with your visit, and if all was to the satisfaction of yourself, then the wedding could proceed."

Olaf looked over at Toork and paused, as he thought for a moment, then he turned to look over at Fraida's crestfallen face. After another short pause, he then agreed. Leif smiled widely, and the two men shook hands to seal the agreement, and the people all began to cheer. A date was then set for some weeks ahead, in order to give both sides time to prepare.

This was not what Fraida wanted, and when Leif sat down she told him so, in no uncertain terms. She wanted it to go ahead now. Leif tried to placate her, telling her they had to respect her father's wishes. Explaining with a smile, that at least this way they would only have to wait weeks, instead of a delay that would certainly have spread over a good number of months.

The festivities resumed with fervour, pleased at the outcome everyone now celebrated the agreement. Olaf jovially bellowed out an order for entertainment and everyone clapped and laughed as they watched the jugglers and acrobats bound across the floor. The acrobats began to jump from table to table as the jugglers performed, and every time a stick was accidentally dropped, a roar of laughter went up from the now noisy and drunken crowd. The performers continued for some time, amidst much laughter and joviality, until finally they collapsed in a heap, fatigued from their exhausting antics. They were all clapped heartily on the back in appreciation, then led away to be served with horns full of ale, which they quickly swilled down to quench their raging thirst.

Throughout the entertainment, Fraida, who was not to be amused, smiled little. Leif, being aware of her disappointment, had the wooden chest containing the gifts brought in. Up until now, it had been inappropriate to present them to her before his proposal was accepted. The array of gifts contained within the trunk, Leif hoped, would in some way help to please and restore, in some part, her good humour.

Fraida, it was plain to see by her despondent looks, was not at all happy with Olaf; or indeed, at the thought of the long weeks she had ahead without the presence of Leif. However, she was not the only one who sat through the night's entertainment finding no joy in the situation. Toork was lost in his own thoughts. He had known this day would eventually come, when they would have to let Fraida go. But a life without her would be dull indeed. It was not in any way something that he or Olaf would celebrate.

The following day, all hands set to unloading the cargo from the ships. Leif, as he stood on the pier watching the last of it being taken ashore, again informed Olaf, that his land had wood in plenty. He suggested after their visit to his

home, Olaf's ships could be loaded with what they could carry for the return trip. Olaf nodded, and at the same time he thanked Leif for his generous offer. He, and his people, would be grateful for the supply of the much-needed timber.

Toork stood silently beside the two men and he watched Leif's men busily prepare their ships for sail. Fraida now approached Leif and in her arms, folded neatly, was the tunic and cloak she had lovingly woven. She held it out to him and his surprise and pleasure at receiving such a gift, made by Fraida's own hand, was clearly shown on his face. Leif was used to giving, but it was not often that he received. This gift showed, in all those weeks spent apart, he must have been in her thoughts.

He smiled widely as he looked down at her, and he said "The next time you see these garments, it will be at our wedding. For I shall wear them then, just for you." However, Fraida did not smile in return. Tears sprung to her eyes as she gazed forlornly up at his face. Leif immediately stepped forward to comfort her, but the dogs being startled by his sudden movement, took up their guarding stance. Dalgar bared his teeth and Volga gave a low growl in warning.

Olaf looked at Toork, and then pointedly at the dogs; because Toork was the only other the dogs would obey. Toork snapped his fingers and the dogs turned, their ears going back to lie almost flat against their heads, as they reluctantly walked over to his side. He held them there, allowing Leif the time he needed, to gently hold and comfort Fraida. Leif enfolded Fraida in his arms and he quietly whispered in her ear, "I go to prepare for our wedding. Fear not, because I will allow no obstacle to stand in our way." Stepping back, he smiled down at her as he released her; but when he looked up, it was straight into the fathomless eyes of Toork. This dark enigma of a man was a puzzle that Leif could not yet solve. He hid his feelings only too well, and Leif felt uneasy that he could not read, even in some small measure, what was in this Toork's thoughts.

Fraida's heart was heavy as she stood watching Leif's boats disappear from view. Glancing round, she directed a frowning look of reproach at Olaf and Toork; then, without uttering a word, with the dogs once again at her side, she turned and walked away. Toork and Olaf looked at each other. Olaf raised his eyebrow and made a small grimace at Toork, and Toork in turn shrugged back. Fraida, with her head held high, walked purposely on. She was intent on ignoring both men and her mind was already busy with plans of how she would pass the time in the weeks ahead. She would try, she thought, to somehow arrange her days in such a way as to make the time she would now have to wait, pass quicker.

The departing ships soon reached the open sea. The wind was behind the large sails, and they stretched and billowed, giving speed, carrying the boats swiftly on. One man stood at each steering oar, while the rest gratefully sat back, content in the knowledge, that the wind would carry them home. Some of the crew now settled down to sleep. Tired out as they were from days of drinking and long nights with little rest. They had feasted well, knowing there would be time enough on the journey home, to catch up with the many hours of lost sleep.

Leif, as he sat back, found his thoughts, like Fraida's, were on the preparations that would be required in the weeks ahead. He yawned, but his head was too full of plans to allow for sleep. Of one thing he was sure though, he would be ready and well prepared for Olaf' arrival. He would make certain Olaf was impressed, because now, more than ever, he was determined nothing would be allowed to stand in the way of his marriage to Fraida. Come what may, she will be mine, he thought with a smile, and stretching, he relaxed before easing himself down to sleep.

Some days later, Kelda alerted the people to the return of the ships; which were as yet still far out to sea. An air of excitement gripped the people and they began to gather on the shore. They were curious to have sight of Leif's new bride, all eager to extend a welcome to her. Vaila however, hung back, watching the scene from a distance. As the boats drew near, the excitement began to fade. The people growing quiet when it became clear that the men were alone. Vaila's heart lifted. Had Leif changed his mind, she thought? The idea that any woman could refuse him, never, for a moment, entered her head. She tried to hide her smile as, hope itself, began to rekindle in the deep recesses of her heart.

The people watched Leif, looking to him for some sort of reaction, but his face remained impassive. The boats tied up and all the men disembarked. Leif then suddenly stopped. Throwing his arms wide, he smiled broadly as he stated, "The wedding will take place here!" Vaila's heart sank as a cheer went up from everyone. The people were all at once relieved that nothing was amiss and they began to clap their hands and talk of the excitement of having a grand feast and celebration ahead. Leif looked round at their happy faces. He thought of how long it had been since they had anything to celebrate. For the first time, he was glad of the change of events. This would bring his people much happiness, he thought, and give them something to look forward to in the weeks that lay ahead.

Kelda jumped about with excitement, having heard the word wedding. She ran up to Leif to give him a quick hug, then turning she ran to Vaila, to hug her. Both Vaila and Leif knew immediately that Kelda had misunderstood. Vaila looked back at Leif with reproach, then putting her arm round Kelda, she led her away, to try to explain what was to happen.

Kelda's eyes looked in puzzlement at Vaila. Vaila sat before her, trying to explain in as clear a way as she could, that Leif's bride would come from another place. Vaila smiled as she talked, struggling hard all the while to keep the quiver from her voice. "This is good," she told Kelda. "We all want Leif to be happy, don't we?" she said with a smile. Kelda was nodding, but Vaila could see the confusion in her eyes and she was not at all sure that Kelda fully understood what was to come.

Leif called a quick meeting with Ragnar and the men. He explained there was much work to be done in the following weeks. "Regretfully," he said, this will leave no time for further raids or for the search for our missing ship this year." Ragnar, at this point, piped in with wry humour, "There will be time enough in the future to continue with our search. At this moment, it is more important that your plan to get yourself a wife is successful!" It was with much laughter that the men then gathered to discuss what could be done to improve the settlement before Olaf arrived.

Over the next few weeks, the settlement became a frenzy of activity. The men constructed a dwelling near to Leif's, of a standard fit for Olaf and Toork. A separate room was constructed within the dwelling for Fraida to use, until the marriage took place. Quarters were made ready for Olaf's crews, and for any of his people that he might decide to bring. Everyone worked hard and the best of what they owned was put on display. Leif's people were proud of the standards by which they lived, and they were eager to show off their wealth to these visiting strangers.

Horses were brought in from the pastures, and after an inspection two of the best steeds were chosen and stabled at the settlement, for Olaf and Toork, for the duration of their stay. Leif picked out a beautiful horse, with speckles of grey, which would be a gift for Fraida. At night he worked at producing another gift for Fraida. He was carving out a chair that would be solely for her. Being a labour of love, he wanted the chair to be special. He took time to carve it ornately, smiling to himself, as the arms began to form in the shape of the two dogs who never strayed far from her side.

Kelda, from her house on the hill, was unable to grasp the reason for all this activity. She nevertheless mimicked the others by sweeping and cleaning all around her dwelling. Every now and then she would stop, and looking round she would laugh loudly. Everyone smiled at Kelda's antics, but Vaila was the only one who continued to visit regularly, going back and forth to help Kelda with her work. Kelda had become very unpredictable when it came to her dealings with people, and the only one she seemed to completely trust was Vaila. The people of the settlement would help Kelda in other ways. They would ask Vaila to use some pretext to get Kelda away from her dwelling, when they wanted to repair her roof or see to the area around her house. They would not go too near the dwelling while Kelda was about. She was so unpredictable, they feared she would cast a curse upon them, owing to her now confused and deranged state.

Fraida, far away on her Islands, was also busy. She stood in her dwelling looking down at the opened, wooden trunks. Already half full with what she would need to take for the start of her new life with Leif. In the background, drifting through the open door, she could hear the noise of the men as they worked at loading the many goods that Olaf had ordered for their journey. Excitement began to stir within her when she thought of Leif. She was happy to think that, at last, she only had another few days to wait before they would be ready to sail.

She smiled to herself as she stretched, and turning, she walked over to look out from her door. She could see, some little distance away, her father and Toork. They were huddled together, sitting on their haunches, looking down at the ground. Toork, a stick in his hand, drew signs quickly on the earth at their feet. Over the years, Toork had taught both Olaf and Fraida, the signs from his language. Although they would never be able to speak it, never having heard it uttered, they both could understand the meaning of the signs.

She stood for a moment, watching from the door. Suddenly, for the first time, the thought passed through her mind that she would be parting from these two men who had been the centre of her life for so long. In all the excitement she had not taken that into consideration, somehow, thinking her life would remain the same. Sadness began to overwhelm her. She felt her throat tighten and tears sprung to her eyes as she thought of the time when they would, undoubtedly, be forced to leave her behind. This thought also brought with it a tinge of fear, and she panicked, as a sudden feeling of insecurity washed over her; with the realization that she would be starting a new way of life, without the two men she loved, being part of it. She had a sudden urge to hug them both, and trying to pull herself together, she left her dwelling and walked towards them, saying," What are you pair discussing?"

Both men, startled, looked round at the same time. Olaf stood up, saying, "Oh just men's talk little one, just men's talk," and at the same time, Toork rubbed quickly at the earth, erasing all the signs that had been before them, and he too stood up. Fraida stepped forward, and putting her arms round her father, she hugged him tight. She then turned to Toork, to hug him, and she also planted a kiss on his large, dark cheek. Both men looked at each other as she turned to walk away." What was that for?" said Olaf, in puzzlement, but with a smile. "Oh just women's talk Papa, just women's talk. It means that I love you both." "Very much," she added, as she looked back over her shoulder.

Later that day, in his workshop, Toork's powerful, dark body, glistened with sweat, in the intense heat generating from the glowing fire. For some weeks now, he had worked in secret, to make a surprise gift for Fraida to present to her on the eve of her wedding. Head bent, he continued working away at the large brooch. The design being in the shape of three swans enclosed in a circle. This was the last piece of the set, and he had chosen to make the set in silver, not gold, because the metal was bright and shining, as he hoped her future would be. The three swans represented "the past, the present, and the future." Together, the three also stood for Fraida, Olaf, and Toork. Because on the day of her marriage, and from then on, the three would become four. To Toork, these swans signified Fraida's purity, and also her gracefulness as a person. Having finished polishing the final piece, he took a rag and wiped the sweat from his brow. Pleased with the result of his work, he placed the brooch in the small wooden casket, which sat on the table at his side. He rubbed the back of his neck and stretching his muscles, he stood up. Looking around as if for one last time, he thought, now I must pack.

CHAPTER THREE

It was Leif's turn to wait and, pacing impatiently, he watched the boats in the distance sail slowly towards his home shores. The early morning air held a chill, but now the wind was thankfully still and the sun had risen to cast a faint warmth over the scene below. Preparations were underway. The fires had been lit under large meat carcasses some hours before, and now the smell of roasting meat was sharpening everyone's appetite; leaving them hungry and eager for the celebrations to begin.

Ragnar joined Leif at the dock to welcome the approaching visitors. Clapping Leif on the back, he grinned, and told him to be patient. "After all, this was your idea" he said, with a laugh.

"Don't remind me," said Leif, smiling, while raising his eyebrows dramatically to the heavens. Ragnar leaned over to say quietly in Leif's ear, "Stop worrying, Olaf will have no objections. He's nobody's fool. He knows well enough you are the better catch. If truth be told, it is I who should be questioning if Fraida is in fact good enough for you!" The incredulous look on Leif's face caused Ragnar to burst into laughter. Jostling Leif in a manly fashion, Ragnar said, somewhat wryly, "You've not had a change of heart then?" "Never," said Leif, smiling at Ragnar's good humour, "she's worthy, believe me," he said, with a wide grin. "That good? Ragnar said jokingly. "Mmm, well if that's the case, then I suppose I will just have to give my consent!" Laughter reverberated from both men as Leif pushed at Ragnar's shoulder.

Leif's people smiled as they watched the two men jostle in fun. In the weeks since Leif's return, their excitement had increased at the thought of his forthcoming marriage. Everyone was consumed with curiosity as they eagerly awaited sight of the incoming bride. They had gathered to position themselves loyally behind their leader and they stood watching, waiting for the boats to reach land. Kelda, when seeing a crowd was gathering at the shore had come down from the hill. She too, stood smiling and expectant at the back of the group, waiting for what, she knew not.

A hush descended as Olaf's longboats, magnificent in their splendour, their adornment being relevant to suit the occasion; finally swept into the bay. The people had their first sight of Fraida, and it immediately became apparent, why their Chief had chosen this woman.

A Princess without doubt, her beauty and stature was breathtaking. Fraida wore a long, linen dress, over which she had placed a softly pleated woollen tunic. The colour being similar to the blue of a clear summer sky. To hold the tunic at the shoulders, she had pinned large, star shaped brooches set with multi coloured gems and they glistened, reflecting the rays of the bright autumn sun. A thick silver chain linked the brooches together and suspended from the centre was a pendant in the shape of a quarter moon. Fraida had deliberately chosen the theme of the sky, the moon, and the stars, representing what they all shared. "No matter where you travelled in life, your culture or your beliefs, all lived under the same."

A finely worked baldric lay across her shapely body and attached to this was a small scabbard enclosing a sword. The hilt was studded and worked to match with the rest of her jewellery and was shaped to fit a woman's hand. Her long, flowing hair, she had fastened back with clasps, which although smaller in scale, were the same design as her brooches. Seeing Leif waiting, she smiled broadly. Her face was alight with the happiness she felt within.

Leif smiled widely back. Olaf's men now pulled in their oars to allow the boats to glide to a halt. The dogs, Dalgar and Volga, wasted no time and immediately jumped ashore. They shook themselves vigorously, but this caused them both to stagger slightly. Their days at sea, aboard a constantly moving ship had left them somewhat disorientated. The restrictions in their movement, through a lack of space aboard the narrow ship, had resulted in the dogs being muscle-bound, and they were glad, at last, to have beneath their paws, the firmness and freedom of dry land.

Olaf and Toork were next to move and stepping forward they positioned themselves either side of Fraida; taking her hands, in order to help her alight. Leif, filled with happiness that this day had finally come, eagerly stepped forward to assist her. He opened his mouth to voice a heartfelt welcome, but suddenly, from somewhere behind, a loud, high-pitched shriek, pierced the surrounding silence; causing everyone engrossed in the scene before them, to jump. Instead of voicing what should have been a welcoming greeting, all that came out of a startled

Leif's mouth was, an involuntary, "What in the name of Odin?"

Ragnar instinctively spun round, his hand on the hilt of his sword. But all eyes had already turned towards the back of the crowd, to Kelda, who was screaming and shaking her tousled head, which she now held in her roughened hands.

Leif and Ragnar looked in question at the people who stood nearest to her, but they spread their arms and shrugged their shoulders, disclaiming all knowledge. Everyone looked to Leif for some direction as to what they should do, but suddenly, before anyone could be stirred into action, Kelda's screaming stopped. Everyone saw her slowly raise her head and her piercing eyes narrowed as she looked over at Toork. She stared at him intently, as if she could not believe what she was seeing. Toork himself did not react to this and he remained still and unmoving. Kelda drew her eyes away from the dark figure, her glance darting quickly around, waiting for someone to speak, to react, but everyone just looked back in stunned silence. Kelda gasped and shook her head in puzzlement, her gaze swinging back to Toork. She glared at him with as daring a look as she could muster, but still she received no reaction. Then with a shake of her head, she turned and with a dismissive wave of her arms, ranting loudly, she began to run back towards the safety of her dwelling, up on the hill.

All eyes now turned to the shadowy figure of Toork. He never exhibited any emotion whatsoever at this outburst. He had grown used to this sort of reaction, as shown by some, at his unfamiliar appearance. It had its advantages when it came to the enemy, because, by now, he was well aware, that the sight of him struck fear into their very hearts. Besides, Toork thought, looking across to see Olaf smiling, it was as clear to him as it must be to the others, that the woman was a poor wretch of a creature.

Leif, now struggling to recover his composure, was deeply embarrassed and he apologised profusely to those before him. Damn Kelda, he thought. He had ensured everyone had been told the tale of Toork's strange appearance in order to avoid such a reaction. Obviously, Kelda in her disturbed state, had not understood. Olaf himself, however, to everyone's relief, just laughed it off; and as he teased his dark friend, everyone laughed, and the tension eased away.

Leif, now growing impatient, finally leaned over and stretching out his arms he supported Fraida, as she stepped from the ship. Once again, as he gazed into her bright and shining eyes, he found himself holding on to her a little longer than was necessary. He had longed for this day in the weeks they had spent apart and he felt loath to release her; but he knew everyone was watching and waiting for him to lead the way. Reluctantly, he stepped back, and extended his arms in a motion for the others to follow. Going forward, he began to walk on, in front, with Fraida, Olaf and Toork. The dogs now ran on ahead, not having the restrictions of the boat, their only interest was to stretch their legs in the freedom of a run. Leif's men, as instructed, quickly moved forward to greet the crews as they stepped ashore.

Olaf looked around, taking in all that was before him, while walking in front with Leif. He was impressed, even at this early stage, at the size of the settlement and the number of dwellings contained within. As they strolled along, Leif explained to Olaf, that his Township was further down the coast. It was large and had many merchant ships visit in order to trade their wares. He explained that his father, with his preference for seclusion, had decided to build his settlement here; just far enough away from any prying eyes. They had sturdy knorr ships, he told him, and they used them to load wood, furs, and various other goods here. They were then transported down to the township. This ensured his people always had a constant supply to trade with visiting ships. They also sailed to other friendly countries, he told Olaf, to deliver goods requested in trade.

Leif began walking slightly ahead, to direct the three to the dwelling that would be theirs for the duration of their stay. Olaf, on entering, was further impressed, as he looked around at the fine furniture and furs. He also noted that care had been taken to put at their disposal, just about everything they would possibly need. Leif showed them the adjoining room that had been prepared for Fraida. The women had been given the task of putting in place what they thought she would require. The furniture was of the best they could provide and the men smiled when Fraida was overcome with delight at the chair Leif had carved as a gift for her. Even Toork smiled as he examined the fine workmanship, finding much humour in the fact the arms were in the shape of the dogs so loved by Fraida.

Now familiar with where they would reside, Leif led the trio to the longhouse, which was larger than most, with a further dwelling alongside to take any overspill of people. The room was already beginning to fill and soon they were seated and enjoying a light meal of bread, meats and cheese, with fresh milk to wash it down. Feasting would begin that night, after the guests had rested from the journey. The safe arrival of the visitors in itself however had already brought a cheerful and festive air to the settlement. Everyone happily chatted while basking in the glow from the crackling logs in the large central fire.

They ate their fill while chatting amicably then sat back to relax. At this point, Leif enquired if they would like to go to their quarters to rest. Olaf declined, saying he would rather stretch his legs after the confines of the boat. Olaf's men opted to start unloading some of the goods from the ships and Leif's men quickly stepped forward with an offer of help.

The offloading was undertaken in good humour. Leif's men smiled when they saw the cargo brought by Olaf. They were more than happy to cart up to the storehouse, casks of wine and barrels of ale brought for use in the celebrations. Olaf had also brought some fruits that, to Leif's curious people, seemed very strange in appearance, as they had never set eyes on them before.

Olaf's men were quick to offloaded some large pots filled with herbs, and others filled with thick, golden honey. Sacks of nuts came next and large blocks of precious salt. Leif was overcome by the amount of precious goods brought by Olaf and he thanked him for the generosity of his most welcome gifts.

Fraida had brought her own loom, and it was carried ashore, along with sacks of fine wool for her weaving. Her clothes, linen, and valuables, ensconced in wooden trunks, were transported up to Leif's large dwelling. Fraida joined the three men who were already there, and she instructed one of the trunks be carried to the dwelling she would share, for a time, with Olaf and Toork. The men smiled at the happiness shown by Fraida, for what was to become, she hoped, her new home.

Everyone continued to work hard, all eager for the unloading to be complete. Knowing, only then, would the feasting and celebrations begin. After a quick check, finally, all the ships were empty. All that was, except for one, which lay berthed behind the others. Olaf had given strict instructions for that to be left as it was; until he instructed otherwise.

With their personal belongings safely ensconced in their quarters Leif asked his three guests if they would like to have a look around the settlement. Fraida, although excited at her new surroundings, declined, saying she would rather go through some of her trunks to unpack her immediate needs. Olaf said he and Toork would gladly accompany Leif.

They left Fraida to her own devices, and Leif asked Olaf and Toork if they wished for horses to be brought. Olaf said they would prefer to stroll and stretch their legs, after the long days spent at sea.

Ragnar was ready and waiting. When he saw them emerge from the dwelling he beckoned to some of his men. To give Leif moral support, they joined the small group to begin a slow stroll around the settlement. Olaf was pleased at what he saw. The extent of Leif's wealth was known, but to see it used in such a way was reassuring. Leif obviously, Olaf thought resignedly, cared as much about his peoples well being, as he did his own.

Fraida had given Olaf no peace in the past few weeks. She had been unusually persistent, continuously urging him for his final consent. This, he steadfastly refused to give, until he was sure the union would be a suitable one. He had no qualms now, and if truth be known, he would be hard pressed to find anyone better suited. There was still, however, the question of leaving Fraida alone in a strange land. The people living here were new to her. Nevertheless, Olaf thought with a shrug, he and Toork together, after much soul searching, had come to a decision about what was one way to solve that particular problem.

Fraida, welcoming the privacy that was lacking on the ship, had the women heat water so she could quickly bathe to freshen up. Excited about her new environment, she then hurriedly unpacked all she would need for that day. She stepped out from the dwelling, intent on having a look around, just as the men returned. She looked directly and questionably at her father. He in turn raised his eyebrows and smiled back. A happy grin spread over her face as, after teasing her for a few seconds with a bland look, he nodded. She ran into his arms and smiling radiantly, she hugged him. The two dogs, thinking this was some sort of game, immediately leapt up and barking loudly, they bound around the embracing pair.

Leif, knowing full well what this meant, breathed a sigh of relief. Over the course of the morning he had tried to relax, but his body had felt tense as if on a knife-edge. Smiling, he turned to look at Ragnar, but instead, his view was blocked by Toork; whose look was unfathomable as he studied Leif's reaction to this news. Leif purposely held his head high and keeping the smile fixed on his face, he stared straight back. However, as they all began to make their way back, Leif felt a slight unease. Once again, he wished he could read what thoughts were in the head of this dark, but ominously silent, man.

However, not all in the settlement were ecstatic with this turn of events, and of those, Kelda was one. After her unbecoming behaviour that morning, she had returned to the safety of her dwelling up on the hill. Here she remained, but she was not in any way at peace. Back and forward she paced, in distracted agitation. Many thoughts were racing through her utterly confused mind and she continued to mutter and fret with no one to hear but herself. The absence of any reaction from the people, to this strange vision of darkness, had left her totally confused.

Had no one been aware of what she saw? she thought. Had this evil vision been clear to her eyes alone? she muttered. These visitors had come and they were accompanied by a strange, dark Demon. She had felt afraid this morning and had run quickly away from the danger down at the shore. But she had to do something to warn her people of the threat that only she, apparently, knew was now within their land.

Her thoughts continued to race. She tried to think of a way in which she could make the people of the settlement aware of the danger in their midst. Enough ill had visited their settlement, she thought distractedly; but this time she had been given a sign. It had been revealed to her eyes alone and so she must act. Suddenly she became still, and after muttering quietly to herself she ran quickly over to her trunk. Throwing open the lid, she searched franticly about until she found what she was looking for.

She removed an urn, which held a mixture of powders. Then she grabbed a box that held herbs, and standing, she ran over and fetched some small white bones that were stacked in a corner. Carrying them to her bench, she set out her measures. Putting them together, she began a strange chant. Lifting her pestle, she ferociously began to pound. Her face was set and her mood intense as she concentrated fully on her grinding. She became oblivious to all. She continued with her chanting and pounding until she was satisfied the whole of the ingredients had been turned into a fine, dusty powder.

She wiped the sweat from her brow; then going over to the other side of the room, she fetched from the cupboard, a small pot urn. She carefully proceeded to transfer the precious powder into the urn and covering it with a small cloth, she sat back, content and with a smile; ready now to await her chance.

Down below in the settlement, it had been declared the celebrations would begin that night. At last, with the final consent from Olaf, it was decided, there would be no further delay and the marriage would take place the following day. Both Leif and Fraida felt impatient. They had already waited too long, and now, being together, they were eager for the union to proceed.

Much work had been done within the settlement in preparation for the arrival of the visitors, and not least, was providing ample food for a large number of people. The women had worked hard in the early hours of the day, and in their eagerness to prove their hospitality was second to none; they had cooked, baked and overseen the roasting of the meats, fish, and vegetables ensuring the long tables had food in plenty for all. Flasks of ale and jugs of wine were placed centrally for everyone to help themselves to whatever drink they chose, as they gathered to wait for the feasting to begin.

The overall mood was light and cheerful. Leif and Olaf's people now happily mingled. Some seated themselves astride long benches, while others preferred to sit on chairs and stools. They laughed and conversed as they began to eat. No one noticed Kelda, whose eyes were searching for only one thing, as she made her way through the crowded room. Kelda crept stealthily forward, quietly weaving in and out between the people, until eventually, she spotted where the dark demon sat. She ensured that she herself remained, like the demon, quietly inconspicuous, until finally, she reached where she wanted to be.

Kelda crouched low behind an unsuspecting Toork. After taking a few deep breaths, she quietly straightened up. She stretched her arm out and with a satisfied grin flicked her wrist, upturning the open pot. Puffs of powder gushed out and drifted down, and Toork, who was just about to take a bite out of a tasty piece of venison, found himself to be, suddenly, and somewhat unbelievably, amidst a blinding cloud of powdery dust. He gasped and drew in breath, but this caused him to cough and choke; so he closed his mouth and at the same time, he dropped the piece of meat he was holding.

Kelda, having unceremoniously dumped the whole of the contents of the urn from above, quickly jumped back. She narrowly avoided contact, because Toork, being momentarily disorientated, knocked over his chair as he leapt to his feet. He coughed and rasped, blinking furiously to try to rid his eyes of the dust. He looked up and out, directing his gaze over to the people sitting before him. Intense outrage and disbelief showed on every line of his angry, white, powdered face.

However, there was no reaction from the room. A blanket of silence had already fallen over the somewhat stunned crowd. Those who had spotted Kelda were shocked, and aghast, when her slight figure suddenly appeared behind Toork. They had watched in horror, unable to move in time to stop her from emptying whatever was in the pot, over Toork's large, dark head.

The people, completely taken aback by Kelda's unexpected actions, found their eyes now drawn away from a glaring Toork; being directed instead to a smiling and unconcerned Kelda, who peeked out from her crouched position, where she had been hiding behind the large figure of Toork. She giggled as she thought to herself, "they can certainly see him now," if the startled looks on their faces was anything to go by. She took one more look at the gaping people, then turned and took to her heels. She ran quickly from the room. Sprinting, weaving and chanting all the while, with her words spilling out and overlapping each other, in her haste to escape.

Everyone stared, motionless, at the furious face of Toork. Some still had the food held half way to their mouths, as mesmerised, they watched this ghostlike face before them. Leif was stunned. Being unable to instantly think of a way to deal with the situation, he turned to look to Ragnar. The noise of Ragnar's chair suddenly grated in the silence as he moved to go after Kelda. Fraida and Olaf, their faces twitching, motioned for him to sit, telling him to leave her be. Fraida looked up at Toork, and the sight of him covered in white dust was too much for her. She struggled hard, but unsuccessfully, to suppress the giggles about to erupt." The poor woman obviously sees you for what you are Toork," she managed to splutter, before finally exploding into laughter.

Toork was, at that moment, not at all amused, and with his face looking like it was set in stone he looked grimly and silently down at a laughing Fraida. Some seconds passed, then his face began to crease, and he too smiled, now able through Fraida's eyes, to perceive his appearance.

Fraida looked over at Olaf, whose shoulders were shaking, before she stood up, and giggling all the while, she helped Toork dust down. She could not stop laughing as she tried to wipe the powder from his face. Leif, now the onlooker, observed how relaxed they all were with each other. The love and affection each held for the other, he could now, for the first time, see clearly showing on all three faces.

Leif, being relieved at the avoidance of what could have been a nasty situation, looked round to locate some of the women. He beckoned to them to bring a ewer of water and cloths to the table, so that Toork could wash to rid himself of the clinging powder. The women came hurrying over and quickly and apologetically, they proceeded to clean Toork up.

Thankfully, the rest of the night progressed without further incident and Leif was pleased when Fraida's attention was fully diverted back to him. He longed to be closer to her, but had to be content for this one last night. Safe in the knowledge that from tomorrow, they would finally be together. From that day forward, it would be he who always sat by her side, he thought, with a satisfied smile. His place would be where Toork sat now, but his instincts told him, Toork would probably find that situation very hard to accept.

The sound of music then disturbed Leif's wayward thoughts and looking up, he saw the musicians, brought by Olaf to entertain, had begun to play. Olaf, smiling, turned to face Fraida to request that she sing. She laughed, then agreed, and the musicians played softly to accompany her sweet lilting voice. This was a pleasant surprise to Leif. The room grew quiet as everyone became caught up in the sound of her voice and in the haunting melody she chose to sing. Leif, as he watched Fraida, found the love for her now deepening in his heart. He began to realise he had a lot more to learn about this beautiful woman, who was very soon to become his wife.

Some hours later, after taking their leave from the feasting, Olaf, Toork and Fraida were walking arm in arm towards their dwelling. Fraida had bid Leif goodnight. Being tired from the journey, they had excused themselves with the intent of retiring early, in order to be well rested for the long day now ahead. Reaching the point where any faint light cast from the torches and fires was left behind, the three continued to walk down a short path to the dwellings, which were under the cover of darkness.

When entering into the blackness, both Olaf and Fraida suddenly became aware of an unexplained light. They swung round to find the strangest of glows emanating from Toork. An unearthly aura beamed out from an unsuspecting Toork's head, startling Olaf, because it looked quite eerie. It gave the improbable impression, Olaf thought with a slight shiver, of Toork's large head somehow floating along without the attachment of his body. This, he knew to be untrue, as they both had hold of Toork's arms. Olaf raised his eyebrows as he looked over at, a just as startled, Fraida. Toork's appearance was already strange enough, without something like this to add to it, Olaf thought with a shudder. What on earth was within the powder the poor wretch had thrown over Toork? he wondered, as he looked over at Fraida.

Both being somewhat mesmerised, they stared back at Toork until Olaf was aware of Toork shaking him urgently by the arm, while looking questionably at him. Olaf looked quickly over to Fraida, and he made a sign with his eyes for her to hold her tongue. He then blustered as he struggled to reply. "Nothing's wrong, nothing at all my friend," he said, to a frowning Toork. Lifting his hand, he brushed it past Toork's head saying, "A moth, just a large moth." Toork went to lift his arm to feel at his head, but both Olaf and Fraida quickly grabbed him again by each arm, eager, before others could see, to hurry him on.

With head bent, Olaf glanced over at Fraida, making a small grimace. Toork's temper, they both knew only too well, could be very unpredictable; and at this moment in time, it was better he remained completely unaware of this strange and unwelcome new look, he unwittingly, and it must be said most definitely unwillingly, now possessed. All Olaf could hope for, was that whatever had caused it, would soon wear off. He would strive to think of ways to hide it from Toork, until that time came.

On the day of the wedding, the preparations started before dawn. Leif was lying awake when he heard his people stir. He listened to the soft murmurs as they quietly set about their work. He yawned tiredly as he turned on his side. Sleep, in these last hours, had proved to be evasive because his mind had been centred on Fraida and on the wedding ahead. Pulling the furs closer, he burrowed into his pillow. He still had a few hours before he had to rise, and closing his eyes, he rid himself of all thought, in an effort to sleep.

In her dwelling at the other end of the settlement, Vaila too, had lain awake for most of the night. Her thoughts had been on Leif and on the hopelessness of her situation. Feeling desolate and so alone, she had cried quietly deep into the night. There was no one to turn to for comfort in her hour of need, because her mother, after years of miscarriages, had given birth to Vaila late in life.

The fact that she was a girl, was no less reason for celebration, in a culture where women were held in high esteem. Viking women were much respected by their men folk and were trusted to run the household and the accounts, both for their homes and businesses. The men folk much preferred the physical side of the business. Be it farming fishing or warfare; and being great men of the sea, liked nothing better than to be free to set sail at a moment's notice.

Being an only child, meant Vaila's time had been spent helping her elderly father in his daily work. But to her, this had been no sacrifice, because she loved the challenge, just as much as she loved both her parents. When they were young, Leif and Jon had often laughingly helped her, as she struggled with the more physical aspects. Completing her daily chores early, meant they all had more time to spend in the company of each other. Being mostly in the company of men resulted in Vaila growing up strong willed and independent, more than able, to stand up for her rights.

However the loss of both her parents within a year of each other, had left her all on her own. But Jon and Leif had always been there for her, and when Jon had been killed, Leif had become the only mainstay in her life. She couldn't remember a time when she hadn't loved Leif. When he told her of his impending marriage, it had all but destroyed her. For the first time in her life she felt vulnerable, and although she showed no outward sign to the people, it had taken all her inward strength to hold herself together.

Fraida's beauty had come as a further shock to Vaila. Her heart had dropped like a stone when, while hiding in the crowd, she had watched this figure of beauty and gracefulness, who had unknowingly stolen her love. When she heard Fraida sing softly in the longhouse the night before, Vaila had felt defeated. It was only then, she accepted within herself, that she could not compete with the woman Leif had chosen over her.

She lay awake on her bed, not knowing how she was going to make it through the rest of this day. Ragnar had asked if she would take charge of Kelda, in order to avoid a repeat of yesterday; especially on today of all days. Frowning, Vaila yawned and shrugged, mentally trying to pull herself together. She had prepared for this day, many times, over these past weeks, she sternly told herself.

Knowing there would be little chance of further sleep, she gave herself no more time to think and rose quickly from her bed. She stood for a moment and stretched, then approaching her chest, she lifted the clothes she had chose to wear that day. Drawing on strength from within, she began to dress with as much care as she could. She would look her best and hold her head high, she thought while working at fashioning her magnificent copper hair. There would be many in the settlement who would watch for her reaction to this marriage. But she, herself, was determined they would see none. Her fierce pride would not allow her to show any sign of a broken heart. She knew as she dressed that deep inside, a little part of her, also hoped that maybe, even if only for one fleeting second, Leif would look over at her and see beauty, then regret that it was not she who stood by his side.

Vaila, now ready, took a deep breath, and opening the door, she left her dwelling. She set off walking quickly in the direction of Kelda's, smiling at the people who were busily going about their work. She was early, but knowing how unpredictable Kelda could be, she wanted to ensure Kelda was presentable and dressed appropriately for the occasion.

Vaila hid her smile when she entered through the door. Kelda, oblivious to everything going on below in the settlement, was unprepared, and in a mess. She sat at her table busily mixing and grinding herbs. The bones of various small animals were strewn all around.

Kelda looked up as Vaila entered and jumping to her feet she immediately started to rant about demons that were within. Vaila, dismayed, had to speak sharply to get the excitable Kelda's attention. Holding on to Kelda's hands firmly, she kept her still while she tried to reassure her. At first, Kelda tossed her head and was unwilling to listen, but Vaila persisted. After some time, Kelda's eyes seemed to clear and Vaila thought she at last understood today was the day Leif would marry, so she released her.

Kelda, leaving Vaila's side, shuffled in her tattered shoes over to her open doorway, where she stood gazing out. Kelda was feeling confused. Leif was to marry, but Vaila would not be his bride. Although Vaila had smiled when telling her this, Kelda could see sadness clouding Vaila's lovely green eyes. How had this come about? she thought, shaking her head in despair. This was supposed to be a day of great happiness, but all it would bring, it seemed, was more pain.

Vaila saw Kelda's shoulders shake. She stood up when she saw tears falling from the sad, lonely eyes. Kelda looked forlornly over at Vaila, then raising her hand, with a choking sob, she motioned for these visitors to go. Vaila went quickly over and placing her arms around Kelda, she hugged her tight. "It's all right Kelda," Vaila said softly," I don't want them to stay either," and stroking the tangled hair back from Kelda's face, being overcome with the same sadness and despair she could see in Kelda's eyes, Vaila found she too began to cry. She hugged Kelda tight, in comfort, wanting to take away her pain.

These two women, who had been left so desperately alone, stood holding on to each other as they quietly sobbed. Both were glad to receive the solace they so badly needed, even if it was only from the comforting arms of the other. Neither had any control over the changes to their lives fate had forced upon them. Changes that had brought with them so much pain. At that moment, their thoughts were of the past. Both secretly wished they could roll back the years, to what was for them, much happier times.

Eventually, all cried out, Vaila stepped back, managing somehow to pull herself together. She forced a smile as she washed the tears from both their faces. Taking charge, she tried to cheer them up by dressing Kelda appropriately for the occasion. Talking all the while, and reassuring a now calmer Kelda, Vaila gently combed and rearranged the tangled straggly hair. She placed the warm cloak Leif had brought, around Kelda's shoulders. Now they were ready to face the world. Leaving the dwelling, she led Kelda down to stand near to the others; who had been instructed to help, by placing themselves to obscure Kelda's view of Olaf and Toork . All in position, everyone now waited for the happy couple to appear.

Leif soon emerged from his dwelling and Vaila's heart ached at the sight of him. His long, blonde, hair drifted in the breeze as he strolled towards the waiting crowd. His chiseled features were relaxed and his eyes glowing with happiness as he glanced around. The silver scribed arm rings he wore and the pendant that hung round his neck, stood out against the rich purple of the tunic, which had been his gift from Fraida. The matching cloak he had also chosen to wear, was fastened back at the shoulder of his tall frame, held in place by a large circular silver pin. His boots, made from the finest of fur, were crisscrossed with thin strips of leather. A narrow leather band hung low at his waist, holding fast his large, ornately hilted, but indispensable knife.

Ragnar walked at Leif's right side and he carried in his hand a small wooden box; a gift from Leif to Fraida. On the lid of the box, the initials F and L were intricately carved and intertwined. The box held a circular necklace made of gold, which had suspended from its centre a small pendant shaped like the hammer of Thor. A gold finger ring to match with the necklace was also in the box. The ring, being a circle, had no beginning and no end and was a pledge of his love for her, which would also, like the circle, be eternal and never-ending.

Being a ceremonial occasion, Hakon walked at Leif's left side. Olaf, who glanced over just as he was turning back to speak to Toork, turned back sharply to look again, when he saw for the first time this ugly and sullen giant.

Leif had always left Hakon behind when they were not going into battle. Hakon was the best man to leave to oversee any heavy work that was required while they were away. They could always rely on him to get the work done. Today, however, loath though Leif was because of Hakon's dour demeanour, he knew in all fairness, that he had to give Hakon his place at his side on such an important occasion.

Toork and Olaf had never before set eyes on Hakon. He had forfeited the feasting the previous night, opting instead to stay in the forest for the felling of the last of the wood needed for Olaf's return trip. Hakon did his job well thought Leif, but if only he would to do it with a little more humour and less seriousness. Leif raised his eyebrows and looked defiantly over at Olaf and Toork, daring them to laugh. They both turned away, but when they glanced at each other, the twitching of their faces said it all.

A hush came over the crowd when Fraida appeared. Leif drew in his breath as he watched her slowly walk forward; once again being overcome by her beauty. Her dress was of the finest silk and with each step it shimmered, reflecting the late autumn sun. A cloak, trimmed with the softest fur, was clasped back at her shoulders, the fine woven material draped in folds down her length. Today her hair was drawn back in a plait interlaced with colourful narrow silk ribbon. Round her forehead she wore a band and attached to the centre was the circle of swans. The two delicate armlets placed high on her arms matched with the circle, but the swans were joined together in a line, swimming into the future, on the waters of life. The two large dogs, who never strayed far from her side, today, wore thick leather collars inset with shiny, round, metal studs.

A cheer arose as the couple joined hands. Leif took from the wooden box, held open by Ragnar, the necklace of gold. He fastened it proudly round Fraida's smooth shapely neck. She smiled up at Leif lovingly when he placed the ring on the finger of the hand he now gently held. A further cheer went up from the crowd as Olaf came forward to present Fraida with her cask, which held the bride price. He kissed her fondly, then followed it up with another box that held her dowry. The crowd clapped, and Toork stepped over to grasp the dogs by the collars. Leif and Fraida turned to lead the way so the celebration of marriage could now begin.

At the longhouse, chairs had been positioned for the couple to sit together. Toork, about to hold Fraida's chair in order to see her seated, found himself preceded by Hakon, who looked over with what seemed to be a direct challenge at Toork. Toork smiled into himself and politely stepped back, allowing Hakon to proceed. The time, Toork thought, when he himself would take his stand, was yet to come.

The feasting was soon under way. Music played while acrobats and jugglers leapt from table to table, entertaining the merry guests. Unknown to Leif and Ragnar, many of the visiting men were showing an interest in Vaila. An unaccompanied beauty indeed, they thought, with her crown of fiery, copper hair. Vaila however, had hung back from the crowd for as long as she could, in an effort to keep Kelda close to her side. Kelda was now at this moment, unavoidably by herself; because Vaila had gone over to the tables to quickly fetch food for them both.

Vaila was trying to hurry, being aware that Kelda, at any minute, could take it into her head to leave her seat and start to wander. So she purposely showed no interest at all in the men who were trying to get her attention. One of the burly visitors however, not content at being ignored, stood up. He swung round, turning his back to the tables where Leif and his company sat and he grabbed at a startled Vaila.

Vaila immediately started a fierce struggle to extricate herself, but it was in vain. She spoke quietly, but angrily, to the forceful man, not wanting to cause a scene, but she found herself unable to detach herself, or to compete in any way with his strength.

Toork, whose eyes were at that moment on Leif, watched as Leif suddenly looked up from Fraida. Leif looked over at the scene, his face immediately set in anger, and he started to rise. Toork turned to look in the same direction to see the cause of Leif's displeasure. Toork, unhindered, having no woman at his side, rose before Leif had a chance and he strode across to where the struggle was taking place.

The man who grappled with Vaila was unaware that Toork was heading in his direction. However, he froze where he stood when he felt the sharp, curved blade of Toork's sword suddenly cradle his chin. He quickly released Vaila, stretching his arms out at the sides as he did so. Toork slowly turned the man around while still holding the sword to his throat. He looked at Olaf's men, then swung his eyes pointedly to Vaila. They all got the message; this was one woman who was not to be touched. He withdrew his sword and the man grudgingly apologised to Vaila. Toork then strode over to return to his seat. He looked at Leif who raised his goblet to Toork in a salute of thanks. Fraida, who had watched the commotion, looked at the beautiful woman now walking away and she began to wonder who this person was.

Vaila, feeling badly shaken, returned to her seat beside Kelda. Ragnar and one of the men carried food across to them, asking at the same time if Vaila was all right? She assured them she was and they left to return to their seats. But as Kelda started to tuck into the array of food before them, Vaila, who was finding it all too much, sat back. She found she now had no appetite for food. It was taking a great deal of effort for her to smile, when all she wanted to do was cry. So she remained silent and became detached from the celebrations going on around her.

Outwardly, she had carried on as normal, but inwardly, she was waiting for the first chance to leave. It was all becoming too much to bear and she did not know how much longer she could keep up this pretence. She sat in abject misery, feeling totally dejected, while looking around at the many happy people eating, drinking and chatting.

As time progressed however, people began to circulate, forgetting about the importance of shielding Kelda's gaze from straying to Toork. Vaila, glancing round, noticed that Kelda, her hand holding food halfway to her mouth, had suddenly become still. People mingled before them but Kelda began moving her head urgently, trying to see that which had caught her eye. Vaila could only assume she must have glimpsed Toork. This was the excuse Vaila had been waiting for. She lifted Kelda's cloak and leaning over, she placed it firmly around the hunched shoulders. Kelda tried to shake the cloak off, while indicating with her mouth already full, that she wanted more food. Vaila grabbed all she could of the food spread before them and holding it in her arms, she cajoled a reluctant Kelda into following. She drew her away with the promise of the food, before Kelda, who was now becoming agitated, could have a chance to make any more mischief. She guided her through the door, leaving the laughter behind, and at that moment, Vaila, in her abject misery, was sure, she herself, would never have cause ever to smile again.

Inside the longhouse however, with everyone unaware of Vaila's distress, the feasting and celebrations carried on. An aura of happiness surrounded the united Leif and Fraida. Love shone from eyes fixed on each other, and at that moment they were oblivious to all who mingled around. They rejoiced in the thought there would be no more parting. They were where they had longed to be, together, at last, as man and wife. Like Vaila, they too were waiting for the time when they could make their excuses and leave, to finally be alone. They longed to be wrapped in each other's arms, but had to be content, for the moment, in just holding hands.

Suddenly, a commotion around the table meant their gaze, somewhat reluctantly, was diverted away from the focus of each other. The acrobats, in order to amuse the happy couple, had come to perform before them. They began to laugh as the jugglers, although trying hard, now dropped more than they caught. The acrobats lost their balance and frequently fell, and there was no doubt, an overindulgence of ale was the cause of their clumsiness.

Gradually, the time did pass, and when the room grew quiet, as the telling of stories and tales began to engage people's interest; Leif slowly stood up, and everyone watched as Fraida followed. Toork, bending over, took charge of the dogs, who strained at the hold on their collars; desperate to break free in order to follow their mistress.

The first Leif and Fraida saw, when they emerged from the longhouse, was Ragnar's grinning face, lit by the torch which he now held high. He swung round so their view was clear, and lining both sides of the path stood Leif's men, creating two winding ribbons of fire, all the way to his dwelling. The men began to cheer and wave their torches. Leif laughed while Fraida blushed. Grabbing Fraida by the hand, still laughing, Leif began to run through the gauntlet of cheering men. When he reached the dwelling, he spun round, and scooping Fraida into his arms, he swung her high. A loud roar went up from the men as he backed into the door, swinging it closed behind him. Leif held Fraida tight in his arms while leaning against the closed door. Their laughing faces were only inches apart. He held her there until the noise of the cheering men ceased. Then, as he gazed into her bright and shining eyes, love overwhelmed him and lowering his head, he brought his lips down gently to meet with hers. Her arms tightened round his neck, the kiss deepened and he made his way over to the bed. Alone at last, they went naturally into each other's arms.

The weeks spent apart had only served to deepen their love and now for them both, the waiting was over. In the hours that followed, their love for each other reached its peak, until finally, at last, in an explosion of feelings, they were united together, forever, as one.

The night proved to be all, and more, than either had expected. Leif woke first, and rubbing his hand over his eyes, he smiled, as he glanced at his sleeping wife. She did not stir, so he lay quiet, listening for any sound of movement. Silence, however, seemed to reign. Everyone must still be asleep he thought with a smile. The prolonged feasting would have carried on well into the early hours of the new day.

He looked contentedly down at Fraida, who lay sleeping in his arms. Snug and warm under the furs which covered them both. He watched her now as her eyes slowly opened. She looked up into his face and smiled at him in a shy and loving way. He grinned and his arms tightened as he pulled her close. Leaning over, he brought his lips down to meet with hers. They had time enough, he thought, before having to rise.

They both woke the second time, to the noise of continuous barking outside their door. Leif jumped out of bed to go and let the dogs in. Fraida watched him walk to the door and the sight of his tall, muscular body, set off a reaction deep inside, which caused her stomach to flutter and tighten.

The dogs bounded in as soon as the door opened and running past Leif, they headed straight for Fraida. They jumped up onto the bed, barking excitedly, because they were overjoyed to be, at last, reunited with their beloved mistress.

Fraida giggled and laughed at their antics and tried to calm them down. Leif returned to the bed, intending to climb back in; but he momentarily forgot what the dog's reaction would be. Dalgar now stood on the bed, towering over Fraida and baring his teeth. He snarled. His guarding stance dared Leif to take just one more step towards his mistress.

Try as he might, Leif could not persuade the dog to back down.

Fraida herself, tried in vain to get Dalgar to settle, but when Volga decided to join her mate and she too bared her teeth, they both laughed and decided to dress and rejoin the feasting, which was, by the noise outside, well under way.

They did little else for the rest of that week, but relax and enjoy the celebrations and feasting, but still both eagerly awaited the time when they could retire and be alone. Every night was better than the last as they became familiar with being in each other's arms. Fraida and Leif's happiness, while in the company of each other, was clear to all.

The days were quick to pass and as it came closer to the time for her father and his people to leave, Leif noticed Fraida was somewhat quieter. Leif was aware everything was new to her, so he spent the following days trying to familiarize her with her surroundings.

On the first day, he sat her before him on his horse. He placed his arms round her as they rode away from the settlement. This enabled her to see more of the land in which she would now live. On the second day, he presented her with her own horse, which was a gift she loved. That day, they rode some way out with Olaf and Toork and a few of the men. The dogs accompanied them on this day, bounding along behind the galloping horses. The day following, they had walked for some distance, glad to be alone and away from the noisy crowd. Leif had hoped this would show Fraida she could be content with his company alone. The dogs had again been with them, running ahead, then racing back, enjoying spending time with their mistress.

However, the dogs were not always this content. Dalgar was still proving to be a problem. When they were all together indoors, he would look at Leif, almost daring him to touch Fraida. Volga was calmer and left the protecting to Dalgar, as long as he could manage the job alone. There had been only one occasion she had bared her teeth at Leif, when he, in fun, had tried to get hold of Dalgar. Leif told Fraida it was only natural for them to resent someone else in her life. He knew it would take time to gain the trust of the dogs and he did all he could to make this happen. But for now, their only option when bedtime came was to shut them out.

So it came to be that every night, both dogs would sit forlornly outside Leif's door, knowing full well their mistress was inside, they would persistently howl. This would continue until Toork, being fed up with listening to the noise, would come and sternly clap his hands, signalling for them to come to heel.

Dalgar and Volga, on the first night this happened, did stop howling, but they sat looking perplexed, puzzling at the sight of this glowing head floating towards them in mid air. Toork being unaware of his strange appearance, found it unusual for the dogs not to instantly obey him, but he shrugged and put the reason down to them being in a strange place. It did take some persuading however, to get them to follow him back to his quarters. Toork thought the dog's behaviour very odd, but eventually after some time had passed, the dogs did settle down enough to stop looking at him in order to curl up and go to sleep.

Apart from Olaf, Fraida and the dogs, there was only one other who had seen the spectrum of the floating head, and that was one of the men. Being the worse for drink, when going out to relieve himself, the man had stumbled and fallen in the dark. He lay prostrate, finding himself on cold ground and unable to move. He muttered away to himself as he tried to muster enough energy to rise up onto his unsteady feet. When he heard the approaching footsteps, he thought help was at hand. He slowly looked up, only to be startled at the sudden appearance of this eerie, ghostlike, floating head. He had reacted by putting his head immediately back down on his hands and he squeezed his eyes tightly shut. He had waited a few minutes, then warily raised his head to look again. This time there was nothing to be seen. Much relieved, he shrugged and laughed to himself and put it all down to the effects of having consumed too much ale.

Toork however, on his way to get the dogs, began to feel the cold from the autumn night air, so he pulled over his head the warm hood attached to his cloak. This had been the cause of the floating heads disappearance, if only the drunk but knew.

Olaf, since becoming aware, of what he hoped, was a temporary outcome of Kelda's powder on Toork whenever he entered into darkness; ensured he himself carried a flaming torch when they walked together at night. This kept Toork in the light, but Olaf hoped fervently the effects would soon wear off before Toork himself was alerted. He was concerned what Toork's reaction to his strange appearance might be.

Apart from this, Olaf and Toork spent the days enjoying their leisure. They had brought with them their much-prized falcons for some days of sport. The birds had been kept in large wooden cases, constructed to transport them safely on any journey over sea. Falconry was one of the pastimes all the men enjoyed and Leif had ordered horses be made available for the visitors to use whenever they wished.

On one of the days, they all decided to ride out together for a day of sport. The men carried their hooded falcons on their arms and Fraida, who was happy to just accompany them, was to ride along at their side. The outing would help clear the mind, they thought, and the peace and quiet would be a welcome break from the noisy crowds still celebrating and feasting. However, unknown to them, this was the day when Hakon had decided to be sociable and of his own volition, he thought he would lead them on a tour of the forest.

They were all seated and just about ready to go, when suddenly into their midst, galloped an ungainly Hakon, sat astride a large unruly horse. He was struggling hard with the animal and brutishly tugging at the reigns in an effort to control the horse and bring it to a halt. The other rider's mounts became skittish in the face of this large prancing stallion, and Fraida, while tightening the reigns, looked over with some surprise at Leif, but after his initial glance back, his face managed to remain void of expression.

Olaf and Toork looked at each other, then away, lest they disgrace themselves by letting loose the laughter this sight brought forth. Turning his horse around, Leif, his face still without expression, acted like there was nothing untoward in this spectacle. He led the way, as they headed off to a clearing set within the vast thickness of the forest.

Hakon rode up in front with Leif and Fraida, and Olaf and Toork, who were themselves expert horsemen, had the pleasure of following behind. They watched Hakon, struggling hard all the way, trying to control his wayward mount. It all became too much for Toork, who had to look away from Olaf. In order to prevent his laughter from erupting, he stopped, and throwing his leg over, dismounted by slipping down the side of the large stationary horse. Toorks shoulders were shaking and he was unable to contain his mirth, when Hakon galloped uncontrollably away into the distance, his long legs sticking out from the unruly horse's side as it decided to go it's own way. Olaf turned back, and bringing his horse alongside Toork, he too dismounted. They both then stooped over the hind leg of Toorks horse, pretending to examine the hoof. Both tried hard for some time, without success, to bring their laughter under control.

Eventually the pair continued on their way and caught up with the others, just as they arrived at a large clearing surrounded by trees. The area was quiet and still, bathed in the warm glow of late autumn sunlight. Toork, who was also a master at falconry, could not let his bird wait any longer. Eagerly he removed the hood, and raising his arm, he set it free. He watched with pleasure his bird soar effortlessly up, ever higher, into the clear autumn sky.

However, Toork's mood, which was light-hearted, quickly began to change as the other birds suddenly came into view. He watched them slowly circle and the sight of the circling falcons made his mind flash back to that day, when fate had deemed his life would change forever. Those painful, unforgettable memories ,suddenly came back to haunt him. His thoughts drifted back to a time long ago. He could almost feel the heat of the warm eastern sun on his head, and hear the laughter of his men, as the birds circled round. All those good men, he thought, who were sadly long dead. He felt the familiar anger and grief swell up inside, but was suddenly jerked back to the present, with a touch on his arm. He looked down at the soft, questioning face of Fraida. This sweet, gentle child, always seemed to know when this sadness and anger was upon him. He smiled, to reassure her, and quickly banishing the painful thoughts from his head, he looked up, just in time to see his bird swiftly swoop down, diving towards its prey.

The time seemed to go quickly and soon they were riding back happy and content, from a day spent in a sport they all enjoyed. Half way through, Hakon even managed to find his way back in order to join them. His horse, having had its head to go where it willed, had tired from its long and strenuous gallop. Hakon now looked around smugly, finally having the wayward horse under his control.

By the time they reached the settlement, they were hungry and thirsty and looking forward to returning to the feasting. They quickly dismounted and some of the men came running over to take charge of the horses, while others took hold of the birds. Turning to go back to the longhouse, they all spotted Kelda. She had her back to them and they could hear her quietly muttering, as her eyes keenly scanned the ground at her feet. She was often searching for her herbs and plants, and at these times she became oblivious to everything around her, as she continued slowly on.

Just as the group was about to turn away, they saw one of Olaf's men, who was very drunk, staggering along the path. He suddenly found his way blocked by the wandering Kelda. Unaware of those watching, the drunk began pushing at Kelda's small frame, shouting, "out of the way Hag!" until she fell over. However, before any of the men could react, Fraida herself had reached the drunkard. With a couple of moves she had him on the ground, her knife close to his throat. Leif was astounded! Toork, who had quickly followed Fraida, smiled as he effortlessly lifted her away. Hauling the man up, he handed him to the other men now at his side. Olaf gave the order for them to remove him and sober him up!

Fraida turned to help Kelda to her feet, only to find she was already standing. She was staring glaringly at Toork. The Demon did not back down, so Kelda tore her eyes away and looked warily around. Without uttering a word, she then took to her heels and ran quickly away, back up the hill to the safety of her dwelling. Leif felt a sense of pride in his new bride, when she turned to Olaf and said, "These are my people now and I won't allow anyone to hurt them!" Olaf apologised to Leif for the actions of the man. Leif smiled, and nodded, then said somewhat wryly, "Fear not, my wife managed the problem very well," to which all the men replied with a hearty laugh.

This was a new side to Fraida that Leif had never seen, and it intrigued him. So later that day, when they were alone, Leif teased and taunted Fraida by pushing at her gently, trying to get her to react. She turned suddenly, and slipping under his guard, she held her knife, still sheathed, at his throat, and she laughed into his surprised face. He held his hands up high for a moment, then brought them down and before she had time to think, he quickly tickled her sides. She squirmed, relaxing for the second he needed, and twisting his leg behind her, he pushed her down, falling with her and landing on top. She was trapped. As he looked into her laughing eyes the mood of them both quickly changed. Leif brought his lips down hard to meet with hers. Lost in the throes of passion, they began to roll fervently about, and pausing only for a moment, Leif dragged the furs down onto the floor. It was some time later, they eventually rejoined the others at the feast.

The day of Olaf's departure, all too soon Fraida thought, finally arrived. She watched with sadness, as the boats were loaded with wood ready for the return journey. Hakon was there to supervise and Olaf's men stared at him in amazement. What they now saw was, what this man lacked in looks, he definitely gained in strength. He worked well with the men. Moving the wood and directing at the same time, how the cargo should be loaded. With Hakon's direction, the men soon made short work of the loads. The cargo was nearly all aboard when the women appeared, carrying boxes of food, flagons of beer and some of milk, for the visiting men to stow on board for the journey.

Fraida stood with her father, her eyes already heavy with tears. Toork hung back. As Leif went over to clasp Olaf by the shoulder, a tearful Fraida left her father's side to walk over to hug Toork. Leif shook Olaf by the hand and smiled, while reassuring him that he would take good care of Fraida. He went on to say, he would do his utmost to ensure Fraida did not suffer from loneliness.

Olaf, with his head bent, remained momentarily silent. Then raising his head he smiled in return, as he replied, "Oh she won't be lonely, that is one thing of which I am sure." Olaf then drew breath, pausing for a moment before continuing. "There was, by the way," he said casually, "one more condition to the agreement of the marriage I have, as yet, omitted to say." Leif's forehead creased in a frown as he looked at Olaf in puzzlement. "Toork stays," Olaf stated flatly, and his face showed no hint of emotion.

Leif, being temporarily shocked at this statement, looked back at Olaf in stunned silence. He could not believe he had heard right, until he looked at Fraida, who was already jumping and hugging Toork in her pleasure at the news. "I cannot, and indeed will not, leave my daughter unprotected," said Olaf. "You yourself, as her husband, can appreciate how precious she is," he further stated, "and Toork and I were decided on this before we came."

Fraida turning, looked over at Leif, but her smile faltered when she saw the anger appear on his face. "She has all the protection she will ever need already here and any that will be required will come from me, her husband," Leif replied angrily. He was furious that Olaf had sprung this on him at the last minute, just before they were due to sail. Turning he walked away to give himself time to think.

Fraida called out to him. He took no notice. Anger was overtaking any other feeling, and at that moment he was trying to control the rage, coursing through his tense body. Toork and Olaf exchanged a look, that only they themselves, could understand. Fraida ran after Leif, pleading with him, knowing by his look, that he had taken this as an insult.

He grabbed the top of her arm as she caught up with him and propelled her along at his side. She immediately was angered by this, but also knew this was not a time when she should retaliate. "Did you know about this?" he grated through his teeth. "No," she said breathlessly, trying to keep up with his furious pace. Trying to placate him, she then went on to tell him," I feel safer with you than with anyone. I don't want Toork as a protector; my faith in you is complete. You have all that is required for my protection. But I would, in all honesty, like for Toork to stay, because he is my friend, my family, someone from my home."

Leif, stopping abruptly, swung round to face Fraida. He looked down into her distressed face and she looked up at him pleadingly. Leif struggled hard to remain angry. The tears welled up and began to spill from Fraida's eyes. She was upset that Leif was angry, but even more so at the thought of her Fathers imminent departure. Unhappy himself, at the sight of her crestfallen face, Leif let out a long sigh. Then putting his arms around her, he hugged her tight. "If it is what you really want," he said resignedly," then Toork can stay." He was not at all sure in himself about this situation, but it was what she desperately wanted; and at this moment in time, he found he could refuse her nothing.

Jumping up, she threw her arms around his neck, kissing and thanking him. Dalgar, on seeing this, began to bark furiously, immediately racing towards them. "Well," said Leif dryly, to Fraida, "I suppose Toork will be useful for something, even if it's only to keep those damn dogs under control so that I can at least hug my wife!"

They walked back and Fraida smiled widely as she ran up to Toork. Olaf strode up to Leif, grabbing him by the hand he thanked him. "This does mean a lot to me, not to mention Toork!" he said. "Besides which, my days of fighting are now drawing to a close; but Toork has many battles left in him yet. He is a good warrior to have on your side, and believe me," Olaf said with conviction, "he makes an even better friend. I will miss him dearly. My only consolation," he said, looking over towards them both, "is that he is here with Fraida".

Olaf swung round and bellowed an order for his men to bring in the one boat that had not yet been offloaded. Leif stood and watched as all Toork's belongings were quickly brought ashore. Leif turned, and for a moment he fixed a steady gaze on Toork's unfathomable face, then he informed him, the dwelling he and Olaf had temporarily shared, could now be his permanently. "Besides," said Leif somewhat wryly, because he was still unsure in himself at this turn of events, "no doubt Olaf will visit from time to time and there will be room enough for you both when he does."

However, there was no time for further talk, as by now, the tide was beginning to turn. So they all proceeded to quickly say their goodbyes. Fraida hugged her father and holding on to him tightly, she told him she wished he did not have to go. Everyone could see Olaf himself was visibly upset at the parting. Turning, Olaf grabbed at Toork's hand, and for a moment both men stared silently at each other, then Olaf suddenly let go. He quickly stepped aboard the boat. There was much sadness on both sides, as the ships pulled away from the shore.

In the last minute rush, no one had taken much heed of the dogs. Dalgar and Volga now ran into the water, looking as if they were ready to jump aboard the ships. They stopped, anxiously looking back at Fraida and Toork, then they looked back at the ships; unable to understand why the boats were leaving without them. Dalgar ran quickly from the water and reaching Fraida, he pulled at her skirts, trying to drag her forward. Fraida stood her ground and tried to grab hold of him, but he freed himself and returned to the water to where Volga still stood.

As the distance between the departing ships and shore lengthened, both dogs barked at the ships, trying to call them back. Fraida called to the dogs, beckoning for them to return to her. Toork managed to grab the wet dogs by the collars, to keep them at his side. They all stood in silence watching the oars of the departing ships move in perfect time. Eventually the ships, with their brightly coloured sails unfurled and billowing freely, picked up speed, all too soon to disappear from view on the horizon.

The crowd at the shore began to slowly disperse, and with the departure of Olaf and his people, the settlement seemed unnaturally quiet. Leif placed his arms around a tearful Fraida, holding her close in comfort. Looking over her shoulder at Toork, he nodded for him to follow, then turning he led them away.

For the rest of the day, in order to keep Fraida's mind from dwelling on the absence of her father, Leif and Toork tried to keep her busy. They let her supervise the moving of Toork's possessions into the building he had shared with Olaf. The large wooden chests that had, unknowingly to Fraida, been put on board one of the boats, were carried up to the settlement by Leif's men. The men looked often at Leif's blank face because they were puzzled as to why Toork was to remain. But no answer was, at that time, to be forthcoming.

CHAPTER FOUR

Later that first night, with the departure of their visitors, the people of the settlement gathered at the communal outdoor fire to drink ale and to quietly chat. Toork sat in abject silence, staring into the fire. He had no way of communicating with these people, and beginning to feel lost in his loneliness, he sighed deeply. Rubbing his hand brusquely over his face, he slowly stood up. Knowing he was not yet ready to retire for the night, he looked at the area around him; then walking away from the circle of light, he entered into the darkness that lay beyond.

He embraced the tranquillity of the solitude, because, as he had expected, he was already missing the companionship of his friend Olaf. He did have the company of these good people, and he knew they were trying their best to make him feel welcome, but to him, they were at this moment in time, still strangers.

The weather, on his first day alone in this land, had been fine. The night remained clear and still. He stopped for a moment to gaze up at the multitude of stars twinkling brightly in the darkness of the sky; then he began strolling slowly and aimlessly along, with his head bent and his thoughts steeped in quiet contemplation.

Eventually he came to a halt. Raising his head, he decided to step over to one of the large, sprawling trees, which lined the path he had chosen to follow. He was a tall, solitary figure, standing alone in the night. In his solitude, his eyes were drawn upwards, towards the glowing fullness of the autumn moon.

Relaxing back against the trunk of the tree, he found his thoughts drifting in the peaceful silence that surrounded him. He remembered happier times in his life, when the soft warm breezes of the Bosporus had brushed against his skin. Although many years had passed, he could still visualize his people going about their business, in that far and distant land.

His thoughts turned to his family and he pictured in his mind's eye his beautiful, gentle wife, his young son and pretty little daughter. They would, no doubt, he thought with a sigh of resignation, stand and look up at the same moon as he; live under that same moon, but sadly, if ever they thought of him, it would be as dead.

He wondered, as he often did, what his children would look like now. With all the time that had passed, they would certainly have grown. His mind always questioned if they would remember him at all. He missed them, and often in his dreams, he would be transported back, to relive the days when they were all together. These were happy times, when they had shared much love and laughter. The carefree feelings of the past, he experienced in these dreams, where everything seemed so real and of the present, would always, he had soon learned, be cruelly shattered, when he woke to the reality of a cold dawn in a newly breaking day.

In the years now passed, when Olaf and Toork had learned to communicate, on winter's nights while sitting by the fire, Olaf would tell Toork he could help him return to his people. Toork however, although saddened, always had to refuse this generous offer. He had not found a way of expressing to Olaf the depth of gratitude he felt towards both him and Fraida. He owed them his life, his very existence, and his debt of honour to them, he knew in himself, could never be repaid.

In the first year after his rescue, he had made a solemn vow. A vow to try to repay these people in the only way he knew how. It was a vow he would have to honour for as long as he drew breath. He knew his only aim was to defend and protect them both.

Toork, looking down, then smiled to himself as he thought fondly of the man who had become his closest friend. The loss of Fraida and of himself would, he knew, leave a great emptiness in Olaf's life.

This change in their circumstances, Olaf had asked of Toork. Knowing only too well Toork himself, would once again be placed in a strange land with unfamiliar people, and with only Fraida to understand him. However, Toork could refuse Olaf nothing. Even more so in this instance. He knew the only way his friend could be at peace, was in being assured of Fraida's well being. To both men it meant self-sacrifice. Their carefully hatched plan, Toork thought with an inward smile, to announce at the last minute that he was to stay behind had worked. It had given neither Leif nor Fraida time to form any argument against it.

Toork began to surface from his reverie when his senses became aware that someone approached. He could hear soft footsteps breaking through the quietude of the surrounding silence. Fraida suddenly appeared at his side. She looked up into his unsmiling face and putting her arms around him, she laid her head against his broad shoulder. "You miss him too," she said, as tears sprung to her eyes. Toork comforted Fraida by cradling her head in one of his large hands, and at the same time he nodded. He softly kissed the top of her head. As he held her, he thought that he would always miss the companionship of Olaf, and no one had been aware of just what this last week in each other's company had meant to the two friends.

Olaf and Toork however, had nothing to fear; because in the weeks that followed, Fraida settled well into her new surroundings. Toork smiled as he watched her. He had never seen her so happy. Leif and Fraida's fragile relationship, which had stemmed from an instant attraction to each other, had now grown and developed into a deep and meaningful love. The more the pair were together, the closer they seemed to become. Leif's people were happy to see their leader return to the fun loving man he once was. They were glad he was no longer alone and was able to share the joys in his life with a woman he so obviously adored.

The laughter of the newlyweds could often be heard echoing around the settlement. Fraida teased and played games with Leif. Always getting her own way, by raising her voice slightly, so that Toork would appear. That was, until Toork saw what she was about and so held back, smiling to himself, as he watched Leif eventually gain the upper hand. In this playing around, Leif soon learned how adept Fraida was with her sword. She was fast, and used many moves unknown to Leif. Toork, over the years, had taught her well. The sword was not just for show; she excelled in its use.

The people, when going about their work, laughed as they caught sight of the pair. The dogs were always barking and leaping round Fraida, as Leif jumped around trying to grab hold of her twisting, evasive body. The place seemed to echo with laughter, now that Fraida and Leif were together.

Vaila watched this from a distance, but unlike the others, it gave her no joy. She had hoped to find fault with this woman. But even she had to admit that, so far, there seemed to be none. Vaila watched Fraida closely, hoping to find some failing in her. Her observations only showed that when Fraida mingled with the people, she showed only kindness and compassion towards those who lived within her new home. Fraida's kindly nature was as instinctive as it was naturally inbred. She never acted as though she was superior to anyone. The people of the settlement were captivated by her soft and gentle charm. Vaila, in her thoughts, could only be consoled in knowing, if she had to lose Leif, at least it was to someone like Fraida.

Fraida herself, had been aware of Vaila's eyes upon her. Vaila, in fact, was the only person Fraida had smiled at, and found her smile had not been returned. On any sudden meeting of the two, whenever their paths had for any reason crossed, Vaila would always look Fraida straight in the eye. Her face would remain impassive, devoid of any expression, then within seconds she would invariably turn around and walk away. Fraida was perplexed at this, but she did remember Vaila from the night of the wedding. At the feasting, she remembered Leif being so angered when one of the men had grappled with this woman, when she stood alone at one of the tables. The incident had stuck in Fraida's mind. So one night when they were lying in bed, Fraida asked Leif to tell her about Vaila.

Leif began by explaining to Fraida, that Vaila was a lifelong friend of his and of Jon. A friend both had a great respect and affection for. Looking down at her with a smile, he carried on to say, "Vaila is a good person, and I place a great value on her friendship." Then Leif sighed and paused, before saying with a slight frown, "Regretfully, a problem arose because Vaila's feelings changed, and she wanted more from me than I could give." Fraida then looked up in question. Leif hesitated for a further moment before saying, "The fact that I chose you and not Vaila to be my wife, resulted in Vaila being deeply hurt. Because of that, our friendship has suffered." Fraida frowned, now beginning to understand the reason for Vaila's behaviour. "However," he said solemnly to Fraida, "I hope with the passing of time, this hurt will fade and that Vaila will look upon me with different eyes, because I miss that friendship and I would like for it to resume."

Fraida, when hearing of this, thought of what it would be like not to have her love returned by Leif. This she would not be able to bear. Although she was glad that Leif had indeed chosen her, she could now understand what Vaila's feelings towards her must be. So from that day on, Fraida continued to smile at Vaila whenever they met. Even though the smile was never returned. When in the company of Leif, anytime Vaila was about, Fraida tried not to show her affection for him quite so much. Respectful now of Vaila's feelings, she did not want to add to the woman's pain.

Unlike Fraida, it took the dogs a little longer to accept this land that was to become their new home. Dalgar was proving to be the most unsettled. In the first weeks after Olaf's departure, he never failed to go, at some point in the day, up on to the headland. Here, he would stand for a time looking out to sea. As if watching and waiting for Olaf and the ships to return. It took the passing of a month, before he stopped going daily to look. Now, only on the odd occasion, when he and Volga were playing together, he would suddenly stop, and look around, then take off and race up to the headland. There he would stand with his head up, ears alert, gazing out over the sea.

The behaviour of both dogs towards Leif did begin to change, but only slightly. They now allowed him more freedom in regards to his new wife, but still, apart from Fraida, they would only take heed from one other and that was Toork.

Nights still proved to be a problem. Having always slept with Fraida, Dalgar being very possessive of his mistress, would become aggressive and not allow Leif anywhere near the bed. So they had no option at night, but to shut the dogs out. The dogs, knowing full well that Fraida was inside, would sit at the door of the dwelling and constantly howl. There was no peace until Toork, growing tired of listening to the noise, would finally lose all patience and go fetch them to lead them away.

Toork himself however, was finding in this new land, the dogs were the least of his problems. He had a bigger problem. It was one he knew he would have to resolve. He was becoming increasingly irritated, and certainly more than annoyed, at the actions of Kelda. She had obviously, Toork thought wryly, because of her sad and deranged mind, taken him to be some sort of demon. Kelda continued to leap out at Toork, at every given opportunity and at the most unexpected times. Whenever he turned a corner, or entered a room, she was invariably there. Infuriatingly, she would always throw one or other of her powders or potions all over him, before quickly running away to make her escape. It was always when his guard was down. When he was unprepared, and Toork's patience was now wearing thin. Some of these potions had the smell, Toork was convinced, of decomposing bodies. Others were the very devil to remove! No matter who tried to reassure her, no one seemed able to penetrate Kelda's own little world. A world in which she had become more active since the appearance of Toork.

Kelda had watched the people closely for some reaction whenever Toork mingled among them. She grew increasingly perplexed when she saw none. In her confused and muddled mind, she could only think he remained oblivious to them; more so because she never saw him speak to anyone. She tried her best to startle him, so he would utter a sound. But to her annoyance, so far this had failed. Not one to be defeated, she was determined not to give up. Now she had taken to wandering about in the early light of dawn to gather herbs, mosses, and anything else she could put her hands on, which she used in these potions destined for Toork.

One day, after yet another incident, Toork decided he'd finally had enough. He had to find a way to show this woman he meant her no harm. So for the next few days, he rose early and managed to remain out of sight, while quietly observing Kelda's routine. He watched closely to see if there was a particular path she followed, because at first sight, she just seemed to drift aimlessly about.

Having noted the general area of her early morning wanderings, Toork, on one of the days before Kelda was up and about, rose early. It did not take him long to find a place where he would be hidden from view and there he waited. When Kelda did eventually appear, Toork crept quietly towards her and grabbing her quickly from behind, his large arms encircled her, lifting her with ease, raising her feet well off the ground.

Fraida and Leif both woke with a start. Before they could even gather their thoughts, the hairs on the back of their necks stood up at the sound of blood curdling and piercing screams. Leif, still not fully awake, stumbled and fell out of bed, while instinctively reaching for his sword. Fraida was quick to follow. They grabbed their cloaks, which billowed out around them as they haphazardly threw them on. The ends trailed behind on the ground, as they struggled to fully cover themselves. In their haste, they bumped into each other running towards the door. Leif put his arm out to push Fraida behind him, but both clasped their swords firmly, ready for the battle they thought was ahead.

On emerging from the dwelling, they could hardly believe the scene before their eyes. Leif pushed back his hair, then rubbed his hand quickly over his face as he looked again at Kelda, who was wriggling furiously in Toork's large, muscular arms. Her small feet were flaying out at thin air. She was screaming for all she was worth. Half the settlement, it seemed, had heard and they too quickly emerged. They ran out like Leif and Fraida, thinking murder most foul was definitely being done. The dogs, who had been shut in by Toork, now started to bark loudly and all the noise added to the increasing commotion.

Thinking Toork had reached the end of his patience, Leif stumbled forward. Fraida reached out to stop him. "He won't hurt her," she said, understanding immediately the scene before her. The people looked over to Leif for his guidance on how to proceed. He held up his hand, bidding them to be still. Following the direction from their leader, they all remained where they stood. Everyone silently watched and waited until Kelda's screams eventually dulled to a kind of squeak.

Kelda, now exhausted from her struggles, suddenly went limp when she noticed the people all staring silently in her direction. Kelda looked pitiful, dangling loosely over Toork's large arms. Fraida felt like she wanted to run over and hug her. Toork set Kelda gently down and turning her round, he planted a big kiss on her cheek.

Kelda pushed him angrily away, quickly wiping her cheek with her sleeve, while glaring fiercely at his smiling face. She hesitated only for a moment, then with a threatening look, she clutched at her herbs in the bag attached to her waist. She looked round at everyone, giving them all an angry stare, then turning, she took to her heels and scurried away.

Toork looked at the gathering of people and raising his eyebrows, he lifted his shoulders and spread his arms wide, and in an unusual gesture for him, he smiled broadly. The crowd, now seeing the funny side, started to laugh, and turning round they began to disperse. Fraida smiled back at Toork and shook her head ruefully. Toork spread his arms again, and raising his eyebrows in question to Fraida, he motioned, what else could he do?

From that time on, Kelda kept her distance. Although she watched Toork from afar, she never tried to work her magic on him again. Kelda, in consolation, convinced herself all her potions and powders combined, had finally done their work. Given the reaction from her people in their acceptance of Toork, her spells, she thought, while pacifying herself, had driven the evil from the demon. She was relieved he now appeared to all, thanks to her, from the earthly realm of the good.

The people of the settlement had accepted, and indeed welcomed, this dark, silent stranger who had come to live among them. They were fascinated by his unusual manner. His strange customs stirred their curiosity. Many in the settlement would stop what they were doing each day, just to watch him rigorously follow a somewhat puzzling ritual. The movements, which were always the same, seemed to be repeated in a set pattern. He continuously moved his muscular arms and legs in a strange, but graceful way. The men thought this ritual, which carried on for some time, must be Toork's way of increasing his strength. Their own strong and muscular bodies were the result of general daily work, coupled with rowing their ships while at sea. These were daily chores that Toork never participated in.

Leif's people, never having seen this before, would watch the ritual to the end, until Toork stooped to lift his curved weapons. That he was a master of these strange swords, there was no doubt. He used them with a swiftness that was almost faster than the eye could see. The men, while admiring his skill, were at the same time glad he stood with them and not against them; because they all agreed, this dark warrior would be a dangerous adversary in any battle.

There was much amusement when Jon's son Erik, now a child of six years, began to attempt to emulate Toork's daily routine. Erik, unlike the other children, was not at all frightened either by the appearance or the manner of this tall, silent stranger. He had developed a fascination for Toork. Each day he would stand near to him and watch his every move. On one of the days, everyone laughed, as he earnestly, but unsuccessfully, tried to follow the pattern of the rhythmic movements. Unlike Toork, his movements were not graceful and flowing and only resulted in him falling down. Never daunted, he rose and carried on, trying ever harder to move in unison with this tall, silent man.

Leif smiled fondly as he watched the boy before him. He was an endearing child. Well liked by the people for his cheery disposition. His colouring was blonde, taken from his mother. But he had his father's limpid blue eyes, that were so clear and trusting. The easy charm that shone out, even at that early age, was all Jon. It hurt Leif sometimes to look at the child, because it brought back so many memories of Jon, and Leif missed his friend badly.

When it came to the part where Toork lifted his swords, Erik then lifted the two sticks he had placed on the ground beside him. He tried to swing the sticks in the same manner as Toork swung his swords. But he soon dropped them when the sticks hit him sharply on the face.

At this point, Leif went over to scoop Erik up and swinging him high, he carried him away; making him laugh so he would forget about the sticks, which Leif thought could do him an injury. Toork seemed to be oblivious to all this and looked neither left nor right. He was steeped in concentration. Aware, as always, of the danger from the sharpness of the curved blades moving so swiftly in his hands.

Since Jon's death, Leif had always ensured he spent time with Erik. He knew if he had a son, and the situation was in reverse, Jon would have done the same for him. He tried to teach Eric what his own father would have, if he had still been alive. He spoke often to Erik about Jon. Of the way they were as children, of the battles they fought together as men. Erik loved being in the company of the older men and he could often be seen following Leif and Ragnar, his grandfather, round the settlement. However, this began to slowly change with the appearance of Toork.

Erik seemed to have found a new hero. He was convinced by Toork's stature and weapons, that he must be a great warrior. So began following him about, chattering endlessly, regardless of the fact he never got an answer. Leif smiled to himself on one of the days, when he heard the boy tell Toork he wished he could speak, so he could tell him about all the great battles he had fought and taken part in.

Like most children of his age, Erik had a great interest in weapons and in anything warlike. He often pestered Toork for a closer look at his strange, but fascinating swords. The first time Toork agreed, the boy tried to feel the blades, but Toork caught his hand in time to stop it touching. He then proceeded to show Erik, using only a blade of grass, just how sharp the edges of the swords were. There was never any emotion shown on Toork's face as to what he thought of this situation with the boy, but smiling inwardly to himself, Toork's thoughts were; at least he had found one friend in this strange land, even if it was only a child.

The following weeks passed quickly and soon the hours of daylight decreased, while the hours of darkness lengthened. A gusty wind came sweeping through the settlement, carrying with it a distinctive chill warning snow was soon to follow. There was a last minute frenzy of activity, as everyone played their part in preparations for the start of winter. Logs were carted from the central stockpile and stacked high near the entrance of each dwelling. Women busied themselves ensuring the larders were stocked with enough food to last the weeks ahead. Grain was stored in a central shed within easy reach, for the daily task of making bread. Flagons of oil were topped up and shared out, for use in the lamps that would burn continuously throughout the long, dark hours of the winter days. Finally, the livestock needed for the supply of milk and eggs, were taken indoors. The rest of the animals moved to a place of shelter.

Leif and Fraida were walking along with the dogs at their side and they shivered and wrapped their cloaks tighter around them, in an effort to ward off the chill. They began to hurry, to return to the warmth of the fire. They spotted Toork and Erik, who were some way ahead. They were absorbed in their task, as Toork demonstrated to Erik, the proper way to perform the moves of his strange ritual. The child, they could see, was concentrating hard in an effort to get the moves right. Leif and Fraida, pleased at the sight before them, smiled at each other, before going on their way.

That night, Toork, feeling the need for some adult company, joined them. They were all sitting comfortably around the fire when, Leif got up to fetch a thick, roughly formed, plank of wood. He asked Toork if he could have sight of his swords. Toork nodded, stood up, and silently handed them over. Leif handled them with care. While judging the weight, he turned them round to examine them closely. Being satisfied, he handed them back and said," I thought I might make a wooden set for Erik. Smaller in scale to suit with his size, before he takes his eye out with one of those sticks!" Fraida laughed, and Toork grinned and nodded. Leif sat down to begin whittling away at the thick block of wood.

Over the next week, Leif worked each night, carving away, bit by bit, until he finished the two perfect miniatures of the ornate swords. When he presented them to Erik, the child squealed with delight, jumping up and hugging Leif tightly, thanking him for the gift. He ran to show Toork, who was just about to begin his ritual. Toork smiled, then placed the wooden swords on the ground for the child, in the same way he had positioned his own. Erik, a grin all over his face, stood at Toork's side as the ritual began. The people were surprised to see Erik could now actually perform the moves in some semblance of similarity to Toork. Unfortunately, Erik was so intent on looking to see if anyone had noticed, that he lost all symmetry and toppled over. The people watching, laughed and clapped before going about their daily business.

The snow started to fall, lightly at first, and it covered the ground in a thin carpet of white. Leif dragged Fraida outdoors, and they laughingly joined with the children, eagerly scooping up handfuls of the drifting snow. They cupped it into tight balls, which they began to throw playfully at each other. The dogs joined in the game, barking loudly, as they leapt in the air in an effort to catch the elusive powdery balls.

Dalgar and Volga, had at last, accepted Leif's presence. Having soon learned, if they refused to let Leif near Fraida, they were removed from the dwelling. At nights, not wanting to be shut out in the cold, they would lie quiet in front of the fire, until the couple began to prepare for bed. Dalgar, never one to give in, would then open his eyes, never moving his head from where it lay on his paws, he would look at Leif and lift his lip, just enough to bare his teeth, while letting out a low growl from deep in his throat. Leif and Fraida would wait for it to happen, then laugh, as they quickly jumped into bed.

The first night the dogs were allowed to remain in the room, Leif found himself waking from a deep slumber. An odd smell penetrated his sub consciousness and when he tried to move, he became aware of a great weight bearing down on him. He opened his eyes, to find Dalgar's face only inches from his own. Still being in the realms of semi-sleep, Leif pushed and shoved until the dog fell to the floor. Turning, he then snuggled into the warmth of Fraida, to drift once more, into the deepness of sound repose.

Within a matter of days, snow, being carried in on gusty winds from the north, fell heavily, and a thick blanket of white covered the settlement. Toork performed his daily ritual indoors. He would never get used to this cold chill sweeping all around ; it seemed to reach into his very bones.

With the worsening weather, people now chose to remain within the warmth and shelter of their own homes and Toork found himself to be alone. Silence reigned all around, and in the lengthening darkness of the days with nothing of interest to occupy his time, he soon became bored. Being alone with his thoughts, gave rise to him dwelling too much on memories of the past, so he decided to struggle through the deep snow, the short distance, to the dwelling of Leif and Fraida. There, the days began to pass as they sat together, enclosed in the warmth, enjoying the company of each other.

Knowing Toork was missing her father, Fraida, as they sat round the fire, related tales of the exploits of Olaf and Toork, in the years they had been together. Leif laughed at these stories. He enjoyed a good tale, and Toork smiled at the memory of times spent with his friend.

Fraida spent many of her days weaving cloth, which she would use to make new tunics and cloaks in the year ahead. Leif worked with his wood, whittling and carving away, until the piece took shape. Toork, lost in his own thoughts, scratched out designs for jewellery, swords or weapons, while basking in the warm glow, radiating from the flames of the crackling fire. Fraida treasured these days. Locked away from the world outside, happy and content, in the company of the two men she dearly loved.

One evening, as they sat eating, Toork lightly scratched some strange markings on the tabletop. Fraida looked at them and laughed. Leif looked over in question? "This is Toork's language" she said, much to the surprise of Leif. "He taught father and I the meaning of these marking's. It has helped my father greatly when trading. For though he cannot speak it, he can mark it and understand what it says." Leif was intrigued by this, and Toork, when seeing his interest, began to scratch out more of the markings, while Fraida explained their meaning. For the rest of the winter it became an ongoing game. Leif would try hard to interpret what Toork marked, Fraida and Toork would laugh together, at the times he got it wrong.

The snow lay deep and thick, but one day the sky cleared and the winter sun shone down on the land below. Leif told Fraida to wrap up to go outside. He then picked up two long, wooden slats he had been working on and he strapped them securely to Fraida's feet. He got himself ready, and strapping on his own, he took Fraida out in the snow. She struggled to remain upright, but laughed with delight, when she found she could glide on the snow without sinking. Leif pulled her along and the two dogs tried to follow. The dogs barked loudly, frustrated that they couldn't catch up, but they were defeated by the deep snow drifts and soon gave up to return to the warmth of the dwelling. Once there, they shook themselves vigorously, trying to rid themselves of small balls of snow, clinging obstinately to their fur.

To Fraida, the weeks seemed to pass quickly, but not for Toork and Leif, who found in their boredom, that the days seemed endlessly long. Leif was becoming restless and he looked for something that would use up his time. He decided to carve snow slats for Toork. At first, Toork was a little apprehensive, but Leif showed him how to strap them on, then both went outdoors while Toork practiced, until he too could use them with ease.

This activity took up only a few of the days and it was not long before they were again bored with the confinement of the dwelling. However, help was at hand in the form of Ragnar, who had decided it was time to go hunting. This short break away from the settlement, was just what all the men needed. Lifting them from the doldrums of boredom, which everyone suffered, when cooped up indoors over the long winter months.

Provisions were prepared, and ensuring Toork and Leif were well wrapped up against the cold, Fraida waved them off. However, they were only gone a few days, when they returned smiling and triumphant, laden with deer and wild boar they had tracked in the snow. The older men were quick to skin the carcasses. The pelts were taken to the store to be cleaned and used at a later date. The women had prepared the longhouse, ready for when the men returned, and the meat was soon roasting on spits, over the large central fire. The people, now bored with their own company, eagerly came together to feast on the spoils. These were times much enjoyed by all who lived within the settlement. They would huddle round, well fed and warm, listening to old stories that, although new to younger ears, to others, they were tales so good, they did not suffer from the constant retelling.

With the women and children's attention now distracted by the stories, the men gathered in a quiet corner at the opposite side of the room, to put together a plan for the last hunt of the season. It would coincide with a date that all Vikings celebrated, the first day heralding the start of spring. At the time of this celebration, the snow would still be deep, and the dark hours still long; but the men knew in only a few weeks hence, they would be released from the confinement forced upon them by the winter weather. They began by forming a set plan. The men would split into smaller groups, and they discussed the area each group would cover. This way, they had more chance of trapping game quickly. Much work had to be done to prepare for the feast, so they all agreed, the less time spent away the better.

Soon, the first day of spring was fast approaching. An air of excitement spread throughout the settlement. Fraida felt her own spirits lift as she watched the people come suddenly to life. The whole place became a hive of activity in the lead up to the spring festival. When the men returned from the hunt, everyone was already busy with their own annually allotted tasks. Fraida joined with the women at the central longhouse. She watched as it was first cleaned, then beautifully adorned, with all the objects used on this special day of ritual. An abundance of food was prepared for the feasting. While the men worked at butchering the carcasses of animals killed in the hunt, the women baked fresh bread to accompany the butter and cheese. Vast arrays of cooked vegetables on large wooden platters, were centred along the tables. Barrels of wine, kegs of ale and mead that had been fermenting these last weeks in the storehouse, were brought to the hall. Flagons were filled from the barrels and placed on each table, as were jars of honey, and wooden bowls full of nuts.

After the elders checked all was as it should be, ready and in its rightful place, with the aroma of roasting meat causing everyone to feel hungry, they all hurried home to change. It did not take long for the men, women and children to reappear, now dressed in their best finery. Everyone gathered together to participate in the spring rituals. When their Gods were appeased, the feasting began.

Fraida sat happily at Leif's side, laughing at the antics of the acrobats and jugglers, as they continued to perform. Vaila purposely sat at the other side of the hall, near to Kelda. She too smiled, because Kelda was clapping and jumping about in excitement. Vaila waited until everyone was distracted, before glancing round the room. She could not stop her eyes from, somewhat reluctantly, straying to Leif. She looked him over, slowly, to assure herself that he was well. He looked happy, she had to admit. That was more than could be said for herself, she thought, with an inward sigh.

Outwardly, Vaila looked as normal, but inside, she hid her pain. She could hardly believe all that had happened in the space of a year. Her heart ached at the memory of the last spring feast, when she was the one sitting at Leif's side. Had she but known then what was to come she thought, and she bit the inside of her lip, in an effort to stop the tears from forming. She missed his company so much. His smile, when he walked in the room. The laughter and all the conversation that only close friends share. I miss everything about him, she thought, breathing deeply. At that point, she raised her head and saw Kelda looking across at her with concern. Shrugging inwardly, she quickly put a wide grin across her face and lifting her hands, she clapped. Kelda, now satisfied, turned back to the performing acts.

In the days following, there was much merriment as everyone made the best of the prolonged feasting. In the daytime, in order to amuse the people, acrobats and jugglers would perform. At night, the musicians played and requests were made for Fraida to sing songs from her homeland. Then it was her turn to listen and enjoy songs the other women of the settlement sang. As the nights progressed, everyone would settle down, and basking in the warmth from the large central fire, the people listened to the elders relating long sagas passed down from generation to generation. Many favourite tales about the lives and battles of all the great rulers and warriors who had been their ancestors.

All too soon, the days and nights of the first week of spring passed The people, tired from the celebrations, began to slowly return to their homes. Here, they would sleep for many a long hour, to recover from the tolls of sleepless nights spent feasting.

It was not until much later, the following week, when the settlement once more came slowly to life. Some of the men began to emerge from their homes and they spoke quietly among themselves, as they made their way through the thinning snow, to the dwellings used as work sheds. Tired now with sitting around, they began to work at restoring their weapons and shields in readiness for use in the year ahead. Others began working again on the small fishing boats that were under construction in the large sheds.

Leif instructed some of the men to assist Toork in setting up his forge and over the next few days, Toork worked alongside them to ensure the layout would suit the way he liked to work. Leif went over to visit him when the forge was up and running and after Toork had shown him all the workings, he took him aside and smiling, he held up a Viking sword and with one stroke, he showed Leif how inferior the sword was in comparison to his own.

Leif looked on in amazement, then bent to pick up and examine the broken sword. He was surprised at the strength of the metal in Toork's swords, which were in fact, much thinner and lighter than his own. Toork, still smiling, then made an offer, indicating in motion, to Leif. Would Leif like Toork to make him a new sword, fashioned like the one he had made for Olaf? Leif was at first overcome at the generosity of the offer and he asked Toork if he had understood his meaning correctly. Toork grinned and nodded. Leif began to express his delight at the thought of owning such a fine weapon and as he accepted, he gave his heartfelt thanks for the kind offer.

In the weeks that followed, the two spent a lot of time together. Leif watched in anticipation, as his new sword began to take shape. Fraida smiled when she saw them huddled at the forge. It made her happy to see a friendship forming between the two. It made her feel less guilty that Toork had been parted from her father, when she knew he had gained a new friend in Leif.

The faint warmth from the early spring sun gradually filtered down to the earth below and the snow began to melt. The men gathered together to watch Leif practice with his new sword. Being lighter than any sword he had previously used, Leif found it gave him greater freedom of movement. Toork practiced with him, showing him moves that could be performed with a lighter weapon. Toork was good, the men thought, while watching him sparring with Leif. They could now see, he was just as proficient with a conventional sword, as he was with his own. The men watched for a time, because they were always willing to learn new moves that would give them an advantage on the field of battle. They then practiced with each other, trying out the moves Toork was acting out with Leif. The children, standing well back from the sparring men, watched in fascination. All longing for the time, when they too, would be old enough to take part in a battle.

With everyone engrossed in the scene before them, nobody noticed the boat sail into the harbour. Leif stopped in surprise, when he saw some of the men from his township approaching. He smiled in welcome. But they, themselves, faltered, because their eyes fixed on this tall, dark imposing figure of a foreigner. Leif turned and trying to put the men at ease, he said, "This is Toork, a new member of the settlement." He smiled as he continued, "He comes with my wife, so not only do I have a new wife, but a new friend also." The visitors remained silent, but they slowly nodded, all the while warily taking in the appearance and stature of the stranger before them.

Leif then turned to Toork to explain where the men had come from. The visitors drew their eyes away from Toork, back to Leif, and one said, "We have come bearing news." Leif took the man by the shoulder and he began walking forward, calling out to the women to bring food and ale, as he and the men, led the visitors back to the longhouse.

When the men of the township were seated and had before them food and drink, they related to Leif that they had news of his father's ship. Toork looked at Leif and saw sadness darken the brightness of his eyes.

But the sadness was closely followed by anger, which quickly spread over Leif's grim, unsmiling face.

The men went on to say trading had started early that year and a few ships had already come in from the sea to dock at the port. The story of Leif's father's ship and the way it had been taken, was common knowledge. Everyone knew that some of the trading ships, while travelling about their business, kept a look out for any sight or sound of the ship's whereabouts. The men then related to Leif, the crew of a visiting ship had told them just as they were leaving port a couple of weeks before, that his father's ship had passed them sailing into the same port they were departing from. This was far down the coast of the lands to the south.

Leif was quiet and sat with his head bent, while struggling to control his rising anger. He looked up and over at Ragnar, then turning, he abruptly instructed the visiting men to make ready two longships from the township. He told them to be sure to crew them with good fighting men. "We will join them as soon as we are prepared and we will sail together," said Leif as he stood. "Do this as soon as you return," and turning, he left the longhouse.

Leif went in search of Fraida. Her heart was instantly heavy when he related the news. She knew only too well what this would mean. The thought of his absence in the months ahead, was hard to bear. When he told her he intended to go as soon as possible, she argued that the weather had not yet settled.

"We won't be beaten by a storm or two," Leif reassured her. "I will find our ship or die in the attempt," he said vehemently. "The longer we wait, the more chance it has of evading us. It is of the utmost importance to my people that we honour our dead, by wreaking revenge on those who deprived us of so many loved ones. Everyone in the settlement lost someone. Kelda lost her whole family. Is there any wonder she is deranged?" he said, throwing up his arms. "With all the pain and grief she had forced upon her. I will never rest until my father's ship is once again at our shore and all those who took her are lying dead, either on the field of battle, or at the bottom of the sea. I will not betray the faith my people have in my ability to achieve this and I swear to Odin, wherever our meeting will be, the outcome will be the same. None will survive," he said, with a finality that was menacing.

Fraida, hurt at the look of sadness now in her husband's eyes, put her arms around him in comfort. "This time when you return," she said softly, "I will be here waiting for you. I will be here at the end of your journey, so that is all the more reason for you to keep yourself safe and unharmed. I know you must do this," she said stroking his face," not only for yourself but for your people. Maybe this time you will find the boat and bring her back," and she smiled as she said, "and then, the people will be able to rest, knowing that justice has at last been done."

Fraida had to think quickly and now she knew what she must do. She waited until later that day, when Leif was busy, before going in search of Toork. She signalled to him to find a place where they could speak, without others hearing. He looked at her with a frown of puzzlement but quickly found a spot. They now stood, out of sight, behind one of the dwellings. Fraida wasted no time and immediately began, by urging Toork, to go on this raid with Leif. He frowned, shaking his head and motioning she would be left alone. "I will not be alone Toork," she said in exasperation. "I have the dogs, and the people, who will take good care of me. What could happen to me here?" she said, trying to urge his agreement to her request. "Besides," she said with a smile, trying to sway him, "I am not really alone."After hesitating for only a moment more, she stated, "I am with child."

Toork stood motionless. He was startled at this news. He was not sure he had heard right. Fraida nodded, but it still took some seconds for the news to sink in. When it did, a smile widened across his face. He put his arms around her in a hug. She looked up at him, as she said, "I have not told Leif this news, because I don't want him to have to think about me. I want him to concentrate fully, on the task before him. So you see why it is important that you bring him back safely to me. I know I can rely on you Toork, to stand by his side, to see that no harm comes to him. That is why I ask this of you."

Toork hesitated for a moment, then frowned as he motioned to Fraida. What if Leif refused to take him? "Don't worry, I will think of someway of persuading him Toork," she said, "as long as I know you are willing to go." Toork nodded and smiled and taking her arm in his, they began to walk back to the centre of the settlement.

Vaila leaned weakly against the side of the dwelling, with silent tears of pain streaming down her ashen face. Her arms were wrapped tightly round her stomach and her basket lay where she had dropped it; with the vegetables spilled out, scattered on the ground. She had been returning from the storehouse with the laden basket and was about to turn the corner of the building, when she spotted Toork and Fraida, walking in her direction. Not wanting to meet them face to face, she had stopped. Her thoughts being, they would pass on. However, she found herself unwittingly caught there, unable to move and hidden from their view, when they halted only paces from where she stood.

She had been inadvertently forced to hear the devastating news Fraida had conveyed to Toork. Vaila now felt physically sick and she tightened her arms around the emptiness she felt deep inside. Tears flowed from her eyes and her heart ached from the knowledge Fraida was pregnant. It should have been me, she thought angrily, gripping at her empty stomach. I should have been the one to carry Leif's child. It was all I ever wanted, she thought, sobbing quietly, as she rocked back and forth. To marry Leif and to bear his children.

Vaila began to despair. This was all becoming too much. She rubbed at her face and quickly turned, leaving the basket where it lay. She set off back to the seclusion of her dwelling. Keeping her head down, she hid her tears from prying eyes and hurried on to where she could mourn in private, for the loss of her love, alone, and by herself.

Later that night in Leif's dwelling, as they sat at the table eating dinner, Fraida glanced meaningfully over at Toork, before drawing breath and saying casually to Leif," Toork wishes to accompany you when you go to look for your father's ship." Leif, who was surprised at this statement, looked up from the food before him and turned to look questioningly at Toork. Toork nodded. Leif smiled, "Thank you for the offer Toork," he said shaking his head, "but I think it would be best if you stayed here with Fraida. She has not been here long and in my absence, I would not like to think of her as feeling lonely in a strange land." Fraida raised her eyebrows as she looked at Leif. "How could I be lonely?" she retorted, in question. "I have the dogs, and I know lots of the people, who incidentally I am sure, will take great care of me while you are away. Toork doesn't want to be left here, with the women. What will he do with just me for company?"

Toork, trying to play along with Fraida, put a doleful look upon his face. A look, that in no way, sat naturally on his strong, silent features. Leif, as he looked suspiciously from one to the other, was unsure that there was not something going on here that he was unaware of.

"There will be other men left here," said Leif, as he continued to eat his food. "But not fighting men Leif," said Fraida, dolefully. Leif, without taking his eyes from his plate, said staunchly, "All our men are fighting men." Fraida, becoming frustrated, grimaced at Toork, and then said forcefully, "Toork has been cooped up here all winter, I say you should give him the respect you afford the other men and let him go with you. My father would wish you to respect what Toork wishes to do."

Leif sighed, and in the face of this argument, he looked up at them both and paused for a time, before nodding. "If it is what you both wish, then I will not say no to your request. I would gladly have Toork stand by my side in any battle, but at this moment in time, my thoughts were for you," he said, smiling at her. Toork also smiled, and nodded, and Fraida said," I will be fine Leif." Then with a satisfied sigh," So be it. That is now settled," and smiling, she grasped her husband's hand across the table, to squeeze it in thanks.

In the days that followed, the settlement became the scene of much activity as the longboats were quickly moved from the shelter of the palisade to be made ready to sail. The women began to prepare wooden boxes for the men to take on their journey. The boxes were stored under the oarsmen's benches and they held spare clothing and cloaks, which the men could change into if they became wet in rough weather. Leif looked at the brightly coloured cloak Toork was wearing. "You had better pack some of my cloaks for Toork, and give him one to wear now," said Leif wryly, "otherwise the enemy will see us coming from miles away." Toork smiled, and Fraida laughed and went to fetch them. Lifting a couple of extra blankets at the same time and folding them, she placed them in Toork's chest along with his furs, knowing only too well, how much he disliked the cold.

All too soon for Fraida, the men were ready to leave. She stood on the shore with the rest of the people. A smile fixed firmly on her lips, masking tears she was struggling to keep at bay. She waved along with the others, as the boats made their way into deeper water. Dalgar and Volga, for once, stood quietly at their mistress's side. They looked from the departing ships to Fraida in puzzlement, wondering why they were again being left behind. Fraida held her composure until the boats disappeared from view. Only then, did she allow her tears to fall, and with a deep, heart wrenching sob, she turned to make her way back to her dwelling. A dwelling that would be quiet and empty, she thought despairingly, gulping back a sob; with the absence of the two men she dearly loved.

Vaila watched Fraida closely and she saw her tears fall as she turned to walk with her dogs back to her home. Vaila frowned and drew in a breath. She was still unsure of what she should do. When Fraida had been busy saying goodbye to Toork, Leif had looked over to Vaila. His eyes had held a request and he had inclined his head as he looked from Vaila to Fraida, then back to Vaila. Vaila knew, immediately, what Leif was asking of her. He was asking her to be a friend to Fraida and to look after her when he was away. Vaila, taken aback at Leif's audacity, had not replied with her eyes, but had looked at the ground instead.

She was so angry that he would ask this of her. Had he no inclination of what it would require for her, to put her own feelings aside, in order to do what he asked, she thought angrily? Confused and angry, she continued to struggle with her raging emotions, while at the same time, she searched for an answer as to what she should do.

Later however, as the boat was pulling away from the shore, Leif had turned once more in desperation to look again at Vaila. Her heart went out to him. Unable to help herself, she caved in. This time she looked directly back into his eyes and Leif gave her a small smile. Knowing her so well, just by the look on her face, he knew she had now agreed to do as he asked.

However, by the following morning, Vaila was regretting having agreed to Leif's request. Her anxiety was increasing and she paced around her dwelling, trying to think of a way to approach Fraida. She could not just casually drop in for a visit, given the way she had avoided any contact with the woman since her arrival. Fraida would find that strange, she thought with a frown, and it could make the situation worse. Vaila cursed Leif under her breath for putting her in such a position. Being unable to think of an excuse, she finally stopped pacing, and with a shrug, decided to just walk over in the direction of Leif's dwelling, in the hope of seeing Fraida out and about.

Vaila was in luck. She spotted Fraida some distance away, walking with the two dogs. Vaila purposely headed in their direction. Eventually the two women came abreast of each other and Fraida, who had been lost in thought, looked up, and was startled to see the other woman standing immediately before her. She hesitated, somewhat confused, and not really knowing how to deal with the situation, she smiled weakly at Vaila. Vaila, shocked at seeing Fraida's beautiful face distorted with eyes swollen from a night spent crying, smiled back.

Fraida, feeling lost and alone, on seeing Vaila smile at her for the first time was unable to stop tears from welling in her eyes. Her face crumbled, tears spilled out and rolled down her pale cheeks. Dalgar straight away began to whine, he pawed at his mistress, unable to bear her distress. Vaila stepped forward, she was unhappy herself at seeing the other woman's pain. Dalgar for once stood back, sensing this woman meant his mistress no harm.

Vaila, after hesitating for only a moment, placed her arms about Fraida saying soothingly," Don't worry, Leif is a great warrior, just like his father before him. He has done this many times," she said softly, "and although his father and Jon are gone, their spirits still stand by his side in battle. He now has Toork, who is also a great warrior, to protect him and keep him safe. Raising her voice slightly, she said, "Then there is Ragnar, who would never allow anything to happen to Leif". Patting Fraida gently, she further added, "Leif himself knows he has everything to live for now. He has you to return to and he would not like to think of you being so distressed." She bit her tongue just in time, as she nearly said it would not be good for the baby, which would leave Fraida wondering how she knew. Instead she said, "So come, please don't cry, he will be alright, as will Toork. They will look after each other, I promise you that."

Fraida, being comforted by the other woman's words, tried to smile. "That's better," said Vaila, smiling in return. "Now, have you eaten this morning?" she said softly. Fraida shook her head. "Well" she said firmly," let us go into the warmth of the fire and we'll both have something to eat," and turning, she led Fraida, with the dogs trailing closely behind, to the dwelling where, when she had last stepped over the threshold, it had been solely occupied by Leif.

CHAPTER FIVE

Toork mouthed a silent curse and huddled closer to the side of the small, wooden tent, hastily erected, in the middle of what he now called "this infernal ship." A ship that seemed to him, to do little other than toss and pitch! Tightening his grip on his sodden cloak, he looked up and his large frame gave an involuntary shudder when yet another wave crashed over the boat. Was there no end to this? he thought despairingly. He then braced himself, waited for the next rush of water to wash over his crouched and shivering body. The weather was torrential, towering waves crashed over the boat in the storm which raged all around. He felt himself to be gravely ill, as the boat, never still, lifted and dropped, while battling to sit atop the swirling waters of a churning sea. He was wet, cold, and constantly cursing the fact he had agreed to come on this voyage.

The longships had sailed unavoidably into the storm on the previous day and by the looks of things now, he thought, glancing up and around, the weather was not about to change.

When the sky had become grey and the winds increased, the crew had taken slats of wood from where they lay flat against the sides of the ship. They slotted them together to form a tent and anchored it to the centre, to give some shelter in the worsening weather. This small tent however, Toork thought ironically, did not afford much shelter when they were being hit on all sides by huge waves. This raging sea was intent, it seemed, in swallowing all that sailed upon her. It would only be still, he thought with a growing feeling of certainty, when all the ships had been drawn deep down into its very depths.

He looked up at the faces of the crew as they battled with the oars, and at Leif who stood at the stern, both hands gripping tight the steering oar, in his struggle to keep them on course. They had no fear these men, a look of fierce determination was on all their faces. In some unfathomable way, it could be said, they were enjoying this battle with the storming sea. They seemed to relish the challenge. Looking upon it as a game, a game that they themselves would surely win.

Toork shook his head. His thoughts differed to those of these sailing men. He himself, was certain the raging elements would never allow them to win, or indeed to ever set foot on land again. They would all, undoubtedly, he thought despairingly, be dragged down into the deep fathoms of a cold and watery grave; never to be seen or heard of ever again. Toork thought fleetingly of the pleasurable trading voyages he had taken with Olaf; they had been nothing like this! They had always sailed to warm climates, on balmy seas of the Middle East. He vehemently wished he was there now with his friend. That very friend who, he was sure, he would never have the chance to set eyes on again.

Leif, from where he stood battling to retain his grip on the steering oar, frowned, he looked over at Toork with some concern. Toork's look and demeanour clearly portrayed that he was ill. Leif and his men were used to weather like this. Being on rough seas bothered them none. Toork however, he knew by the look of him, would not be able to stand much more of the boats pitching and tossing, as it continued to ride high on the swell of the waves.

On any other voyage, regardless of weather, the boats would continue to sail on until they reached their destination further down the coast. They would always keep to the deepest waters, too far out for any lookouts on land to warn of their passing, until the fall of night. Then they would use the cover of darkness to sail unseen to shore.

However, looking at Toork now, Leif knew he would have to make for dry land soon. It was still daylight, but if they waited until dark before trying to slip ashore, they would be in danger of coming aground on one of the many rocks hidden by the depth of water surrounding this area of land. He looked up at the darkening grey of the stormy sky. There would be no moon to be seen that night, to light their way to shore. Of this he was sure. The boats had made little headway in the face of the wind, so, taking all aspects into consideration, Leif knew there was no other way but to strike out for land now; while enough daylight still remained for them to navigate their way through the many jagged outcrops of rock.

There was an estuary a bit further down the coast the boats could make for, he thought resignedly. Where they could row upstream, hopefully unseen in the dim light of the raging storm. He knew little of the dangers in this area, having never had cause to land here before, but he knew the coastline and that was what concerned him now. With his mind being set on this course of action, Leif wasted no more time and turning, he shouted over the wind to one of the men to bring the torches.

The torches the boats carried were made of thick staves of wood, wrapped around one end were oil soaked rags and rope. The men huddled together to try to form some shelter as they struggled to get the torches to light. Eventually the rags smouldered and the flames sprung to life. When the torches began to glow, they quickly strapped them into the brackets at the stern of the ship. This would signal to the other boats to follow in their path. One of the crewmen then moved to join Leif at the steering oar where, with the strength of both men, they managed to swerve the boat round to head in the direction of shore.

As they neared land, the men pulled hard on the oars. The water here was not quite so turbulent as out on the open sea, but it still took all their skill to manoeuvre the boats past intermittent formations of treacherous, jagged rocks. Moving slowly, they took as much care as they could while being tossed around on crashing waves. They used their oars as levers to push against the rocks when the boats drifted too close, the crews fully aware of the grave danger of going aground. Leif's ship led the way. Carefully steering a path through a jutting outcrop of rocks. The other boats followed in its wake.

Eventually, after much care in manoeuvring, Leif's boat managed to reach calmer waters. He waited only long enough to ensure the other boats made it through, before heading downstream to the start of the estuary. The men were now tired and exhausted from their efforts, but they continued to row quickly, in order to reach a haven where they could shelter until the hours of daylight had passed. Only then would they feel safe, when cloaked by the darkness of night.

Leif expelled his breath in a sigh of relief, feeling some of the tension lift from his shoulders when all the ships safely reached the mouth of the estuary. Waiting until they came as close as they dared to each other, he hurriedly shouted above the noise of the wind. He gestured to the crews they would now row some way upstream, where he would signal to the two boats from the township, the place where he wanted them to berth. The crews understood his message. Leif's two boats would row deeper into the narrow estuary, travelling further upstream; keeping the boats apart, in order to give reinforcement in case of attack. The men were all aware of the danger of being seen in the few hours of daylight that still remained. The sooner they could be hidden, sheltered by the banks and tall reeds the estuary provided, the safer they would feel. They all, as they rowed, drew on the last bit of strength from their tired bodies. Using what remained of their energy to move the boats swiftly, to a place where they hoped they would be hidden from enemy eyes.

As soon as Leif's boat berthed at the side of the bank, Toork stepped off onto dry land. His legs buckled and his head swam. He sunk down onto his haunches. Putting his head in his hands as he crouched, at that moment, he thought he would never again step aboard any sailing ship. Leif's men remained on board. They were now too exhausted to move and they sat with their arms draped over the oars, gasping, drawing in air to their aching lungs. They began to look warily around and then at each other. They could only hope they had moved with enough speed into the shelter of the reeds and rushes to avoid being seen. The last thing their tired bodies needed at this moment in time, was a battle.

Leif quickly opened Toork's trunk and removing the furs, he jumped ashore. He spread them out on the ground, and taking Toork's wet cloak from around his body, he told him to lie flat on top of the furs. "It will stop the swimming in your head," he told Toork. Then added, "I'm sorry your first voyage with us is turning out to be such a bad one. But unfortunately, this was just an unforeseen storm." This was of no consolation to Toork, whose thoughts at that time were, first and only voyage I hope! However, Toork, who was worn out, gave up on all thought and he gratefully laid his tired and ill body down. He sank into the welcoming softness of the thick, warm fur and the tension which held his body in its grip, immediately started to ease. Spreading his arms out at his sides, his hands groped at the grass beneath, and looking up at the sky above, he sighed deeply, thanking the gods he was once more on dry land.

Leif, having gone back to the boat, now returned with two blankets from Toorks trunk. As he covered the prostrate figure of Toork, he told him he would bring him some food. Toork shook his head vehemently in refusal, then brought his hand up quickly to his forehead, as the movement caused the dizzying sensation to sweep once more through his aching body. Leif said, "I'm sorry Toork, but you must eat. Believe me, I know if you do, these ailments you have will soon go." Toork however, did not believe him! The very thought of food, at that moment, caused this unwelcome feeling of nausea to once more rise up and wash over him.

Leif, ignoring Toork's wishes, brought over from the boat, bread and cheese with milk to wash it down. He sat there insisting, until Toork eventually gave in and grudgingly forced himself to swallow the food. Leif, satisfied, then returned to the boat. Wrapped in the furs and blankets, Toork's body soon warmed up and his eyelids grew heavy. Unable to stay awake any longer, he closed his eyes for the first time in twenty-four hours. The drone of the men's whispers faded as he drifted into the still and peaceful realms of exhaustive sleep.

Toork woke sometime later, when it was dark, with Leif bending over to ask if he now felt better. Toork shook himself awake and after thinking for a moment nodded, surprisingly, he did feel much more like himself. The dizzying sensation had gone, as was the awful feeling of sickness raging through his insides. "Good," said Leif quietly. He then asked him if he wanted to remain where he was, or come aboard the boat to sleep. Toork, now feeling for the first time in days that he was once again in the land of the

living, motioned he would rather stay where he was. Leif nodded, then standing up, he returned to the ship. Toork watched Leif take the couple of steps to the boat, where the men, after having eaten, were themselves preparing to bed down for the night. His last sight before drifting off to sleep, was of Hakon, settling himself down not far from where Toork lay, at the prow of the ship, next to Leif.

Leif, while Toork had been asleep, had explained to the men his intentions for the following day. The boats would set off at dawn, making use of the first light to steer their way out to sea. This was relatively unknown territory to them, so they would leave the area as quickly as possible and sail further down the coast. Leif had a bad feeling about this place. He felt the whole area was too open, therefore leaving them vulnerable to attack. The men agreed. They much preferred to be in familiar territory, where they knew from which direction danger would come. So before settling down they prepared themselves for an early departure on the following day.

The men, being worn out from their exertions, slept soundly. At the break of dawn, Toork was the first to wake. However, he found himself surfacing from sleep with a feeling of unease and for a moment he felt strangely disorientated. He struggled with his thoughts, trying to remember where he lay. He held his breath as he slowly opened his eyes. The first he saw. was the barely visible outline of their ship. Its form now beginning to emerge in the creeping, grey light of early dawn.

He expelled his breath with a sigh of relief. But in that same instant, an inexplicable feeling of impending danger suddenly rose up and it was so strong, it overwhelmed him. His body tensed, and he immediately became alert and on guard as he strained to listen. He tried to identify what had caused him to wake from his sleep. He may not be able to speak, he thought wryly, but there was nothing wrong with his hearing. Turning his ear to the ground, he held his breath and listened. But just as his brain identified the noise to be many footsteps trampling on the ground, he heard rustling coming from the bank above. He sat up quickly. Throwing his blankets aside he, at the same time, kicked out at the boat.

His foot met with a sleeping Hakon, who on finding himself on the receiving end of the unexpected blow, immediately woke with an angry bellow. This in turn woke the rest of the men who, when startled with the noise coming from Hakon, themselves became instantly alert. Toork only had time to rise to his feet before the first of the enemy swarmed over the bank and they were quick to surround him. He stood there alone, facing this unknown enemy. He suddenly realised he was without his swords, which in his haste to get ashore on the previous day, he had left aboard the ship. His brain went into overdrive. Raising his leg, he swung out. Keeping his powerful leg extended, he spun round and the force of the kick brought those closest to him tumbling down. He quickly grabbed at another who lunged towards him, and holding the head locked in his strong arm he, twisted it sharply. Hearing the bone snap, he loosened his grip and the body dropped to the ground.

The men at the front of the boats raised their shields to protect the crews from flying missiles. Hakon, on seeing the numbers of men pouring over the banks, leapt ashore to help Toork. He shouted at the same time for the boats to, "Go, get out of here now!" Leif's answer was an immediate "No!" and just as he too tried to jump off the boat to take on this enemy hoard, Ragnar grabbed him and held him back. Ragnar, while struggling to retain his hold on Leif, shouted to the men of both boats to pull away! Leif told the men to stop, but Ragnar bellowed, "Row!" and the men obeyed.

Leif struggled fiercely, as he tried to jump from the ship. One of the others had to help Ragnar hold him back. The crew at the front of the boats held fast their shields, and the men at the rear rowed for all they were worth. The boats quickly skimmed over the water, moving swiftly out of range of the enemy's arrows.

They all, having been abruptly woken only minutes before, hardly had time to gather their thoughts. In stunned silence they looked back at Hakon and Toork, who, with the enemy still swarming over them, were continuing to fight on. Hakon was lifting two at a time and smashing their heads together, before throwing them into those who came behind. Leif's heart was pumping in rage. He was furious at Ragnar, but Ragnar shouted back at him. "We will find another way! I will not lose you the way I lost your father and Jon! There is at the moment, too many of the enemy and too few of us!"

Leif could not believe what was happening! He watched Toork and Hakon continue to battle the hoards surrounding them. He was furious with himself. How could he have lost Toork in what was his first voyage with them? How could he have lost both men, without even a blow being struck by him in retaliation? All these thoughts raced through his head. He looked back to see the pair of large, courageous men, who were heavily outnumbered, being finally overcome and taken prisoner. Leif had suspected they would be worth more to the enemy alive. Two men, of this rare calibre, would fetch a good price when sold on as slaves.

Leif momentarily put his head helplessly in his hands. How could he have allowed Toork to be taken prisoner after what the man had endured in the past? He thought, distraught with despair. Then hearing shouts, he looked up and his raging anger spilled over in the form of a roar; which he let out through gritted teeth. The hoards had now turned towards the rapidly departing ships and waving their weapons, they laughed and jeered in celebration, of what they thought, was the defeat of these heathen Viking invaders.

Leif knew in that moment he could not let this enemy win. He had to think fast. His body was too tense and bringing his clenched fists up to the sides of his head, he squeezed hard, in an effort to control the rage washing over him. At the same time, his brain desperately searched for a solution.

Looking back, he could now see from a distance, the number of fighting men the enemy had. He reckoned, taking in the crews of their two boats positioned downstream, the enemy still outnumbered them two to one. They could take them easily, he knew, with only two of them to every one Viking. It was how they would do it was the problem. Leif was wise enough to know, if they attacked face on, there was every chance the enemy would, in retaliation, instantly kill Toork and Hakon.

Leif then watched the jeering hoards scramble back up the banks. He saw them start to walk across a meadow. They seemed to him, to be heading in a southern direction. A plan began to form in his mind. He suddenly turned to the men and shouted, "Row as quick as you can men! We will see who has the last laugh this day!"

The crews on the boats berthed further downstream, jumped up in alarm, at the speed Leif's ships were moving down the estuary. They grabbed at their weapons and shields, ready for what they thought was about to come. Leif's crew slowed up and as the boats came abreast of each other, they stopped. Leif quickly explained what had happened. The men dropped their weapons and immediately took to the oars, positioning themselves to row back upstream. Leif shouted, "We are not going back!" Ragnar and the men looked at him in stunned silence.

Leif had a plan. He knew every bit of this coastline. Being a man of the sea, no matter where they travelled, he always took a mental note of any rivers or estuaries, where they could, in emergency, berth the ships. Every time they sailed down this coast, he had noted the areas they might use at a later date. He was now glad that he had. Raising his voice so everyone could hear, he began to explain to the men what he intended to do.

Further down the coast, not far, was another bay with a small estuary. The estuary was too narrow for their boats to travel up, but at the mouth, there was a place where they could easily hide their ships. They would have to row quickly, Leif told them, using all the strength they could muster, because they had to leave this waterway and go down the coast to the other. Once there, they would go ashore and travel on foot to place themselves in the path of the oncoming enemy. A murmur now arose from the men, who were impatient to be off. Fully understanding Leif's strategy, they did not tarry. With no further explanation needed, they took to the oars. All four boats quickly began to pull away.

They moved with great speed and knowing time was against them, they rowed for all they were worth, until they were back in among the reeds of the second estuary. Wasting no time, they jumped out and hauled the boats up onto the banks. Placing their helmets on, they hastily lifted their shields and weapons. Next came their cloaks. Purposely woven with wool dyed to match the colour of grasses, making them harder to spot when covering any distance. They threw these loosely over their shoulders and set off running inland. Keeping together and maintaining a steady pace, they soon reached the place where they would take up their stance.

The men crouched low as they hurried to take up their positions. Leif placed them well apart. Each of the four crews began their formation, which would be in the shape of a wedge. Leif and his crew would face the enemy head on. Two formations would position themselves either side of the advancing men. Ragnar and the other crew would remain hidden in the long grass until the enemy had passed; then would attack from the rear. This way, they would have the enemy surrounded. This formation stance was used in any battle where they were outnumbered. It gave them a slight advantage. With shields up, they moved forward like four arrows driving straight into the heart of the battle. This caused much confusion and split the enemy into smaller groups, making them more vulnerable. The double-edged swords the Vikings carried, allowed them to slice at their enemy from both sides The axes they used were large, with rounded blades, strong enough to slice through any armour.

Leif gave instructions his group would be the first to move, and at this point the other formations should follow. He and his men would aim to push forward as quickly as possible, in the direction of Toork and Hakon. One thing in their favour was, with Toork's colour, and both men's height, their position should be easily spotted. Leif's main objective would be to try to reach the two captives, in order to rescue them, before the enemy had a chance to strike them down.

Leif's men, now ready and in position, drew their cloaks over their bodies and crouched low, waiting for the arrival of the advancing army. They did not have long to wait. In the silence of early morning, they heard the voices of the rabble making their way towards them. The army marched unaware, straight past Ragnar's crew, who lay hidden in the tall grass, towards Leif and his men, who were positioned directly ahead. Leif's men remained silent and still. Leif would wait until the enemy was almost upon them, before he gave the order to attack.

Leif, as he stealthily looked up at the advancing hoard, could see the gods were now on his side. Toork and Hakon, with their hands tied behind their backs, were being pushed and jostled along in front of the oncoming rabble. Leif and his crew, although ready, still waited in silence until the last possible moment. Then Leif roared, "Now!" With this signal, all four crews jumped up roaring fiercely and quickly advancing. The startled enemy stunned and disorganised, were completely unprepared for these Viking warriors, who were only feet away and coming from all sides

Toork's reaction in the melee and confusion, was instantaneous. He swung round and his back and tied hands he faced towards Leif, while at the same time he kicked out at the enemy closest to him. Hakon, a bit slower in reacting, also turned, and using his head, he butted the man facing him with such force, everyone heard the crack of breaking bone.

Leif, with one swipe, cut the ties that bound Toork and quickly put his own sword into Toork's hand. Leif used his axe to swing out at the advancing enemy while Toork, gripping the sword tightly, swung round to slice through those now attacking from the side. One of the others cut the rope that bound Hakon and knowing what was coming, quickly jumped out of the way when he placed an axe in Hakon's large hand. This, Hakon swung with such strength a path appeared in front of him. The enemy fell, three at a time, to the ground.

Leif's crew quickly regrouped in formation. All four formations, now in their position of attack, began to move slowly forward. They drove through the enemy hoards, splitting them up and cutting them down. The enemy became frustrated and confused, finding this Viking formation almost impenetrable to their weapons. The two rows of shields, held up in front in each formation, made it nigh on impossible for their own blows to strike home.

Leif's men, still keeping to their arrowed position, soon met in the middle, and turning, with shields held up, they began working outwards. At this point, a few of the enemy left standing, began to fear for their lives. Dropping their weapons, they quickly fled from the field of battle. The others who were brave enough to stay, fought on, only to suffer the same fate.

Leif and his men, finding they had run out of adversaries, finally lowered their shields to gaze upon the blanket of bodies now littering the field. Looking around, they felt no remorse. These men, who lay dead at their feet, were the very ones, who themselves, had no compunction that morning, about attacking men while they lay in sleep. If the Gods had not been with Leif and his men, the outcome of this day could have been very different. "Laugh now," said Leif coldly. His voice lacking humour, as his eyes scanned the corpses that lay all around.

Leif then turned to look at Toork and Hakon. Seeing cuts and bruises from the time of their capture, he asked if they suffered further harm. Both men smiled and Hakon said with a rare spark of wit, "We are now!" He then looked about him in surprise, as Leif and the men burst into laughter. Shaking his head, Leif patted him on the back as they turned to start making their way back to where they had left the ships.

They walked quickly and soon reached the place where the boats were berthed. They were about to step aboard when Leif, with a grin, called out to the other crews to follow his ship.

He knew of a little uninhabited Island that lay further down the coast. They could berth at the lee side, where the ships would be hidden from view for the time they needed to spend ashore. They had to reorganise themselves and dry out clothing saturated in the storm. Besides, after the events of the past few days, Leif knew the men would more than welcome some well-earned rest. The boats sailed out of the mouth of the estuary and Toork moved over to position himself next to Leif. He then motioned a gesture of thanks to Leif for coming to rescue him. Leif looked at Toork and made light of it as he said wryly, "If, on my return, I had to tell Fraida that I had lost you in such a way, then knowing my wife, I would have all too soon been joining my friend Jon in the realms of Valhalla!" Both men laughed, as they thought of Fraida's reaction, if Leif had found himself to be in such a situation.

Fraida, at that moment in time, fortunately, knew nothing of the whereabouts of the men. A number of weeks had passed since the ships departure and although she missed the two men desperately, especially Leif, she had settled down to everyday life in the settlement. The weather had greatly improved and today the sun shone warmly on the land below.

That morning in the light of the good weather, she had decided to make a start on dying wool she would need for her weaving. Having something to focus on would make the time pass quicker, she thought, sighing despondently. This would keep her occupied in the weeks ahead. Toork, if he continued to sail with Leif, would require new cloaks of his own of the same colour worn by Leif's men, when they set out on raiding voyages.

Toork's cloaks had all been woven by Fraida, in the bright colours of his choosing. But his stature, coupled with the brightness of his cloaks, ensured he was a figure who stood out in a crowd. What Fraida didn't want, she thought with a smile, was for the eyes of the enemy to be focused solely on him when he was in the midst of battle.

Fraida knew she would have to work the wool, to dye it and make it ready to weave the lengths of cloth needed for the new cloaks. Earlier that morning she had given instructions for one of the outside fires to be lit and a few of the men had willingly come forward to position her large pot, which contained the water she needed to boil, over the fire.

When she was younger, Toork brought back from a trading trip with her father, a box, which contained, what looked to her, to be nothing other than large grains of sand. Toork, at the time, had laughed at her expression. But later, he demonstrated what these wondrous grains could do, when dissolved in hot water in a large pot. If she first steeped her wool in this solution, then transferred it into the pot containing the dye, her wool would always take on a much brighter and deeper hue. The use of this solution, enabled her to achieve the many bright colours with which to make the cloaks that Toork preferred. However, this wool she would dye today, needed to be of a much softer and paler hue. So this time, she did not follow her usual procedure of steeping the wool first.

While the women servants worked at preparing the wool, Fraida gathered together ingredients she thought she would need for the dye. This being a colour new to her, she hoped the mixture would give her wool the colour it required.

Fraida put on her apron and stepping out from her dwelling, she glanced up at the sky. She stopped and smiled and took a moment to enjoy the warmth from the late spring sun. Strolling over to the pot, she lifted her paddle and sighing with contentment, she slowly stirred the thick mass of wool simmering within. However, when Fraida bent over to look at the wool closely, to see if it was ready for the dye, she was unaware she had an audience.

Kelda had returned from her daily wanderings, her pouches now full with all she had gathered. The sight of a very large pot bubbling away over a well-stocked fire, had stopped her in her tracks. Her interest was caught, and held, by the fact that no one was near at hand. This caused her to think the pot may have been abandoned. She stared at it intently, while quietly muttering questions, which she in turn, answered herself.

Kelda became slightly agitated when she spotted Fraida walking towards the pot. She watched her closely when she stirred the contents within. This fuelled Kelda's interest even more and she began to fidget; desperately wanting to see what this large pot could possibly contain. She stood hidden from view at the side of one of the dwellings and her eyes remained fixed on the vessel; convinced now it was ready made for her, suspended as it was, over a nice glowing fire.

Fraida, oblivious to Kelda's interest, decided on close inspection, the wool was now ready. So putting down the paddle used to stir the contents, she turned and walked back to her dwelling, in order to fetch the dye. This did not take long, but when she emerged shortly after, she came to a sudden stop. She was startled at the unexpected sight of Kelda bent over the pot and she gasped, when she saw her throw handfuls of, she knew not what, into the bubbling mixture.

Dalgar was off on his daily run, where he would chase and catch hares. But Volga had chosen to stay close to Fraida. Her eyes, until now, had been lovingly watching her mistress go back and forth, while she herself lay stretched out, basking in the warmth of the sun.

Now however, she rose quickly to her feet. With her ears alert and head to the side, she looked in puzzlement at this strange person muttering quietly as she bent over her mistress's pot. Volga's tongue lolled out from her open mouth as she panted in the heat of the sun. She turned her head to glance over to where Fraida stood, with a look in her eyes that showed her mistress she was unsure of what she should do.

Fraida smiled to show Volga nothing was amiss and then softly patted her skirt. The dog walked over to take up a stance by her side. Some of the servant women came running over when they looked across and realised what was happening. Fraida silently held up her hand to stop them in their tracks.

They all stood where they were, watching in disbelief, as Kelda bent to lift the paddle that lay on the ground at her feet. Smiling gleefully, Kelda gripped the paddle with both hands and muttering faint rhythmic sounds under her breath, she stirred at the unknown mixture Fraida's pot now contained.

Fraida, at this point, did not know whether to laugh or cry. She grimaced when she thought of all the time spent in careful preparation that had now gone to waste. Unsure of how she should deal with this, she, in the end, could do nothing but stand back and hope Kelda, who unfortunately suffered from confusion of the mind, would soon lose interest in this particular pot which happened to contain her wool.

Eventually, after some time had passed, Kelda stopped stirring. The muttering sounds faded away and she stood gazing somewhat dazedly into the pot. Nodding to herself, she then looked up and glanced furtively around. For a matter of minutes she stared in silence at the servant women, then seeming to lose all interest, she abruptly turned and wandered off.

Fraida waited until Kelda was some distance away before beckoning to the waiting women and together they returned to the pot. "This should be interesting," Fraida said, as they bent over to look into the bubbling mixture. She was sure in herself, even before looking, that her wool would be ruined. However, fishing out some strands of the wool with the retrieved paddle, to her surprise she found it was the exact colour she had wanted!

Fraida, studying it closely, began to wonder to herself if there was a chance of salvaging the wool. She smiled and decided she would have to try. She told the women to fish it out of the pot and spread it on the grass to cool off.

It would take some time to pick out the odd bits of bone from the wool, and all the grasses and herbs that had become entangled in it Fraida thought with a smile, but she was pleased it was now the colour she herself would have tried to achieve. Could it be Kelda had not forgotten her skills but had known what she was doing, Fraida thought later, as she sat in the sun with her servant women, working with them as they tried to remove all the bits from the tangled mass of wool.

The following morning Vaila came early to visit Fraida. The two women were laughing at the story Fraida told of Kelda and the pot on the previous day, when Dalgar came bounding in. He began barking to get Fraida's attention. Pulling at her skirt he tried to drag her outside. "What is it?" she said distractedly, still laughing. She ruffled his ears and kissed his head.

Dalgar persisted and both women began to wonder at his antics. They stood up and followed the dog outside. From the doorway, they saw a crowd of people beginning to make their way down to the shore. Dalgar set off running towards the gathering crowd, but every now and then he would stop and look back and bark for the women to follow.

Fraida felt her heart immediately lift. Could this be the men returning early, was her fleeting thought? She looked over at Vaila who had suddenly become quiet and she saw the smile had now left her friends face. Fraida shrugged her shoulders and looked at Vaila in question. Then grinning, she hooked her arm in Vaila's as she said, "Let us go and see who comes." Fraida could sense Vaila's reluctance, but she pretended that she couldn't and dragged her along regardless.

When they reached the shore the people, all smiling, parted to let them through. Fraida stopped short as her eyes looked directly at the unexpected sight of her father's ship pulling in to berth. Taken by surprise, her breath caught in her throat; but she hesitated only for a moment before starting to run. She reached Olaf's open arms just as he stepped from the boat. Bursting into tears she threw her arms round him, hugging him tight, unable, at that moment, to speak for sobbing.

Olaf was alarmed. This was not the welcome he had expected. He said softly to his daughter, as he hugged her," What ails you child, are you so unhappy in this new land?" She shook her head as she tried to speak, and finally she did manage to say," I've missed you so much." "I have missed you more," he said to her quietly in return. He patted her back as he held her, giving her the time she needed to calm down. "Come," he said as he looked down at her with a smile minutes later. "Where is my friend? I have missed him too.""Toork is not here father," Fraida said, drawing in her breath. Still with a slight sob she carried on to say, "He has gone with Leif to search for his father's ship.""Ah," said Olaf nodding, "now I see the reason for your tears. Have you been lonely?" "No, not really," said Fraida, and now she smiled. "The people here have looked after me well, but nevertheless I do still miss the men." Fraida then turned to look at Vaila, in order to introduce her. She wanted to say that the woman had been a good friend to her, but Vaila was nowhere in sight.

Vaila, on seeing Olaf had arrived, quickly left the shore as someone had to instruct the women to start preparing food for their guests. She also wanted to send some of the women into Toork's quarters to freshen up the dwelling, because she expected Olaf had come for a short stay.

The settlement sprung to life at the unexpected arrival of the visitors. The longhouse was soon prepared and the older men who had been left behind, instructed the women on the needs of Olaf's crew. Everyone was pleased at this surprise visit because it dispelled the boredom now setting in with the absence of most of the men.

Fraida took her father up to her dwelling where they found Vaila awaiting their arrival. She introduced Vaila and explained to her father that Vaila had looked after her since the departure of Leif and Toork. Olaf smiled, nodding, he thanked Vaila for the care she had bestowed on his daughter. Vaila felt shy and embarrassed. Shrugging it off, she told them she would now go, seeing they had the company of each other. Olaf smiled and urged her to stay for a while, to eat with them, as there would be plenty of time for Fraida and him to be alone.

The women quickly prepared some food and the three then ate together in the privacy of the dwelling. As they chatted, they could hear laughter coming from the direction of the central longhouse. Vaila expelled a small sigh of relief. Being of proud people, she was now content in the knowledge, regardless of the absence of Leif and the men, that Olaf's crew were obviously enjoying the hurried hospitality provided by the people of the settlement.

Fraida's happiness at being in her father's presence once more was clear to see. Her eyes were bright with joy, her smile wide, as she looked fondly at this large man whose company she had missed so much. Olaf explained as they ate that his visit would only be a short one. He was about to set off on a trading mission, but wanted to call in to see them all before he left. He had been lonely, these long winter months, he told Fraida. He had badly missed the companionship of herself and Toork. But seeing her now, he bellowed jovially, had done much to lift his spirits.

Fraida smiled as she leaned over to squeeze her father's hand which lay on the table. "It is a pity that Toork is not here to enjoy your company also," said Fraida. "He will be sorry he missed your visit." "No matter," said Olaf, laughing. "He is probably having a better time where he is! I will call again before the year is out, when I return from my trading voyage. I will be bringing back some fine goods for trade and no doubt Leif will want to do business. So I can visit and trade at the same time," he said, smiling widely at Vaila and his daughter.

They finished eating their meal and Olaf stood up and stretched. Turning to Fraida he said, after having suffered the confines of the boat he had a need to stretch his legs so, would she like to accompany him on a short walk. Fraida, smiling broadly, gladly hooked her arm through her fathers and they left the coolness of the dwelling to step out into the warmth of the sun.

They began to stroll slowly along, accompanied by the dogs, who, being overjoyed to see Olaf, walked one at either side of the couple. Father and daughter chatted happily to each other as they made their way through the settlement. Olaf told Fraida his news, then listened as she told him about what they had all been doing in the months since his departure. She informed Olaf that Toork had made Leif a new sword, and that both men had now become friends. This pleased Olaf greatly, as he had secretly worried that Toork would not feel settled in this new land.

They continued on their walk and eventually made their way back to Fraida's dwelling. Once indoors and now alone, Olaf remarked to Fraida that this life was suiting her well. She looked healthy, and had indeed filled out a bit, he said smiling, as he spread his arms. Fraida blushed, then being unable to hold back her news any longer she hesitated only for a minute before blurting out," Leif does not know this yet, but Toork does. I am with child," she said, grinning widely at her father.

Olaf sat back for a moment. A look of disbelief on his face. He then jumped up and, with a bellow of joy, went over to Fraida to put his large arms around her; enveloping her in a gentle hug. He looked down at her in question and said, "Should not Leif have been the first one you told?" She looked up at him with a slight frown on her brow, "There were reasons as to why I told Toork first." Not wanting to tell her father she had urged Toork to go on the voyage with Leif, she then said," anyway, I wanted to surprise Leif with the news on his return." Her father, being so overcome with joy, accepted this without further question.

That night, Fraida accompanied Olaf and his crew to the longhouse where entertainment had been arranged to amuse the visitors. Olaf spent the whole of the night with a wide grin on his face. He looked often over to his daughter, with whom he shared this wonderful secret, and she, in return, smiled just as broadly back.

Vaila, unknown to Olaf and Fraida, also shared their secret, but her mind was at this time elsewhere. She was fully taken up with trying to watch Kelda, who she had managed to cajole into accompanying her to the longhouse. Vaila wanted to be sure she could keep her eye on Kelda in case she took it into her head to cause mischief to their visitors.

It was fortunate that earlier that day Vaila had taken her leave from Olaf and Fraida to allow them some time together alone, because that was when she had inadvertently stumbled across Kelda. She had spotted Kelda angrily muttering to herself while pacing back and forth in an agitated state. If their paths had not crossed, then Vaila would not have been forewarned and Kelda would still be walking freely about, planning goodness knows what!

Vaila had hurriedly approached the distressed Kelda to comfort her and at the same time to question what it was that had made her so upset. Kelda, returning from her wanderings, had instantly recognised this ship now at their dock to be the one that had brought the dark demon into their midst. She told Vaila she was looking carefully around, just in case they had decided to bring another!

Vaila, at the time, could not help but smile inwardly at this and putting her arm comfortingly around Kelda, she spoke softly to her. She tried to explain to Kelda who Olaf was. He was a friend that wished them no harm. But by this time Kelda had worked herself into a state. She was having none of it and had dismissively shrugged Vaila off.

Kelda had stormed away, shaking her head, refusing point blank to listen to reason. Vaila followed, to attempt again to reassure her. All the while using conciliatory words she hoped would calm Kelda down. But Kelda just muttered angrily, preferring in her confused state to remain highly suspicious of Olaf and his crew because to her they were still strangers.

Kelda continued with her ranting. Throwing up her arms and accusing Vaila and the others of being blind to danger while the men were away. It was clear to see, it was all up to her, Kelda, to ensure no danger would befall anyone within the settlement.

It was at this point Vaila, who had managed to keep calm throughout, became concerned. She knew what Kelda could be capable of and she became secretly alarmed when she saw Kelda had got herself too worked up to be easily pacified.

Vaila quickly realised, if she was going to get anywhere with Kelda, she would have to change tact. So, in a turnabout, she started to agree with her. Leaning slightly over, she whispered secretly in Kelda's ear that she was probably right. Vaila could now see she herself had been too trusting. Maybe the two of them should go to the longhouse that night, to keep watch, in case of anything untoward happening.

Kelda had stopped her muttering in order to turn and look closely at Vaila. She had studied her with piercing eyes while giving herself the time she needed to think. Vaila, holding her breath, had kept her expression impassive until Kelda, her excitement growing at the thought of this secretive plan, smiled widely.

Vaila had built on this, and carried on talking in a low voice until she persuaded Kelda to return to her dwelling. She told her to go home and change, and to wait for Vaila to pick her up. Kelda, finally giving in, had bobbed her head and turned to hurry away, looking around her surreptitiously all the while, in case others were watching.

Vaila had expelled her breath in relief that Kelda had finally fallen for her ploy. But because of her inability to reason with her, she would have to inform the people of the settlement of Kelda's feelings towards the visitors. Being only too aware of the mischief Kelda could cause, Vaila assigned a few of the women the task of keeping an eye on the highly unpredictable Kelda. This would be when she herself had to be otherwise occupied in seeing to the needs of their important guest.

Because of this, later that night in the longhouse, Vaila had to show two faces. A friendly one to Fraida and her father, and a blank one to a distrusting Kelda, who, at the start of the night, sat glumly at the end of one of the tables looking suspiciously around.

However, as the night progressed, much to Vaila's relief, Kelda's mood lightened as she happily tucked into the array of food the people put temptingly before her. She looked up sporadically to glance around but thankfully was soon distracted by the various acts of entertainment. Vaila knew Kelda well and she could sense she was at last beginning to enjoy the evening. Vaila then looked secretly over at the others and gave a slight nod. Everyone was relieved. They had succeeded, this night, in taking Kelda's mind off any further demons.

It was much later, after an uneventful evening, when Vaila escorted a happy Kelda back home to her dwelling. While walking the short distance, Vaila took the opportunity, because of Kelda's lightened mood, to continue to talk in a positive manner about how good the night's entertainment had been; in the company of their new friends. Kelda's head nodded in agreement. Later, as Vaila settled herself down to sleep, she felt somewhat relieved that another probable incident had now been cleverly averted.

The following morning however, Kelda woke abruptly from her sleep. Her eyes flew open. But instead of rising, she lay motionless staring up at the wooden struts high above on the ceiling of her dwelling. Her brain, in these first few minutes of awakening, was already active and she began muttering quietly to herself. Plotting and planning in the recesses of her mind. What potion might she use to trap any new demons that may have slipped unawares on to their shore? she questioned inwardly and with a smile. She had been unprepared, she told herself, when the last one had come. But they would not catch her out a second time, she thought excitedly. Because this time she was ready and on the lookout for any threat they might bring.

Suddenly, with a grin, she threw the covers aside. Rising from her bed, she quickly began to dress. Stopping only long enough to eat a little food, she then scrambled about in each of the dimly lit rooms within her lonely dwelling. Wanting to be prepared for any eventuality she took every potion and all the powders she could find and stored them haphazardly about her person.

Now ready for her mission Kelda hurriedly left the coolness of her dwelling to step out into the rising warmth of the early morning sun. Her eyes screwed up in the glaring brightness. She lifted her arm to shade them, while glancing up at the cloudless sky. Feeling slightly weighed down with all the various pots and pouches, she pulled at her clothes to try to distribute the weight. Not quite succeeding, she shrugged dismissively, and regardless of the heaviness of the load, set off, staggering ever so slightly, down the small hill to the settlement below.

Her first few hours were uneventful. She was content to just drift around the outlying areas enjoying the welcoming warmth of the sun while searching for her elusive demons. That, however, was before her sharp eyes spotted Olaf and his crew, accompanied by the men, making their way towards the forest for a day's hunting.

Kelda stopped in her tracks to stare at the departing riders. Suddenly an idea began to form in her mind. She stood silent for a time, but too many conflicting thoughts crowded her brain. So shaking her head distractedly, she began to mutter absentmindedly to herself.

Where was the best place for a demon to hide, she asked of herself? She was not supposed to go near the ships if she was on her own, this she knew. But who would know; she argued with herself, if no one was here to see?

A plan began to develop, and with it her excitement increased. But she held back, because she was wise enough to know this could mean trouble if she was caught.

Time passed as she deliberated, but she only succeeded in talking herself into a state of confusion. In the end, now totally confused, she shrugged her shoulders, and despite the weight about her person, tried to straighten up. She made a decision to throw caution to the wind and without further ado, she began to make her way down to Olaf's ship. Moving quickly, and in the absence of any onlookers, Kelda soon reached the shore. Scurrying along, she made her way surreptitiously towards Olaf's boat.

Unchallenged, she finally reached the ship. With her excitement mounting she smiled gleefully as she proceeded to go aboard. Glancing furtively around to check the coast was clear, she crouched low and tried to stay hidden as she began to creep quietly about. Under her breath she softly chanted one of her spells, commanding the demons to show themselves. She stopped now and then to listen, while dragging at the hindrance of her clothes which were laden down with all she had stored about her person. She continued, making her way slowly along the deck of the ship; weaving in and out among the cargo. She looked nervously around all the while. Exploring further, she soon realised there was nobody onboard, and nothing that could stop her walking the length of the ship. Freely, at her will.

Smiling widely she straightened up and stood with her hands on her hips looking all around. She began chanting her spell, quietly at first, but she remembered she had no need for stealth. So her voice increased in volume and she waited expectantly for something to happen.

Nothing appeared and she began to frown. Delving into a pocket she produced one of her powders. Holding her arm outstretched she twirled, laughing, relishing the drifting cloud of dust as it was caught by the breeze and scattered all about.

Once more she came to a standstill. Her hands gripping at her potions, ready for what was to come. She listened intently, and her piercing eyes scanned the ship, but nothing stirred. Now she began to get annoyed. If there was unseen demons lurking aboard this ship, then she, Kelda, would soon seek them out, she muttered angrily to herself. So the volume of her chanting increased, becoming much louder. After stopping to look around to find there was still nothing visible, she started to run somewhat dementedly about the ship.

She began, in her anger, to use all her powders and potions. Moving aside any of the cargo she could shift, she scattered the mixtures in every nook and cranny. She continued to stop every few minutes, loudly chanting out the words of her spell, words that commanded any demon to dare show themselves to her!

By this time, any demon lurking in the shadows would most certainly have been frightened out of his wits at the eerie sight of the ghost-like apparition of Kelda. Her spiky hair was covered in a cobweb of drifting powder. Her dark, piercing eyes stared out through a film of fine white dust which had settled on her, now ashen, face. Dregs of the assorted lotions had run down her tattered dress and the fine dusty powders now drifted in an aura around her thin, scrawny body.

Vaila stepped out from her dwelling, in order to go and check on what food was to be prepared for their guests that evening. She was walking along deep in thought when suddenly, just for a brief moment, she heard a vaguely familiar sound drifting in on a gust of wind. She stopped, frowned, then stood alert and listening. Hoping against hope, that all she had heard was the cry of a bird. She waited, then she heard it again. The faint sound of chanting confirmed her worst fears. Her heart sank at the implications. Her eyes began to scan the area around her, but Kelda, unfortunately, was not within her sight.

Vaila became uneasy. She began to panic, wondering what on earth Kelda could be doing. Abandoning the task she had first set out on, Vaila decided instead to go in search of Kelda. She set off in the direction the sound seemed to be coming from. The chants grew louder the nearer Vaila got to the shore. Vaila's view was suddenly clear. She gasped in horror when she saw in the distance, the white ghostly figure of Kelda, leaping and jumping about dementedly on Olaf's boat.

Vaila immediately called out with urgency to some of the other women, shouting for them to follow her, and without further thought she began to run. Her intent being, to remove Kelda as soon as possible from Olaf's precious ship.

Vaila reached the boat just as Kelda was stepping ashore. She looked in disbelief and complete dismay, at the mess Kelda had made of the, what was once, pristine ship. Vaila was speechless with shock. She put her head in her hands to shake it in despair. Her heart was thumping in her breast at the gravity of Kelda's actions. She then looked up and almost screamed as she shouted angrily at her, "What have you done!"

Kelda however, was in a state of elation. She showed no remorse. Instead she put her hands defiantly on her hips and grinned widely as she nodded towards the turmoil aboard the ship. Vaila gritted her teeth and drew in her breath; trying to resist the urge she had to grab Kelda and to shake some sense into her. Instead she turned to the women and quickly said, "I have no need to tell you that all hell will break loose if word of this deed done today reaches the men. If even a hint of it reaches their ears, then this is one ship that will never leave these shores!" Vaila knew all the men who sailed out to sea were highly superstitious in regards to anything pertaining to their ships. She was wise enough to know Olaf's crew would be no different. She ordered those who had run down behind her to get as many of the women as they could to help, quickly, in order to clean up this mess before Olaf and his crew, or any of the men, returned.

She then grabbed Kelda by the arm, and dragging her all the way back to her own dwelling, she proceeded to berate her, while trying to clean her up. She did not want any of the men to see Kelda in this state, or they would become suspicious and question what she had been up to. Kelda hardly listened, being in a state of bliss at having succeeded in carrying out her plan. Her thoughts were far away in a recess of her mind and she stood smiling, congratulating herself on a good days work.

That night the settlement was unnaturally quiet. The men were tired after spending the day hunting, but thankfully they were unaware the women were also worn out from their frantic efforts to restore the ship to its original condition, before Olaf and his crew returned.

Following this episode, Vaila gave strict instructions for someone to accompany Kelda on her wanderings for the remainder of the time the visitors were here. She wanted, she sternly told them, to avoid any such happenings again. Those who had been given the task of keeping their eye on Kelda explained, with all the men being out on the hunt, they mistakenly thought there was no danger of Kelda causing mischief while the visiting crew were absent.

With a close eye being kept on Kelda, the following days passed without further incident, but they seemed to go too quickly for Fraida. Her father and the men had spent one of the days hunting, killing game, now being cooked for them to take on their journey. Another day was spent with Olaf choosing, and the men loading, some fine fur skins, which Olaf would take with him to trade. He also took a large wooden box full of trinkets. These were items much sought after in trade. Combs, some made from deer antler, some made from walrus ivory. Carved pins, brooches and arm-rings of silver. Some had large pieces of amber shaped and set within them, but he also requested a large pouch be filled with small beads of amber, because the fiery stones were popular with women. He would exchange all these for goods the people here requested, then would return with them later in the year.

Business now completed, Olaf devoted the last day before his departure solely to Fraida. They had taken the horses out for a few hours in the morning, with Olaf insisting, because of Fraida's condition, the pace be no more than a gentle walk. Fraida was already tearful at the thought of her father's departure, but Olaf promised he would return later in the year. If not before the arrival of his grandchild, then shortly after. The time would soon pass with the return of the men, he told her with a smile. Then there would be the coming of the child for them all to look forward to. These words were of some comfort to Fraida. She began to smile, and her father hugged her as he said jovially, "Come, let us enjoy the few hours that still remain."

All to soon however, it was time for Olaf to leave. Fraida now stood with Vaila at her side, tearfully watching her father's ship once more depart from their shores. Vaila put her arm comfortingly round Fraida's shoulders and they, along with the people, waved until the boat disappeared from view.

Fraida, remembering her father's words of comfort, set her mind forward to when the men would return. She thought of what she could do meantime to prepare for the arrival of the baby. In the days following her father's departure, she kept herself busy by continuing to weave the cloth needed for Toork's cloaks. She now wanted this work finished so she could begin weaving some soft blankets for the child soon to come.

Leif and his men, unaware Olaf had visited their shores, were back aboard the ships and once again at sea, continuing their journey south.

After the battle they had sailed down the coast until reaching the isolation of the small Island. Here they quickly berthed, and while some of the men pulled the boats onto the shore, others set off to explore the surrounding area. Once the all clear was given, they quickly gathered driftwood and lit some small fires. Having fought a battle on empty stomachs the men were now ravenous. They had trailed lines to catch fish on the way to the Island, and while these cooked on stakes over the fire, they gathered gulls eggs, shellfish and crabs. Being seasoned travellers they were used to making the best of what was available. These would help eke out the remainder of their food.

Over the next few days, using the warmth from the fires and the heat from the sun, they dried their wet clothes by draping them over frames made from sticks of driftwood. As each item dried, it was folded neatly and put back in the wooden boxes, leaving room for the drying of the rest. The wooden slats, used to make tents in the centre of the boats when the weather was bad, had been spread out to dry in the heat from the sun. By day they worked at getting the boats shipshape. At night they rested, sitting around the small fires, drinking the last of the ale and listening intently as some related tales of war.

Having had a few days rest, and with the boats now rigged up and ready for sail, on the last day they gathered round the fires to discuss what would be their next move. First on the agenda for discussion was the need to replenish their food stocks.

Leif, in a jocular mood, had raised his voice so everyone could hear. He said with a widening smile, "I know where there is a plentiful supply of food, ready cooked and there for the taking." The men looked over at him in question, but he continued to just sit and smile. Ragnar himself began to smile when realisation dawned on where Leif's thoughts lay. "Think back to our first raid of last year," Ragnar said wryly to the men. The two crews that had accompanied Leif on the previous year burst out with laughter. The crews from the township looked on in puzzlement.

Ragnar then related the story of their raid to the place of the chanting Monks. All the men had laughed heartily on the telling of this tale. Ragnar, in question to Leif, then said, "Ah, but would this work out the same a second time around?" "I don't know," Leif had replied with a smile, "but it would amuse me greatly to try again and see if it did."

All the men laughed and nodded in agreement. "We would have to ensure the timing of the raid was the same as last year, just before dawn," Leif said stoically. He then carried on to say, "If we set sail at sunset, we would reach the place within a couple of days. We could cook fish here to wrap and take with us to eat on the way. Having only fish to eat for two days is not great fare, but I know this place has food in plenty. If things don't go according to plan, then," he said spreading his arms while grinning, "we will just take it by force." The men all cheered and laughed because, now feeling restless, they were eager to move on. Having agreed on what would be their next move, each man set to work on their own task; quickly preparing for the continuing journey south.

Toork sat at the stern of the ship in the company of Leif. The boats sailed close together, gliding silently through the still waters, while cloaked by the blanket of darkness that came with the night. Toork looked up at the outline of Leif's silhouette in the faint glow of the waning moon. Leif stood tall. His strong hands gripping tight the large oar as he steered the ship on its continuing journey. Toork marvelled at how these men could always steer a true course. Even in the blackest of nights, when it was impossible to see any familiarity of landmass.

He watched Leif as he constantly looked to the stars shining in the vastness of the sky. At times Leif would also look over the side of the ship, studying the pattern of the waves and watching which way the water flowed past the boat as they sailed swiftly on. They must know the oceans well these men, Toork thought. To be able to find their way with only these small things to guide them.

The sails on the boats were hoisted, but with only a slight breeze, some of the men continued to row while the others slept. They changed shifts every few hours to ensure their progress through the dark waters was maintained, because for everything to go according to plan, they had to cover the distance set by themselves before the journey began.

One of the men came to take over the steering oar, to allow Leif some time for sleep. The boats would reach their destination in the early hours of the morning, when it was still dark, before dawn. To carry out the raid they would set out as soon as the ships reached land. With this in mind, Toork followed Leif and he too settled down to sleep. Wanting to be well rested before the raid on the following day.

Both men woke when the ship came to a sudden halt. Some of the crew had already jumped ashore to anchor ropes to the side of the banks to stop the boats from drifting. Leif rubbed his hand over his face, then watched as the men took down the masts and hurriedly furled the sails, so no part of the ships showed above the tall reeds lining the banks of the estuary.

The men went quickly about their work. They kept their voices low, whispering, knowing any sound would carry in the still silence of early dawn. With the boats secure, the men going on the raid now moved to get ready. They would not take any chances in case it did not work out the same as before. So all donned their helmets and shields and carried their swords. All except for Hakon and a few of the men, who carried wooden boxes they could fill with food to transport back to the boats. Leif did not need all four crews for this small raid, so he opted to take some men from each ship. That would allow those who had not been on the previous raid to gain knowledge of the whereabouts of this place; in case they had need of it in the future.

They set off into the darkness. Toork walked stealthily at Leif's side and the rest of the men followed close behind. They did not travel fast, just kept to a steady pace as it was hard to see what lay underfoot in the dark. It wasn't long before the faint sound of voices, chanting in unison, reached their ears. The men put their hands quickly over their mouths, trying to suppress the noise of the laughter as it threatened to erupt. They did not want to give any warning of their approach.

Toork, ever silent, was highly amused. Looking round at the men, he smiled to himself as they continued to travel on. Like before, they approached the building stealthily and this time not knowing what to expect, they crept silently through the back door.

The men all stopped and stared. Once again surprised at the abundance of food before their eyes. Hakon, now feeling hungry, did not wait about. He quickly grabbed some bread and cheese from the table and crammed it into his mouth. He lifted one of the jugs of milk to swill it down. As he drank from it, one half went down his throat, the other half spilled down his front. The rest of the men followed his example and began to quietly help themselves from the laden tables. Ragnar opened the chests. He quickly began to fill them with food. He grabbed at large joints of cooked meat, some from the boar, some from the cow and sheep, large cooked birds, he threw them all in the trunks. Some of the men lifted urns of milk, others found the sacks which were now hung behind the door. They filled them with large cheeses, loaves of bread, apples from the barrels. Hakon and his men were quick to leave, to start back to the boats. They carried the large sacks of food, milk urns, and now full to brimming wooden boxes with them.

Leif silently beckoned to Toork, Ragnar, and the remainder of the men to follow. Keeping close together they crept through the narrow hall. Leif motioned for the men behind him to halt. They stood silent and unmoving until the chanting stopped. Leif, gauging the time to be the same as before, crept up to peep round the door. The large room was now empty. He beckoned again for the men to follow. They stepped quietly into the newly vacated room where they all took time to look around.

Items of gold and silver were spread across the stone altar, replacing the ones they had taken the year before. The gold cross, Leif could see, was not so big or impressive as the one it replaced, but still, it was good bounty. This cross was adorned with some fine gems that could be removed before the gold was smelted down. The gems could be set in jewellery, the gold used for coins and adornments. He pointed to it and with a nod of his head, he directed the men to pick it up, along with all the other icons and chalices spread about the altar. Smiling, they quickly obliged. Making their way down the aisle, they managed again to creep in silence out through the large wooden doors.

Looking round at each other, they held their hands tight to their mouths. They started to run. Trying to get as far as they could from the building. But in fact they did not get too far because, one of the men was unable to stop his laughter from bursting forth and he came to a halt. That was enough to set them all off. Staggering to a halt, thinking of what had just transpired, the more they looked at each other, the more they laughed. They laughed so much that tears ran from their eyes.

In an effort to bring himself under control, Leif had to turn away from the men. He bent over, and with his hands on his knees he shook his head, trying to fight his laughter. Then he happened to glance up. His eyes, as he cast them around, caught sight of a vague outline, and without thinking, and still laughing, he strained to look at what was starting to emerge in the creeping grey light of dawn.

He straightened up. His laughter began to slowly subside as he looked at the outline of the large building in the not too far distance. His thoughts began to clear as he stared at the view before him. This is what they had missed in the darkness of the raid the year before, he thought. Suddenly it all began to fall into place.

The surprising abundance of food, for what seemed to be a small number of people. The dwelling they had just raided, it was obvious to him now, held the supply of food for those who lived within this large building, now visible before his eyes.

He turned to the men, who had just about brought themselves under control. With a grin, he pointed behind him in the direction he had just faced. The men grew quiet as their eyes scanned the area, until they saw what Leif had spotted a few minutes before. Raising their eyebrows, they looked at each other and they too began to smile.

Suddenly they all crouched down. Two horsemen emerged from the large gates. They watched as the riders set off at a gallop, riding towards the west. Leif motioned to the men to start quickly back to the ships. They ran the short distance in record time. All the men who were waiting at the ships leapt up, startled, as Leif and the men came crashing through the reeds to jump back on board.

They dropped the loot into the wooden box at the stern of the ship.

Leif began to quickly explain what they had just seen. "Anyone in the mood for a battle?" he said with a grin. His men smiled and replied with a hearty, "Need you ask!" They dropped the food they were eating and reached for their shields. "We have to move quickly," Leif continued as he reached for his own weapons, "while there is still an element of darkness, we can creep up unseen and surprise them."

Leaving just a few men on board each ship, in case of the need for a quick departure from the area; the rest set off at a quick pace back the way they had come. When the building was within sight, they crouched low as they ran forward, so that their silhouettes could not be seen by watching eyes, ready to raise an alarm. They straightened up just before they burst through the gates. With their spirits high, they roared loudly and quickly advanced.

At first, the sudden noise and sight of Leif and his warriors caused shock and confusion to those standing within the squared courtyard; but the people who lived here reacted quickly, because they were trained soldiers who fought wars for their Christian faith. Reaching for their swords they shouted an alarm urging their comrades to wake up and join them. Leif and his men though, these soldiers would soon find out, were not mere serfs who were easily frightened, but warriors who too had a God of their own. "Thor," their god of war.

Both sides advanced fearlessly into battle, shields up, their swords striking out, they met face on. The courtyard soon filled with the sound of clashing weapons as more of the enemy rushed from within the building to join in the battle against the invaders. Toork, unknown to Leif's men, also served a different god and he had fought men like these Christians before. He quickly advanced towards the ever increasing numbers of the enemy. His curved swords moving so quick the soldiers only had a chance to glimpse the weapons before they were struck down.

Hakon, noting Toork's prowess with his swords, not wanting to be outdone, looked at Toork before swinging his own weapon, his axe, with all his might. He began to swing it round in a half circle, bringing a number of the enemy down with the force of each swing. Toork took up the challenge. The two men soon became caught up in competition against each other, forgetting their sole aim in battle was to protect Leif.

Leif very soon found himself to be almost surrounded by the enemy, who, in a tactic of battle, had proceeded to quickly separate him from his men. In an effort to isolate him, they pushed forward forcing him to retreat to the other side of the courtyard. Leif turned to position himself with his back to the wall. Raising one arm, he used his shield to protect himself from the reigning blows of the enemy. He then used his other arm to swing round his sword, which he brought down in anger and with tremendous force. But as soon as he struck one down, another took their place.

Ragnar, as he battled with the men before him, looked frantically around for Leif. His eyes finally located Leif's position and on seeing he was surrounded, he bellowed out a loud warning to Hakon.

Toork and Hakon, on hearing Ragnar's shout, both swung quickly round. Their eyes searched the courtyard but it was now full of fiercely battling men.

They tried hard to locate Leif. They eventually saw where he had taken up his stance against the surrounding enemy, and they could see he was only just holding his own.

Hakon immediately started to swing his axe, Toork stood by his side. Both fought fiercely to clear the enemy from their path. They gradually made their way over to where Leif was, at that moment, surrounded, and with his back to the wall. Ragnar had also started to fight his way through; he struck men down and knocked them aside as he made his way forward, his only aim now, to aid Leif.

When they found themselves back at Leif's side, all four men then quickly formed a circle. Keeping their backs to each other they began to slowly rotate, this enabled them to bring down many of the enemy while they edged themselves into the very centre of the battle. Leif's men, on seeing this formation, began to do the same. With their shields up, each little group then became impenetrable to the enemy's sword. They battled on, striking out with their swords and axes, till less and less of the soldiers remained standing.

Leif, as he fought on, suddenly found his eyes being drawn upwards, to where a large cloud of smoke had appeared, drifting up towards the sky. This was from a fire they themselves had not lit. By the position of the smoke it looked to be a fire set in an inner courtyard. The thought that this could be a signal of distress had just passed fleetingly through Leif's mind when suddenly, one of Leif's men sounded the horn of retreat.

Leif's immediate thought was, what is he doing? We are winning, there is now very few of the enemy still standing! He looked over to where the sound originated. He could see a small group of his men standing at the large gates. Now being clear of the enemy, they were looking out and beyond. One of them was gesturing that men on horseback were approaching from the west. Leif and the others then began moving quickly together, striking out at the small number of the enemy remaining in their path.

As Leif and his men reached the gates they could see in the distance many riders on horseback heading in their direction. Leif shouted the order for all the men to return to the ships. They set off, running quickly, back to where the waiting ships lay ready. The men, who had been left in charge of the longships, had remained alert and watchful for any sign of their return. As soon as they saw Leif and the men running in the distance, they prepared the boats for immediate departure. The men clambered aboard and the boats were soon moving swiftly down the estuary out into the sea beyond. They were well out of reach by the time the horsemen reached the point from where the boats had made their quick departure.

Leif and his men however, regardless of this, were well satisfied with what they had achieved that day. They had struck a blow at the enemy in revenge for what had been done to their loved ones. Now they were aware of this place, where many of the enemy were situated, they made a vow they would return; but next time they would bring more men and they would wipe them out completely.

For the rest of that day the ships stayed well out at sea. Keeping clear of any landmass they sailed away from impending danger, continuing on their onward journey, to a destination further down the coast.

Out at sea the wind was with them and they raised the sails, which at first flapped, but before long, stretched and billowed and strained at the ropes as the material became taught. The four boats, now with the wind to carry them on, soon picked up speed and all the men were able to sit back and relax. The food was now shared out. They smiled and talked as they ate, content with the added satisfaction of knowing this fine food they were able to enjoy had been at the cost of the enemy.

After eating their fill, some of the crew talked of the day's events. Others settled down to have a short nap. It was some hours later, as night drew in and darkness fell, when the crews worked together to turn the boats, to swiftly make their way inland to berth at more familiar shores, where they could settle down to sleep in relative safety.

Some of the men had minor injuries from the battle of that day and although the wounds were not thought to be serious, Leif knew they would still need attention. As they berthed for the night, Leif set about switching round the crews. The injured men, along with some older trusted crewmen, were now put together in one ship. Leif then ensured they stored aboard enough food for the journey home. He switched about the wooden boxes holding the items of gold and silver taken in the raid; putting the full boxes in the boat that would now sail home.

Leif told all the men the three remaining ships would spend another few weeks looking for his father's ship, before making their way back home. He asked Toork if he wanted to return on the ship now ready to set out for home the following morning. Toork, having enjoyed once again being in the heart of a battle, refused. He opted to remain with Leif and his men. Leif then checked with the others that everything was now prepared and ready for the following day before he too, settled down to sleep. They slept soundly that night after the exertion of the early morning raid and the battle that had followed. However, they all felt refreshed when they woke the next day, and in the darkness before dawn, the boats took to the water. The three boats sailed with the ship that was returning home, until they reached the vastness of the open sea. They all watched it go safely on its way before hoisting their own sails, then turning their boats, they set off in the opposite direction.

CHAPTER SIX

Leif sat upright and awake at the stern of the ship. He smiled at the sight of Toork's large frame, and that of some of the men, as they lay crouched and sleeping in any space that was available. Most of the room on the ship had been taken up by the carved oak chairs and benches acquired in the last raid. The people who lived within the dwellings they pillaged always seemed to have the best of furniture, which the men found useful for their homes. Loath to leave any behind, they would squeeze onboard every last piece they possibly could. The smaller items taken in the raids, the silver and gold cups, wall hangings, kitchen bowls and clay pots did not take up much room. These were stored in the wooden boxes at the prow of the ships, but the chairs and benches had to be stacked wherever there was space.

Leif yawned and stretched. Rubbing his hand over his face he looked landward. At last he could see in the creeping grey light the familiar outline of the dwellings of the settlement. His eyes felt heavy and he shrugged as he tried to shake off the tiredness now washing over him. The nearer they got to home, the less he had been able to sleep. He had sat upright for most of the journey, preferring to give his sleeping space to the men who had the task of working the oars. His lack of sleep however was now catching up with him and he was struggling to keep his weary eyes open.

His thoughts, on the long voyage home, had been of Fraida. He liked this feeling of excitement when returning home, which came with the thought, she would be there waiting for him at the end of their journey. He was surprised at how much he had missed her company and was eager for the ships to made good speed on their return trip, because he was now impatient for her to be wrapped once more within his arms. He would not have long to wait now, he thought, glancing over at the dwellings. A feeling of thankfulness, that at last, they had reached their journeys end now swept over his tired and aching body.

The men pulled at the oars, bringing the ship to shore. They looked over at Leif with a smile. They too were glad their journey had now come to an end and they wearily let the oars rest so the boat could glide into berth. Leif grinned back at them. Standing up, he quickly jumped ashore with the ropes. The slight thud of the boat berthing at the dock woke Toork and the others. They yawned and stretched and rubbed at their eyes. Easing themselves up, they shrugged as they tried to shake off the residues of sleep. Everyone rose to their feet, glad now to be able to step ashore. Some of the men turned, ready to grab at the ropes being thrown from the other two ships as they pulled into berth behind them.

They all gathered on the shore and Leif told the men to leave the boats as they were, with the goods remaining on board. There would be time enough to unload later in the day he told them, yawning, after they all had some well earned rest.

The men, being tired after their long trip, heartily agreed. Turning, they left the boats behind and set off walking together towards the settlement. Toork accompanied Leif and he motioned to him a reminder he was not to tell Fraida of his capture at the very start of their journey. Toork was aware the tale of this event would upset Fraida, given she was the one who had talked him into going, and as only he knew of her condition he did not want her to worry unnecessarily. Leif just laughed, and thinking Toork's reasons to be different, he once again agreed. They then continued walking in silence. Being the very early hours of dawn no one stirred as everyone made their way quietly to their homes.

When they reached the door to his dwelling, Leif lifted his hand in the gesture of a wave, and parting from Toork, he quietly crept in and made his way directly to the bedroom. He stood looking down at Fraida as she lay in sleep, with her lovely hair spread over the pillow and her arms thrown out at her sides. On seeing her, the overwhelming love he felt for her suddenly rose up to swamp his tired body. Dalgar, who was on the bed beside Fraida, had sat up when Leif entered the room. Leif quietly ruffled his ears, then tugged at him in an attempt to remove him from the bed. Leif smiled to himself as the dog tried to resist, but giving in, he jumped down and walked slowly across to flop down beside Volga, who had not bothered to stir but had chosen instead to remain where she lay, in front of the dying embers of the glowing fire.

Leif tried to make no noise as he quietly undressed, but when he crept into bed Fraida stirred. Her sleepy eyes slowly opened, only to look straight into his smiling face. Fraida's heart leapt with joy and she immediately turned towards him. Leif slipped his muscular arm around her soft body, but in the next moment he suddenly stopped and became still. He jumped back and threw down the covers, looking in shock at the full, rounded mound of her pregnant body. She burst into laughter at the look on his face, then her smile widened as the look changed to one of wonderment when he realised what this meant.

He gently touched the bump. She stroked his hair as she told him she had known of her condition before he left, but had wanted to keep it a surprise for when he returned. To say Leif was surprised would be an understatement. He was, at that moment, overjoyed. A grin spread over his face and his eyes lit up when he realized that, at last, he would soon be a father. He told her, as he enfolded her in his arms, he would not have left her had he known of her condition. She laughed and replied by saying, that was the very reason she did not tell him.

They lay at first just snuggling close, gently kissing as they talked. Both wanted to take time to savour the feeling of being wrapped once more in the arms of the other. Fraida, who was now wide awake, did most of the talking. She was quietly telling Leif about her father's visit when suddenly, she realized Leif had not replied. She raised her head from his chest to look into his face and smiled when she saw he was asleep.

Finding himself warm and cosy in the comfort of his own bed, Leif had been unable to shrug off the overwhelming fatigue now swamping his tired body. Although he tried to fight it, his eyelids closed of their own accord and he quickly sunk into the realms of deep sleep. Fraida smiled as she watched him. She felt ecstatically happy, content in the fact he was now home and lying here by her side. She lay awake next to his sleeping body, only extracting herself once from his arms in order to rise and let the dogs out. She then quickly returned to the bed. He did not stir as she snuggled once more into the cradle of his muscular arms.

It was some hours later when Leif woke. Finding Fraida's soft warm body still beside him, he grinned. With a smile he tightened his arms around her. For a moment they just gazed into each others eyes, but the passion they had for each other was quick to ignite and without hesitation, Leif brought his lips down hard on hers. They found their need for each other intense, the months spent apart had only served to fuel their desire. Locked in the throes of passion, they clung desperately together. Oblivious to all, but the moment in hand, emotions rose to overwhelm them, until they were again united as one, in the finality of the act of deep, meaningful love.

Sometime later, when the intensity of their need had somewhat abated, their hunger for food forced them to rise. Leif was first to dress. Having had enough of listening to the constant barking of the two dogs, he stood up and walked over to the door.

When the door opened the dogs came bounding in. Dalgar, after directing a look at Leif, went straight inside to be with his beloved mistress, but Volga wagged her tail and walked over to Leif. This took Leif by surprise and he bent down to cup the dogs head in his strong hands. He was pleased at least one of the dogs now trusted him enough to want to be in his company. He smiled as he stood up, and leaving Fraida to dress at her leisure, with Volga at his side, he left the dwelling.

Feeling happy to be home, he began to stroll through the settlement. The smell of meat roasting reminded him of his hunger and he stopped for a moment to watch the women busily preparing food for a feast to celebrate their return. He then continued with his walk. He could feel the warmth from the sun on his head as he took time to look around, satisfying himself all was well with his people.

Ragnar called over to him. He was laughing, nodding and pointing to draw Leif's eyes towards the direction of the hill. Leif looked up to see Kelda, her slight figure bent almost double under the weight of one of the carved oak chairs from the boat, which she precariously balanced on her back. She struggled with trying to keep the chair aloft because of constantly tripping over one of the wall-hangings trailing from her arms. Leif was not able to contain his laughter at the sight of the quick witted Kelda, who had decided not to wait, but to choose for herself before anyone else had a chance to look. He set off in her direction in order to help.

He soon caught up with her and reaching over, he deftly lifted the chair from her back. She quickly spun round, grabbing at the chair and refusing to let it go, but then she realized it was Leif and she suddenly grew quiet. Leif smiled down in compassion at the waif like figure before him. He told her gently that it was alright, as the chair had been brought back for her. Kelda promptly dropped the wall-hanging and clapping her hands with joy, she smiled widely as she leapt about in excitement. Leif set down the chair and bending, he picked up the wall-hanging. Rolling it up tight, he placed it in Kelda's arms. Picking up the chair and holding it in one hand he then took her arm with the other. He proceeded to walk slowly with her back to her home.

When they reached her dwelling she insisted Leif put the chair down at her door. She dropped the wall-hanging and promptly sat down on the chair. She grinned widely as she sat there, legs dangling, arms resting along the sides. Leif's heart ached as he watched her pleasure at such a small thing. He gently stroked the hair back from her forehead and bent to kiss her cheek. She smiled up at him, then as some of the people happened to walk by, she jumped quickly to her feet. She stood proudly, hands resting on her chair, as if to say, look what I've got, this is mine.

Leif smiled and slowly shook his head. Leaving her to enjoy her spoils, he began to walk back down the hill. Glancing back, he saw she had again sat on the chair, and was now grinning and patting the wall-hanging which was draped over her thin and scrawny body.

Volga, on seeing her mistress and Dalgar standing at the bottom of the hill, now left Leif's side and set off in a run down the hill to join them. Vaila also stood at the side of Fraida, both of them watching what had transpired. As Leif joined them he frowned and said,"Kelda needs some new clothes, the ones she has on are in tatters. Why has no one seen to this?" Vaila replied defensively that she had tried to get her to wear new ones and to throw the old ones out. But Kelda had stubbornly refused, insisting that if her boys returned she wanted them to recognise her. So until then she would continue to wear the same clothing as when they left.

Leif shook his head ruefully and said they would have to figure out some way round this. Fraida said she had some good tunics that no longer fitted and fur boots and shoes, Kelda could have those. Vaila said, getting her to accept them and wear them was the problem. After a few moments Leif said thoughtfully," I think I know of a way." He went on to say he would go with Fraida to fetch the tunics. He told Vaila to wait for a short time before telling Kelda that some of the women were about to go down to the boats to look at what had been brought back. Leif then called over to a few of the women who were near at hand. He quickly told them what he wanted them to do.

When Kelda reached the ships, the other women were already on board. They stood together in a group exclaiming about these fine wool tunics and linen under-dresses which they held up in front of them. One was holding a pair of fine fur boots, another shoes, and Kelda stood silently at the side, watching their actions closely. She watched as each of the women put their garments down, to turn away as if to look for something else. It was then when she took her chance.

Vaila remained on shore, she stood out of sight waiting until Kelda, with her arms now full of the clothing, came within reach. Vaila then approached her, smiled and enthused about the lovely clothes, while at the same time she asked Kelda, "What did you managed to get?" Kelda grinned somewhat slyly, then she hunched her shoulders and beckoned for Vaila to follow her to her dwelling.

When indoors, Kelda gleefully began to show Vaila her spoils and while congratulating her, Vaila managed at the same time to persuade Kelda to try on a set of these newly acquired clothes. They fitted perfectly. Vaila stood up so that she could fix the shoulder brooches properly to Kelda's new over-tunic. She took the opportunity to whisper in Kelda's ear, "We better put these clothes away in your trunk, just in case the other women try to get them." Kelda began to nod eagerly. She let Vaila go to her trunk, as she herself was too busy spinning slowly around admiring her new clothes.

Vaila quickly, but surreptitiously, removed all the old clothes that were in the trunk. Bundling them together, she furtively stuffed them under her tunic. She replaced them with the new ones and standing, she grabbed the others that were on the floor. Making her way quickly to the door, she said she would have to run as she had left something cooking over the fire.

Vaila smiled to herself later when she threw Kelda's old clothes onto the smouldering logs of the fire. Kelda would have no option now, she thought with satisfaction, watching the flames. She would soon find out she had nothing left to wear but the newly acquired garments.

Later that afternoon Leif, accompanied by Fraida and the dogs, entered the longhouse, only to find everyone else already seated and waiting for the feasting to begin. Leif had a big grin on his face. He quickly swung Fraida round to face him, and raising his eyebrows he looked at the men, his hands pointing at her swollen belly. All the men cheered and leapt to their feet clapping. The dogs, unaware of the reason for the commotion, barked loudly. Fraida, blushing, began to laugh. She pushed at Leif playfully before turning to walk to her seat.

Toork rose, and feigning surprise he put his arms around Fraida in a gentle hug of congratulations. He then looked down at the sweet face of this person who he had missed so much. She hugged him tight, telling him she was so pleased he had now returned. She looked well he thought. Studying her, he could see in the few months while they had been away, she had changed, and matured. To become if anything, even more beautiful.

As they sat eating, Fraida informed them of the visit of her Father. Fraida saw Toork's look of dismay at having missed him. She reassured him he would still be able to see Olaf. He had promised to return for another visit before the year was out. This pleased Toork, as he was eager to see his old friend once more. He could not wait to communicate to Olaf the adventures he had experienced on his journey with Leif.

He and Olaf, in the early days, had been in some fierce battles together, but as time had passed and Olaf aged, these had become rare. Toork himself, being younger, had worked at keeping his body in fighting condition. After his experience of the past, he would never again allow himself to be left vulnerable to any enemy that had the misfortune to cross his path. If he were to die in battle, then many of the enemy would go with him. If he was ever again to be taken captive, they would soon find they could not hold him for long. Being captured by the enemy on this last trip had bothered him none. He already, if Leif hadn't come along, had a plan of escape all worked out in his head. What had concerned him was the fact he knew Hakon's reactions would be slower. He would probably have had to leave him behind and find some way of rescuing him once he himself was free. However, he thought to himself, it had all worked out well in the end, with the appearance of Leif.

The feasting began and was already well under way when Vaila entered with a now well dressed and happy Kelda at her side. Vaila made a sign with her eyes to the company not to laugh, because although it was the height of summer, Kelda had chosen to wear her new, thick fur, winter boots. This she did with pride. Everyone had to hide their smiles when Kelda kept stopping, and grinning, and looking down at her feet.

Fraida called Vaila over to sit with them. Some of the women came to take charge of the smiling and strutting Kelda. When Vaila was seated, Leif leaned over the table to squeeze her hand. He smiled at her openly while thanking her for seeing to Kelda, and for her care in looking after Fraida when he was away.

Vaila, who's heart still leapt at the touch of Leif, steeled herself to show no emotion. She looked at the couple who sat smiling before her and while allowing a small smile to show on her lips, she shrugged in an offhand way and replied it had been no bother at all. Leif, who knew Vaila only too well, immediately realised by her reaction that she still had not returned to her old self. He sat back, his smile slowly fading. He wished she too could find happiness like he had. He knew some good men who had shown an interest in Vaila. She had great beauty and would make a good wife, but she had spurned their interest and seemed to prefer to stand alone.

Vaila herself knew she could find a husband tomorrow if she so choose, but she knew in her heart there would only ever be one that she wanted. That was Leif, the one she could never have. If she could not have him, then she would have no other.

Over the following days, Leif and his men began checking to ensure everyday life in the settlement was proceeding as planned. Work on the goods used for trade continued, along with the farm work needed to produce their food for the year ahead. Leif knew he would have to take a short trip within the next few weeks to his Township, to see how they progressed. He wanted to see how the boat building was coping with demand. They had good craftsmen who built strong ships from the wood they harvested. These ships were much in demand. The orders for them ever increasing. He was thinking they would have to build another boatshed and look to getting more tradesmen skilled enough to work on constructing the ships. However, at the moment he was enjoying being back in the company of his wife. So this could wait for a few weeks yet he thought, smiling to himself.

Leif heard a loud bellow, and turned to see Hakon beckoning to him. He walked over to where Hakon stood looking at a large tree trunk which lay directly at his feet. Leif had asked Hakon, who knew wood like no other, to find him a trunk big enough to allow him to carve out a cradle. Both men crouched down to examine the trunk and then standing, Leif clapped Hakon on the back saying, "Well done." It was a fine piece of wood, exactly what he was looking for.

Hakon, knowing Leif was satisfied, called to some of the men to come and lift it. He told them to carry it over to Leif's woodshed.

Later that night, Leif spent a couple of hours stripping the bark and preparing the wood ready for carving. He looked at the trunk. Now it was stripped, he could see it was big enough for two cradles. He decided to make one for indoors, the other slightly bigger with a hood, so his child would be shaded when lying outside in the sun. He could start working on the wood in secret, on the following day he thought. The designs were already forming in his mind. He smiled to himself when he thought of how delighted Fraida would be when he presented her with the cradles.

Toork, unknown to Leif, had also decided to work at producing a gift for Fraida. It would be something he could give her after the event of the birth he thought. An item of jewellery to raise her spirits. He sat in his workshop at his bench scrawling out designs, and his thoughts were lost in the years that had gone, all too swiftly, by. The child who had pulled him back from the dark shadows of death was now a woman. She, herself, would shortly be giving life to another. It gave him pleasure to be here with her now, watching her enjoy the happiness that she so richly deserved, through her marriage to Leif.

It was some weeks later, when Leif stepped back to look with satisfaction at the two cradles, now finally ready. He was pleased with the work he had just completed. After running his hands carefully over both cradles one last time, he lifted them, one in each hand, and left his woodshed to go in search of Fraida.

As he walked back towards their dwelling, his attention was drawn to Dalgar who had taken up a stance on the headland. The dog was barking loudly as he looked out over the sea. Leif wondered what had caught his eye. Putting the cradles down, he strolled over to where the barking dog stood. Looking out, he saw a ship far out in the distance. Cupping his hands over his brow, he narrowed his eyes to scan the horizon. Moments later he began to smile. This will please Fraida, he thought to himself, when he recognised the ship to be Olaf's. Clapping Dalgar on the head, he turned and went back to where he had left the cradles.

On the way to his dwelling, Leif called out to some of the women, notifying them Olaf's ship was on the horizon. He instructed them to start preparations for the imminent arrival of the visitors. Entering the dwelling, he lifted both arms to hold out the cradles to a surprised Fraida. She smiled widely and clasped her hands together, exclaiming with delight, when she saw the two beautifully carved and ornate little cradles he had made for their child. He set them down. She threw her arms round his neck, kissing him, thanking him for such lovely gifts.

Finding it difficult to bend over, she sank to her knees to examine the cradles closely. She was thrilled at the two little beds, and now she could not wait for the time when the child would arrive. She could picture in her mind's eye the baby sleeping within, wrapped snugly in the soft blankets she had long since finished weaving.

Leif smiled fondly down at his wife. Bending he put his arm around her to help her to her feet. Lifting the cradles he carried them over to place them on the table. She would find it much easier to examine them there, he told her with a smile. She looked at the cots in great detail and kissed Leif once more before turning to go excitedly to her trunk, where she had stored the baby's blankets and furs. Leif did not mention the approach of her father's ship. He knew she would want to go down to the dock to greet him, and in the warmth of the afternoon sun, the effort would drain her energy. He intended to fetch Toork to accompany him to welcome Olaf, then they would bring him up to the dwelling and surprise Fraida.

Leif kissed her forehead then left her happily unaware, busily preparing the cradles, making them ready for the baby. He quickly walked over to Toork's dwelling, only to find he wasn't there. Turning, he crossed to his workplace. Toork looked up as he entered. Leif, with a smile on his face, said, "Your friend Olaf comes. His ship is just about to dock." Toork threw down the tool he was holding and immediately got to his feet, a broad grin spreading over his face. His smile exposed strong white teeth and they looked stark against the shadowy darkness of his dusky skin. He reached out to grab at a sweat rag and wasting no time, he used it to wipe his face and hands. It took very little time for him to get ready and they were both soon heading down in the direction of the dock. Leif explained on the way he had not told Fraida, preferring instead to surprise her with the appearance of her father.

They reached the shore just as Olaf's boat drew in to berth. Olaf grinned widely and bellowed out a greeting. He jumped from the ship and rushed over to engulf his dark friend in a bear hug. Toork in turn, clapped Olaf heartily on the back. Their delight at seeing each other was plain to see. Olaf then turned, looking round for Fraida. Leif came forward with his explanation that he intended to surprise her. Olaf grabbed at his hand and shook it, at the same time he clapped Leif on the shoulders.

Olaf's men began to disembark just as Ragnar arrived. The men looked relieved to be coming ashore. "Have you been on a long journey?" Leif asked Olaf, looking at the heavily laden ship. Before Olaf could reply, there was a loud creak, then a twang, and to Leif's surprise one of the planks on the ship, for no apparent reason, suddenly sprung out. Toork looked at Olaf, and Olaf's men looked warily at each other. Leif looked at Ragnar in question and said "I have never seen that happen before, have you?" Ragnar frowned and shook his head in reply. Leif stepped onto the ship and crossing to the area, he knelt to examine the sprung plank. Looking at it closely, he could see no obvious flaws to cause the wood to act in this way.

Olaf then said with more than a hint of concern, "The reason we sailed straight here, instead of first returning home, is due to the fact our journey has been the strangest I have ever encountered on my travels. Up until now, this," he said waving his arm at the boat, "has always been a good strong ship. But on this last voyage, there have been many strange happenings onboard. Planks have continuously sprung, strange noises are heard," he said with a shake of his head. "I tell the men it is the wind blowing through the sails, but they question as to why they have never heard these noises before?" Olaf then frowned, and splaying his arms he carried on to say, "Some have even sworn they saw eerie lights in the darkened corners, and I tell them it is the ale making them see things. But it has caused the crew to become jittery when onboard, and now they do not want to continue to sail on her. So you see my dilemma, I urgently need a new ship."

Leif looked slowly around the boat as he got to his feet. "That is not a problem," he said, nodding towards the palisade where a number of knorr ships were berthed. "Later today I will tell the men to bring over one of the ships and we will transfer all your cargo onto the new one." Olaf clasped his hands together and bellowed "Splendid!" He grinned as he looked over at his men, pleased his problem was going to be so easily solved.

His men looked much relieved and they too started to smile. It was just as well Olaf, and indeed all the men present, were blissfully unaware Kelda had been aboard the ship before it took its leave from these very shores. No doubt she herself would have been more than pleased to hear the use of all her spells and potions had achieved the desired affect.

Olaf's crew began to disembark, so the four men left them to it and turned to head back towards the settlement. Leif told Olaf he was about to take a short trip downriver to his township, to deliver a figurehead he had finished carving. He wanted his boat builders to attach it to a new longship, he said smiling, one that he intended to add to his own fleet.

Leif then had an idea. "Yourself and Toork could make the trip with us and we could sail your old ship down to my boatyard," he stated while nodding. "I could ask my men to examine her to see if they can identify any fault. The planking is still good on her and we could look at what would be salvageable if we have to take her apart," he said amicably. " We could sail back on the new longship. It is but a short journey," he continued," but as I have other business to see to, it will mean an overnight stay. My people will expect to have this chance to show their hospitality. I think you would enjoy seeing the township as it has much to offer. It is always busy with traders," he remarked. Olaf smiled and said he thought the idea a splendid one. He would enjoy going on a voyage with Toork again, "even if it was only a short one," he said with a laugh in reply.

They reached the door of Leif's dwelling and Olaf entered first. Fraida looked up to see her father, large as life, standing there with his arms outstretched beckoning to her. She gasped in surprise and smiling with joy, she went over to him as quickly as she could. The other three men stood where they were, to give Olaf and Fraida time to hug each other in welcome. Fraida then ushered them in and the servant women hurriedly set the table with jugs of ale, bread with butter and cheese. The men spent the next two hours chatting and giving each other news of what had transpired since they last met. Toork sat listening, but every now and then he would make signs on the table to question Olaf when he wanted him to expand further on the subject being discussed. Everyone's mood was light-hearted. Fraida was very happy when she looked at those she cared so deeply about. They were relaxed, laughing and talking with Ragnar their friend, and she was pleased they were together, here, in her home.

Leif brought up the subject of his intended trip and Fraida said yes they all must go, but make it soon as there was not a lot of time now before the baby would come. She wanted them near at hand when she gave birth. Leif suggested maybe they should go tomorrow. They would only stay away one night, but going this soon would leave nothing to chance. The others all agreed. It was decided they would go now, have the new knorr ship brought over to the dock and Olaf's cargo transferred, so his ship would be empty and ready for transportation the next day.

The people of the settlement were excited and pleased at the goods

Olaf had managed to exchange for the furs and trinkets they had given him to trade. Olaf smiled widely when he brought forth many gifts he had purchased for Fraida. He gave her pots full of new herbs. She gasped in pleasure at two beautiful ornaments made from a fragile composition called glass. These would not be for daily use Olaf said, because they would shatter if dropped, and their cost was more than he liked to pay he said with a laugh! Everyone gathered round to examine and wonder at these glass items never before seen, Olaf grinned proudly at his daughter. Olaf had also brought Fraida leather shoes that fastened with straps, and little silk fashioned slippers both for her and for the baby. He then brought forth a roll of lightweight, colourful woollen material he thought would be ideal for making small clothes for the child. Olaf then produced with a flourish, a thick woven carpet that he spread on the floor. This was to enable her to walk about barefoot at night, when having to rise to see to the baby, he stated proudly. Fraida was excited and thrilled with all these lovely gifts from her loving father. She reached up to hug him in thanks.

After the offloading of the ship was complete and everything was back in order, they sat down to eat in the longhouse alongside the people. They did not stay late into the night, but excused themselves from the feasting, to ensure they had ample sleep. They intended to leave early the following morning. Leif had sent one of the small fishing boats down to the township with a messenger, to give notice about his intended visit and to inform them about his accompanying guests.

At sun rise the next day, Leif and the others began preparations for their intended journey. Some of the men went to Leif's work shed to fetch the figurehead, in order to stow it onboard. Leif watched Fraida's face as the figurehead came into view. She stared at it in surprise. She looked over at Leif and smiled broadly, clasping her hands together in joy. Everyone began to laugh at this large, wooden carving that was an exact replica of Dalgar.

"With his temperament," Leif laughingly explained, "if he had not been a dog he would have been a warrior. So I decided he should have his rightful place at the head of one of our warships." Fraida was thrilled that the figurehead of her hound would accompany Leif when he went off to war. She asked the men to lower it, so she could examine it close at hand. Leif had indeed caught the likeness of the dog, Fraida thought, as she looked at the carved features. She laughingly kissed and patted the figurehead for luck, before the men raised it again in order to carry it to the boat.

Fraida insisted she went down to the dock and she stood smiling and happy as she waved the men off, knowing they would soon return the following day. As she walked slowly back to her dwelling, Vaila came to join her. She took Fraida's arm to give her some support for the walk back. They entered the dwelling and one of the servant women brought them a drink. Fraida was pleased to see Vaila and she told the woman to bring out all the lovely gifts her father had brought so she could show them to her. The two women spent the next hour happily going through them. They tried on the silk slippers and Fraida insisted Vaila should keep a pair that fitted. She would not take no for an answer. She also told the women to bring some pot jars which she filled with spices for Vaila. "I have more than enough," she insisted, when Vaila protested. " If I ever run out, which I doubt very much I will," she said laughing, looking around her, "then my father will fetch me more." Vaila in return, then insisted she would cut some of the fine woven material Olaf had brought, and take it with her to sew some clothes for the baby to wear over the coming winter months. If they both sewed clothes, Vaila said, then the child would soon have enough to see it through the first year.

Unknown to Fraida, Vaila had already spent her nights happily sewing together some small fur lined skin boots, a little fur jacket with a hood and mitts to match, so that she would have a gift for her friend when the baby came. She could not wait for the baby to be born. She had long since decided, if she could not bear Leif's children herself, then, she would do the next best thing, and accept and love any child Fraida and Leif were to have together. They would become, to her, the children she would never have.

Vaila, all be it reluctantly, now found she had a great affection for Fraida. Against all the odds, she had grown to respect and like, very much, Leif's new wife. Their bond of friendship was growing and although she tried constantly to put Leif from her mind, she knew in her heart, that her feelings towards him had not changed. Regardless of this, Vaila knew she herself, would do nothing to cause any rift between the two. She was a person who believed in loyalty between friends, and she would not bring hurt to Fraida.

The two women passed the day happily in each other's company. Kelda, having decided to keep away from the noisy boisterous men she had heard laughing in the longhouse, remained locked in her own little world in her dwelling up on the hill. She sat curled up on her large oak chair, alone but content, in front of a warm and glowing fire. The temperature at night was now beginning to fall, leaving a chill. She snuggled closer into the soft woven blanket that had been among the gifts left today, at her door. The people were kind, was her fleeting thought, because when goods were traded, they always ensured she got her fair share.

She finished eating the last of her soft, buttered bread and stretching out her arm, she randomly lifted one of the pots from the table at her side. The people had left her a few pots of herbs and spices. Holding the pot to her nose, she smiled to herself, while taking in the pungent scent of the fresh green herb. Her thoughts were on nothing in particular, and she was content to just sit awhile, to absorb the warmth radiating out from her glowing fire. Gradually however, darkness began to fall, but just as she thought she would have to rise to light her lamps, she began to feel strange. She tried to move, but found she could not. Her eyes were drawn to the flickering flames that suddenly and inexplicably shot up from the embers of the smouldering logs in the ebbing fire. She found herself entering into a trance like state. Her concentration increased as she focused solely on the images now appearing within the leaping flames.

The first she saw was a smiling child, whose little arms were outstretched towards her. This she could see was not one of her twins, because it was a girl. A girl child with dark hair she thought, with puzzlement, as she leaned closer towards the flames. Kelda smiled back at the child in the fire. A girl child for her? She questioned of herself. Kelda could feel much happiness coming from the child, and for the first time since the loss of her boys, she felt a faint stirring in her tired and aching heart. Suddenly, the vision started to fade. Kelda muttered a quiet "No," as she tried to hold on to the picture of the child.

An ominous black cloud now swept over the flames and Kelda's mood quickly changed. Her head began to agitate from side to side as she tried to see what lay behind. The prow of a ship suddenly broke through the swirling blackness, entering into the light, and the smoky cloud cleared to reveal a picture of her smiling twins, aboard a ship, and they too were holding out their arms towards her.

The pain was too much for Kelda to bear. She threw off the blanket and jumped from the chair. Grief began to overwhelm her. Holding her head in her hands, she quietly whimpered and paced in despair. Suddenly she stopped. She looked up and over at a cloth bag that lay on her wooden chest. She stood still for a moment, then rushed over to grab at the bag, carrying it over to the table.

Pulling her chair to face the table, she sat with the bag before her. Her hands began to rub over it, moving it back and forth, and the contents rattled as they tumbled together within. She concentrated hard and softly chanted, then suddenly, without warning, she upended the bag and the contents spilled wide across the table.

The rune stones clattered and tumbled as they hit the hard surface. Kelda stood, bending close she peered at the markings visible on the scattered stones. The child was there, the markings on the stones showed she was somewhere near. Kelda was puzzled. She turned to look shiftily around her, then shaking her head, she leaned over to study the ones that had landed further across the table. This child would come soon. She would bring much happiness Kelda could see, by the depiction of a large stone showing a ray of bright light.

Kelda sat down abruptly. She frowned as she tried to fathom what message the stones were trying to convey. Who was this child? Where was she coming from? She knew of no child, she muttered while trying hard to think. She rose to her feet once more, but when she leaned over, she now saw death and the child in blackness. What mix-up was this? she thought in anger! She had suffered the death and the children in blackness. Why were they trying to tell her what she already knew? But subconsciously, even after all this time, her mind still adamantly refused to accept what the rune's were trying to reveal.

She quickly swept her arm angrily over the table, clearing it of all the runes, which fell tumbling to the floor. Ignoring the stones, leaving them where they lay, she grabbed at her blanket and made her way to bed. The picture of the child however, stayed with her as she lay trying to sleep. It began to calm her, making her smile. Eventually her eyes slowly closed. Content once more, she drifted off into the realms of sleep.

Unlike Kelda, Leif, Olaf, Toork and Ragnar were themselves, at that moment, far from sleep. They had been given pride of place in the longhouse of the township. Everyone who was anyone now attended the all night feast held in their honour. They had sailed into the docks of the township that day, only to be met by a large welcoming party. Vikings loved nothing more than feasting. This was as good an excuse as any to enable them to show off their high standards of hospitality.

The figurehead of Dalgar had been offloaded and taken away to the boatyard, where craftsmen now worked at attaching it to the ship Leif would sail home on the following day. Olaf and Toork were whisked away to be given a tour of the places of interest, to allow Leif and Ragnar time to meet with the elders in order to discuss business. They tried to make the meeting as brief as possible, but even then it took a couple of hours. Olaf and Toork however were bothered none, as they had been well looked after in the absence of Leif and Ragnar. Having attended to all urgent business, the men eventually met up. Together they happily continued their walk through the township. Unknown to them, the tour had been arranged to end at the central longhouse, where a feast was laid out and ready to begin.

The four men, and the small crew accompanying them, were in fact, at that moment, all laughing at the entertainment. They were, by this time, more than a little drunk. Mead, ale, and good wine flowed freely, and they were being constantly urged to drink up and be merry. After all, they told each other, they knew that not to participate in this good hospitality could leave their hosts offended, no one wanted that!

They were all enjoying the boisterousness of the mixed company. There was much laughter as they continued to drink, talk, and feast throughout the long hours of the night. However, time was quick in passing. All too soon the light of a new day came suddenly with the dawn. Leif and the others started to yawn. Now realising the lateness of the hour, tiredness began to creep in. However, just at that time, some of the men of the township, whose boat had only just returned to berth, came to join in the celebrations. They burst into the longhouse calling out a hearty welcome to Leif, who they had not seen for some time. There was much laughter and jesting from these men. Life was put back into the party, so shrugging off their tiredness, more drink was then poured and the feasting started afresh.

It was very late in the afternoon when Leif realised, that whilst they had been enjoying the pleasurable company, the hours had flown by. So he stood up and tried to stop himself from swaying as he stated, they really would have to leave. There were shouts of, "No, not so soon!" but Leif, while laughing, insisted. Many of the drunken people were willing to accompany them to the dock. They found themselves half carried by the crowd as they made their way back to the new longship, which had now been floated and made ready to sail.

Leif, Toork, Olaf and Ragnar stumbled and fell onto the ship. All the gifts that had been given for Fraida, and the new baby to be, were piled on board. The crew by this time were so drunk and tired they wondered to themselves how they were possibly going to sail this ship home! They managed however, somehow, to haphazardly row out of the docks, to many cheers and shouts of "Don't make it so long before your next visit!" They all waved back at the receding crowd. Leif, feeling light-headed, sat abruptly down. He put his head in his hands and groaned, as he muttered to himself, "it will take me long enough to get over this one!"

Leif rubbed his hands roughly over his face, trying to gather his wits. He looked wryly over at Olaf and Toork who were already dead to the world, and Ragnar not much better, but he couldn't follow suit because he knew it was his responsibility to ensure they all made it home. He looked at the crew and he could see they were trying to remain upright while struggling, somewhat in vain, with the ropes. He got unsteadily to his feet and fumbled as he tried to help the men raise the sail. Somehow they managed between them to first raise the sail, and then to fasten it down, and after concentrating hard to make sure they were pointing in the right direction, unable to stay upright any longer, they all gave in and collapsed in a heap.

It was just as well the journey was only a short one, otherwise there is no saying where the ship would have ended up. Fraida, who had been watching all day for the return of the ship, finally saw it appear just before dusk. Dalgar's head was proudly silhouetted, but she couldn't understand why the boat seemed to be drifting about in an odd manner. The oar strokes were in no way synchronised and she puzzled as to why the oars seemed to be waving in the air and not in the water. Hakon, who was down at the dock, had also been watching, and he laughed gruffly when he caught sight of the ship. He knew immediately what the problem was. He quickly called to a few of the men and they set off in one of the small boats to row out to the drifting ship. The men clamoured on board to take over the oars. With that, the ship was soon steered into its dock.

Hakon and the men then hauled Leif, Toork, Olaf and Ragnar ashore. Hakon, after calling for more assistance, managed to have them all taken to their homes. Leif smiled weakly at Fraida as he was half carried in the door. Olaf and Toork both waved and grinned lopsidedly at her as they were helped to their dwelling. Fraida burst out with laughter at the sight of the three drunken men. She shook her head as she instructed Hakon to carry Leif to his bed.

Two of the men followed Hakon in. They carried between them a very large basket filled with the gifts for Fraida and the baby. They lifted it onto the table. As the three men left, Hakon said to Fraida he would continue to work close by and he would be near at hand in case she needed help. "If he falls out of bed," he said gruffly, "just give me a shout." Fraida laughed as she thanked him, but said she thought by the look of Leif he would certainly sleep soundly till morning! Little did she know, as she watched Hakon walk away, that it would be she who would wake Leif long before morning came.

Fraida, still smiling, then closed the door. She walked slowly over to see what was within the large basket the men had placed on the table. She began to exclaim softly in delight when she found it contained many gifts. She stood for some time examining and appreciating all that had been sent by the people of the township. She hoped Leif had thanked them for what seemed to her, so many lovely gifts. She then took her time fixing through the gifts. She walked back and forth stowing them away in various trunks and chests throughout the dwelling. Her back began to ache from being on her feet so long. She sat down to rest, but after having a drink of milk, tiredness began to overtake her and she decided to make her way to bed.

As Fraida climbed into bed she had a sudden twinge, so sharp it made her wince. Thinking she had stood on her feet too long, she gingerly positioned herself on her back. She lay still, waiting to see if it would happen again. No other pain was forthcoming. So after a few minutes, she turned onto her side and smiling, she drifted off to sleep beside her drunken husband who, at that moment, was himself out cold and dead to the world.

Leif began to surface from a deep sleep, because someone was roughly shaking him. He felt dizzy, his head was swimming and he groaned and shrugged while trying to shake them off. Much to his annoyance, the shaking continued. Faintly, through the drunken haze, came Fraida's voice. He opened his bleary eyes to darkness. For a moment he wondered where he was. Then Fraida spoke again, a bit louder this time and he remembered he was home. He tried to open his eyes wide, at the same time he tried to listen to what she was saying. He felt he had only been asleep for just a few minutes, but in fact it had been a good few hours. Fraida shook him again and said urgently "Leif it's time." His brain struggled to make sense of the sentence." Time for what," he thought? "Ugh," he uttered as he tried to lift his head. "Leif wake up," Fraida said again, "the baby is coming."

Her words finally penetrated the cloud in his brain and Leif now understood. He shot up and swung his legs out over the bed. He groaned as his head immediately started to swim. He could not stop his body from swaying uncontrollably to the side. He, right away, forced himself to his feet. Staggering to the large ewer which stood on the chest close to the bed, he gripped the sides, and bending over he immersed his whole head into the water in an effort to sober himself up.

The shock of the cold water made him gasp. It did help some, but by the gods he felt ill! He grabbed a cloth and rubbed it over his dripping hair and at the same time he went straight back to the bed. Sitting down abruptly, he put his arm around Fraida in a comforting embrace. He held her close and asked softly if she was okay. She lifted her head, and after having watched his actions, she smiled at him and said, "Yes, but are you?" Leif grinned down at her as she carried on to say, "I need you to fetch Vaila and the women."

Leif kissed her gently, settling her down on the bed before going to wake the servant women. He struggled hard to get his thoughts in order before instructing some to go and assist Fraida. Others he told to quickly work at building up the fire. Both dogs by this time were sitting up looking bewildered, watching Leif and the servants hurriedly move about in the darkness, disturbing the peace and silence which normally reigned in the middle of the night. Leif was quick to light each of the oil lamps throughout the dwelling. Then, taking one with him, he immediately set off to fetch Vaila.

Leif quietly opened the door to Vaila's house and with the lamp lighting his way, he walked over to where he knew her lamps were situated. From the flame on his, he lit two. Going over to the bed, he bent over and quietly said, "Vaila," in an effort to wake her. Vaila, subconsciously, on hearing Leif's voice, thought she was dreaming. With her eyes still shut in sleep, she smiled widely up at him.

Leif's heart, when he looked down at her, ached when he realised how much he had missed that friendly, open smile. This, he thought, is the first time she has properly smiled at me since I told her about Fraida. He leaned over and kissed her forehead. Then he spoke again. This time it brought Vaila out of her dream state.

Leif straightened up at the same time Vaila's eyes flew open. She suddenly sat bolt upright when she realised he was really there. Leif explained Fraida had sent him to fetch her, as the baby was coming. Still clutching the covers up at her neck with one hand, Vaila ran the other through her hair as she tried to shake herself awake. Leif turned his back to her and said he would wait until she dressed and accompany her back to Fraida. Vaila jumped up and quickly threw on the clothes lying closest at hand. and soon they were both hurrying in silence back to Leif's dwelling.

Leif waited by the fire while Vaila went in to see Fraida. Vaila came out and said to Leif that, yes, the baby was definitely coming. She informed him he would have to leave the dwelling and take the dogs with him as they could not do with them being underfoot at a time like this.

Dalgar whined a bit when Leif took both dogs by the collar to escort them out. Although it was still dark, being the middle of the night, people were moving about the settlement. Some of the women had been sent for by Vaila, so their husbands came out to light up the large central fire to give warmth to those who had to wait. One of them patted Leif on the back and led him over to a bench others had carried out and positioned near to the fire. Leif took the dogs with him. A horn of ale was put into his hand but when he took a swig he was nearly sick. He handed it back and asked for milk instead. The men laughed, knowing full well what state he had returned from the township in only hours earlier.

Leif then remembered Olaf and Toork. He smiled to himself mischievously, and standing up he began making his way over to, what had now become, Toork's dwelling. If he had to be up, then they should be too, he thought with a grin. He deliberately banged loudly on the door, shouting out as he threw it open. Toork, being startled, shot up from his bed before he was really awake. He stumbled and swayed before sitting abruptly down. Olaf came staggering through from the other room, one hand held to his aching head. Covering him was a blanket, half of which was haphazardly wrapped around him, the rest trailing on the ground. "What in the name of Odin!" he bellowed, then he groaned. Leif stood quietly smiling, before stating smugly, "the baby is on its way." Olaf groaned again. "What a time to come," he said trying to shake himself more awake. "I am outside at the central fire if anyone would like to join me," Leif said, and smiling wryly, he walked away.

The three men sat silently on the bench in front of the glowing fire. Olaf was leaning forward with his head in his hands. It had been so long since he had consumed the amount of ale and wine he downed yesterday, that he had forgotten how ill you could feel in the aftermath. He now deeply regretted celebrating with so much enthusiasm. If he had thought for one minute the child would come early, then he certainly would not have imbibed so freely, he thought, inwardly groaning.

Ragnar suddenly appeared in front of them, grinning, and looking none the worse for wear. He gave Leif a celebratory clap on the back. Nothing seemed to affect Ragnar, Leif thought enviously, putting his hand up to nurse his own aching head. Ragnar began to laugh at the sorry sight of the trio before him. He called to a few of the men to bring over water and some bread. He told a doubting Leif, Olaf and Toork to get it down them and they would soon begin to feel better.

In the hour that followed, more and more people gathered together to join with the group; all of them wanting to give support to Leif while he waited for the birth of his firstborn. An air of excited expectancy began to take over and sure enough, after drinking the water and eating the bread, the three men did, eventually, begin to feel better.

Olaf stood up to stretch his legs, and after yawning he began to pace about. His thoughts went deep. He was somewhat edgy and a little scared regarding his daughter's well-being. He had not told the others of the fate of his own lovely wife; Fraida's mother, who died while giving birth to his daughter. Olaf, at the time, had been thrown into deep despair and had in fact never recovered from the loss of his loving and gentle wife. He, in consolation, from that moment on, had centred all his attention towards raising their only child in the way her mother would have wished. Fraida was in appearance, the mirror image of her mother. But where Olaf's wife had been older and frailer, Fraida herself was strong and healthy. That was what he, at that moment he told himself staunchly, had to hold on to.

The two hounds, having long since given up trying to figure out what was happening, had settled themselves down at Toork's feet to bask in the warmth from the glowing fire. However, a loud groan came from the direction of Leif's dwelling. Both dogs, recognising it to be coming from their beloved mistress, suddenly shot up. Dalgar bounded over to the door, Volga followed. Dalgar began to bark, snarl, and scratch frantically at the door in an effort to gain entry.

Fraida's voice was faintly heard calling out to Dalgar that she was alright. Dalgar stood, head to the side and ears perked up, staring at the shut door. He then turned his head to look at Volga who was at his side. Both dogs stood looking at each other for a few moments, unsure of what to do, until Volga suddenly flopped down, facing towards the door. She put her head on her paws, but kept her ears perked up as she again stared at the door.

Dalgar however was not to be settled. He bounded over to Toork and stood looking up into his face then over towards the door. Toork shook his head and clicked his fingers at his feet as a sign for Dalgar to lie down. Dalgar was having none of it though, and he ran back to the door. He stood there for a while, then after getting no joy from Toork, the next one he ran to was Olaf. Olaf ruffled Dalgar's head and spoke soothingly to the dog, telling him everything was fine. Dalgar was not convinced and he ran back to take up his stance at the door of the dwelling.

Leif, while watching the antics of the dog, was thinking time seemed to be slow in passing. He knew how Dalgar was feeling because he too wished he could be at Fraida's side to ensure all was well. Feeling, for once, helpless, Leif stood up to stretch his legs and he began pacing back and forth.

One of the elders, sensing tension was beginning to affect those who waited, laughingly called out to Leif that his father would be looking down from the heavens on this night. Everyone laughed, then agreed. On the back of this, the elder immediately launched into a tale of Leif's father's bravery, in a particularly fierce battle, when he was a young and strong warrior. This tale sparked people's interest and the tension began to ease as everyone gathered round to listen. Some of the women had prepared food and it was passed round. Milk and ale was poured for those who wanted it. The crowd now happily settled down to listen to the tale, to while away the time before the event of the birth.

It was not long after however, another groan came from within the dwelling. Dalgar again became agitated. Leif stood up, and leaving the crowd sitting around the fire, he walked over to where the two dogs were stationed at the door. He sat down on the ground beside Volga and he leaned back against the building. He began to talk reassuringly to the dogs. Both seemed to listen as he talked. The fact that Leif had joined them seemed to settle Dalgar and he walked over to sit down in front of Leif.

Both dogs watched Leif's face as he quietly talked. The dark figure of Toork then appeared, and he too sat down at Leif's side. Olaf, from where he sat at the fire, looked over and smiled to himself at the sight of the waiting group at the door to the dwelling. All who sat there loved his daughter in their own special way, but none, he knew, loved her as much as he himself did.

The blackness of night gave way to dawn and finally they heard a baby cry. Toork looked at Leif and a smile spread over his dark face as he quickly got to his feet. Putting his hand out, he helped haul Leif up from where he sat next to Volga. The dogs stood staring at the door, listening to this strange noise coming from within.

Everyone waited. The silence was such you could have heard a pin drop. A bright ray from the newly rising sun shone on the door of the dwelling at exactly the time Vaila pulled it open. She was holding in her arms a baby swaddled in a blanket. Dalgar took his chance and immediately slipped behind Vaila as she stepped forward to hand the soft bundle to Leif. "It's a girl" she said. The whole settlement broke out in a cheer. Either sex was much welcomed in the birth of a Viking, because unlike many other cultures, women played a strong part in Viking life. They were much respected, and they managed the finances of the home and many of the businesses within their society.

Leif turned back towards the crowd, grinning, while looking proudly at his daughter through the rays of the rising sun shining down on her. Bringing up his arms, he gently kissed her. Then holding her high, he said "I will call her Rayna, bringer of light!" Another massive cheer went up from the crowd. Olaf and Toork, both grinning widely, moved forward, eager themselves to have sight of this child of Fraida's.

The crowd waited, then they too all surged forward trying to get a glimpse of the baby. Vaila held up her hand and called out as she took the baby from Leif's arms. Volga was still at Leif's side and she looked up in question at this bundle being passed over.

"Fraida is well," Vaila called out, as she smiled at everyone. "Now go to your homes to get some sleep and allow her to rest." Olaf and Toork went to enter the dwelling but Vaila put her hand up and held them back. "That goes for you too," she said. "The women are still working with Fraida, so you cannot see her yet. Go home and get some sleep," she told them."You can see her later today." To say Olaf and Toork were disappointed would be an understatement. But they could see the determination on Vaila's face. They both shook Leif by the hand and Olaf clapped him on the shoulder before, with some reluctance, they turned to go back to their dwelling. The crowd too, satisfied at having seen the outcome of the birth, now began to quickly disperse.

Leif said to Vaila in jest, "I take it you are not going to try to stop me from seeing my wife." Vaila replied with a smile and said over her shoulder as they both turned to enter the dwelling, "As if I could." She did however ask him to wait for a few minutes until they had Fraida settled. So Leif sat down at the table and Volga waited at his feet. The next they heard was a growl from Dalgar. He appeared with Vaila leading him by the collar out to Leif. Leif laughed as he took hold of him. "You just had to be the first in to see her," he said, as he looked down at the dog. The dog looked up at him, feigning innocence, and Leif said, "Settle down now. We will all get to see her shortly."

Leif, accompanied by the dogs, was eventually allowed to enter the room. He stood looking over at a pale, but smiling Fraida. She was sitting up in bed with their child wrapped and held in her arms. Standing still for a moment, he smiled as he took in this vision before him. He was suddenly overwhelmed with feelings of pride and love for this woman who was the mother of his child.

Leif then walked across and as he sat on the bed, he put his arms possessively round his wife and newborn child. He kissed Fraida tenderly. The two of them could not believe the happiness they felt when looking down at the face of this little girl who was part of them both. They looked in wonder at her. They quietly talked until Leif could see Fraida's eyelids drooping, she was struggling to stay awake. Leif then removed a sleeping Rayna from her mother's arms and placed her gently in the cradle positioned at the side of the bed. Turning back, he settled the tired, but happy, Fraida down to sleep. He kissed her forehead before leaving the room.

The servant woman had prepared another bed for Leif in the main part of the dwelling. After having helped himself to something to eat he decided, before he lay down himself, to look in on Fraida again. He slowly opened the door. Dalgar was lying quietly by the side of his sleeping mistress's bed. However, he was surprised to see the gentle Volga in a guarding stance by the baby's cradle. She looked over at the door as it opened, then seeing it was only Leif, her eyes went back to watch the sleeping baby. Leif smiled to himself as he closed the door. Volga, it seems had found a new role in life. He wondered what Fraida would think of her clever hound when next she woke.

At the time when everyone else was settling down to sleep, Kelda, who was in her house up on the hill, abruptly woke up. In her dreams she heard a baby cry and it seemed so real she sat up to look around. Her searching eyes slowly scanned the dimly lit room. However, apart from her, the room was empty. Throwing off her covers, she rose and searched the dwelling. Everything still remained as it was when she had gone to bed the night before. Shrugging her shoulders, she then wandered over to get herself something to eat. She could see the sun was up and wondered why, on that morning, she had overslept.

After hurriedly dressing, she stepped out from her dwelling. She stood as she normally did, stretching, with her hands on her hips, looking down at the settlement, but suddenly she became still. She sensed something was amiss. For a few minutes she tried to figure out what was wrong, then realisation dawned. Where was everyone? Normally at this time the settlement would have come to life and many of the people would be milling about seeing to their daily tasks. But looking down she could see the settlement was deserted. Where had everyone gone she wondered? She began to panic.

Half running down the hill, she reached where the other dwellings were centred. She spun around looking for any sign of the people. Going over, she opened one of the doors and entered without knocking. She stood looking down at the people sleeping in their beds, then opening a number of other doors, she could not understand why everyone was asleep.

Going hurriedly over to Ragnar's large dwelling, she opened the door and unhesitatingly walked in. Ragnar was asleep at the table. His head cushioned on his folded arms. Kelda approached him and shook him hard. He stirred to look up sleepily at a gravely concerned Kelda. "A spell has been cast on our people," she whispered agitatedly to Ragnar. "Everyone sleeps," she said urgently to him. Ragnar rubbed his hand over his face and shook himself awake. He stared blankly for a moment into Kelda's face. Then it dawned on him everyone had forgotten about Kelda. Being up on the hill, she would have slept through the events of the night before.

Sitting up, Ragnar stretched his arms and yawned, then rising to his feet, he put his arm around a very worried Kelda. He sat her down and poured her a drink of milk which he placed in her hand. "Everyone sleeps Kelda," he said in his gruff voice, "because they were up all through the night." Kelda waited while she thought for a moment, then stuttered "Why? I heard no noise," she said, with a puzzled look on her face. Ragnar replied with, "Because Leif's wife Fraida gave birth in the early hours," he stated. Ragnar then yawned tiredly before carrying on to say, "In fact, at the very break of dawn this morning," he said with a smile.

Kelda took some moments to let this statement sink in. She was not even aware that Fraida was expecting a child. But then, suddenly, Kelda's mind began to race. The message from the oracle began, at last, to make sense. "Was it a girl child with dark hair?" she exclaimed, as she turned to Ragnar. He looked down in puzzlement at Kelda, who for some reason, unknown to him, had now become excited." It was a girl child, yes," said Ragnar, "but as to the dark hair, I don't know, because I have not yet laid eyes on the baby."

Kelda clapped her hands with excitement and lifting her milk she downed it in one swill. She stood up smiling. Pushing Ragnar out of the way, she went hurriedly towards the door. Ragnar smiled and shook his head as Kelda left his dwelling. What was in Kelda's mind now was beyond him. These days it was difficult at anytime, for anyone to know what Kelda's thoughts were. Shrugging his shoulders, Ragnar again stretched, then walking over to the bed he lay his tired body down. Still smiling to himself, he turned to snuggle up close to his warm and peacefully sleeping wife.

Kelda quickly made her way through the deserted settlement, over to where Leif's house stood. She began to pace impatiently back and forth at the front of the dwelling. She could hardly contain her excitement and was desperate to have sight of the newborn child. Why doesn't everyone wake up? she thought, as she continued pacing. Suddenly she came to a halt. She stood staring fixedly at the door.

Kelda turned and looked warily around, to ensure no one was about.

Then creeping quietly over, she stealthily opened Leif's door. She hesitated only for a moment, listening for any sound, and hearing only silence, she smiled and promptly entered the dwelling.

Having had very little sleep in the last forty eight hours, Leif continued to sleep soundly. He never stirred when Kelda stopped to smile down at him. Glancing around the room she then crept over to another door. Opening it quietly, she peeped in. Volga looked over as the door opened. When she saw it was Kelda, she silently brought her lips up to bare her teeth. Completely undeterred at the sight of the dog, Kelda quickly entered the room. She had no conception of fear. She knew only the pain of grief, and she walked over to where the child lay in her cradle.

Volga turned to look at her sleeping mistress, before looking back at Kelda. She again snarled quietly, showing her fierce, fang like teeth; but Kelda just reached out her hand distractedly to unconcernedly pat the dog on the head. Kelda leaned over to look at this dark haired child. She saw the baby was awake but lying quietly, with her newborn eyes, only able to distinguish shadows, open. A big grin spread over Kelda's face and she brought her hands up to her mouth in case she made a noise in her excitement. She stood there for a few minutes looking down at the child, then she threw a silent kiss towards the baby, before turning to quietly leave the room.

Kelda crept out of the house and went some distance away before she allowed herself to jump excitedly about. It was beyond her understanding why the child was shown to her through the oracle. She only knew she had a really good feeling when she looked at the child, sensing she would in some way, come to be of some importance to her.

Fraida woke in the afternoon and opened her eyes to find Toork sitting on a chair at the side of her bed. One large arm was taken up by cradling the baby, but his other arm was stretched out so his hand could gently hold hers as she lay in sleep. Fraida smiled at Toork and asked of him, "Is she beautiful?" Toork grinned and nodded. Bringing his hand up, he swept it down over his face and pointed at her. "She looks like me?" Fraida said, as she laughed. Toork nodded. Toork then lifted his eyebrows in question. Fraida replied contentedly, "Yes, I am fine Toork, and I cannot express to you how happy I feel. I have Leif who I love so much," she said softly with a smile, and now I have the baby who is part of him". Toork smiled back and nodded. Then he stroked her hair back from her forehead with his large, dark hand. He smiled broadly, content now to see all was well with regards to her. He was just handing the baby over to Fraida, when they heard a bellow from the other room. Toork grimaced and Fraida said, "What ails Father?"

What the silent Toork could not relate to Fraida was, that when he himself had woken up, it was to find Olaf still asleep. So he had quietly dressed and sneaked out instead of going first to wake his friend. He had wanted this time to himself, to have peace to gaze upon the baby and to ensure in his own mind Fraida was well.

Everyone had still been asleep when he quietly entered the dwelling. Creeping in, he had lifted the baby from the cot. Toork had held the child gently in his large, muscular arms. Smiling down at her in the quiet and peaceful surroundings, his thoughts had returned to when he once held his own children. He thought again of his wife, and of the beautiful daughter he had lost. His heart grew heavy, but then he looked down at what he had gained, Fraida. Placing a chair beside the bed, he sat in silence, cradling the baby in his arms, quietly reminiscing while patiently waiting for Fraida to awake.

Olaf now burst furiously into the room saying, "Make way for the grandfather Toork!" Toorks shoulders were by this time shaking as he laughed at how he had duped his friend. Olaf took one look at him and then he too burst into laughter. "Let me, the grandfather, now be the last in line to hold my granddaughter," he jested, as he strode across the room. Olaf's bellow had woke up Leif, who on hearing the jest from the next room, now stood at the door saying, "And I am the father! When do I get to hold my daughter?" and everyone laughed again.

While Olaf and Leif's attention was centred on the baby, Toork unfastened a pouch from his waist and handed it to Fraida. She looked up in question as she began to open it. Toork just smiled. Fraida gasped when her eyes settled on two beautiful, large cloak pins designed to look like miniature swords. The long blades were made of silver with ornate scrolls down their length. The bar between the blade and the hilt was delicately worked in gold. The hilts themselves were silver and each one had a beautiful amethyst orb, set in a claw. Fraida held the hilt of one between her fingers, holding it up like a sword. The reverse side of each brooch had indented signs of the hammer of "Thor," and the stick-like figure of a boy was on one, and a girl on the other. Fraida laughed with delight and she thanked Toork for her lovely gifts. Olaf and Leif turned and immediately exclaimed themselves when seeing the design and workmanship of Toork's gift to Fraida. Toork just stood back smiling. For him the pleasure was in the reaction from Fraida herself to his gift.

Fraida had many visitors in the days that followed. Vaila came with a basket full of small clothes and Fraida took particular delight in the little fur set Vaila had finished making. She told her friend she could hardly wait for the winter months when the child would be old enough to wear the little set. This pleased Vaila greatly to see her friend's pleasure at the gift made lovingly by her own hand.

Olaf and Toork came to see Fraida every day. They would joke as they jostled with each other as to who would be the first to hold the baby whenever it stirred. Leif and Fraida laughed in private at the sight of these two large men, who would sit watching the cradle, willing the child to wake. The only time Fraida and Leif had the child to themselves was in the evenings, when they could sit in peace and quietly enjoy this amazing little bundle of softness. They would laugh at the expression of intentness on the little face when Fraida sang softly to her. The baby's eyes would then move, trying hard to focus on the laughing shadows above her.

A feast was prepared to celebrate the birth of Leif's firstborn. It carried on for many days. Some in the settlement remarked on the change they could see in Kelda. She was often seen smiling and humming to herself and the people began to wonder why. Kelda, unknown to the others, had already seen the child, only that one time, but she was happy to wait for the time when she could, on her own, look upon it again. To know the child existed was, in itself, enough to make Kelda happy.

It was not long after the celebrations when Olaf's crew became restless. They had been away from home for many months and the celebrations reminded them they had families of their own. It was time they returned to their own loved ones they stated, who were patiently waiting at home. Olaf, although reluctant to leave, could understand the needs of his men. So it was with a heavy heart, that he again prepared to set sail. He would have preferred to spend more time with his daughter and granddaughter, but needs must. He would just have to look forward to visiting in the spring.

Fraida, so soon after the birth of her child, was still very emotional and she wept at her father's departure. Leif however, soon comforted her by telling her to think forward to the spring when her father would return. By that time, their child would be old enough to welcome her grandfather with a smile. He told her to think of Olaf's delight at that. Fraida smiled then, her thoughts having been taken from the departure of her father, to thinking of what now lay ahead in the year to come.

Two weeks later, Fraida ventured out for the first time with her newborn child. Being a warm, autumn day she carried the baby in her arms, loosely wrapped in a fine wool blanket. Vaila saw Fraida leave her dwelling and quickly went over to join her, for a short stroll through the settlement.

It was not long before both women became aware of a hovering Kelda, who seemed to be continuously bobbing up and down behind them. Fraida could see Kelda was trying to get sight of the child, so she turned and held the baby up for her to see. Kelda though, would not come up close to Fraida and she stood agitatedly wringing her hands. Vaila asked Fraida if she could hold the baby, and taking her in her arms, she approached Kelda to show her. The look of joy on Kelda's face, when looking down at the child, surprised both women. Kelda, hesitatingly, gently touched the baby's tiny hand, and to Vaila's surprise, the child seemed to smile. The child was too young to smile, so she must have wind Vaila thought, and it would be more of a grimace because of that.

However, this smile pleased Kelda even more. She skipped away, clapping her hands in delight. Both women stood watching her departure in puzzlement. "Very strange," Vaila said to Fraida, as she handed Rayna back. "That's the first I have seen Kelda react positively to any situation since the loss of her husband and sons", but unable to guess the reason for Kelda's strange behaviour, both women smiled, shrugged and continued on their way.

A few days later when Leif walked briskly home from the dock, having given assistance and advice on a ship needing urgent repairs, he thought the weather was now on the turn. He gave a slight shiver. There was a definite chill to be felt in the night air he thought, drawing his jacket closer together. Tomorrow he must ensure the people begin preparations for the winter months, which were all too fast approaching, he thought, as he quickly strode along.

Keeping this in mind, he woke early the following day. Rising quietly, he left Fraida and the baby sleeping soundly in their warm and cosy beds.

Leif walked through the settlement giving orders to the people concerned. Very soon the settlement became a hive of activity, as everyone began preparations for the winter season now closing in.

Later that morning, Fraida questioned the work going on around the settlement, given that, on most days the sun still shone. Leif then explained that once, on a previous year, they had been taken off guard and caught out with the early arrival of snow. That year the weather had proved to be particularly fierce. It had caused a lot of problems, particularly with the livestock, and they had lost many of the animals. So now they left nothing to chance he said, and always started preparations early.

The wood was already being stacked high at each dwelling. Some of the men built crates, which they filled with logs, and these were put inside Kelda and the other widow's homes. The women who lived alone would use these if the snow became too high outside, causing it to be difficult for them to open their doors. Sacks of grain were distributed to each house along with blocks of cheese, butter and dried salted fish; which could be boiled until they were soft enough to eat. Boxes of vegetables were stacked in corners and covered with earth to preserve them. Large casks were filled with enough oil to keep each house lit in the long, dark days and nights of the oncoming winter. A milking cow was tethered in the space at the back of a room in each dwelling, to give a constant supply of milk. Each had a few hens that scratched among the hay at the cow's feet. Sheaves of fodder for the cows were stacked high up in the lofts, which gave the added bonus of lining the roofs and keeping the dwellings warmer. The rest of the cattle and livestock were brought closer to home, so they could be easily moved indoors to the large sheds when the weather worsened.

The temperature had dropped, but the snows had not yet arrived, when Leif decided they would have a feast. Fresh meat grew scarce in the depth of winter. People were unable to move about and had to make do with what they had. So it was decided a hog be killed, along with a bullock. Both carcasses were roasted outside over the open fires and a good deal of the meat was consumed in the two days of feasting. The rest was divided equally to ensure each dwelling would have roasted meat to eat in the week ahead.

Toork continued with his daily routine indoors, in the warmth that his dwelling provided. He would never, he thought as he watched Eric, get used to this chill that seemed to cut into his very bones. The boy Eric had much improved in his movements and had not, as Toork first thought, soon grown tired of them. He now tried to practise every day along with Toork. The tall silent stranger that was Toork, had grown used to his company, and enjoyed it, even though the boy did chatter on.

However, this year their time together indoors was cut short because the winter snow arrived with a vengeance. Carried in on the tail of a raging Norse wind. The snow did not fall in a gentle flurry, taking days to build up like in other years, but came down thick and fast in relentless blizzards, which continued blowing, without easing, in the weeks that followed.

The people, prepared for winter, were already cosily ensconced in their dwellings when this happened, sheltered from the storms which raged all around. With movement being restricted, everyone was quick to accept the solitary existence severe bad weather brings. Soon the only noise heard within the settlement was the continuous howl of the fierce, Norse wind.

CHAPTER SEVEN

Fraida secretly treasured the solitude in those first weeks of winter, when the severity of the weather kept everyone isolated in their homes and they were left solely on their own. She enjoyed very much having Leif and the baby, not forgetting her hounds, all to herself. It was in this time the bond between them took on new meaning and the love she shared with Leif now, if it was possible, only increased.

However it was not to last, as on the fourth week Toork, being weary of his own company, decided to brave the elements and struggle through deep drifts and falling snow in order to try to reach Leif and Fraida's. When Leif opened the door, they both burst into laughter at the sight of Toork. By the time he reached them, he was fully covered with snow and was not amused as he tried angrily, and in vain, to shake the most of it from his cold, shivering, body.

Fraida and Leif quickly ushered him into the warmth of the fire and it soon improved his mood when they gave him hot broth to warm his insides. When Rayna woke from her sleep, Toork, without hesitation, went over to lift her from her cradle. He was surprised at the change in the baby in the weeks since he last held her. Rayna looked up at Toork, her eyes studying this large dark face looking down on her, as if waiting for him to speak. He put his smiling face close to hers. Her little hand came up to grab at his hair. He nodded his head, then jerked it up, causing the hand that grasped his hair to move with him. The baby immediately gurgled. Leif and Fraida stopped what they were doing and smiled as they listened to their child laugh. Toork jerked his head again and Rayna gurgled once more. From that time on, this became a game between the silent Toork and Rayna, whenever he held her. It was always guaranteed to make her laugh.

The hunting trips that year were few and far between. Although Toork hated the cold, he wrapped up well and joined the men in the hunt just to relieve the tedious boredom caused by the forced restrictions in movement the blizzards caused. The men kept the trips short and did not stay away from home for long, returning as soon as they had a kill.

The carcasses were dragged back through the snow. On these occasions, the meat was prepared solely by the men. They cooked the meat in the longhouse and when it was ready to eat, they brought everyone from their homes. These were times when they ensured all who lived within the settlement had remained free from ailments, and when they catered to the needs of the most vulnerable living among them. Some of the younger men used these times to clear the animal waste, replenish everyone's stocks, and clear snow from the stacks of wood outside the widows houses, refilling the wooden crates, replacing the wood the women had been forced to use.

At the first of these gatherings, Rayna sat on her mother's knee. Her little head turning constantly as she tried to take in everything before her. The many people, and the place itself, was new to her. Her eyes and ears tried hard to absorb all the new sights and strange sounds.

Kelda, unnoticed by anyone else, could not take her eyes off the baby. She shuffled her way closer to Fraida. As the baby swung her head round her eyes fixed on this bobbing head, whose hair stood out in all directions from a lined, but grinning, face.

The child's expression however remained at first impassive as she took time to study the excited Kelda. Kelda raised her hand up to her face and gave a little wave. The bracelet Kelda always wore on her wrist was made from numerous bleached animal bones and they rattled together when Kelda waved her hand. The baby's eyes swung to the bracelet, then looked back at the face and smiled. Kelda was ecstatic. Both her hands came up to her face as she tried to contain her excitement. The bracelet again rattled and the baby giggled, thinking this was a game. Fraida smiled and looked down at the chuckling child in her arms. She followed her eyes, trying to see what was making her laugh, but Kelda swung quickly round leaving her back facing the pair and Fraida was none the wiser.

At each of the few gatherings held that winter, Kelda always managed to make some contact with the child. The child's eyes, when she saw her, always went to the bone bracelet worn on Kelda's wrist.

To everyone's relief, after the severe weather of that winter, the snow at last began to melt when a weak, but faintly warm, spring sun slowly surfaced for the start of another year. Everyone emerged from their homes smiling, glad at last to be released from the confines of their dwellings. The sound of people's voices could be heard all around, and

as the men set to work in the sheds, the women took the chance to visit each other for a much longed for chat and to catch up with news.
Vaila, as she walked towards Fraida's, was excited at the thought of seeing and holding Rayna again. Each time she had seen her at the gatherings, she could not believe the change a month or two could make in the child's appearance. Vaila carried with her a little cloth doll she had passed the time making in the long weeks of winter, and some small dresses, with tunics, that would fit the child in the summer months that lay ahead.
Leif was out with the men and Fraida was thrilled to have the company of her friend again. Rayna could now sit up on her own, in her little cradle. Vaila went straight over, and kneeling down, she held the doll up in front of the child. Rayna studied it closely, then smiled. Vaila placed it in her hands. Both women laughed as Rayna immediately put it to her mouth. She began to gurgle and jerkily shake the doll about. Seeing Rayna happy and content, playing with her new toy, both women sat down at the table and the servant woman brought them refreshments.
Vaila started to remove the clothes she had made from her basket and Fraida excitedly looked at each one. She was thrilled with the little tunics Vaila had made for Rayna and she leaned over and hugged her in thanks.
Everyday life in the settlement soon began to take on its normal routine with the daily work required at the start of a new year. Within a couple of weeks Fraida thought it warm enough for the child to be placed outside in the fresh air for a little while, in the wooden cradle with the hood. She dressed Rayna, to keep her snug and warm, in the fur outfit Vaila had made. Fraida placed the child in the cradle, and being something new, she smiled as Rayna's head twisted and turned to inspect the inside of the hood. Volga followed Fraida outdoors and took up her usual stance at the side of the cradle. Kelda, who had been patiently waiting for this day, stood hidden at the side of one of the sheds and she watched the movements of Fraida closely. She stood silent and still, watching, until Fraida walked back to her dwelling. She could hear the child gurgling at Volga, who was at that moment looking in over the edge of the ornately carved cradle.
Kelda, when she saw her way was clear, crept forward. She reached the cradle and looked down at the baby, who was now struggling to stay awake. Her eyes had become heavy from watching clouds drifting slowly across the sky. However, her little eyes shot open at the appearance of

Kelda's face, which now obstructed her view. Kelda clucked softly at the child and nodded her head. A grin widened over the lined and tired face. The child smiled, then made gurgling noises as if trying to speak. Kelda put her hand in the cradle to touch the child gently on the face. Volga stood up, baring her teeth. She began to growl low in her throat. Without taking her eyes from the child, Kelda again reached over to pat the hound distractedly on the head, but this time, the bones that hung from her wrist bounced off the disconcerted dog's nose.

Kelda raised her arm and Rayna, spotting the bracelet, became quiet as her eyes fixed on it. Kelda lifted her hand and shook it, to rattle the bones. Rayna began to laugh. This game went on for some time then Kelda, being overcome with excitement, leaned in the cradle to kiss Rayna on her soft cheek. She then tried to straighten, but Rayna's little hand now had hold of her wayward hair. Kelda tugged gently, trying to free herself, but Rayna held on tight and gurgled and laughed. The more Kelda tugged to free herself, the more Rayna held on. She laughed and gurgled loudly at this familiar game she played with one other, that was Toork.

Fraida came to the door of the dwelling to see what her child found so amusing. She was surprised to see Kelda bent over with her head in the cradle. Volga looked over at her mistress then back at the cradle and she growled and bared her teeth as she again looked over at Fraida. Fraida put her hand silently to her mouth in a gesture for the dog to be quiet, then waved her hand in a downward movement for the dog to lie down. Volga was not happy but she did what her mistress instructed.

Fraida then stepped back into the shadows and quietly watched, hidden from Kelda's view. Kelda, having tried in vain to extract herself from the baby's grip, removed her bracelet and held it up, dangling it and rattling it in front of the baby's face. Rayna soon let go of Kelda's hair, grabbing for the bracelet instead. Her little hand grasped the bracelet and held it tight. Kelda tried again, at first in vain, to pries the little fingers loose. Eventually however, with patience, Kelda did manage to gently loosen the child's grip, but as she straightened and put the bracelet back on, the child's face began to crease. She started to cry at the loss of, what was to her, a new toy. Kelda, now perturbed at the crying baby, looked around her in consternation. She tried to hush the child with bobbing and laughing, but the child would have none of it. There was nothing else for it, Kelda thought, but to give her what she wanted. So removing the bracelet, she held it out to the crying child. Rayna immediately stopped crying when she spotted the dangling bones. She smiled as her little hand came up to grasp the rattle from Kelda's hands. Kelda stood for a few minutes studying the now happy child, then bringing up her hand she gave a little wave before contentedly continuing on her way.

Fraida waited until Kelda was well out of sight before going over to the cradle to look in at the child. Rayna had now given in to tiredness and had fallen fast asleep, but still clenched in her little hand was the bracelet of bones. Fraida reached out and gently tried to take away the cluster of bones. The child stirred in her sleep and tightened her grip. Fraida withdrew her hand, deciding meantime, in case her movement woke Rayna, to leave the bracelet there.

Leif, returning from his work shed, smiled when he saw the outdoor cradle and he crept over to look in at his child. He frowned slightly when seeing the bunch of bones clasped tight in the sleeping child's hand. He looked around him, wondering where on earth they had come from. He went into the dwelling to inform Fraida of what the child held and Fraida told him what had transpired with Kelda. She told Leif that as soon as the child woke up she would remove it and give it to Vaila, so she could return the bone bracelet to Kelda.

Both parents however did not take into consideration the strong will of their child. When next Rayna woke, Leif went out and carried the cradle, with the child still in it, back to the dwelling. She giggled and laughed up at her smiling father while jerkily waving about the rattling bones. Leif set the cradle down and lifted Rayna out, to place her on her mother's lap. Fraida removed Rayna's fur hat, then tried to take the bones from the small hand before removing her jacket. Rayna's little face creased in a frown. She looked up at both her parents who smiled and made conciliatory sounds trying to distract her.

Fraida managed to take the bones which she handed to Leif, but Rayna's eyes followed them. Fraida removed the coat and leggings but Rayna twisted and turned her head in order to keep her eyes on her new toy. Leif put the bones into his pocket, but as he turned to walk away, Rayna started to cry. She twisted and turned in her mother's arms, refusing to be fed, and instead held out her arms to her father.

Leif walked back and lifted the child from a struggling Fraida. Rayna immediately smiled, and then leant over in her father's arms to look down at his pocket. Both parents looked at each other, being astounded at their child's show of astuteness. Fraida lifted Rayna's little cloth doll and waved it in front of the child, hoping to distract her from the bracelet which was still in Leif's pocket. The baby however, lifted her arm and swept the doll away from her vision. She leant over again to look, first at the pocket, then back at Leif.

Rayna studied her father's shaking head as he said no, and her little face creased and taking a deep breath, she began to cry. Leif and Fraida tried everything they could think of to distract the sobbing child, but she would not be consoled. After putting up with this for a full half hour, Leif then took the rattle from his pocket. As soon as Rayna spotted it, she immediately stopped crying. She hiccupped as a grin spread over her blotched little face, and Leif, being unable to resist his child's smile, gave in and returned the rattle to her eagerly grasping little hand.

That night, Leif began to carve out of walrus Ivory, as good a replica as he could, of the bone bracelet. He worked night after night doing each peace individually, until he was sure they were smooth and shiny. Fraida strung them together, in the same order as Kelda's bracelet. It was just over a week later, while Rayna was asleep, that they switched bracelets.

Both parents held their breath the next morning when Rayna woke. They watched from the side as, using her little arms, she grasped the side of the cradle and somewhat wobbly pulled herself up. Her eyes searched the blanket for her toy. Smiling she lunged forward to get it in her grasp. She lifted it and put it to her mouth, but straight away she brought it back down in front of her and her face creased as she studied the ivory rattle. She put it up to her mouth once more then down again in front of her.

Rayna then looked up at her parents who began to talk unconcernedly as if nothing was wrong, but the child was not easily fooled. She threw the toy from the cradle. Fraida and Leif could not believe it. Eventually, sometime later, being tired of the child's constant crying, they gave in and returned to Rayna her bunch of bones. After getting her own rattle back, Rayna then accepted the one her father had made. She sat for some time with one in each hand, giggling and gurgling at the sound as she brought both clashing together in front of her.

The weather began to improve as the weeks passed and Ragnar and Leif were down at the dock seeing off the second knorr ship now filled with more cargo for Olaf. Lief's men stood about watching the ship go out to sea. Leif began to notice the restlessness in their eyes as they looked from the departing ship over to the longships berthed in the shelter of the palisade. Leif looked at Ragnar, and he could see by his manner he had also noticed the men were showing signs of discontentment. Leif felt a slight guilt, because for the first time in years he had been content and happy to stay at home. He knew many of the men were still angry and dissatisfied that the murdering thieving cowards, who had deprived them of so many of their friends and family, were still at large.

He asked Ragnar to walk back with him. Leif started the conversation by saying, "I have not, nor will I ever, forget about Jon, or my father come to that, and the way in which they were killed." Ragnar looked over at Leif in question as he paused before continuing, "Maybe it is time for you and I to sit down so that we can try to work out a plan which would help in the search for their killers?" Ragnar stopped. He looked sideways at Leif, and putting his arm around Leif's shoulder, he smiled wryly as he said, "I think that would be a good idea, because, you know, this settlement cannot be at peace again until we have had our revenge on those who have deprived us of so much." Leif nodded, knowing in his heart that Ragnar was right. Both men carried on walking and they discussed where the best place would be for them to meet to work out their plan.

Later that day, without mentioning anything to the men, Leif went to Ragnar's dwelling to meet with him. They talked of what their plan of action would now be. They discussed the areas where they had searched for their ship in previous years, plus all the places where it had been seen. They tried to work out if there was any pattern to the route the elusive ship followed. If they could work out an area where the ship might regularly pass, they could berth there, hidden in readiness, waiting to spring a trap on the ship as it sailed past.

With this in mind, they continued for the rest of the day to formulate a plan. Both agreed to start preparing the long ship's now for their planned trip, but they would delay sailing until the knorr ship returned from Olaf's, because some of their best seafaring men had sailed aboard her.

That night, Leif told Fraida about their planned journey. She became quiet and he watched as the tears gathered in her eyes. He stood up, and going over he enveloped her in his arms. "I will try my best to find our ship this time, to put an end to this once and for all," he said, and she nodded as she hugged him. Knowing until that happened, every year, they would spend these months apart.

There was much to be planned in the week ahead and with the news that everyone wanted to hear, the men eagerly set to work. The longships were brought over from the palisade. After Leif and Ragnar checked them over, the men began preparing them for sail. The weather was growing increasingly warmer and everyday Rayna sat outside in her little cradle watching the bustle going on around her. Kelda came to see her each day. The child began to watch for her coming. Whenever she spotted Kelda in the distance, the child would start to gurgle, laugh, and wave her arms excitedly about.

After spending some time with the child, Kelda would then leave to go on her wanderings. It wasn't long before Rayna began to strain and pull herself round to look from the side of the hood of the cradle, and her eyes would watch Kelda until she was out of sight.

Eventually the child could sense when Kelda was about to wander off and she began holding both arms up in a motion for Kelda to lift her. Kelda at first just shook her head and held the little hands in hers. However, on one of the days, when she saw Rayna's face crease as if to cry, Kelda gave in to temptation and lifted her from the cot.

Rayna was ecstatic. She gurgled and laughed as her little hands came up to touch Kelda's cheeks. Kelda closed her eyes, her heart warming at the touch of the soft little fingers moving over her face. She stood with her eyes closed, just savouring the moment, until she felt something tug on her skirt. She looked down and Volga was growling low in her throat while tugging for her to put the baby back. She looked into the baby's laughing face for a minute more, then she kissed her and placed her back in the cradle. Fraida watched all this from the shadows, as she always tried to do when she knew it was time for Kelda to appear. Now she had a child of her own, Fraida could understand the heartache the poor woman had been forced to endure. The thought of losing Rayna was too much for Fraida to contemplate. Her heart went out to Kelda, for the loss she had been forced to endure.

Vaila visited Fraida often and although Rayna loved her and all the attention Vaila bestowed upon her, both Leif and Fraida noticed, with some consternation, that no matter who held the child, if Kelda appeared, Rayna would strain to watch until Kelda disappeared from her view. The child seemed to have developed a growing fascination for this bedraggled and lonely figure. Fraida would look at Leif at these times, but Leif could only shrug, unable as he was to understand and answer Fraida's unspoken question.

Kelda's antics up on the headland told the people their knorr ship was on the horizon. Some of the people began to gather on the shore. Leif walked over to the banks to look out. He soon spotted the other ship sailing close behind. A grin spread over his face when he recognised it to be the longship of Olaf's. He went to call Fraida and lifting the child in his arms, they set off together down to the dock.

Toork was there before them. He smiled as Rayna held out her arms to him. He took the child and kissed her before holding her up high so she could see the incoming ships. She gurgled, laughed, and kicked out her little legs in her excitement at being held so high. As the ships came in to dock, Toork lowered his arms to point out Olaf to the child as her grandfather disembarked.

Olaf bellowed his usual greeting, which made Rayna jump. She frowned and tightened her arms round Toork's neck as she studied this big blustery stranger. Seeing the uncertainty on his granddaughter's face, Olaf turned instead to Fraida. Rayna watched as her mother ran into Olaf's arms and she watched her smile as Olaf hugged her before swinging her round. She then saw her father smile and laugh as he too greeted Olaf.

Olaf then turned to come quietly towards his granddaughter. He stood in front of her smiling, pleasured at the resemblance which reminded him so much of Fraida when she herself was just a child. Rayna's face was impassive as she studied this strange new person standing before her. Olaf lifted his neck pendant and chains and rattled them in front of her. Rayna's face creased into a smile. She stretched out her hand to try to grasp them. Olaf stepped back though and held out his arms to Rayna. She hesitated for a moment, till he again rattled the chains, and then she went forward into his arms. Olaf kissed and hugged the child often as they walked back to the settlement, but Rayna's attention was fully taken up by the many new toys hanging around her grandfather's neck.

Fraida took the child from her father's arms when they entered the dwelling, so he could sit to eat. She placed her outside in the sunshine in her cradle. They gathered round the table and the servant women walked back and forward laying out food and drink for them all to consume. There was much jollity and laughter in the hour following his arrival as they all chatted and exchanged their news. Eventually though, Olaf stood up from the table. Going eagerly towards the door he said, "Where is my granddaughter? I have brought her some toys." Fraida jumped up and ran to stop her father before he reached the door.

He looked at Fraida in question. She held him back as she explained about Kelda. He looked at her in puzzlement and taking his arm she walked with him towards the door, where they both stood in the shadows watching Kelda spend time with the child.

Olaf stood quietly watching and was surprised to see the delight the child seemed to derive from the solitary figure of the delusional woman. Was this a good thing he thought to himself? The woman certainly, he could see by her smiles, got as much pleasure from the child as the child did from her, but she was delusional, and unpredictable he would have to say, but for the time being, while the child was in sight of the dwelling, and with Volga to guard her, maybe it could be allowed. Fraida then dragged him away and they returned to the table, where the talk and laughter resumed.

Later in the day Leif carried Rayna in to see her grandfather, who took from his pocket a circular spinning top. He smiled at Rayna as he set it in motion and her little eyes were mesmerised when she watched it spin across the floor. Leif sat her down and they all laughed as she immediately lunged forward. She toppled over, but proceeded with strong determination on her little face to try to propel herself forward in order to reach the spinning toy. Olaf derived much pleasure that afternoon from playing with the child, but soon, after all the excitement this day had brought, she grew tired and tetchy. Fraida took over and fed her and settled her down for the night.

One of the men came to inform Olaf his trunk had been brought up from the ship. He took his leave to go and freshen up for the feast in the longhouse, which would be later that evening. After his and Toork's departure, Leif told Fraida he was glad her father had chosen this time to visit, because he would be company for her when they left to go on the raid. Fraida smiled and agreed. Leif wondered if Toork would choose to stay here now Olaf had arrived? He said to Fraida he would remember to ask him later that night.

Everyone had gathered in the longhouse, and having satisfied their hunger, it was a relaxed atmosphere in which they all sat talking in general and supping their ale. Leif brought up the subject of their, soon to be, planned departure. He remarked casually to Olaf that he was glad he had chosen this time to visit, as they themselves were about to depart on a predetermined raid. However, no sooner had he finished the sentence when, to his surprise and dismay, before he managed to get another word out, Olaf threw up his hands and bellowed, "A raid! Splendid! Did you hear that," he blustered as he called over to his men, "we are about to go on a raid!"

Leif, stunned into silence at this statement, sat back as Olaf's men cheered. Leif turned to look sideways at Fraida, who was looking back at him with some surprise. Leif grimaced, and shrugged. Fraida began to frown. Fraida looked over at Toork who also shrugged and himself raised both eyebrows when returning her look.

Leif, now being unsure of how to proceed, then began to say," Of course, you and your men are welcome to come along, but, if you choose to stay here to spend some time with Fraida and the baby," he trailed off somewhat hopefully. "Nonsense, nonsense," Olaf bellowed, "I can spend all the time I like with them when we return," he stated, now overcome with excitement at the thought of the forthcoming journey. "Besides," he said turning to pat Toork on the knee, "it will be wonderful to be in a battle again with my old friend Toork by my side, this is something I have sorely missed."

Fraida, by the cross look on her face, did not think this was so wonderful. Toork as he avoided her eyes, was, for once, glad he did not have the means to voice an opinion.

Ragnar by this time was also looking over at Leif with a questioning look on his face. Leif rose casually from the table to make his way over to explain to Ragnar what had just happened. Ragnar started to laugh at Leif's growing consternation. "Well this trip will certainly be interesting if nothing else," Ragnar said giving Leif a consolatory clap on the back. "Think of it this way," he said as he bent to Leif's ear, "the more the merrier," then he burst into laughter at the set look on Leif's frowning face.

For what remained of the evening, Leif was aware of his wife's angry look whenever her eyes met his. Later when alone in their dwelling, she told him, in no uncertain terms, that she did not want her father going on any raid. Leif explained to her it was no fault of his. He was certainly not going to be the one to upset her father by telling him he had to remain here with her. Fraida then said angrily that if he would not tell him, then she would.

However the following morning Olaf was far too excited by this turn of events to listen to anything his daughter had to say. She stood looking out from her dwelling, shaking her head in exasperation as she watched him leap about in front of Rayna, who was laughing as he waved his treasured sword about in a jocular manner. "Look at him," she said to Leif, who stood by her side. "He thinks it's all a game." She left Leif's side and walked back into the room. "I have enough to worry about when thinking of the safety of you and Toork without having the added worry of the well-being of my father," she retorted with some concern. "Don't worry, I will look after him," Leif said resignedly, "I promise you that." "And who will look after you?" she said angrily. "Toork will," Leif said. Fraida drew in an exasperated breath and said, "And who will look after Toork!" "Hakon of course," said Leif throwing up his hands. Fraida let out a hiss between her gritted teeth as she turned her back on him. "You always have an answer," she said angrily, and at this, Leif walked over and put his arms around her. He began to softly kiss the back of her neck. Fraida's insides melted at his touch. But she still swung round angrily in his arms, determined to have her say. He was ready for this, and before she could utter another word he brought his lips down hard on hers. She struggled with him for a few minutes more, then gave in and circled her arms around his neck. The cause of the argument was soon forgotten when the emotions stirred up by their love for each other quickly overtook their senses. It was with reluctance they broke apart when Olaf bellowed outside for Leif to join him. "This will have to wait until later," Leif said with a promise as he softly nibbled Fraida's ear. Letting her go he reluctantly went out to join her father.

The following day, the camp was a hive of activity as the boats were made ready for their departure. Ragnar looked sideways over to Leif, a wry smile spreading over his face when Olaf, who had brought with him large casks of ale, ordered the casks be distributed among the boats setting out on the raid. Leif returned Ragnar's look by raising his eyes to the heavens.

The women busily prepared food for the men to take on the journey, while Ragnar took Olaf's crew with him to the armoury. They were given the choice of other weapons they may need for the battle south.

There was a growing excitement among the men, but at the same time the women, who were the ones left behind, grew increasingly quiet. Fraida had finished the cloak's made from, what she called Kelda's wool, and she insisted her father and Toork left their own cloaks behind and took these instead. Both sensing Fraida's displeasure at the turn of events, did not argue but gave in willingly to her demands. Last minute checks were made that evening by Ragnar, Leif and Hakon to ensure everything was as it should be. Then the settlement grew quiet as everyone retired early, in preparation for the departure of the ships on the following day.

Their goodbye's all having been said, Fraida stood with Rayna in her arms and her hound's at either side. Vaila stood at her back. Everyone from the settlement turned out to watch the ships pull away from the shore. Rayna studied the tears now running down her mother's face, then turning in her mother's arms, she stretched out towards her father, Toork, and Olaf, who stood at the stern of the ship. All three men, at the same time, felt their hearts wrench at the realisation of what they were leaving behind. Olaf coughed gruffly, trying to dispel the sudden lump in his throat. Leif bit the inside of his lip, then lifting his arms he waved both hands at the sad face of his watching wife and at the empty outstretched arms of his small daughter. Toork tried, but failed, to smile, and Rayna started to cry and made little noises to the departing men who did not come back to hold her.

This made Fraida worse and she began to cry in earnest. Vaila herself was upset at seeing them this unhappy. With tears in her own eyes, she drew all the men an angry look. Taking the crying child from her mother's arms, she began walking with her back to the settlement. Volga left Fraida's side and went with Vaila to follow the child, but Dalgar stood fast at the side of his mistress. Fraida stood unmoving, her long flowing hair drifting about in the breeze. Tears continued to fall from her eyes as she watched the ships until they faded from view.

She turned, Dalgar walked close by her side, softly nudging her as he tried, in the only way he knew, to consol her. Together they walked slowly back to her dwelling. Approaching it, she was saddened by the thought that her home never seemed to be the same without Leif being there beside her.

She walked in to see Vaila sitting at the table waving the doll while trying to amuse Rayna. Her face crumpled as she looked at her friend. Vaila, not wanting the child to see her mother so upset, ran outside where she placed Rayna in her cradle. Leaving Volga by the baby's side, she then returned to give comfort to a sobbing and distressed Fraida.

It was some time later, when Fraida had finally calmed down, when the woman remembered Rayna had been left outside in the cradle. Failing to hear any noise coming from her, both women rushed to the door. Fraida's heart leapt when she saw the cradle was empty and no sign of Volga.

Stepping out into the sun they heard a gurgle and looking up, they could see Kelda, a short distance away, sitting on the grass in the sunshine with Rayna on her lap. Kelda was picking wild flowers and holding them out to Rayna, telling her their names. Rayna seemed to be listening and laughed at each new one Kelda held out to her. Volga lay at the bottom of Kelda's outstretched feet. The two women, seeing the little group happy and content, decided to leave them as they were.

The first few days after the men's departure, Fraida missed Leif badly. It took her much longer this time to settle into a routine. Even the baby seemed out of sorts, but Vaila visited every day. She thought of many things to do to distract her friend, but it was Kelda who always managed to settle Rayna down, making her laugh, even when all else seemed to have failed.

Meanwhile the ships, having the wind behind their sails, had journeyed far, and it was with relief they now neared their destination. It was this last lap of the voyage that was proving to be the most tiresome. The wind had dropped, and having entered a period of calm, everyone was beginning to suffer from the doldrums. To make any headway at all, they were forced to take to the oars. With the absence of any breeze, the men were beginning to feel the strain that comes with rowing in the heat of the midday sun. Each day had brought a rise in temperature. The further south they sailed, the hotter it became. It was hot, a bit too hot for some. Most of the men had stripped off what they could of their clothing.

Toork was the only one who was perfectly content. He lay back with his eyes closed, absorbing the heat beating down from the, high in the sky, summer sun. This reminded him of home. He could sit forever like this, dreaming of times gone by. This feeling of peace and tranquillity was too good to last he thought, smiling to himself. He was right, because his reverie was soon disturbed by the bellows and laughter emitting from a bored Olaf.

Before leaving the settlement, Ragnar had taken charge of Olaf's ship and crew. He had insisted Olaf sail with Leif and Toork. This had pleased Olaf greatly. He now stood at the side of the ship calling over to his men. Olaf knew they were nearing their journeys end and he was calling for the three ships to break out the ale. Leif was unsure this was a good idea, but it was uncomfortably hot he thought, wiping the sweat from his brow. He himself, as well as the men, had a raging thirst. Leif looked over at Toork who slowly raised his eyebrows in question. He then looked over at the other ships as they sailed closer. Ragnar was waiting for some sign from Leif. When Leif nodded, all the men cheered. Leif grinned as the men fetched their drinking horns. It would do no harm he thought to himself, as their voyage was nearly at an end.

It was the middle of the afternoon when the boats made for land. Normally Leif would wait until the fall of night, but the sun was hot and his men were merry, so better reaching land now while they were sober enough to do so; therefore avoiding any damage that may occur to the ships in their effort to reach the shore.

The boats berthed without incident, but as soon as the sails were furled and the masts fastened down, all the men threw off the remainder of their clothes and jumped into the welcoming coolness of the water in the estuary. Toork and Olaf quickly stripped down to linen undergarments and they too leapt into the cooling water. Ragnar and Leif were the only ones left on the banks. Leif was, by this time, a bit concerned about the noise coming from the frolicking men.

Ragnar looked around him, then reminded Leif this area was not one they had found inhabited before. Nevertheless, both men went to unlock the weapons chest and they carried some of the weapons over to the side of the bank. "Better safe than sorry," Leif said to Ragnar, as they walked back and forth with the heavy weapons and shields. By the time they were satisfied enough weapons were at hand, the sweat was pouring from them both.

Leif stood facing Ragnar, a mischievous grin slowly spreading across his face. He began, hurriedly, to remove his clothes. Ragnar, grinning in return, took up the challenge. It was not long before both men raced towards the water, both diving in at the same time.

Over the next two hours, the men forgot about the object of their journey. They continued to frolic in the water and only came out in order to sup more ale. But the heat was so intense they did not linger long and were quick to return to the coolness of the water. It was the hottest day that Leif, Ragnar, or the men could remember. Certainly too hot to sit waiting aboard a ship.

Toork and Olaf were the first to tire of the game. They decided to sit on the banks to rest awhile, so they waded through the water to reach the shore. Toork walked over to the boat to fetch the cloaks Fraida had given them and putting one around his dripping body, he then carried the other over to drape around Olaf's shoulders. Olaf was sitting on top of one of the embankments, a big grin on his face as he watched the men frolicking in the water below. He was loving the company, Toork could see. He smiled at his friend as he took the empty drinking horn from his hand, to go to the boat and refill it.

Toork was smiling as he walked back to Olaf, until he saw Olaf suddenly lurch forward. Toork faltered in his stride. He saw what looked to be an arrow bounce up in the air behind his unaware and defenceless friend. Toork immediately dropped the drinking horns and began to run. His gut reaction was to call out a warning, but the only sound to come out of his mouth was a hollow grunt.

Ragnar and some of his men were about to come ashore for more ale, but they had stopped to laugh and jest and spray each other with water. Ragnar, from the corner of his eye, saw Toork drop the horns. He swung round as Toork started to run. Looking up in puzzlement, he saw Olaf slumped over. He saw Toork launch himself at Olaf, landing on top of him, just as two arrows struck home, but thankfully, bounced off. Ragnar immediately roared a warning and rushed from the water. Ragnar hesitated on the shore for only a moment, but realising there was no time to don their clothes he called for his men to follow. They ran to take up their shields and swords. Everyone ran from the water and some were armed within minutes.

Toork rolled down the embankment taking Olaf with him. They came to a halt and Olaf pushed him off, unsure for a moment of what had actually happened. It took but a second however for him to see his men running for their weapons, and Toork, after hauling Olaf to his feet, started running towards the ships in order to arm himself. Olaf then followed.

Olaf's men immediately started firing their arrows over the embankment at the unseen enemy. Ragnar and his men ran to the slope at the side of the embankment. They scrambled up, crouching down, they began to run along among the long reeds and grasses, hoping to remain hidden so they could attack from behind and drive this unseen enemy forward, into the waiting arms of Leif and the rest of the, now armed, men.

A large band of fighting men, who were marching north, had heard some noise coming from the estuary. The leaders had instructed a few of the guard to go forth and investigate. They reported back that a number of empty Viking ships were berthed at the banks, and that the crews were bathing in the water, unarmed and unprepared. The leaders had all grinned as they visualised having the means to transport their men north by ship, instead of having to walk all the way in this confounded heat. Unknown to Leif and his men, at that point they had advanced forward, their eye being on what they thought was an easy target. However, these men could never have had the misfortune of doing battle with hardy Vikings before, or they would have deemed it wiser to carry on walking.

Ragnar and his men came creeping up behind the band of fighting men just as they were nearing the crest of the embankment. Leif and the others, who held their shields up to deflect the shooting arrows, were ready and waiting on the other side. Ragnar roared out as he and his men rushed forward. Leif, hearing the cry, led his men up and over the bank. The enemy, being startled, were slow to react, so shocked were they at the sudden appearance of all these armed, but naked men, who were behaving in a somewhat berserk manner. They were waving their swords wildly and roaring dementedly as they ran towards them. This was a sight never before seen. These men were surely mad, they thought, looking around in disbelief. They must be, to fight naked against a heavily armed enemy. But this same army hesitated too long and before they even had a chance to raise their weapons, the Vikings were upon them.

It was all the time Leif had needed. They struck into the very heart of the enemy before they could gather their wits. Olaf swung out with his sword and Toork stood at his back. Toork felt a blow to his arm and he looked down to see a sword had struck both his and Olaf's cloaked arms. The weapon had, to his surprise, caused no harm. Toork swung round and he brought the man down. Another lunged at Olaf, but the enemy sword refused to pierce the cloak. Olaf looked momentarily at Toork in question, then shrugged as he also brought his sword up and struck his assailant down.

Leif looked over from his position behind Hakon, to where Olaf and Toork stood battling side by side. He could see both men were fighting fast and furiously, bringing down many of the enemy in the process. Being satisfied they were more than efficient in their battle skills, he pushed the over enthusiastic Hakon to the side, so he himself would have the chance to strike out at the enemy. Hakon, as usual, stood in front of Leif, ensuring as few men as possible were able to pass his swinging axe in order to reach his leader.

Being naked in no way inhibited the men from giving their all on the field of battle. In fact, some began to prefer this state of undress as it gave more freedom of movement, but no doubt the amount of ale they had consumed was a contributory factor to their high spirits and lack of fear in facing this enemy. However the enemy themselves were deeply shocked at these mad, naked Viking's and even more shocked with the ferocity with which they fought. The scene was one that many would not believe. A band of naked Vikings taking on a small army.

Some were not prepared to stand and fight these men who they had previously thought would be an easy target. They took to their heels and ran. The rest, who were sandwiched between Ragnar's men and Leif's in front, could not escape. They continued to battle for their very lives. It was to no avail however, as the Vikings, as always, stood fast and fought on, until all those who had the affront to attack them, were no more.

Eventually, all sweaty and bloodied, Leif and his men lowered their shields and swords. They were all breathing heavily with the effort of battling with so many in the heat of the day. Leif looked over to Ragnar and said," That was a close call." Ragnar, who did nothing in half measures, was bent over with his hands on his knees trying to catch his breath. He grinned wryly and nodded back as he said to Leif breathlessly, "You're telling me."

Leif looked round for any casualty's they may have suffered. He was more than relieved to find, apart from a few arm and leg wounds sustained by some, there was none. "You did well men!" Leif shouted out. Everyone then began to laugh as they made their way back over the embankment.

Olaf was in a state of high excitement, knowing he had performed well in what was his first real battle in years. Toork however, stood silently to the side. His thoughts went deep as he fingered the cloak about his shoulders. It felt like a normal cloak, he thought, rubbing it between his fingers. However, his eyes had shown him it was not. Olaf and he had been struck a number of times, with different weapons each time, but non had penetrated the material of the cloaks. This was not normal, this much he knew. It was just as well they had decided to don the cloaks when they did, or the outcome for them both on this day could have been very different, he thought, confusedly.

The men were much quieter this time, when they entered the water to wash down. It felt good as they immersed themselves fully to wash off the sweat and blood. They did not linger for long in the cool water but came out to dry themselves, and to dress. Some started fires. Soon the fresh fish, caught on the journey down, was set on stakes to cook over the fire. The smell of the cooking fish made them all realise how hungry they were. The wounds of the injured were seen to first. Then everyone gathered round the fire to eat and relax. Leif, while eating, knew they would have to move on, because the unfortunate incident of today would have alerted the people of this area to their presence. This was the place he and Ragnar had worked out where the missing ship might pass, but they could no longer sit it out here, because their presence and position was now known and that could leave them open to attack.

Leif called Ragnar over to his side, while the men supped their ale. Together they quietly planned their next move. They decided to set sail the following morning before dawn, while it was still dark. They would shift base to a place further down the coast. Sailing out to sea in the early hours would prevent soldiers who had flown the field of battle from seeing the direction in which the boats sailed. The decision on where to berth they decided to leave for the moment. They would look first at what opportunities any new area might reveal.

The next morning, under cover of darkness, the boats took to the water. Olaf was impressed at the stealth of Leif's men as they silently drew away from the banks of the estuary. When they were far enough out at sea they hoisted the sails, and only then, did they allow themselves time to sit back and relax. They gathered round to eat what was left of the bread and cheese, washing it down with a horn of ale. The sun came up and the temperature began to increase, but today a cool breeze drifted over the ships from the open sea. The men took it in shifts to lie and snooze while the billowing sails carried them south.

It was early evening when they turned the boats towards land. They all knew of a wide estuary where they had berthed in previous years, but they had only used it as a stopping point and had always stayed close to the mouth. They had never carried out any attacks in this area and Leif had a mind to sail deeper into the estuary to see what lay ahead. As long as their way out to the open sea was clear, in case of the need for a quick getaway, he knew it could afford them some opportunities for raids.

In the half light of dusk, as soon as the hazy outline of land became visible, the men lowered the sails. They worked quickly to furl and fasten them down. The rowers took to the oars and as darkness fell, they steered the ships into the still waters of the estuary. The ships proceeded with stealth, to row inland, keeping to the centre of the broad waterway. Leif's ship led the way and he stood looking out from the prow as they rowed upstream, guiding the other ships who followed in their wake. He spotted a place ahead where the bank was steep and covered with many reeds and rushes, dense enough to disguise their presence. His silhouette motioned to the other ships to follow and they glided towards the sloping embankment. The boats slid silently to a halt and some of the men jumped off with the ropes to anchor the ships down. Everyone worked in silence to avoid the risk of being discovered, until they could look at what dangers surrounded them in this new area.

Ragnar joined Leif and Toork. The three men scrambled up the bank. They cast their eyes over the skyline, in the far distance they could see the outline of dwellings. Leif turned to scan the opposite side of the bank, but for as far as the eye could see, there lay only stretches of land. Toork put his head to the ground and the others remained still as he listened for any sound. He shook his head and the three then scrambled down. Leif gave the go ahead and the men relaxed and spoke quietly among themselves as they set about lighting a few small fires. They erected the tents from the centre of the boats round the small fires to prevent any light from projecting into the darkness. When the fires began to glow, they set about cooking the fish, which the men ate in stages, until they all had their fill.

It was a warm, balmy evening and the men gathered in groups around the small fires, listening to Olaf and his men as they told tales of the many mysteries of the Far East. Toork, as they settled down for the night, remembered only too well his last trip with Leif, so this time he slept aboard the ship, with his trusty swords held close to his side.

The next morning, early, at the break of dawn, Leif and Ragnar again scrambled up the bank. They remained still while studying the smallholding of dwellings that lay in the distance. As the light increased and the view began to clear both turned to each other and smiled. There in the centre was a large building. Silhouetted against the skyline was the sign of a cross. They looked again all around in the increasing light of day, to ensure the surrounding area was clear. Leif began to smile. Ragnar grinned while remarking they could not have picked a better spot. They scrambled down and gathered the men around. The men were now hungry and wanting food other than fish. So it was decided that although daylight had dawned, they would raid the smallholding. If they all donned their cloaks they could sneak up through the tall grasses before having to reveal themselves. Olaf became excited at the thought of another raid so soon after the last battle. However, Toork made sure that in his excitement Olaf did not leave anything behind. He checked Olaf had all his weapons before covering his shoulders with his cloak.

They set off in line, one behind Leif and another behind Ragnar. Crouching low they made their way somewhat slowly at first, through the squelching, boggy ground that lay beneath their feet. However, the closer they got to the smallholding the firmer the land became, and this allowed them to quicken their pace. They split into groups as they neared the dwellings and they could see pigs scrambling around in pens close to the houses.

It was still early and very few people were out and about. They straightened up, and began to run. Those who were going about their business still did not notice what was about to befall them. When they did, it was already too late. All hell broke loose as they burst through the doors of the dwellings. Leif, Ragnar, and some of the men, made straight for the building displaying the sign of the cross. Their intentions, as always, to make these people pay. They fought their way forward, striking down those who chose to remain in their path, but there was no fighting force here, so very soon none were left standing. Silence fell once more in the little village and the men began to search around. The women and children had took to their heels and ran for cover, but that bothered them none because food was what they were after.

They gathered up bread, cheese, butter, eggs, and ewers of milk from the dwellings. They took birds that were strung up in a yard, and Hakon and a few of the men grabbed two of the pigs, while others scrambled about gathering chickens. Leif and Ragnar found a cask of wine in the dwelling with the cross. The men lifted the gold cross and chalices, and some fine cushions, before removing the tapestry's that hung on the walls. They set fire to the dwelling with the cross, but left the rest of the homes intact for the women and children to return to.

Back at where the ships were berthed, they built up the fires. Knowing the pigs would take some time to cook, they prepared them first, setting them on stakes over the larger fires. They cooked the birds and chickens to eat there and then. They boiled the eggs to eat with the butter and bread. Having eaten they felt refreshed. Some of Olaf's men decided to scout the surrounding area. They were soon back with some fine fa birds shot down with their bows and arrows. They continued to cook what they could of the food that day and each ship was restocked with enough provisions to last the week ahead. With the pigs not fully cooked guards were posted around that night. Preparations were carried out to ensure the ships were ready for sail on the following day. They would remain at sea in the week that followed and cover as much of the coas as they could, to search for any sign of the missing ship.

It was some months after the boats departure, when Kelda alerted the people to their ships return. Fraida's heart leapt in her breast and she ran to the bank to look out at the three ships in the distance. It was with relief she saw they were all intact. However she, along with the others sighed deeply, because they had hoped against hope, that this time, they would recover Leif's father's ship. Everyone knew this would not be an easy task. It was a strong ship, capable of sailing anywhere. The chance of it being in the right place at the right time, was faint to say the least.

Fraida ran back to her dwelling. Rayna, now being up on her feet, was tottering towards Volga, but Fraida scooped her up. She struggled in her mothers arms as Fraida quickly changed her into a clean tunic. Wiping her little face and hands she then combed through her wispy hair. She quickly brushed her own long hair, bringing it down from where she had pinned it up that morning. Her stomach had butterflies at the thought of seeing Leif again. She smiled happily to herself, and picking up her child she set off down to where the ships would soon dock.

The men were all weary from their long journey home. They sat cramped in ships that were full to the hilt with goods taken in the raids. However they all brightened up at the sight of their loved ones waving from the shore. Leif, Olaf and Toork all stood up and waved. Fraida, who held the child up in her arms, pointed to them as she said their names. "Look," she said repeatedly, "Papa, Toork, and Grandpa." Rayna's brow came down and she studied in silence the incoming ships and the three men who stood waving.

Fraida wondered, because young children had very short memories, i. Rayna would still recognise the three men before her. Leif was the first to jump from the ship. Setting Rayna down, Fraida watched as she immediately tottered towards her Fathers outstretched arms. He scooped her up and cuddled her tight, loving the familiar feel and smell that only ever came from the innocence of a small child. He then looked into her face but she turned to look behind him. She leaned over his shoulder and stretching out her arms she said the word "Oork."

Everyone stood stunned, in silence, as the child smiled and repeated the word. Tears sprung to "Oork's" eyes as they all realised she had spoken his name. Walking over, he took the child from her father's arms and swung her giggling body, high, before then bringing her down to hug her. Leif looked over at his wife, thinking he had forgotten just how beautiful she was. He rushed over and scooped her up in his arms. She hugged him tight and kissed him, feeling so relieved and happy he was home. Olaf smiled while watching this reunion from behind. Then he bellowed forlornly, "What about me?" Everyone laughed and Fraida rushed over to hug him, and Toork put Rayna into his waiting arms. The happy group then set off walking back to the dwellings, chatting excitedly about the difference they could now see in the growing child.

The people of the settlement helped the crews to disembark. They took from the ships the slaves Olaf had acquired in the last raid, in order to feed and freshly clothe them. These prisoners were very quiet and subdued, in fear of what would befall them. Little did they know they would be far better treated where they were going, than they had ever been as supposedly free serfs of the noblemen in the land they had just left. The Vikings looked after their slaves well, they fed them and clothed them. Gave them dwellings to live in, and in return, they always worked hard.

The returning men ate but a morsel of bread and a little milk before giving in to sleep. With all the men in bed, the noise of excited chatter ceased. The people of the settlement used this time to prepare food to celebrate the men's safe return. As always, carcasses were set to roast over fires. The feasting would carry on for some days, and they would need enough food to see them through. The air was soon filled with the smell of roasting meat, and freshly baked bread which the women baked and piled high. Plenty of vegetables were put on to boil, because for the men on their journey, these would have been scarce. The longhouse was swept and the tables set with ewers of milk, ale, and wine. Pots of honey were placed on each table with large blocks of butter and cheese. The women worked hard and did their best to ensure everyone would eat well that night.

Later that evening Toork smiled to himself as, fully satisfied, he now sat back. He had eaten too much, he knew, and his belly was now full to bulging, but he had not been able to resist the fine spread before him. Fraida leaned over to kiss his dark cheek and she whispered, "Thank you for looking after father, and for keeping him safe." He leaned forward and hugged her, then holding her arm he motioned to her, by touching his mouth, that he needed to communicate.

Fraida sat closer to him as he drew his marks on the table. He was asking about the cloaks. "The cloaks that I gave you and father to take with you?" she asked with a slight frown. Toork nodded." Were they not warm?" she questioned, not fully understanding what he wanted to know. Toork nodded repeatedly, then he drew some signs again on the table. "What did I use to make them?" she said uncomprehendingly. Toork nodded fervently. Fraida thought for a moment, then said, "The only thing that was different was the preparation." Then she went on to tell him laughingly, of Kelda's part in the dying of the wool.

Toork nodded slowly, now beginning to understand. What they thought was a sadly delusional seer, was in fact someone who, in some way, did have certain powers. She must have, he stated to himself, otherwise who could explain the protective properties in the two cloaks? Fraida, looking at Toork's thoughtful face, asked again if the cloaks had served their purpose? Toork nodded and grinned, thinking to himself, Fraida would probably never know just how much of a purpose with which the cloaks had in fact, served the two men.

Olaf and his crew stayed at the settlement for two weeks more, but the weather began to change. Olaf deemed it was time for them to head for home. One of the knorr ships was brought over from the palisade to be loaded with timber, furs and livestock that Olaf's people would need for the winter ahead. That day, Leif took Olaf and his crew out on the hunt. The game they caught was butchered up and put in barrels of seawater brine and placed onboard the knorr for Olaf to take to his people. All the goods taken by Olaf's men in the raids was transferred to the knorr ship, so the crew would have more room on their own boat on the journey home.

Olaf was very pleased and more than satisfied, with what he had to take home to his people. With the ships now ready, everyone gathered at the shore to say goodbye.

Olaf looked forlornly back from his departing ship and turned his thoughts to the many experiences this journey had brought. He would have some good memories to mull over this winter when he sat alone at his fire, he thought with a smile. Hopefully the winter would not seem so long. With this in mind, he gave a final despondent wave to those he had to leave behind. The long, dark nights would soon pass, he told himself, watching his men raise the sails. There was the spring to look forward to, when he would come again to visit them all.

Following Olaf's departure, the settlement again returned to some semblance of normality. Everyone quickly settled into their daily tasks, but the hours of daylight lessened as the hours of darkness lengthened. So the men set to work preparing for yet another winter, that inevitably, would soon be upon them.

CHAPTER EIGHT

Rayna sat cradled in her father's lap, her sleepy eyes watching the flickering flames of the fire as they cast shadows on the circle of men basking in the warmth from its glow. An aura of excitement hung in the air. Rayna could feel it as she looked around the Longhouse. It was still very dark outside and cold, because deep snow lay thickly on the ground.

Sometime earlier, Papa had woke her from her sleep, whispering to her that Mamma was having her baby. She had smiled up at him, still dazed from sleep. He had lifted her from her cot bed, wrapping her warmly in her furs and blanket, before carrying her into the main room of the house. Vaila was there, so was Toork. Both of them had smiled at her fondly.

Papa then told her they were going out in the snow to walk to the longhouse; where they would sit in the warmth to wait until the baby was born. She had heard her Mamma moan and had looked with some concern at her father, but he had carried on smiling and told her everything was alright.

Toork carried a flaming torch and led the way as they left the warm dwelling to enter into the coldness of the night. Vaila had stayed with Mamma. Dalgar had wanted to stay too, but Toork had led him by the collar and Volga had followed.

The snow was very deep, but Papa held her high in his arms out of its reach. The sky at night looked different. This was something that was new to her. She had looked in wonder at the bright stars sparkling in the dark sky above and at the big glowing orb of the moon. She had never seen the settlement in darkness before. It looked strange and unfamiliar glistening in the moonlight under a covering of deep snow.

It was only a short walk to the longhouse. They had soon reached it to find Ragnar already there, along with a lot of the men. He had come over and patted her on the cheek as he smiled into her face. When Papa sat down one of the women had given her a cup of milk, then handed Papa a horn of ale.

Everyone was smiling and happy. After a while, some of the men began to tell tales of big battles. These battles, they told her proudly, had been led by her other Grandpa, a man who was brave and fearless they said. Sadly, he had died before she was born. She had felt special, being the only child among all the grownups. She had listened to their stories and clutched her cloth doll while fingering her bracelet of bones she always carried with her. She had listened intently to the men as they stressed the importance of dying with a sword in your hand. Without it you could not enter Valhalla, which was a wonderful place you went to when you died in battle, where you joined with all your ancestors who had gone before.

Rayna glanced over at the women who were passing around food. The place grew quiet as the men began to eat. Rayna looked at Toork, but he was not eating because he was pacing about. He smiled at Rayna and her Papa nodded to him to come over. He came and lifted her from her father's arms, but then Papa got up and he started to pace about.

They wanted the baby to come, she thought. Dalgar sat staring at the door; Rayna smiled, because she knew he was waiting for it to open. Rayna loved him just as much as she loved Volga, but she knew Dalgar did not like to be far from her Mamma. Not like Volga who would always come with her and Kelda on their walks, when they wandered around gathering herbs and wild flowers, some of which Kelda used when making her potions. She missed the company of Kelda, who she had not seen since the snow came. "Will Kelda be alright?" she said to Toork, forgetting for a moment that he could not speak. She looked up, Toork nodded and smiled. She smiled back and put her little hand up to gently touch his mouth, then she kissed his cheek. Toork hugged this child who he loved. She had just the same gentle qualities as her beautiful mother, he thought, with a smile.

Suddenly the door opened. Rayna saw Dalgar rush out, as Vaila, accompanied by one of the men, came in. She was smiling as she said to Leif, "You have a son." All the men cheered. Ragnar went over to clap a grinning Leif heartily on the back. Leif quickly finished what was left of the ale in his drinking horn and putting it down, he came over to sweep Rayna up. He said to her with a big grin, "You have a baby brother."

Rayna was very excited, as they struggled back through the snow, at the thought of seeing their new baby. She had been waiting a very long time for him to come. She would be four years old this summer and for some time she had wanted a brother or sister to play with. She played sometimes with Eric and the other children. Papa had made her wooden sword which Eric showed her how to use. But Eric was nearly eleven. He would soon tire of his game with her and leave her to go and play with the older boys. The rest of the children would follow, but she was not allowed to go away from the dwelling; unless she was with Kelda. Anyway, she thought, I always have Kelda to spend time with and now they both would have a new baby of their own to play with.

Leif stood with Rayna at the bedroom door. Fraida was sitting up in bed, holding the new baby in her arms. She looked over and smiled. Leif shook his head from side to side, a grin spreading over his face. His heart swelled with pride and a feeling of joy swept through him at the sight of his wife and newborn son. He walked across the room. Setting Rayna down, he leaned over to look into the face of the new arrival in their family. "He is so like you," Fraida said laughingly, as he looked down at the baby whose hair was as fair as Rayna's was dark. Leif kissed Fraida lovingly. Lifting Rayna, he let her see her new brother. She kissed the baby gently on the cheek and marvelled at how soft his skin was. She held up her bracelet of bones and rattled it in front of his little face. Leif and Fraida laughed. Fraida said to her daughter that he was still too young to have any toys, but in a few months he would, without doubt, love to see her bracelet.

Her father then set her down and sat on the bed to talk to Mamma. Rayna walked round the bed to the other side where Dalgar sat staring wistfully up at his mistress. Rayna put her little arms around Dalgar's neck. She cuddled him as she spoke to him soothingly, then she kissed him and stroked his head before going over to cuddle Volga, who sat at the door with a somewhat confused look on her face.

They called the baby Olaf, after Fraida's father. Fraida was so pleased when Leif had suggested this. She knew her father would be ecstatically happy when he came to see the new child. "The next one," Leif had said laughingly, "we will name after my father." Fraida retorted back with a laugh," What if it's a girl?" "The one after that then," he said, grabbing her playfully.

Fraida was glad the child had been born in the winter because it gave them all time to bond together, alone, in the confines of their home. In the weeks following the birth, Vaila was the only one to visit, everyday at first, to help Fraida with the baby. Each morning the men took it in turn to escort her through the thick snow, then back again to her dwelling which she would return to at night.

Vaila, from the moment he was born, adored this little boy who was so like his father. The love she felt for him at first confused and overwhelmed her. Each morning when she awoke she could not wait to see him and hold his soft little body in her arms. Rayna, there was no doubt she did love, but for some unknown reason the feelings she had for this child were much stronger.

When it came to the time Fraida did not need her every day, the days in between her visits seemed to be so slow in passing. She willed them to go quickly just so she could hold the baby once more in her arms. No one was happier than she when the snows began to melt, heralding, at last, the start of a new spring.

There was one other though, who felt just as pleased at the coming of spring and that was Kelda. She had missed Rayna so much in the long winter months and she could not wait to see her.

She had whiled away her time by making herself a new bone bracelet, to replace the one Rayna now wore, but that did not take long. She decided to make them both amulets from a rare and precious stone she had possessed for many years. The stone had healing properties, this Kelda knew, and it was pretty, with streaks of pink running in veins all through it. She had parted the stone, making two pieces. Over the weeks she spent time boring holes so she could thread them with thin strips of leather she had previously prepared. In each stone she carved a rune symbol, one that gave protection to the wearer, all the while she chanted a spell. In the days that followed she continued to grind the stones until they were smooth and shiny. She was very pleased with her work and could not wait to see the look of pleasure on the child's face when she presented the gift to her.

Kelda would eagerly open her door each day now, just to see how much the snow had melted. She could see movement in the settlement below, because some of the men were already moving about, but she knew she would have to wait until her way was clear before she herself ventured out.

Finally, on one of the mornings when Kelda opened her door, she jumped about with excitement. Rushing back indoors she grabbed at her cloak and quickly wrapped it around her shoulders. Then she stopped for a moment to think. She had better put on her fur boots she thought, and not go out in her thin leather slippers. She ran to fetch the boots. Sitting down, she hurriedly put them on. Standing up, she again made for the door, then she remembered she had nearly forgotten the amulets. Rushing back in, she grabbed at the little pouch that held them. At last, she made it out through the door.

Vaila had set out to go to Fraida's and on her way, she spotted Kelda hurrying down the hill. She smiled to herself as she thought of how pleased Rayna would be to see her. For the last few days the child had continually questioned when Kelda would be coming down.

Vaila quietly told Fraida when she entered that Kelda was on her way. Fraida called Rayna and she began to dress her in her warm furs. Rayna was puzzled and asked her mother if they were going out? Fraida just smiled and said to the child, "You are, but just for a little while."

Vaila lifted Olaf. She wrapped him in a blanket to keep him warm. He was now a few months old and he gurgled up into the smiling face looking down at him. He was truly beautiful, Vaila thought, looking at his little fat cheeks and his clear blue eyes. She softly stroked back his blonde wispy hair and kissed him.

When Fraida opened the door, Rayna was at her side. Her face lit up when she saw Kelda impatiently pacing up and down. Rayna immediately ran towards Kelda's outstretched arms. As Kelda hugged her she closed her eyes to savour the touch of the child's cheek against her own. "We have a new baby Kelda," Rayna said excitedly. " His name is Olaf, after Grandpa." "Oh," said Kelda, clapping gleefully, sharing in the excitement of the child. Both then looked over at the door where Fraida stood, Vaila was now at her side, holding the baby.

Fraida, smiling, motioned for Vaila to take the baby outside, so she could show him to Kelda. Vaila, as she reached them, took the blanket down so Kelda could see the child clearly. The smile that was spread across Kelda's face however, now began to fade, because a pain that was only too familiar stabbed right at her heart. She froze as she stared down at this smiling baby who, with his wispy blonde hair, reminded her so much of her own boys when they were both young. Old memories began to surface, bringing with them all the pain she tried so hard to block.

Rayna had been looking at Kelda's face for some minutes now, waiting for her reaction, when, to her consternation, she saw a tear roll down the lined and saddened face. "It's all right Kelda," the child began to say urgently, not knowing the reason for Kelda's tears. "It's our baby, yours and mine. I will share him with you," she said as she tugged, then hugged, her sad friend. Vaila felt awful. Her heart went out to Kelda when she realised what had been in Kelda's mind. Kelda came out of her trance at the urgent plea from Rayna. She shrugged, and smiling through her tears she said "Of course you will, and he is the most beautiful baby. We are really lucky to have him," she said half chokingly, trying to swallow the lump in her throat. Rayna looked at her for a moment, then she took her hand. She was happy now Kelda was smiling again. She led her off in the direction of their walk. Vaila watched them walk away hand in hand, with Rayna chatting excitedly as she noticed the bone bracelet on Kelda's wrist. "You have one too," Rayna said, "now we can be the same."

Vaila returned to the dwelling. She explained what had just happened to a questioning Fraida, who had viewed the scene from the door. Both women felt sad for poor Kelda, and as they looked down at the happy, gurgling child, they now realised the pain Kelda must have felt.

That first day, Rayna and Kelda did not stay out too long. There was still a chill in the air, but Kelda was satisfied with the little time she spent in Rayna's company. She was thrilled at Rayna's reaction to her gift. Rayna had exclaimed in delight and immediately put the amulet round her neck. She stood looking until Kelda put on hers. "Now we really are the same," Rayna said laughingly, holding up Kelda's wrist to look first at the bracelets on both their arms, and then at the amulets round their necks.

Later that day, both Leif and Fraida were forced to examine the lovely stone that hung from their daughter's neck. Neither had seen a stone like it. It was a very fine stone indeed they both agreed. The unusual veins of pink almost seemed to glow. Rayna then told her father she wanted something to give Kelda in return for her gift. She asked her father if he would make a stool for Kelda, like the one he had made for her. Leif laughed and said of course he would, but he explained to Rayna that Kelda would have to have one taller and wider than hers. Rayna thought for a moment, then she agreed, and said, "As long as it is nearly the same."

Leif did not mind in the least doing this for his daughter. He knew Kelda would derive much pleasure from an unexpected gift in return. Leif was not wrong, because later, when he helped his daughter carry out the stool, Kelda jumped up and down with delight at such a fine gift. Rayna was pleased Kelda was happy. After some discussion between the two, a decision was made to keep the stool at Rayna's house; so when Kelda came down in the summer, both would have their stools to sit on when they sat outdoors by the baby's cradle.

The heat from the spring sun began to increase as with each day it rose higher in the sky. Olaf came to visit. With bellows of grandfatherly pride, his delight at his new grandson and the naming of the child could be heard all around the settlement. Toork, Leif and Fraida looked wryly at each other, laughing at his predicted reaction. He informed them however, he could only stay for a week. He and his crew were about to set off on a journey to the east, on a trading mission. Spices were now in short supply, in both settlements, and it was time, he said jovially, for further trade. He would take with him some boxes of trinkets he said, from Leif's people, and trade them for whatever goods they requested.

However, although it was only to be a short visit, Fraida was pleased to see her father again, just as much as he was pleased to see her. She still missed him a lot. It bothered her to think of him all alone without the company of her and Toork in the long, dark nights of winter. She had suggested to her father, now she was settled with a family of her own, Toork could return as company for him. Olaf would have none of it. His daughter's well-being was paramount to him. It was only the presence of Toork that gave him peace of mind where she was concerned.

Olaf had brought presents for his grandchildren. Among the gifts was a fine ivory rattle, which he gave, with glee, to the new baby who was his namesake. For Rayna, he produced with a flurry, a little wooden cart on wheels. It had a long, straight handle she could pull behind her when she went out to gather, his words, "her bits of grass and old bones!"

Rayna was thrilled with her cart, as was Kelda. They took it with them that very day. Leif, Fraida and Olaf laughed, when later that afternoon, they watched the pair walk up the hill to Kelda's home trailing a full to overflowing cart behind them.

That year, after some in-depth discussion, Leif and the men decided not to go on raids, but to stay at home. If there had been any reported sightings of his father's ship, they would have set sail and journeyed south. But these past years, because of their continued absence in the summer months, work on the settlement had been neglected. More houses were needed for those who wished to marry, coupled with the urgent repairs required on most of the dwellings already standing. There was much work long overdue. All the men had to be present when new buildings were erected, to ensure each of the dwellings be completed before winter set in. Needless to say, the women were more than pleased, that this year at least, their men would stay at home.

Kelda had been teaching Rayna the names of all the plants they gathered. Now she began to explain their uses. This was something Rayna took a great childlike interest in. She would watch Kelda intently as she mixed the different ingredients in a large pot suspended over the fire. She could even chant some of the spells, the more common ones that Kelda used a lot. On one of the days, Kelda was explaining to Rayna how important it was for her to learn about the healing herbs; just in case anything untoward should befall her, because then the settlement would be without a healer. Kelda turned away to pick up something from the table. Rayna surprised her by saying in her childlike innocence," but Kelda, nothing will ever happen to you, because I will always be here to look after you." Kelda's back was to Rayna, and she became still. A lump came into her throat as she looked down at the table. She smiled to herself, feeling a warming in her heart for this little one, who was the only person she had left in the world to love.

Vaila and Fraida, to Rayna's delight, had sewn little pouches just like the ones Kelda wore. They strung them on each side of a leather strip that tied round Rayna's waist. Kelda was pleased at their thoughtfulness. She filled the pouches for Rayna, each one with a different mixture. Their use she explained carefully to Rayna. However, Leif and Fraida were a bit perplexed when on one of the evenings Rayna, while playing by herself, sat on her stool by the fire busily stirring her small pot while chanting a spell. Leif looked at Fraida with a frown and he said quietly," She becomes more like Kelda every day." Fraida however could not stop laughing. She said to Leif with a smile, "It can do no harm, she is learning about the plants that heal." Leif was not fully convinced he wanted Kelda to have so much influence on his daughter, but that was soon to change with the turn of events on the following day.

Leif strode into his dwelling with a grimace of pain on his face. He sucked in his breath and bent over while looking up at Fraida. His arm was stretched across his body, his hand tucked tight in his armpit. He continually cursed under his breath. He had been momentarily distracted while hammering a trunk of timber in place on one of the new dwellings, he told her through gritted teeth. He had missed the wood and hit his hand instead.

Fraida rushed over and grabbed the arm in order to see what damage had been done to his hand. The dark bruising was already beginning to show. Rayna, who had rushed to her mother's side in order that she too could see, took one look at the hand, then quickly ran over to get her little pot which held the mixture from the night before. She grabbed a cloth which she dropped into the pot, then rushing back to where her mother and father still stood, she said, "Mamma, let me see Papa's hand." The pain was so bad Leif distractedly tried to shrug Rayna off, but Rayna insisted. From her pouch she quickly took a clump of herb. Putting it gently on his hand, she then covered it with the potion soaked cloth.

In the space of the first few seconds, the pain was excruciating. Leif gasped and collapsed into a chair while looking disbelievingly at Fraida. His other hand reached over to pull the cloth off. But he was suddenly distracted by the odious pungent odour of the herb Rayna now waved under his nose. He began to protest angrily, trying to rise from the chair. But at that point the deep intensive throbbing suddenly started to ease. Leif became still. After looking at the hand for a few moments more, he finally expelled his breath in a sigh of relief.

Rayna held the cloth gently in place. She watched her father's face relax as the pain decreased. "I don't believe this," he said to Fraida, "this is actually working." Fraida herself then began to relax. She smiled down at her daughter. Rayna said to them both in a matter of fact way," Of course it works, Kelda showed me how to do it." Leif looked up at Fraida who shrugged her shoulders as she smiled, but from that day, both parents began to look upon what they thought was Rayna's childlike play, in an entirely different way.

In the ensuing summer months, the men remained hard at work. However, on some of the warm, hazy days, Leif would take the odd afternoon off to spend it alone in the company of his wife. These were opportune days when Vaila would come to "borrow" their son, and with Rayna away on her wanderings with Kelda, they would find themselves alone. Leif would look questioningly at Fraida. Smiling they would hurry to fetch their horses to ride out together into the peace and solitude of the forest.

Sometimes they could not escape without Dalgar, who would insist on following. He would happily run alongside the horses until they dismounted, then watch as they harnessed their steeds to a tree. Fraida and Leif would stroll along, arm in arm, in the cool shade the trees provided. They would laugh all the while at Dalgar, as he ran back and forth eagerly exploring all this new ground.

Other afternoons they would managed to escape without him. They would walk deep into the forest, away from any prying eyes, and it was here that Leif would laughingly drag Fraida into a hideaway under a canopy of thick, sprawling branches arching out from a wide girthed tree, and there they would make love. Both treasured those stolen times when they were together, completely isolated, alone in the company of each other.

Motherhood suited Fraida. She grew more beautiful in the passing of those early years. Leif loved her deeply, as she did him. Sometimes when she was busy and unaware he would watch her, and thank the gods for steering him to her home, for bringing them both together.

It was later in the summer when Leif stepped back to wipe the sweat from his brow. He and the men looked in satisfaction at yet another dwelling just completed. It was hot work in the heat of the sun. The women hurried over to give drinks to each of the men. Thankfully, Leif thought with a sigh, they only had one more dwelling to build. Leif took a swill from his horn, then turned to the men to state firmly, "I think it's time we all had a few days rest." The men smiled, murmuring their agreement. Leif called out jovially, "Let's have a summer feast," and everyone cheered.

Preparations were soon underway. The noise of chatter and laughter was a welcome respite from that of the constant bangs of many hammers. Everyone entered into the spirit of the celebration. They came dressed in their best clothes to the gathering, to enjoy these few days of rest.

Kelda sat next to Vaila on a short bench in the longhouse. She yawned as she leant back against the edge of the table. She was beginning to tire. It had been a long day, but for the first time in a long time she felt happy and content. She had enjoyed the day of feasting and entertainment. Turning, she looked over at Rayna, who sat on her father's lap. Smiling fondly at the child, Rayna smiled and waved back. Kelda's glance then swung to Fraida, who sat at Leif's side, the baby happily twisting and turning on her knee. Yes, it had been a good day Kelda thought, nodding to herself. It pleased her to see all her people gathered together and happy.

Kelda sat back, scanning the room, smiling all the while to herself as she watched everyone happily converse as they ate. She was relaxed and content, thinking of nothing in particular, when suddenly, the hairs on the back of her neck stood up. The strangest of feelings overwhelmed her. She frowned, and shook her head. She felt no pain she thought, but in the next instant, she was aware of something untoward holding her tightly in its grip. It made her gasp, and she jerked forward on the bench. For a few seconds she struggled to breath. She gulped in air, in an effort to compose herself. Shaking her head she tried to glance around, all the while looking for a sign. She found her eyes reluctantly drawn upwards. They narrowed as they fixed on a dark wispy cloud beginning to form above. She froze and drew in breath. Closing her eyes she tried to blank it from her mind, but when she opened them the cloud was still there. Thickening, swirling and drifting in a menacing manner. It seemed to appear from nowhere. Kelda quickly glanced around the room looking for a reason, but everyone continued to behave in a normal fashion. Her heart began to thud in her breast. Her insides began to churn, and a feeling of dread swamped her body. She looked down, averting her eyes from this bringer of doom. After rubbing her face roughly with her hands, she looked upwards again, but the dark cloud was still there, hovering now, above all her people.

She looked quickly round the room at people's faces, looking for any sign that others could see it. Everyone seemed to be unaware of what was above them however, and continued unconcerned, laughing chatting and eating. She looked back to where the cloud still hung, suspended in mid air. Why was she the only one who could see this, she questioned of herself? Refusing to look at it, even for a minute more, she gripped her head in her hands and closed her eyes tight.

Within minutes she felt a tugging at her arms. Looking down she saw Rayna at her side, questioning what was wrong. Kelda looked up, then quickly glanced around the room. But the cloud was nowhere to be seen. She shivered, trying to pull herself together. Shrugging she smiled at Rayna. Lifting her onto her lap, she said with a smile "Nothing is wrong, nothing at all," and she gripped the child tight. She could see Rayna was not convinced, so she kissed her cheek and said dismissively, "It was nothing more than a passing pain in my head." But Kelda, deep within, was at that moment fighting hard to bury what she had just witnessed. At the same time, she tried to convince herself it really had been nothing more than a passing pain.

Kelda's feelings were mixed in the weeks that followed. At certain times when she wandered through the settlement she would have to stop, because this feeling of dread would swamp her body. It left her drained. She tried hard to shrug it off, but she could sense something bad was about to happen; especially as these episodes began to increase. She would not, she told herself sternly, consult the oracle, because these sensations would pass. Every day she tried to convince herself they were only manifested from her fear of something happening to her people, and to the child she had grown to love. But deep within her subconscious, Kelda was in fact frightened. Frightened of what the oracle might be trying to reveal. After all that had happened in the past, she was unsure she had the strength to face any danger that may lie ahead, or the ability to deal with the pain and grief arising from any consequences.

Kelda began to wake up in the dark hours of the night, in a cold sweat. The powers she possessed tried to show her in sleep, what in the daytime, she constantly tried to deny. On one of the nights she rose and angrily threw more logs onto the fire. She felt chilled, but she still refused to admit to herself the reason. However, Kelda should have known, the foretelling of destiny, be it good or bad, would not in itself be falsely denied.

Kelda dragged her chair nearer to the warmth and sat down abruptly in front of the smoking fire. The logs began to burn. As Kelda looked into the intermittent flames she found, suddenly, she could not move. She tried now, struggling with her thoughts, to fight off the familiar feelings that came before the psychic trance. She was screaming inside with rage because she wanted to jump from the chair. But no matter what she did she found she was unable to move. The logs crackled and hissed. Through the smoke and leaping flames came the missing ship. The sign of death hung low over its frame; the drifting spirits of those who were lost, shrouded the ship in a thick, black mist. Silent tears began to fall from Kelda's eyes. She tried to call out to the spirits of her loved ones, but they were so far away she could not reach them. Her heart now began to ache at the emptiness of her arms, at the enforced solitude of her solitary and meaningless life. Grief was the cause of her tears. They streamed from her eyes, and although she was unwilling, she found herself unable to look away from the flames. What they showed her next made her breath stop. She tried even harder, but failed, to turn away.

It showed the settlement in turmoil. The dwellings were burning and bodies of her people lay strewn all around. Kelda gasped, struggling to breathe, she tried to make sense of what was being revealed. This could not be so, Kelda thought, her heart pounding! Where were all the men? Leif would not allow any harm to come to his people. He would give his life for them, as would Ragnar, and even come to that, the "dark demon."

Her eyes continued to search through the flames, then she heard the sound of drumming hoofs. It filled her with dread. A prolonged, high pitched screech began to emit from the logs. Through the smoke and the mist, a golden chariot from the very halls of Valhalla swept into her view. The eyes of the horses pulling the glowing chariot were red and wild. They reared in fury and tossed their long manes as they fought to free themselves from the restraints of the reigns, held tight by the dark and ominous hooded figure standing behind. Their legs flayed out in mid air. Bringing their hooves down hard, their tails flew out behind them as they galloped towards the settlement.

Kelda stared at the faceless figure in the long drifting cloak. She watched the cloak billow out when the chariot began its sweep through the settlement. Kelda screamed out in protest. Leaping forward, she put her hand into the fire to try to stop them from taking her people. A black cloud immediately descended over the fire, blocking her view. Slowly, she slumped back in her chair. She continued to stare into the fire, but from that moment on, no other revelation was forthcoming.

Kelda breathed heavily as she tried to gather her thoughts. She did not feel any pain from the burn on her hand, so distraught was she at what the fire had revealed. Slumping forward, she put her head in her hands. Her shoulders shook as her tears flowed. She shook her head in despair; her repeated whisperings of, "no!" echoing around the emptiness of her lonely room. She sobbed for some time, then began to question, "Why would the gods allow this to happen?" Hadn't they suffered enough she thought? It was now when her anger began to surface. She sat up with a determined look on her tear streaked face. When was this catastrophe supposed to happen she questioned of herself? She would not allow it she thought angrily, gritting her teeth in determination! She herself was not without power; she would use all the powers that were within her, and more, to try to thwart any disaster that would be likely to befall them.

Feeling a faint glimmer of hope, Kelda now jumped from her chair. She immediately winced, as for the first time she felt the pain from the burn. She went over to her chest, and while she dressed her burnt hand, she thought of all she must do. She must not allow herself to become distracted, she told herself sternly. It would take every bit of her concentration to focus on what was required, to enable her to carry out all that she planned. She stayed up for the rest of what was left of that night. She felt no tiredness when methodically searching through her dwelling, checking on all she had, while thinking of all she would still need to gather in order to avert what was yet to come.

Dawn broke and Kelda sat down to nap. When next she woke, the sun was high in the sky. She hurried to dress. She grabbed at some food and ate it on her way down the hill, all her thoughts taken up with what she could lay her hands on that day.

Rayna was outside her dwelling with her little cart, patiently waiting for Kelda to join her. Kelda faltered as she looked down at the child. She was not sure if she should take Rayna with her today, knowing as she did what she must do. "Today I must go alone Rayna," Kelda said, distractedly, to the child. Rayna looked up at Kelda, not understanding why she was to be left behind. Her little face creased unhappily. Kelda, after a moment, thought she may need the child and her cart after all. "Alright, you can come with me, but you must stay where I say and not follow me. Do you understand?" she said with some urgency, to the child. Rayna nodded repeatedly, only too glad that Kelda was now going to take her along.

They set off. As both hurried along, Rayna asked Kelda what was wrong. "Nothing," Kelda said somewhat abruptly. Then at the look on Rayna's face, she said with a smile, "Nothing, child," and patted her comfortingly on the head. "It is just that I have to go somewhere you are not allowed to go, to gather things I am going to need." "I can help you gather things Kelda," said Rayna somewhat pitifully. "Of course you can," Kelda went on to say, stopping to bend and hug the child. " I will show you what other things I need, and you can gather them up and put them in your cart for me. That will be a great help," she said apologetically, to the child.

They went further that day, to a place Kelda had never taken the child before. Rayna looked around with interest, at this new place Kelda had brought her to. Kelda told the child to stay where she was. She herself walked over to the brink of the cliffs to look over.

"We are not supposed to go near the cliffs," Rayna called out, somewhat concerned, when she saw Kelda looking over the edge. "Yes, yes, I know," replied Kelda, waving for the child to stay where she was. Kelda walked slowly along the edge until she saw what she was looking for. She then returned to Rayna. Taking her by the hand, she walked with her until she found the place a particular small, but rare, flower grew. She showed it to Rayna, who studied it intently. "Over this area of ground you will find some small clumps of this flower," she said to Rayna."What I need you to do is to take a few flower heads from each clump, and put them carefully in one of your pouches. Can you do that for me?"Kelda said smiling. Rayna looked up and nodded."Then," said Kelda as they walked to another area, "gather some of these grasses and herbs and put them in the cart, along with anything else you find that you might think useful."Rayna again nodded, understanding exactly what Kelda meant. "Now," she said as she gripped the child's arm, "whatever happens, whatever you hear, and no matter how long I take, you must not," "not," she emphasized, "come over to the cliff edge to look for me."Do you understand?" Kelda said, looking directly at Rayna's face . Rayna again nodded and said, "I promise I won't Kelda." "Good girl," said Kelda. "Now stay here and do what I have asked and I will try not to be long." Taking one last look around, Kelda then made her way over towards the edge of the cliff.

Rayna removed from the cart the bread, cheese and small urn of milk her mother always gave her, for her and Kelda to have when they had a rest. She put them safely to the side. Then going forward, she began to search for the clumps of little flowers.

Kelda reached the cliff, looking over, she studied which way would give her the best foothold on her way down. Her heart pounded when she looked at the distance to the bottom of the cliff. It would be a long way if she fell. Many years had passed since she last ventured over the cliff, but she could not let her fear stand in the way. Drawing in her breath, she steeled herself and put her nervousness aside. Hoping wryly that she could still manage the arduous task.

She carefully lowered herself over, her feet all the while searching for firm footholds before she allowed herself to move on. It took some time, but she edged her way over to the particular nest she had her sights on.

She held on with one hand, while her other hand groped in the nest. She removed the bones she could feel within and carefully put them in one of the pouches strung round her waist. She removed the feathers next and the broken shell of an egg, then a piece of the nest itself. When they were all safely within her pouches, she began to move the other way. Her eyes searched all the while for the plant imperative to her strongest potion. It was small, and hard to see. You had to be almost upon it before you saw it, but she had a bit of an advantage, because she already knew in which area it grew.

Kelda smiled when she at last came across the small plant. This would be a bit more difficult she knew, as it was only the tiny roots of the plant she would need. She took her time and gradually scraped and dug with the long nails of one hand, until she had prised the small plant loose. She breathed a sigh of relief when it was successfully tucked in her pouch. She stood for a few moments gripping the cliff face, taking a short rest,. Then, after looking up, she began to make her way back towards the top.

Kelda hauled herself up and over, onto solid ground again. She lay still for a moment to catch her breath. She lifted her head and looked across to see Rayna, now standing where she had left her, looking worriedly over her way. Kelda stood up and went towards the child. A big grin spread wide across her face. "See now," she said, "I told you I would not be long." Rayna herself then smiled and ran forward to take the old woman's hand."

I have gathered a lot of good things for you Kelda," she said as she dragged her over to see what was in the cart." I found a very big spider's web and I folded it carefully and put it in my pouch". Kelda was really pleased and told Rayna the web was the very next thing she had on her list for them to find.

Both then sat down to rest. Rayna brought over their bread and cheese. "This is good," said Kelda, as they sat in the sun munching away. Rayna agreed. Then Kelda said with some seriousness, "You must not tell anyone we have been here today, or about what we gathered, otherwise they will not allow you to come out with me again." Rayna went quiet, then shook her head and said she wouldn't, but after a moment she said, "Something's wrong isn't it Kelda?" "What makes you say that?" Kelda said, somewhat falteringly, to the child. "I had a bad dream," Rayna said. Kelda immediately put down her bread and placed her arm around the child. "What you had was only a dream," Kelda said.

"I love you and I would never," never," she repeated, "let any harm come to you. I would use all the powers I have to protect you," she said, squeezing the child tight. "Even," she said in desperation under her breath, "if it meant my own life be taken in place of yours."

Rayna's little voice then broke through Kelda's drifting thoughts."Kelda, you are squeezing me too tight." Kelda let go instantly, they both laughed, and Rayna reached up and kissed Kelda's lined cheek. They carried on eating their food. When they finished, Kelda told Rayna to start packing up. They would go home as soon as Kelda fetched this one last thing.

Kelda left the child and walked over to some distant rocks. Moving a few boulders she found what she was looking for and carefully picked the small fungi that grew in the damp grass that lay underneath.

On their way back, Kelda patted Rayna affectionately on the head. The child had done well today, she thought, to walk such a distance on her little legs. "Tomorrow we will not go out," she said to Rayna, " because I will have to start making some potions with what we have gathered today." "Can I come up and watch?" Rayna said in return. "Of course you can," Kelda said, smiling down at the child.

In the week that followed, Kelda spent her time carefully separating and laying out all the ingredients she would need. Rayna watched. She learned from Kelda the expected outcome of what some of the ingredients, when mixed together, could do.

When everything had been prepared and set out in proper order, Kelda lit the fires; one indoors, one outdoors. In order to get the best result from their properties, each group of ingredients could only be boiled at certain times of the day and night. Some had to be boiled when the sun was strongest and at its highest point. This process she explained to Rayna, while they rushed back and forth between the fires.

Leif, from his vantage point on the roof of one of the dwellings, began to wonder what the pair was up to, as he watched them scurrying back and forth. Later that evening, he asked his daughter why she and Kelda were rushing about at Kelda's place and not going out on their walks. After a moment, Rayna replied casually they were just using up some of Kelda's plants and herbs gathered earlier in the year, so Kelda would have room for all the late summer ingredients they had yet to gather in. Thinking of all the times he had seen them with the little cart full, Leif had no reason not to accept this explanation.

Soon, one particular potion was ready for use. Kelda put it in separate pots. Then each day, she and Rayna walked slowly about the settlement, secretly dripping the liquid onto the ground. On one of the days, when they turned a corner, they bumped into Vaila and inadvertently spilled some on her. Luckily she failed to notice.

It was not long before the people, who were working out and about, began to wonder why they could smell a strange, pungent odour. They questioned each other as to what was the cause, while looking in puzzlement all around . Kelda could see everyone was growing suspicious, so she told Rayna they would have to stop for a while, to give time for the smell to fade.

Kelda however, continued to work at night when Rayna was not there, on a potion she wanted everyone to drink. She used her strongest spells on this mixture, hoping the powers within would be enough to avert what was to come. She had not yet worked out how she would get the people to agree to drink it; but she knew she had to find a way.

Kelda's chance came when, after completing the building work, Leif ordered another feast. This is where everyone would be gathered together. By now the days were becoming shorter, there was a chill in the air, and they all knew the winter would not be long in coming.

Kelda explained to Rayna what it was she wanted her to do. She gave Rayna a container of the liquid, which the child then hid in her tunic pocket. Kelda went to the longhouse with another small container hid in her hands. Kelda sidled, unnoticed, over to the ewers of ale. She dropped a good portion of the liquid into each of the jugs standing on the tables. Rayna watched, then Kelda nodded to her. The child casually walked up to where her parents were sat, with Toork and Vaila seated at either side.

They did not notice Rayna as she slipped some of the potion into each of their drinks. She even managed to slip some into baby Olaf's cup of milk. She then went over to Kelda, where, after screwing up her face when drinking some of the potion herself, Kelda held the cup to Rayna's lips.

There was a shout and all hell broke loose as people began to drink from their horns. They all spat out, and Fraida herself, being the first to drink at their table, spat out the vile mixture. Toork looked immediately over to Kelda. He saw Rayna's face screw up as she drank from the cup. He ran over and knocked the cup from Kelda's hand, but there was only a little left within . It spilled onto the floor, and no one noticed Volga walk over to lick it up.

Kelda ran from the room. Uncaring what people thought, hoping at least some had swallowed her potion. Rayna tried to follow Kelda, but Toork would not let her. He scooped her up, and her little body struggled in his strong arms. She fought against him but he just smiled and raised his eyebrows, while his head shook in a motion of "no". He carried Rayna over to her father. Leif questioned Rayna about what she had put in their drink. She answered defensively that it was only a potion to protect everyone. From what? her father questioned of her. From harm, Rayna answered resolutely. Leif laughed as he scooped his daughter from Toork's arms, and he said as he swung her up, "Papa will protect you from harm little one, you don't need a potion for that."

Leif then turned to Vaila. He told her to go fetch Kelda. Everyone knew Kelda's intentions were good, but they laughed, when Leif said what they did not need was for them all to be laid low with problems of the gut. Vaila returned with a subdued Kelda. Rayna asked her father if she could go over to sit with her. "Only if you promise not to drink any more of Kelda's potions," he said with a grin. Rayna promised him she wouldn't, before quickly turning to run over to a happy Kelda's outstretched arms.

On the second night of the feasting, Fraida told Toork and Leif about her concern for her fathers absence. "He should have returned by now," she told them. "The weather is beginning to take a turn for the worst. If he is to visit before making his way back home, then he will have to come soon." Toork began to frown when he thought of his friend, hoping himself nothing was amiss and that no harm had befallen Olaf. Leif said in reply, "Yes, come to mention it, Fraida is right. Her father should have been here by now." He carried on to say they would wait a couple of days yet. If he still did not arrive, he would meet with Ragnar to see what could be done. This statement somewhat placated Fraida and Toork.

The following morning however, all Fraida's fears were confirmed. A small boat arrived with some of the elders from her home. They told Fraida Olaf's boat had already returned to the Islands, but Olaf and most of the crew were seriously ill. They appeared to be suffering from high fever and delirium. Being able to get no sense at all from their leader, the older men had decided to sail here to inform Fraida of her Fathers condition. Fraida became very upset at this news. She began to cry. Leif, as he comforted his wife, told the men they had done the right thing. Toork paced about in agitation. Leif grabbed at his arm and told him he would sort it out. Leif called to Ragnar to ask him to gather everyone together for a meeting.

Everyone gathered in the Longhouse where Leif then asked for volunteers. His plan was to sail to Olaf's Islands, taking two ships. His own ship would bring Olaf back for Fraida to look after. The people who sailed in the other boat would stay on the islands for the winter, to help Olaf's people tend to the ailing crew until they were back in good health. Many were quick to come forward to volunteer, some good women as well as men. Taking no time, and keeping one eye on the weather, everyone immediately set to work loading the ships with all they would need, wanting no delay and to make a hasty departure.

Rayna ran up to Kelda's, to tell her that her grandfather was ill. Kelda asked "With what." Rayna explained what she had heard the grownups say. Kelda thought for a moment, before going over to one of the pots on her dresser. She told Rayna to throw some logs on the fire to build it up. Taking one of her smaller pots, she threw in some dried bark taken from a tree. After hesitating for a minute more, she then added some little yellow flower heads and some big green leaves. She put them on to boil. She told Rayna to continue to stir the mixture while she fetched some small pots. After an hour or so the potion was ready. Rayna watched as Kelda poured it carefully into the pots.

Kelda fetched a basket. Placing the pots within, she and Rayna then hurried down to the settlement. They soon found Leif. Kelda explained, as she handed over the basket, that he must give Olaf and his men a little of this mixture as soon as they arrived. This should be repeated three times in the day, she went on to say. One pot he should keep to give Olaf on the way back, the rest he should leave for the men who were to remain on the Island. Leif hugged Kelda in thanks.

Kelda however, just stood hovering hesitatingly. Leif looked at her in question. "Are you sure you should leave?" Kelda said, as a strange feeling of nervousness came over her. Leif, thinking Kelda's concern was for himself and those accompanying him, said, "The weather at the moment is relatively calm, although cold. I must do this for Fraida. We will not be away long, I promise. We will take it in shifts while at sea. I hope to make a straight turnaround when we reach Olaf's."

Fraida stood with baby Olaf in her arms, wrapped warmly in a blanket. Vaila stood at their side. She watched the departing ships with some concern. A worried look was on her face. Kelda stood with Rayna, waving back at those on the ship who were leaving. Rayna walked over and took her mother's hand, squeezing it tight. "It will be okay Mamma," she said."Papa will make everything all right."A solitary tear ran down Fraida's face and she hugged her daughter against her side."You are right, he will" Fraida said. Her hope that Leif would not be too late to save her father, deepened.

That night, Kelda sat in front of the fire. Ever since the boats departure, she had been troubled with a feeling of unease. The feeling was growing stronger by the minute and she found she was unable to shrug it off. She began to go over in her mind all she had done in the previous weeks, trying to convince herself it would be enough to divert any danger that may befall her people.

Lifting a stick she poked at the fire, causing the logs to flare. She wanted to see if there was anything more she needed to know. She focused on the flames. Again they did not disappoint. To her consternation however, the first to come was the swirling black cloud. It was still there she thought, half in anger, half in concern. Suddenly though, while staring at it with her thoughts in confusion, the cloud parted, and this time instead of seeing the settlement in turmoil, she saw the missing ship. But now it was bathed in a light, golden glow. Her spirits were elated when she saw both her sons, standing at the bow, smiling, with their arms outstretched towards her.

Kelda's heart lifted. She had always known they would return to her she thought; no one could tell her different. But had she managed to avert the catastrophe, previously shown? she wondered, frowning worriedly. The cloud had dispersed to reveal the ship in a golden light, so she must have had some success, she reasoned. She continued staring at the fire, but the cloud failed to reappear. However, as she sat back, for some inexplicable reason, deep inside, she still had this feeling of unease.

The crews on the departed ships worked shifts and made good speed. In a matter of days they reached Olaf's. The sight of the sick men and Olaf however, told them they had not come a moment too soon. Olaf was so fevered he was not even aware of their presence. His people were distressed and pleased help had at last come. The visiting crews set to work right away and Olaf and the men were given their first dose of Kelda's medicine. Leif, helped by Toork, forced some liquid down Olaf's throat. They bathed him in cool water and changed his tunic. Only then did he stop his ramblings. Soon after, he sunk into a deep sleep. "This is good," Leif told Toork. "With some luck, we might break the fever that grips him."

Toork however looked back at Leif. His expression showed he was very concerned. "Don't worry Toork," Leif said, "we will pull him through this." Both men then prepared a bed for Olaf aboard the ship. Leif had brought blankets and furs. They erected the wooden tent over where Olaf would lie. Leif told Toork as soon as they were sure order was being restored where needed on the Island, then they would sail." The sooner we get him home to Fraida, the better," Leif said, "and besides, Kelda, once she has seen him, may have other medicines that can help."

Keeping to the timetable Leif had promised, they set sail that night with, a still fevered, Olaf on board. Toork sat at his side, constantly bathing sweat from his sick friends face. Leif looked worriedly over at the pair. He was more concerned than he cared to show to Toork. The sooner they reached home the better; he thought quietly to himself.

CHAPTER NINE

The weather grew increasingly colder. At the township, a boat on its last trip of the year had docked, bringing with it some worrying news about Leif's father's ship. The men aboard the trading ship said they had seen the boat two days previously, sailing in these waters. The elders of the township could not believe this news, but the crew on board the visiting ship stated it was definitely the missing ship. They knew the ship well, they said, having traded at the township for many years. The elders had to agree this was true and immediately called a meeting. It was decided that, without further ado, two men would travel up to the settlement to carry this news to Leif. It was also agreed, while the messengers were away, two of the longships would be prepared for sail, ready to accompany Leif. Their best fighting men would be put forward as crew.

Due to the urgency of the situation it was agreed, for speed, the men would travel in one of the small boats berthed in the harbour. It was manned by some strong rowers who would take no time at all to reach the settlement.

They arrived, expecting to talk to Leif that same day and were concerned to find Leif and the men absent. In fact, they began to worry because so few people were now left in the settlement. Not wanting to alert the women to the fact the boat was in these waters, in case of causing pain and upset, the men stated they had just come on a visit. It was explained to them about Fraida's father and both men were relieved to hear Leif would soon return. However, when talking just to each other, the two men decided, given the information they had, to go back to the township. They would instruct the two longships with the fighting men on board, to sail immediately they were ready, up to the settlement, so the few people remaining had some protection until Leif returned.

On the trip back the elders could see the weather was beginning to turn, the force of the wind was greatly increasing. The sooner they could get these ships ready the better, they thought, while looking up at the darkening sky.

The storm came sweeping in that very evening. Accompanying the howling wind was rain, and it poured from the heavens. Fraida, as she sat cosily by the fire with both children at her side, hoped Leif and his ship would be out of the storms reach. If her father was ill, the last thing he would need was the boat to be pitching and tossing in a storm, she thought worriedly. However, what Fraida did not know was, another ship sailed in these waters. Gripped in the throws of the storm, at that moment, it was looking for a place to berth for shelter.

The storm raged throughout the night, but Kelda slept soundly. She woke to silence, the storm had now passed. It was still dark, just before the break of dawn. Kelda wondered, as she lay there, what had woke her from her sleep? She felt strange, confused, and had an overwhelming urge to rise and go outside. Still in a dream like state, she rose somewhat unwillingly, from her warm bed, and began to dress.

Leaving her dwelling, Kelda set off down the hill. She tried to gather her thoughts and shake off this confusion, but her brain refused to function. Suddenly a strange orange glow spread across the sky, bringing with it a sprinkling of light. She looked down below and her heart leapt in her breast at the outline of the figurehead of the ship berthed at the dock. It was a figurehead forever etched in her memory. The silhouette of the magnificently carved sea horse stood outlined in the glow cast from the murky orange sky.

Kelda gasped and stared for a moment in disbelief. She took to her heels, running down the hill, all the while gaining speed. As she neared the shore, her eyes lit up and a smile spread across her lined and tired face. They had returned, just as she always said they would. She ran towards the ship, with arms outstretched, aching to, at long last, welcome her husband and sons back into the comfort and safety of her open arms.

The fact that these figures emerging from the boat in no way resembled her family, did not penetrate through the elated haze of Kelda's confused and muddled mind. She was completely oblivious to the gravity of the danger she faced. The blow to the side of her head came as a great shock. One of the barbarians lifted his arm and brought the hilt of his sword sweeping down sideward, to rid them of this crazy woman who stood with arms outstretched, blocking their path. Kelda had no time for further thought. Her legs gave way and she sank slowly to the ground. The blackness of oblivion quickly overwhelmed her, swallowing her up, until she knew no more.

Fraida struggled to surface from sleep. Subconsciously she was aware all was not as it should be. She opened her eyes to find it was still dark. Dalgar was trying to wake her by tugging and pulling from the bed, the furs that covered her, leaving her cold.

Looking over, she saw Volga facing the door. The dogs hackles were up, her teeth were bared. A continuous growl, given in warning, was coming from low in her throat. Fraida shot up, becoming instantly awake. She sat motionless, alert and listening. The behaviour of the dogs had caused fear to rise up and now it washed over her in waves.

Leaping from the bed, Fraida reached over for her small sword. Her heart was pounding. She gulped in air when she realised she had been holding her breath. She motioned for the dogs to protect the children. They moved over to stand by the beds; only then, did she creep stealthily forward to the closed door.

Opening it slowly, Fraida found her nostrils immediately filled with the smell of stale, rancid sweat. Her heart leapt in her breast with shock when she saw a menacing silhouette standing before her. Looking huge in the half light of dawn.

With no time for thought, her reactions were spontaneous. Her moves perfected by the many years of training from Toork. She threw the door open wide, to give herself the room she needed. Bringing her leg up, she kicked out as hard as she could. The man bellowed as he doubled over to grasp his groin. Without hesitating, taking her chance, Fraida brought her sword up and quickly slit his throat. As he keeled over onto the ground, she swiftly sidestepped, and with heart pounding, she came face to face with another figure who now lunged at her.

She quickly brought up her sword and thrust it under his ribs with as much strength as she could muster. She twisted the sword as Toork had taught her, before withdrawing it. Then bringing up her arm, she plunged the weapon hard, into his neck. She watched the man fall to the ground. Taking time to breath, she looked down to see many shadowy figures descending upon the, as yet, unaware settlement.

She feared for Vaila, who she knew was on her own, and for Kelda. But she could not help them now, because she had to protect the children. Her thoughts raced as she tried to think of some way of getting them to safety.

Fraida moved quickly. She went back inside to where Rayna was now awake and sitting up, whimpering in fear. "Mamma?" she said in question. The dogs looked up at Fraida from where she had ordered them to stay. "Hush," Fraida said to her daughter, as she kissed the top of her head. "Rayna put on your slippers and cloak, as quickly as you can," she said, while lifting the baby from his cot. Grabbing a blanket, she quickly wrapped it round him. Throwing on her own cloak, she drew it around to hide the baby she held in her arms. Turning, she grasped Rayna by the hand and they quickly ran from the building.

As they emerged into the cold, morning air, she glimpsed from the corner of her eye, a burly figure running towards them. Her cloak billowed out behind her and it hid the child who ran at her side. She could not stand and fight these invaders, like she wanted to. Her main priority was her children, who she had to get to safety. She would try to make it to the forest, she thought somewhat frantically, where she could hide among the density of the many trees.

The dogs ran with her, staying close to her side. Dalgar, sensing the danger to his mistress, suddenly veered off. Turning back, he ran towards the menacing figure, who at that point, was gaining ground and closing in. Fraida carried on running as fast as she could with Rayna at her side. She called out in vain, trying to get him to return to her. She was overwhelmed with anguish and fear for her fierce and loyal hound, who she knew would defend her to the death.

Dalgar took a flying leap at the one who dared to threaten his mistress. He went straight for the throat. But as the man turned his head, Dalgar's teeth fastened instead on his ear. He bit down hard. The man screamed and tried to throw the dog off, but Dalgar held on. The intruder managed to bring up his knife, and in a frenzied attack he repeatedly stabbed at the dog. Dalgar however, would not give in. He continued, through his pain, to try to wrestle the man to the ground. But the knife soon found its mark, piercing Dalgar straight through the heart.

Fraida heard Dalgar's deathly howl. She screamed out in anguish, "No!", and in that moment her heart felt like it was breaking in two. She wanted to turn back and kill the murdering invader, so she could hold close in her arms her beloved Dalgar, but her legs still carried her forward, fear for the safety of her children carrying her on. Volga, however, when hearing Dalgar's howl, left Fraida's side. Turning back she ran to his aid.

Vaila woke abruptly from her sleep. Fear washed over her when she heard screams and shouts coming from somewhere outside. She jumped from her bed, slipping her feet into slippers before running to the door. Opening it cautiously, she gasped in shock when she saw the mayhem now taking place. She could not believe that which was before her eyes. The settlement was under attack!

Her hands flew to her head as she tried to think of what to do. Fraida and the children were in danger! She knew it was imperative that she warn them! Her only thought now was how to reach them. Hesitating only for a moment, she threw open the door and ran quickly from the dwelling, round to the side, because she knew of a back way through the buildings where she could hopefully avoid capture and reach them before the invaders.

As she swung round she caught a glimpse of young Eric valiantly fighting to defend his mother and grandmother. She prayed to the gods as she ran, to keep Fraida safe, and Rayna, and her dear little Olaf. She would not be able to bear it if anything happened to them. Where had these invaders come from? How had they managed to find the settlement? she thought fearfully, as she ran with all the speed she could muster.

Vaila, breathing heavily from her strenuous run, turned the corner of Toork's dwelling. She suddenly stopped short. Her heart pounded at what lay before her. A large figure with blood pouring from the side of his head, wrestled fiercely with Volga. A sob rose in her throat at the sight of Dalgar, who lay on the ground in a pool of blood. She saw from the corner of her eye the cloaked figure of Fraida, running for her life. At the same time, she saw the figure bring up his axe, and watched as Volga too fell to the ground.

Feelings of anger and rage, at the fate of the two dogs, suddenly overwhelmed her. She knew she had to help Fraida and the children escape. She ran forward, what happened next made her heart leap with fear in her breast. She saw this figure of evil raise his axe high, aiming it at Fraida. She launched herself at him, hoping to reach him in time, but the axe had already left his hand and was travelling with speed towards its target.

Vaila wrestled with the barbarian, to avert his attention from Fraida. Her rage and anger gave her strength. She scratched at his eyes, regretting she had no weapon she could plunge into his evil, black heart. She was determined not to let him reach Fraida and the children. She fought as hard as she could, punching and kicking him, hoping to bring him down. Suddenly her body jarred from the force of the blow to her head. It was applied with such strength she was thrown like a rag to the side. She hit the ground hard and an explosion of pain vibrated through the whole of her being. Waves of blackness washed over her. Her last thought before she was drawn into a deep pit of darkness, was of the fate of Fraida and the children.

The barbarian, enraged by the loss of his ear, had raised his axe and threw it with all the strength he could muster in the direction of the cloaked figure running ahead, whose hounds had inflicted his injury. Fraida felt the thud as the full force of the axe hit her back. It pitched her forward, slicing through her like a knife in butter. She felt herself topple. Her cloak billowed out as she fell, hiding the children who fell with her.

The invader, after he had dealt with the ferocious Vaila, stood for a moment looking up at Fraida. He wanted to be sure his weapon had found its target. Seeing her unmoving, prostrate figure, he now lost interest and turned away. Grabbing the unconscious Vaila with one hand and clutching the side of his head with the other, he began dragging her back down towards the others who still battled below.

Fraida struggled to surface from an enshrouding blanket of darkness. It was trying to overwhelm her. She could hear screams from the mayhem still taking place in the settlement below. She opened her eyes to Rayna's little face which was all wet from tears. Fraida tried hard to speak. "Shush, my little one," she said with some difficulty to Rayna. "You must not make any noise, don't let them find you," she said in a weak voice.

Fraida lay still and unmoving in the grips of fear and pain. Then she realised the noise was not coming from Rayna, but from the baby, who was cradled in the arm beneath her. He was making strange whimpering noises. She moved her hand gingerly up to feel his head. With every small movement her pain increased.

She felt his soft, little head and it was wet. She knew it could only mean one thing. Please, not her baby, she cried inside herself. Her heart pounded in her breast as she felt the large boulder his head must have hit when she fell. Fraida was suddenly frightened for the fate of her son. She said quietly to her daughter, "Valhalla for Olaf, Rayna," hoping the child would understand, but the expression on Rayna's face showed she was confused.

Fraida was finding it took a tremendous effort for her to speak. Her voice, she knew, was fading. "My brooches," was all she managed to say to the child, but with that, Rayna now understood. Using as little movement as possible, so the men would not know she was there, she loosened the large brooches Toork had made in the shape of small swords, from her Mammas cloak. Putting one first in her Mammas hand and folding her fingers over it, she then felt down for Olaf's little hand. There was only two small swords, but she would hold her own hand over Olaf's and hope that the Gods would take her too. She did not want to be left alone while her Mamma and baby Olaf were taken somewhere out of her reach; where she herself would not be allowed to go.

Suddenly Fraida was struck by a moment of fear, and a small gasp escaped her. She could feel herself slowly fading. Her senses told her the end was near. She was frightened of going forward, all alone, into the unknown. She was worried about Olaf, who lay still in her arms. She hoped he would survive this to grow up happily with his father and sister. She tightened her grip on the brooch as visions of her life began flitting through her brain. She saw herself as a child, playing with her father. As she gazed up at the smiling face looking down at her, she wished she was back there now, being held in the comforting safety of his large, open arms. Visions of when Toork came into their lives appeared. She wanted to call out to him, knowing he would keep her from harm. Other fleeting images took over and continued, up to the time when she met Leif. She held on to, and focused on, the vision of Leif. She thought of how much she loved him. Her heart screamed out when she realised she would be parted from him forever in this life.

Please, please, she said to the powers that be. She hated the thought of having, ever, to leave Leif. A solitary tear spilled from her eye. It ran down her now pale and ashen face. She loved her daughter and wanted to see her grow. Her heart ached as she struggled to lift her hand up to touch Rayna's little face for, what she knew, would be the last time. She did not want to die. She tried to muster the strength to fight against it. Then she shivered as she grew cold; she could feel the blackness again closing in. Suddenly Dalgar, her Dalgar, appeared before her. He started licking her face, making it warm. She smiled lovingly up at him, as the final darkness closed in around her, for the very last time.

Rayna tried not to move and lay as still as she could. She had been lying there, in the cold, for what seemed a very long time. She had watched the snowflakes fall from the sky and they had settled on her face. She was too frightened to move to brush them away. They had soon stopped falling and she had looked across at her Mamma, who was asleep again. There was no sound from the baby, who had stopped whimpering. Silence now reigned and she felt very cold and frightened. Where was her Papa? She thought. He needed to come to help Mamma. She tried to stop her teeth from chattering, to make no noise. Rayna began to think about Kelda. She wanted her there, to be beside her. Kelda would soon be coming. Her spells would work, making it all be as before, she thought, in her childlike innocence, while trying in some way to comfort herself.

Rayna lay unmoving and still, waiting for someone to come. But after some hours had passed, when her little body had grown numb, her eyes became heavy. She began to feel very tired. She looked across at her mother's lifeless, pale face, she mouthed the word Mamma, but getting no reaction and being too weak now to fight it, she gave in and closed her eyes. Her small head lolled to the side, as she too sunk into the darkness of oblivion.

The amulet Kelda had given her, still lay around her neck. It was only now it flickered, as the powers within tried to hold on to the last, small vestige that remained of the dying child's life.

Leif sat wide awake aboard the ship. He had not been able to sleep. He sensed an inexplicable strangeness in the air. It gave him a feeling of unease. He was glad to see the break of dawn, but when the sky turned an unusual colour of orange, it increased his feeling of doom. He shivered and rubbed the back of his neck with his hand. He looked over to see Toork watching him. Toork drew his cloak closer around him and the look on his face revealed, he too felt the same. What strangeness was this?, Leif questioned of himself. This overwhelming sense of foreboding? Both men looked over at Olaf, who lay muttering in his fevered oblivion. Was it some kind of omen, to foretell Olaf was not going to survive this accursed ailment? Leif thought, trying in some way to put a reason to these ominous feelings.

Both men, each being lost in their own thoughts, jerked somewhat, when the strangest of sounds came from the figurehead of Dalgar. They quickly turned and looked up to see the carved eyes of the figurehead glowing, like the strange orange of the sky. Both, at the same time, began to rise to their feet. While looking at the sky, Leif saw a vision of Fraida. He quickly shook his head, but when he looked back, the vision was still there. She stood with her lovely hair blowing around her, baby Olaf cradled in her arms. Leif felt the blood drain from his face. His heart all but stopped. He glanced over at Toork, only to see he was looking up at the same place. Leif quickly looked back, but the fleeting vision was gone.

Toork raised his hands to the sides of his head and motioned as if he was trying to cry out. What did this mean? Leaf thought, frozen to the spot. A feeling of panic gripping his breast. He looked over again at Toork, who was now urgently shaking the men awake. Ragnar woke up. Sitting up, he looked over at Leif in question. Leif could not move or speak, struck dumb with an overwhelming feeling of fear. His brain refused to accept that which his eyes had seen. Ragnar, seeing the tortured look of fear on Leif's face, jumped up and going over he shook him. "What's wrong, what's happened?" he said urgently to Leif. Leif gasped and gulped in air. He was unaware, up until that moment, that he had been holding his breath.

"Row quickly," Leif managed to get out, "something's wrong at the settlement." "How? What?," Ragnar stuttered while looking from Leif to Toork, who was pacing with his head in his hands. "What has happened?" Ragnar bellowed as he shook Leif. "How do you know?" "Don't ask," Leif managed to say, as he bent over gulping in air. "Just do what I say." Seeing the state his leader was in, Ragnar now turned to the men and roared, "Row, row for your lives."Now!" he bellowed, as the men looked at him in confusion. "Something is wrong at the settlement," he called out, "so get moving!" Some of the men, after looking at each other, then rushed to raise the sails. The others positioned themselves at the oars and started to row. Ragnar, for the first time, noticed the colour of the sky. "By the gods, What?" he said, when looking up and all around. He trailed off as he looked over at Leif's white, ashen face.

Vaila slowly emerged from the darkness. The dull, throbbing pain in her head, made her want to vomit. She opened her eyes at the same time as she lifted her hand. She found her hair wet and sticky with blood which oozed from a deep, gaping wound at the side of her head. She became aware of movement. As she gathered her thoughts, she realised she was lying on the deck of a ship. She kept her head still and moved her eyes around, trying to locate where she lay. Her eyes swung round and fixed on, what was to her, a familiar figurehead. She was on Leif's father's ship! She frowned, the pain in her head increasing as she tried to figure out how could this be so?

She looked across at the people who were sitting further down. She recognised Eric, who was bleeding from a wound on his arm and leg. Also his mother and grandmother, who sat at either side, trying hard to stem the bleeding. Vaila's eyes continued their search. She could see she lay near to the side of the ship. She felt dizzy and weak but began to wonder if she could muster enough strength to get up onto her feet, where, if she was quick enough, she could take the few steps needed to launch herself over. She did not know how long she had been unconscious. But she would rather die in the sea, she thought to herself, than be taken from her home to end up, who knows where. Life would have no meaning for her anyway, she carried on thinking, if she was away from her home and those she loved.

She tried to give herself the strength to concentrate through the pain. She was aware, because of the way she felt, that she could be overcome by the darkness again at any moment, and then, she knew, it would be too late. Without thinking further, and with one immense effort, she suddenly leapt up and ran the few steps needed. Stepping up on to the side, she quickly jumped into the sea.

Waves of shock from the chill of the water surged through her body as she was drawn down into the depths of the cold, blue sea. She let herself sink deep, knowing she would have to stay under long enough to escape further capture. She flayed with her arms for as long as she could. Then propelled herself to the surface, where she gasped for air, because her lungs, by this time, felt they would surely explode.

Breathing heavily, she moved her wet hair away from her eyes. Looking round she saw, with relief, the stern of the ship as it continued to sail on. Treading water she then turned and saw land, in what she hoped was not too far a distance.

The shock as she entered the water had brought all Vaila's senses alive. Her will to survive suddenly became strong. She immediately started to swim. Putting all thoughts of the pain and the cold from her mind, she concentrated instead on getting back to Fraida. Over the distance she covered, she gave herself the strength and stamina to go forward by visualising the soft, warm bundle that was Olaf.

She swam on, head down, until she could feel the strength once again ebb from her body. She tried hard to will her body to reach the shore. Just when she thought she could fight off the exhaustion no more, she looked up and as her legs went under, she felt her toes touch ground. She flayed out in desperation with her arms, propelling herself forward, until her whole foot could stand on the ground. The water was still up to her neck, but sobbing weakly, she forced her body to walk forward. Just a little bit further, she kept telling herself, until she reached the safety of the shore. She sobbed to herself when she finally reached the beach. Dragging herself from the water, she walked but a few steps before the huge effort it had taken began to take its toll. The piercing pain in her head made her gasp. For a moment she staggered with exhaustion, but suddenly the darkness rose up to engulf her. With all thought blanked out, she toppled over into oblivion.

Later that day, the crew on the boat had land in their sight. Leif kept his eyes fixed on the headland, willing Kelda to be there. He saw the rest of the men look up, then at each other. Her absence causing a feeling of deep foreboding in them all.

They sailed towards the shore. Everyone jumped up together when they saw the smouldering buildings near to the docks. "What the?" Ragnar bellowed, then trailed off as they looked at the devastation the settlement had sustained. Leif looked over at Toork, who stood at the bow, ready to take a leap ashore. The look of anxiety, coupled with the sheen of sweat on his dark, frowning face, caused Leif to shudder. He felt sick with fear. His brain repelled the thought of the unthinkable. Whatever had happened, she would be safe, he told himself repeatedly. She could defend herself, Toork had thankfully seen to that.

The men did not bother to approach the dock, but rowed the ship straight to shore until it ground to a halt on the beach. Toork immediately leapt ashore, Leif followed. The rest of the men jumped off at their back, leaving the sick Olaf where he lay. Everyone saw Kelda lying outstretched and bleeding, but they all ran on. Each needing to see what fate had befallen their own loved ones.

No one, when confronted by the stricken settlement, had thought to look the other way. They failed to notice the two longships from the township quickly approaching their docks. The men from the township looked in shock at the burning buildings. They watched as Leif's boat rammed into the shore.

Toork ran like the wind towards Leif's dwelling, bypassing the devastation scattered all around. Leif was not far behind. Leif, as he neared his dwelling, felt hope rise, as his eyes took in the two invaders lying dead at his door. Fraida's small sword embedded in the neck of one. Toork emerged hurriedly from the dwelling. Jumping over the two bodies, he continued to run on.

Leif, who's brain was now numb with fear, hesitated only for a moment, then he began to follow. He saw Toork bend down, his cloak hiding what was at his feet. Then Toork stood up and again started to run. Leif, for the first time, knew real fear as his eyes took in the two dogs lying side by side in a pool of blood. His insides screamed out "no!" But for some reason all that left his mouth was a whisper. He reached the dogs and quickly bent down, saying "Dalgar, Dalgar," sadly, as he stroked the heads of the now lifeless hounds at his feet.

Leif stood up. Again he started to run in the direction Toork had gone, when all of a sudden a loud, somewhat inhumane, noise of pain and anguish began to echo through the settlement. This drawn out wail was like no other sound Leif had ever heard. He stopped momentarily, while his tortured mind tried to figure out what it was. The power then drained from his body when he realised it could only be coming from one person. Leif gulped in air. He was struggling to breathe. He sank to his knees because his legs were no longer able to support him. His body was trying to tell him what his brain fought to deny, the reason for the long, drawn out, lamentation.

Ragnar and his son Sweyn were running behind Leif. They came up, one at each side, and they hooked their fallen leader under each arm. Lifting him, they dragged him on. They stopped running when they saw Toork, who stood with his cloak billowing out and his head back, his face looking up at the sky as he wailed to the heavens in rage and anguish. He held in his outstretched arms the body of Fraida. Her legs hung lifelessly down. Her arm was thrown out from her side. Ragnar was frozen in shock. He looked at her head which lolled back, inert, in the crook of Toork's arm. His eyes stared at her beautiful face, pale and wan. Her lovely hair, still vibrant and alive, fell down in a thick curtain to drift in the wind.

Ragnar gasped, and shook his head in disbelief at the sight of the large axe embedded in her back. His eyes swung round to where the two children lay. Olaf in a pool of blood, Rayna dead at his side, her little hand grasping and holding on to that of her brothers. This took only but a second to take in. Ragnar looked then at Leif who was still being held up by both men. Leif's face was contorted, his mouth open as he tried to scream out, but no sound came. Ragnar realised the very breath had been taken from his leader. He swung round and bellowed "Breath!" to Leif. He shook him hard, trying to make him take in air. Leif's head swam and blackness descended, blanking out the scene before him. He heard Ragnar's voice fading in the distance. He tried to take gulps of air because his body was labouring to breathe. Ragnar then caught Leif as, slowly, he sunk to the ground.

The men from the township ran quickly ashore to help. The first one they saw was Vaila, lying unconscious on the shore. They fetched blankets from the ship. While some stayed with Vaila, the others ran further along. They came across Kelda. They knelt to feel if she was still alive.

Vaila surfaced from her unconscious state with the men dabbing at her hair, trying to gently dry it and see the extent of her wound. Some were rubbing her arms and legs trying to warm them, another was forcing wine down her throat. She coughed, and spluttered, and began to wretch. Her head throbbed. One of the men took off his fur jacket and helped her put it on. Vaila could feel the warmth from the man's body still in the garment. It seeped into her cold arms. She struggled as she tried to get up. The men helped her to her feet. At first she felt very dizzy and nauseous. They stood at each side to support her. She told them urgently she had to get to Fraida. The men looked at each other over the top of Vaila's head, knowing the news would not be good, but she was insistent. So they supported her, one at each side, as she started walking towards the settlement; heading in the direction of Leif's dwelling.

Kelda had also gained consciousness. She was utterly confused as to why she was lying on the ground on the shore, with men who she recognised to be from the township towering over her. They were deeply concerned about her welfare, because her scrawny hair was red and plastered to the side of her head, from the blood still seeping from a gaping wound.

Kelda was unaware of the fate of Fraida and her children, because at that moment she was struggling to gather her thoughts. How had she come to be down on the shore, she thought, struggling to sit up? Then she looked over in horror at the scene of the burning buildings before her. How had this happened? Had everything she done been of no consequence? She shook her head, trying to organise her thoughts in her confused brain. Raising her head she managed to look further. She could see all the new buildings still stood, where she and Rayna had walked around scattering their potions. Rayna! Now her thoughts turned to the child. She had to get to Rayna!

Pushing the men aside, she got unsteadily to her feet. She swayed about dizzily. The men grasped at her arms. She shrugged them off. Struggling with the blanket they had placed around her, she managed to put her hand into one of her pouches and she took from it a herb. Putting it to her nose she took a deep breath. She gasped, her eyes watering as the pungent odour enveloped her senses. The men watched her shake her head. Then, with one half of the blanket covering her, the other half trailing behind, she staggered off in the direction of the settlement. The elder, who knew Kelda only too well, shook his head and nodded for two of the men to accompany her. It was blatantly obvious to him she was still, "not in her right mind."

Vaila, supported by the men, followed the sound of the strange wail. She gasped in shock at the sight before her. Her heart immediately dropped into the very pit of her stomach. Her head swam as the blood drained from her brain. Stunned, she put her hands up despairingly to her head and started to scream "No! No!" repeatedly, in fierce denial. She stared in horror at Toork, who now knelt with the dead Fraida still in his arms. Tears streamed from Toork's eyes, and the strangest of sounds came from his mouth, because for the first time, he was trying, with great effort, to talk soothingly to the dead Fraida.

Vaila's breasts heaved with deep, heart wrenching sobs. She looked with distress at Leif, who had collapsed and was now held in the arms of a tearful Sweyn. Ragnar's back was towards her as he knelt in front of the dead children. Vaila only saw Rayna. She staggered forward, crying out, to kneel at her side. She sobbed as she touched the child's cold, pale face. Then she saw that which Ragnar's body hid from her view.

She screamed out again at the sight of baby Olaf, lying in a pool of blood. His little face ashen and lifeless. She shook her head pleadingly as she looked into Ragnar's face, but the tears streaming from his eyes gave her no hope. She looked down to see the small sword grasped in his little hand. Ragnar, she could see, was at that moment, trying to unfold the small hand of Rayna, who still held on tight to her little brother.

Ragnar gently prised Rayna's small fingers open and he loosened the grip. Not hesitating, Vaila pushed Ragnar out of her way to lift the baby into her arms. She stood up, and grasping the baby hard to her breast, she turned round and round agitatedly, willing the life to return to his little body. She moved her arms down and looked at his, still lifeless, little face. She started to scream out. Her heart felt like it was breaking in two as she again in desperation grasped him close in her arms. The scream, drawn from the very depths of her stooped and shaking body, came out like a croak. All the men who looked on helplessly cried themselves as the enormity of what had happened began to grip them.

No one in their grief noticed Kelda, who, after taking in the scene before her, with a gasping sob, rushed over towards her little Rayna, who lay pale and still spread out on the cold, hard ground. Kelda knelt down and quickly clutched the cold and lifeless little body. She shook her, looked at her, then clasped her to her breast. Kelda began to sob deeply and uncontrollably while continuously rocking the dead child back and forward comfortingly in her arms.

Suddenly though, through her tears, Kelda noticed the amulet hanging from her lined neck was now emitting a faint glow. She stopped rocking. Drawing in her breath, she became still. She lowered her arms and looked hard at Rayna. Then she saw a very faint flicker from the stone around the child's neck. She put the child's head to her ear, but she heard, or felt, no breath. The stones could not be wrong, she thought to herself. With a sob, for the first time she now began to hope. Calling one of the men to her, she told him to quickly lift the child.

Just as the man stood up with the child in his arms, Leif roared out. Surfacing from the blackness holding him in its grip, the men quickly helped him to his feet. Pushing them out of his way, he rushed over and knelt down in front of Toork, who still held Fraida in his arms. Leif cradled Fraida's still and lifeless face in his hands. Repeatedly kissing it, shaking it, willing her to just open her eyes and look at him. He looked up at the tear streaked face of Toork, who, in a motion of finality, shook his head. Leif roared "No," and standing up, he swung round to face Vaila; who was sobbing uncontrollably, the baby held close in her arms. He grasped the face of his small son, planting small kisses of comfort on it. With tears streaming from his eyes, he then turned to Rayna. "Not Rayna, not my little Rayna," he bellowed, sobbing brokenly. Suddenly, the range of emotions coursing through Leif's body combined to form an uncontrollable rage. It left him with an overwhelming urge to kill someone. Half deranged with grief, he withdrew his dagger and swung round. But Ragnar, seeing the rage and confusion on Leif's face, quickly grabbed at his arm. Leif fought fiercely with Ragnar. Knowing Leif was not in his right state of mind, Ragnar bellowed for some of the men to come and help him. The men rushed forward and together they wrestled the knife from Leif's hand.

Kelda stood watching, understanding all too well Leif's grief. However, she did not have time for this, she knew it may already be too late for Rayna. So putting her hand in one of her pouches, she withdrew a phial. Walking over to the men struggling to hold Leif in their grip, she poured the potion down the throat of Leif, whose mouth had remained open as he cried out in grief. Leif spluttered, for a second he looked at Kelda, then his body went limp and his eyes closed as he drifted again into the darkness of oblivion. Ragnar looked at Kelda in question while trying to support the body of Leif. "He will sleep," Kelda replied to the question in Ragnar's eyes. Then after a moment she said, "for a long time." Ragnar nodded. Hoisting the limp body of his leader over his shoulder, he began walking back to Leif's dwelling to lay him down on his bed. Sweyn put his arm round a sobbing Vaila, steering her to follow in the path of Ragnar.

Kelda then beckoned for the man holding Rayna to follow her. They too hurried down into the settlement. However, as they passed the two dogs, Kelda felt heat emitting from her amulet when it suddenly glowed red against her throat. She stopped to think for a moment. She looked down at the two hounds who lay dead on the ground. She knelt down and felt Dalgar. The dog had definitely passed on, there was no life there, she thought. Leaning over she felt Volga, who also seemed to be dead, but as her hand touched Volga, the stone again began to glow. Beckoning to one of the other men she told him to pick up Volga, instructing he too should follow her. When they reached Leif's dwelling the men hesitated, but Kelda said, "No, no," they were to follow her. The men were unsure, but at that moment Ragnar emerged from the dwelling. Taking in the scene before him and seeing Kelda insist, he told the men to do what she asked. If anyone could salvage anything from this black day, then it could only be Kelda, he thought, as he watched them hurry away.

Kelda ran ahead of the men. Rushing into her dwelling, she grabbed some blankets and furs. She dragged the table over near to the fire and made a bed on it for Rayna. Then throwing some covers on the floor at the side, she made a bed for the dog. The men walked warily in. She told the first one to lay Rayna on the table, instructing at the same time that he quickly light her fire. While she wrapped Rayna in the blankets and furs, she told the other man to take the furs and blankets lying on the floor and do the same with the dog. The men looked at each other but they did what she said. The fire took hold, but it was slow to burn. Running over, Kelda grabbed a pot from the dresser. She ran back and threw the contents onto the fire. Both men jumped back in shock as the fire suddenly exploded into life. They looked warily at each other. Kelda then turned and shooed them out. They left willingly; glad to be leaving the presence of this strange, disturbed woman.

Kelda's thoughts however, were not on the men, but on the child who lay before her. Kelda rubbed at Rayna's little face, trying to make it warm. There was no reaction. So Kelda rushed over and threw more logs onto the fire, building it high. She then scurried over, breathing heavily now with all her exertion, and she lifted one of her potions. She studied it for a moment, knowing what she must do. Lifting it to her lips she took a large swig. She grimaced and grunted as it burned all the way down her gullet. Holding her breath she ran back to Rayna. Opening the child's mouth, while holding her nose closed, Kelda blew her hot breath into the child's mouth as hard as she could. She stood back and waited, then she did it again. She repeated this a number of times until her head began to swim. Swaying back dizzily, she plonked herself down on the chair.

Kelda put her head in her hands to give herself time to breathe. Then she heard it, the faintest of sounds. She jumped up and found she still swayed as she leaned close into the child. Rayna was breathing, just. She stayed there, close, listening, until she was sure the breathing was regular, then she began to tire. She sat down and gave a small sob, expelling her breath in relief.

After giving herself a few minutes to rest, Kelda withdrew the herb from her pouch once more. Her eyes again watered when she took a large sniff. She had to keep her wits about her because there was still the dog to see to, she thought. She looked once more at Rayna. She tucked the furs and blankets closer around her body before turning to the dog. Kelda examined Volga's wound, then she gathered together all she would need to dress it. Hurrying over to the dresser, she lifted the potion. She looked at it again, trying to give herself the courage to take another swig.

She downed it quickly and tried hard to stop herself from throwing up as she ran back to the dog. She repeated with Volga what she had done to Rayna, but her breast heaved each time she had to blow into the dog's mouth. Not waiting for a reaction this time, she carried on to dress the wound. She finished by covering the dog with furs, tucking them around her to keep her warm. Exhausted now, she sat down. She drank a large cup of cold milk to rid herself of the taste of the potion. Out of the corner of her eye she saw a small movement. Looking over, she saw the slightest of twitches in the dog's ear. She rubbed her hand over her forehead, sighing in relief. She grimaced, as she accidently touched the forgotten wound at the side of her head.

Taking a short time to rest, Kelda then took some warm water from her pot that always sat at the side of the fire. Putting it in a bowl, she dipped her head in slowly. The water turned red. She threw the water out, then continued filling the bowl and rinsing her hair until the water ran clear. On the last rinsing, she added some leaves and flower heads to the water. She stirred it for a time, to allow the properties of the plant to be released. Then after rinsing one last time she used the same water to wash her face and hands. Sitting close to the fire, her hair soon dried. Slowly, she began to feel well again.

Kelda knew however, there would be others down in the settlement still needing her help. So after looking once more at Rayna and the dog, to check they were still breathing, be it faintly, she began to gather all the potions she could get her hands on in her dwelling. She placed them about her body. The room was now warm. To keep it that way, she stacked more logs on to the fire. All this Kelda had achieved in a very short time.

She was about to leave to go back down to the settlement when her door flew open and there stood Toork. Kelda looked at him for a moment as he stood framed in the doorway, then she said calmly, "The child lives, so does the dog, but only just." Toork flew into the room and Kelda shouted at him to close the door to keep the heat in. He went back and closed the door. Then going over to Rayna, he placed his large black hand lovingly on her head. Tears flowed from his eyes in relief. The child was still too far gone to know he was there, but he could see she was alive. He kissed her cheek softly, then going over, he knelt down at Volga's side. He touched the dog softly on the head. Putting his other hand over his eyes, his shoulders shook as he silently sobbed.

He slowly stood up, then suddenly he swung round and looked at Kelda with an expression of a question clearly showing on his dark face. She did not know what he was asking. Not waiting for her to try to understand, he grabbed her by the hand and pulled her towards the door. When leaving the dwelling, he made sure he shut the door. Keeping hold of Kelda's hand, he dragged her hurriedly along behind him. Her feet ran in tiny steps as she tried to keep up with his long stride.

Toork had finally carried Fraida back to her dwelling. He held her close while Ragnar removed the axe from her back. When the men laid Fraida out on a bed, Ragnar had gone outside and thrown the weapon. It landed and embedded itself where he meant it to go, at the side of his dwelling. They had taken the baby from Vaila, to place him in his mother's arms. Dalgar, they draped at her feet. Toork had removed from Dalgar's mouth, the ear still gripped in his teeth. He studied it for a moment, before slipping it into the pouch at his waist.

It was only when Fraida had been properly laid out that Toork noticed Rayna and Volga were missing. With a frown on his face, he had shook Ragnar, motioning where was Rayna? Ragnar had told him. He rushed up to Kelda's intending to return Rayna to her mother's side. When he reached the house on the hill he could not believe this delusional woman had, in fact, worked a miracle.

Ragnar shot round, and a very pale Vaila looked up from where she sat on the chair, when Toork crashed through the door into Leif's dwelling. He dragged Kelda over to the bed where Fraida and the baby lay. Grabbing her arm, he urged her forward. Kelda looked up at him in puzzlement. He pushed Kelda forward, while nodding towards the bed. Kelda was confused. Toork put his head in his hands in frustration. Then after a moment he looked up, and gasping, he then started to breath heavily in and out as he pointed at the bed. Kelda nodded slowly, now she understood.

Kelda leaned over and put her hand on Fraida's forehead. Tears of sorrow began to run down her lined face, then she felt the baby. "I am sorry," she said quietly to Toork, "I can do nothing for them. Their life's blood has run out, and there is nothing left. "Toork swung round with his head in his hands, he cried in despair, then turning, he grabbed Kelda and shook her; pleading with his eyes for her to do something. Ragnar stepped in to calm Toork down. Vaila again started to cry. "They have passed on, gone to the Gods," Kelda stated, "and unfortunately it is beyond my powers to bring them back," she said regretfully, with tears in her eyes. Kelda then looked over to Ragnar. She told him Rayna and Volga lived.

Ragnar hugged Kelda. Vaila jumped up with a gasp, wanting to go to the child, but she swayed dizzily and fell back down onto the chair. "They need to stay where they are," Kelda stated firmly. "Where there is warmth. They need peace to allow their strength to slowly return. I do not want Rayna to be reminded of all this," as she looked at Fraida and the baby, "and of all that has happened. I will keep her with me up on the hill, away from the settlement, until she is strong enough to return."

Kelda then looked with concern at Vail. Her face was ashen and her teeth now chattered. She watched Vaila shiver and pull the blanket closer around her. Kelda said to Ragnar, "Vaila needs attention, I need a fire and hot water." Just at that, Vaila suddenly cried out, "Ragnar I forgot," she babbled, "they have Eric, his mother, and your wife, along with the others, aboard the ship. It was Leif's fathers ship!" Ragnar stood, at first stunned. Then his thoughts began to race as he tried to take in this information. He had sent Sweyn to look for his family while he dealt with Leif. Having lost Jon, he was fearful of what he himself might find. His heart lifted in hope, at least he knew they were still alive. "You must go after them now," Vaila said urgently, "before they have had time to go far."

Ragnar went to run from the dwelling, but Kelda called out for him to wait. "Get me to a fire and I will look for any signs," she said to him. One of the men was just about to enter Leif's dwelling. He stated they had prepared the other buildings left intact, to house the injured, they had lit fires in them all. Kelda told the man to lift Vaila and to bring her along. Toork elbowed the man out of the way and lifted Vaila effortlessly in his strong arms. They all then hurried to the nearest dwelling. The room was warm, with a well built fire. Kelda ran over to it and Toork placed Vaila in a chair. Kelda took some powder from her pouch and threw it on the fire. The fire smoked at first, then as Kelda looked into it, she saw a y shaped estuary. There was a large building at its mouth and on it she saw a strange sign. It was a sign she did not recognise. She shook her head, then looked back into the fire. The sign was still there. She struggled to understand its meaning. Then the face of Toork appeared. She turned to look at Toork, then back at the fire. The others crowded round at her back. They all stared into the fire too, but they saw nothing.

Kelda straightened up. She turned to explain to them what she had seen. She told Ragnar he would have to sail close to the shore, as there would be a sign at the mouth of the estuary, only the dark one would know. Toork himself had not intended to go, he did not want to leave Fraida. Kelda, sensing his reluctance, said flatly, "There is no more you can do for those that are here. Eric needs you now." Then going into her pouch, she took out another phial. "If the weather worsens, sip at this. You will need to remain alert so you don't miss the sign." Toork nodded and took the phial. Both men then hurried from the dwelling.

Kelda could now turn her attention to Vaila. She took water from the pot at the side of the fire and gently washed Vaila's hair, just like she had done her own. After checking the wound was clean and sealed, she helped her over to the bed. Kelda heated some milk on the fire and put a few drops of the potion in, so Vaila would sleep soundly. She made Vaila drink it all. Then she covered her with furs and blankets and Vaila was asleep before Kelda even left the dwelling.

As Kelda walked away from the door, she saw some of the men carrying Olaf, who, up until then, they had forgotten still remained aboard the ship. She followed them to Toork's dwelling. When they had finally lifted the deliriously fevered man onto a bed, she stood looking down at him. How lucky he was, she thought, to be unaware of all the death and destruction the people of the settlement had suffered.

Kelda heated some milk on the glowing fire, like she had done for Vaila. She put drops of the potion in, enough to make him go into a deep sleep. First though, before she held the cup to his lips, she put on his tongue a few drops of a remedy she knew tasted vile. This should break the fever, she thought. Even in his delirium, Olaf screwed up his face. She quickly held the milk to his lips and made him drink. He too began to grow quiet as the potion started to work its magic. Kelda watched as he slowly slipped into the realms of a dreamless sleep.

For the hours of daylight still remaining, Kelda continued administering to those who had managed to survive the unexpected attack. In between, she went back and forth to her dwelling to check on Rayna and Volga and to stock up the fire. Her feet were dragging and she was very tired. There was no other potion she could take to keep her awake, she thought worriedly. When, much to her relief, the woman arrived from the township.

Kelda, more than willingly, now left it all in their hands. Pulling on the little energy she had left, she made it thankfully back to the peace and calm of her dwelling. She checked on Rayna and the dog as soon as she entered. Then after throwing more logs on the fire, she lay down, and closing her eyes, she quickly drifted into a deep sleep.

Kelda woke some hours later to knocking. Rising up, she went to open her door. Standing in the dark was a smiling woman holding a basket of food. Behind her, a man carried an urn of fresh milk. Kelda stepped back and they entered. As they unpacked the basket, the smell of freshly baked bread and roasted meat made Kelda realise how hungry she now was.

Kelda stood smiling at the pair, then out of nowhere, sadness suddenly rose up to overwhelm her. She stared dazedly around her. Tears welled up in her eyes when she remembered everything that had happened over two short days. Unbelievably, two nights ago, she thought, nothing had been amiss. Her people had been safe in their homes. Fraida, her baby, and Dalgar, were at that point, still alive.

Kelda looked at the two people before her. Her face creased in sadness and she began, only now, to sob at the enormity of it all. The woman dropped her basket and stepped forward to enfold Kelda in her arms. She too sobbed at the consequences of the terrible tragedy that had befallen the settlement. Kelda sobbed for some time, until suddenly she remembered Rayna was in the room. Pulling herself together, she withdrew from the woman's arms. She assured them hurriedly she would be alright and saw them to the door.

Kelda's appetite had suddenly left her. Going over, she looked down at the child who lay on the table. Rayna's eyes were now open and tears streamed down her pale little face. The child mouthed the word "Kelda," but no sound came out. She is too weak to speak, Kelda thought. Folding Rayna in her arms she said, "Shush, everything is alright, you are safe with Kelda now. Kelda has made everything alright," she continued, stroking at Rayna's hair. "I have brought you up here with me, to make you well. Look," she said, "I have even brought Volga up to keep us company." Rayna turned her head to look at Volga, who lay covered and asleep in front of the fire.

Laying the child back down, Kelda tucked the furs around her. She carried on to say, "You stay there and I will make us both a nice drink of milk." Kelda then spoke continuously to the child as she heated the milk at the fire. She stirred in some honey, then taking a cup of the warmed milk to Rayna, she held the child up so she could drink from it. Kelda then broke off some of the freshly baked bread. She dipped it into the milk to make it soft, then she made the child slowly eat it. Rayna was still very weak however, and soon her little eyes began, once more, to close.

Kelda laid her gently down and tucked the furs closer around her. After assuring herself Rayna was asleep, Kelda went over to the dog. Volga's eyes were open, but she lay still as she looked up at Kelda. Kelda fetched a bowl with some of the milk that was now just barely warm. She put in a few drops of a potion that would help the dog after the blood loss. She added just one drop of the sleeping potion. She did not want Volga to try to move, given the wounds she had. The longer the dog was still, the better the chance for the wounds to heal. Kelda spoke quietly but soothingly and lifted the dogs head as gently as she could. But with Volga's wounds, any movement hurt. She gave a little yelp. Kelda held the bowl to her mouth and her tongue came out to lap up the milk. Laying Volga's head back down, still talking soothingly to her, Kelda then stood quietly watching, until the dogs eyelids flickered, then slowly closed.

Kelda sat by the fire, going through the motions of chewing meat she did not want to eat, but she knew she must to keep up her strength. She leant over and threw more logs on the fire. After assuring herself all was well, she went back to her own bed where she soon fell into a deep sleep.

Ragnar and Toork were aboard one of the longships, crewed by men from the township. It was dark, but the wind was up and the sails were billowing. They were making good speed Ragnar thought, watching the boat as it skimmed over the dark water. He knew Leif's fathers ship well and was aware, being a knorr, it would be slower than the longship. He hoped fervently they would be in time to rescue his wife and Eric his grandson, along with all the others.

He turned to look over at Toork, who was wrapped in furs and fast asleep. Just as well, Ragnar thought, as he knew this dark, silent man did not like rough weather. Besides that, he continued to think, sleep was a refuge from grief. Ragnar rubbed his hand over his face. How had all this happened? he despaired. Why now?, and why that ship?, one of their own. If only they had managed to find it these past years, then this could all have been avoided. In fact, if only Olaf had not been ill, then they would still have been at the settlement. What was the meaning of it all?

he thought sighing. However, what was done was done. Unfortunately there was nothing he could do to undo it; so all the if's and buts were futile, he thought, now feeling the onset of a headache.

Ragnar stood up and stretched, looking over at the others, who like himself, were still awake. Everyone was silent and sombre. They were still in shock, like he himself was, at what had just happened. There was one thing he knew, he thought, as rage coursed through him, these murdering barbarians would pay dearly for what they had done. Even if they had to search to the ends of the earth in order to find them. There would be no giving up this time. He would personally see to that, he thought with unwavering determination. Grabbing a blanket, he wrapped it roughly around himself as he settled down to sleep.

Making full use of the strong winds, they kept the boat at full speed. By the following afternoon they spotted land. Ragnar turned the sails so the boat would veer nearer to the shore. They sped down the coastline. All the while, Toork stood at the side watching for any sign. He was beginning to worry it would grow dark and they would have to stop. There was no sign of the ship, but that was not what Kelda had told them to watch for, he thought with some consolation.

Ragnar began to slow their boat down, just slightly, as he knew they would soon be approaching a y shaped estuary. At its mouth, he was aware of a small township, with a dock. He did not know how many people lived there, but he was confident enough to know his men were fierce when challenged.

They sailed close and Toork's eyes searched. Then he saw it. It was a sign he had taught young Eric, it looked like it had been drawn erratically in blood, at the side of a dwelling facing the sea. Toork made an involuntary grunt and waved his hand urgently to Ragnar. Ragnar immediately swung the boat round towards the dock. They would not have seen the sign if the boat had sailed further out from the shore Toork thought. So Kelda had been right.

The people on land began to scatter when they saw a Viking ship full of armed men swiftly approaching. The boat swung into the docks and most of the men, with their shields held up and swords in hand, jumped quickly ashore. Toork and Ragnar led the men to the building, going forward, they crashed through the door.

The men who sat around the fire jumped up in fright. There, tied together on the floor, was Eric and their people. Some of the Vikings ran forward, ready to strike the men down, but Ragnar bellowed to wait. He walked over to his wife and lifting her, he hugged her. "Did these men hurt you?, he said quietly to her as he gently stroked her hair. " No," she replied with a sob of relief, "it was the others that came to the settlement." Ragnar then bent down and lifted his grandson to his feet. Eric said, "I knew you would come Grandpa, and I hoped Toork would too. That is why I made the sign from the blood on my arm, while our captors discussed terms."

"Good thinking," Ragnar said to his grandson. Then as Ragnar looked at Eric's wounds, Eric went on to say, "I tried to stop them Grandpa, but there was too many. Even so," he carried on enthusiastically, "I still managed to send some straight to the bowels of hell!" Ragnar smiled wryly. "I saw that," Ragnar said to his grandson, and patting him on the head he said, "You did well."

Ragnar then walked over and grabbing the one that looked like the leader by the neck, he began to question him. The man was terrified because Ragnar's strong hand was tightening on his throat. He protested vehemently, with arms waving, they did not know these were Viking people, as it was a Viking ship that brought them in. They had only taken them to use as slaves, he gargled as he trailed off. Ragnar loosened his grip and asked which way the ship had gone and how long ago? The man told him. Ragnar again grabbed the man by the scruff of the neck and he said "If ever, you are knowingly offered Viking people again, you buy them, then you send word with one of the trading ships that you have them here. You had better look after them well though, maybe then you will be reimbursed for your trouble. But, if I ever, ever, hear that you take them and sell them on, then I will come looking for you myself. Do I make myself clear?"Ragnar bellowed in a resounding voice. The man repeatedly nodded, then as Ragnar released him, he, along with the others, being frightened out of their wits, tried to placate the Vikings by rushing over to untie all those still at the side of the building.

Ragnar, when they returned to the ship, told everyone to wait before they boarded. He had to think. He knew if they left now, they could easily catch up with the fleeing ship. He looked round at the people they had just rescued, knowing he could not take them along, but on the other hand, he could leave them here and pick them up on the way back. But, he continued to think, there was also the question of what Leif would feel if he was not there to take his revenge on those who had murdered his family. Would it be enough for him to know he had done that for him? He was unsure of what to do. He then looked out at the water, at the worsening weather. He did not want them all to be stuck here because of the weather, unable to sail. There would be the burial of Fraida and he knew Toork would not want to miss that. Ragnar rubbed his hand tiredly over his face .

He walked over to Toork and explained his dilemma. Toork shook his head vehemently, and mouthed the word Leif. "Yes, that is what I thought too," Ragnar said, "Leif would want to be there. It is his right," he conceded. Ragnar thought for a further minute, trying to formulate a plan. He called for the men to gather round.

"What I am going to ask," he said, "is for Sweyn and four others to stay here, and to travel south for the winter. There will be no more leaving things to chance. I need the men who agree to stay to use any means at their disposal to find out where our missing ship goes." Toork at that, began to nod in

agreement. He placed his hand on Ragnar's arm to get his attention. Toork then took a full pouch from his waist and he spilled out onto his hand some of the gold coins it contained. He poured them back in and then handed it to Sweyn.

Ragnar nodded and said, "Use this to get lodgings, and for any bribes you might need, try to blend in with the people." Ragnar looked at his men and carried on to say, "We need to know the whereabouts of the ship, where it berths for winter, so that in early spring we can attack. This time we will have it. I mean to have no more wasted searches," he stated, with gritted determination. Sweyn agreed with his father and four good men eagerly stepped forward to volunteer to stay with him.

The five men put their shields back on the boat, but they kept their short swords with them. They donned their cloaks and took a couple of wooden boxes from the ship, filling them with clothes and blankets. Everyone else climbed aboard the ship. The men watched from the dock as the ship set sail, then turned to disappear into the darkness.

Once they were far enough out at sea, Ragnar and the men began to see to the needs of their traumatised people; giving them food and drink before settling them down to sleep. Ragnar's wife held on to his arm as he covered her with furs. She asked why Leif had not come.

Ragnar had to tell her, quietly, about Fraida and the children. She cried out in shock, unable to believe what had happened. When the news sunk in Ragnar held her close as she wept.

Back at the settlement, Kelda lay awake on her bed. She too was filled with grief and sadness and felt she did not want to rise. How were they all ever going to get over this? she thought. The thought of the heartache the child and Leif would have to endure was unimaginable. What a waste of life. How could destiny have allowed this to happen to such a beautiful, loving and caring wife and mother; as well as the sweet little boy with his whole life stretched before him? There had been far too many deaths already within their small community, she thought, as silent tears of sadness ran from her eyes. Kelda then heard movement in the next room. Sighing, she tried hard to pull herself together as she rose, heart weary, from her bed.

Kelda walked into the room to find Rayna up and sitting at the fire, stroking Volga's head. She smiled at the child and going over, she knelt beside her. "Volga was hurt," she now explained to Rayna, "by the bad men who came to our home, but I have dressed the wounds," she said, "and you and I will look after her until she is better." Rayna slowly nodded and then she looked up. Kelda looked down at her pale, little face and Rayna mouthed the word "Mamma?" Kelda bit down on her lip to stop the sob rising in her throat. She said to the child, "She is down at the settlement," before then getting up and going over to the dresser.

It was not a lie Kelda thought, keeping her back to the child, because she could not stop her tears from falling. Fraida's body was still down there, but she could not bring herself to tell Rayna about her mother. "Don't worry about anything now," she said to Rayna, wiping her sleeve roughly over her cheeks, "because you're Papa, Toork and Ragnar are back to protect us. They will not allow anything more to happen to any of us."

Kelda then turned back to Rayna. She saw Rayna was mouthing words, but no sound was forthcoming. Rayna suddenly stopped speaking, as she realised for the first time there was no sound coming from her mouth. She put her little hand up to her throat and Kelda ran over to her. "Don't worry about that just now dear" she said, kissing the child and holding her in her arms. "It will come back, it is because you are still weak, after being so ill." She smiled down at Rayna, who after looking at her for a few minutes, hesitatingly gave a small smile back. "Now," said Kelda brusquely, "let's all have something nice to eat."

Further down the hill, Leif at that moment, opened his eyes. He lay for some seconds, confused, trying to think of how he came to be in his bed. Then this great weight hit him in the chest with a thud. Memories of what he had witnessed flashed before his eyes. He gasped as he sat up, then he doubled over.

He looked from his bent position over at the closed door, fear overwhelming him when he thought of what he would find on the other side. A cold sweat broke out on his brow. He still did not want to believe any of what he had seen. Hoping somehow, this was all just a bad dream. That when he opened the door, everything would be as before.

Taking a deep breath, he rose to his feet. Going over, he threw open the door. Hakon and Vaila, startled, looked up at him in surprise. He looked back at them before his eyes swept round the room to where Fraida, Dalgar, and the baby now lay. His heart dropped first into his stomach, then rose to lodge in his throat. At first he could not move. Then, taking large gasps of air, he put his hands up to his head in anguish. A great rage overwhelmed him and he let out a roar. He shook his head violently in denial, moaning "no" in despair. His shoulders began to shake and his chest heaved. There was the sound of harsh, rasping sobs as tears of agony began to flow.

Vaila rushed over to him, sobbing, for his pain and for his loss. After a few moments, in his deep overwhelming grief, he pushed Vaila away. He walked, somewhat unsteadily, over to where his wife and baby lay. He looked down and for the first time, saw Fraida in a way he had never seen her before, still, inert, and lifeless. His heart felt like it was breaking in two. His legs felt weak. He dropped down onto a chair that had been placed by the bed. He put his arms around Fraida and Olaf, grasping them tightly to his breast, never wanting to let them go.

He stroked Fraida's hair and told her softly, in an anguished voice, he was sorry he had not been there to protect her. All the while he sobbed, tears streaming down his grief stricken face.

He gently held his son and kissed him. Then standing up he walked to the end of the bed to stroke the ears of what had been a very brave dog. Looking down, he could see Dalgar's many wounds, proving he had fought fiercely in defence of his mistress. It was more than he himself had done, he thought guiltily. He had not been here to defend his family when he should have been, and he would suffer the consequences of that for the rest of his life.

Dalgar was lucky to be able to go with Fraida to that other world he thought, grief stabbing again at his heart. It was just as well, because Dalgar would not have survived long without her; he would have wasted away when denied of his beloved mistress's presence.

Leif sobbed, in that moment he was glad Fraida and the baby did not have to cross over alone. As long as Dalgar was at their side, Leif knew they would have all the protection they would need, in that other world, out of reach, where he himself could not follow.

It was only at this point Leif noticed Rayna and Volga were missing. He swung round and said to Vaila with a sob, "Where is Rayna."Vaila told him, "At Kelda's," and as Leif frowned, Vaila quickly said with a small, shaky smile, "Leif, Rayna and Volga live, Kelda managed, somehow, to bring them back from the shadows." Leif looked shocked, hardly able to believe this news. He felt the ache in his heart, ever so slightly, ease. He sobbed and rushed to the door, only to stop suddenly and turn back.

He rushed into the room where Rayna slept, to lift her cloth doll and bone bracelet from the floor where they lay. Rushing back, he went out the door and ran all the way to Kelda's. He threw open the door, breathing heavily. Kelda was sitting by the fire with Rayna on her knee. Rayna turned her head and said, "Papa," and Leif did not notice that no sound came out. He rushed over and scooped his daughter up into his arms, to hold her tight. His shoulders shook, tears of relief flowing from his eyes. Kelda got up from the chair and went over to the other side of the room.

Leif sat down and held Rayna close in his arms. Rayna pushed herself back and she mouthed to her father, "Mamma?" Leif looked over at Kelda, realising now that his daughter could not speak. Kelda made a motion with her eyes for him not to remark on it. Rayna put her little hands up, one on each side of her father's face, and pulled him round to face her.

Rayna mouthed her question again. Leif looked down at the face so like her mothers, and silent tears ran from his eyes. He tried to pull himself together before speaking. He breathed deeply, then told Rayna her mother and brother had gone to that great place, to join with the Gods. Rayna's face creased in pain. Leif carried on to say, but they would be alright because they had Dalgar with them. Tears began to trickle down Rayna's little face and she shook her head in denial at what her father was saying. Kelda had to turn away, because she could not hold back her own tears when seeing the child's pain.

Leif, trying to comfort her, continued to say they had been allowed to enter Valhalla because she had been a very clever girl. She was the one who put the little swords in their hands, and her Mamma was really proud she had managed to do that. Rayna looked up at her father through her tears and she nodded.

Leif carried on to say, "Mamma has Olaf and Dalgar with her. I have you and Volga with me. That is what the Gods wanted. They did not want to take you too, or I would have been left here all alone."Rayna, in her innocence, believed this story. Putting her arms around her father's neck, she cuddled him tight. Leif held her until her sobs began to ebb. He stroked the hair back from her face and told her she was to stay up here with Kelda, until she was better. "You will like that, wont you," he said to his daughter. Rayna nodded and a smile came on her tear streaked face. "Look what I have brought you," he said, holding up her doll and bracelet. This caused another smile, Rayna took them from his hand.

Leif then stood up. Placing Rayna back on the chair, he went over to Volga. "Poor girl," he said gently, lifting back the dressing to look at her wounds. "You were a brave girl," he said to the dog, stroking her head. Then after kissing her, he got to his feet. He walked over to Kelda and hugged her in thanks for giving him back his daughter. "I wish I could have done the same for your wife and son," Kelda said sadly, a solitary tear running down her tired face. Leif, as he looked at her, could only now understand the state of mind this awful grief could cause. Leif walked over and kissed his daughter goodbye. He then left the peace and quiet of Kelda's dwelling, to go back down to the settlement, to the sorrow awaiting him below.

Later that day, after learning of Toork and Ragnar's absence, Leif requested Vaila tell him all that had happened, as much as she knew. Leif found it very hard to keep himself together. When he was told the ship had been his father's, it only made things worse. He sat with his head in his hands despairingly, and like Ragnar, started the, "If only," until his head also ached. Why had the Gods allowed this to happen? But he too could find no answer that made any sense at all.

The restoring of order to the settlement continued. Some of the men approached Leif to ask where he wanted Fraida buried. They would have to start preparations soon to lay their people to rest. Leif could hardly bear to think about it. All he could say to Hakon was, "Somewhere close," because he wanted to feel Fraida was always near. Hakon gave a gruff reply and clapped Leif on the back saying, "Leave it to me."He went out behind the house into the forest and found a spot not far from their home. He took Leif to the spot. Leif agreed, that in the shade of the trees, it would do very well. Hakon marked out the large square himself, insisting he alone would dig out the borders, only then, did he let the other men join in .

Leif ordered Rayna's small bed be taken up to Kelda's until things were more settled. Vaila, at the same time, took up some of the child's clothes so she could change. Rayna saw Vaila enter. She ran into her arms, clinging on tight, refusing to let go. Tears streamed silently down Vaila's face as she hugged the child close. She felt anger inside that it could not be her mother's arms the child had run to. Why, oh why, could the Gods not have taken me in place of Fraida she thought dispiritedly, sometime later, when sitting in front of the fire with Rayna still in her arms and Volga at her side.

Vaila stayed at Kelda's with Rayna for the remainder of that day. She did not leave until Rayna had fallen asleep in her arms. When she placed the sleeping child on her bed, she looked down at her fondly. She felt somewhat concerned about Rayna's loss of voice. She hoped fervently this was only a temporary affliction , caused by the shock of all that had happened.

The next morning, Ragnar's boat returned. The men had used all their strength rowing, to ensure the boat would return in time for the burials they knew would take place on the following day. Toork, as he stepped from the boat, felt desolate. There was now no Fraida to return to. Already it was having an effect, not to have her standing here with the dogs waiting to welcome them back. He visualised her beautiful, smiling face. Tears began to well in his eyes and he felt a great weight drag at his heart. That feeling, he was certain, would remain with him always. Fraida had given him back his life when he teetered on the brink of death. He had not been able to do the same for her. The fact that he had failed to protect her, in her hour of need, would stay with him forever.

Olaf, who was still unaware of what had happened, now had long spells where he was conscious, but he was still very weak. He questioned where Toork was and why Fraida had not come to see him. Everyone just looked at the floor and muttered inanely in answer to his many questions.

They eventually told Leif Olaf was now conscious and asking where everyone was; but Leif could not go to see him, to tell him of his daughter's death. He knew how much Olaf loved Fraida and he knew what this news would do to him. At the moment, Leif had enough trouble himself trying to get through each day, trying to struggle against a strong urge to kill himself, without having the added burden of Olaf's grief. That task was left to Toork and Ragnar.

Ragnar spoke to Vaila first, to find out what she knew about what had happened. Then he, along with Toork, went to see Olaf. A smile spread over Olaf's face at the sight of his dark friend, but it quickly began to fade when he saw Toork's face. Toork fought the tears welling up in his eyes, but it was to no avail and they spilled over to run down his dark face. Olaf had never seen Toork show any kind of weakness, let alone cry. His heart began to thump in his chest at what could be the cause. Toork turned away to try to hide his pain from his friend. Olaf then looked at Ragnar in question and Ragnar, at the look on Olaf's face, struggled to try to tell him. Everyone heard Olaf's cry as he bellowed out in pain. Leif put his head despairingly in his hands and his shoulders shook as he quietly wept.

Olaf, although very weak, insisted Toork and Ragnar help him up from his bed so he could go to his child and grandson. He cried out again at the sight of poor Dalgar who had suffered the same fate as his daughter. Olaf all but collapsed at the scene before him. Toork and Ragnar carried him to the chair at the side of the bed. There he sat weeping for the rest of that night, Toork and Leif sat with him.

The following morning, the burials began. Leif carried Fraida to her grave, alongside Toork, who carried their son. Olaf wanted to carry Dalgar, but they would not let him because he was still far from well, Ragnar carried him instead.

The men stepped from the dwelling to find their path lined on either side by a procession of men bearing torches, to light up the start of Fraida's journey to the afterlife. Leif faltered for a moment, because memories of the day when he and Fraida wed suddenly began to surface. He felt the weight of his grief dragging him down. Tears welled up and ran from his eyes when he thought of that day when the body, he now held in his arms, had been so happy and full of life. Hakon stepped forward to silently offer support, but Leif shook his head and steadied himself, then took the first step. The small group made their way towards the grave. The men bearing torches turned two by two as they passed to follow in their wake.

Fraida was laid out in the centre of the large square. Baby Olaf was placed safely in her arms. Dalgar they positioned at her side. Leif gently stroked her face before he put around her neck, the gold necklace with the hammer of Thor. He fastened the bracelets of swans Toork had made for her wedding day, on her arms. Olaf put in the glass ornaments he had brought her from the east, the ones she had always loved.

Toork and Ragnar fetched her loom, which they placed at the end of the grave. Leif carried over a casket and set it down at her side. He had been deeply upset earlier, when he had filled it with some of her prized possessions. He put in the casket some gold coins, her ivory combs, the disc that reflected her beauty. He also placed in the box many of the carved bone pins he himself had lovingly made in the shape of animal heads. He put in a pair of fur boots and silk slippers, in case she would need them, and her long, silk ribbons. A ewer, filled with wine, was placed in the grave, along with food, bowls and cups for her and Olaf. Leif then placed next to Olaf his wooden toys, so he would have something to play with in the afterlife.

Only when Fraida was laid out and ready, did Leif fetch Rayna. Rayna cried as she mouthed "Mamma," at Leif. He carried her into the grave so she could kiss her mother and brother goodbye. Placing Rayna down on her feet, she bent to kiss them both. Everyone who watched felt a lump rise in their throats, when she placed her treasured bone bracelet in her little brothers hand, her doll in her mother's arms. Leif, with tears streaming down his tortured face, carried a small wooden box, and taking Rayna, he then knelt down at his wife's side. He twisted a long lock of Fraida's hair and taking his knife, he cut it off. He put it in the wooden box, telling Rayna this was for her, so she would always have a part of her mother with her. He stood up, Rayna then pointed to the baby. Kneeling down, he cut off one of Olaf's blonde locks, placing that in the box alongside her mothers. Rayna then pointed to Dalgar, Leif hesitated, but Rayna insisted, so he cut some hair from the dog and put that in too. Then Rayna went to Dalgar and she stroked him, tears running down her little face all the while. After she kissed him, Leif lifted her and handed her up to Toork so that he himself could climb out of the grave.

Leif watched his men place a covering of wood over the grave, to complete the burial chamber. He could hardly bear the pain, because he knew this would be the last time he would have sight of his beautiful wife and the son they had both adored. He forced himself to carry on watching as they covered the grave with earth. His thoughts flew back to the time when his father had been killed, when anger and rage had dampened down his grief, but this time he could not depress the overwhelming anguish washing over him in waves. It drowned out all other feeling and left him physically weak. Life breathed in his body he knew, but his soul and heart was dead. At that moment he willed his breath to cease, so he could be reunited with what had been everything to him. Fraida's smile could light up his life, now, nothing had meaning without her.

As was the custom, a feast had been prepared, to celebrate the passing over to the other life of Fraida and the child. Everyone followed Leif as he drifted down to the longhouse, but no one felt like celebrating. Leif, when seated, remained silent and morose. Then with a look of despair, he lifted his drinking horn and began to drink, a lot, in an effort to dull the pain wrenching at the very core of his heart. Vaila too, remained silent and detached from it all. She herself began to down much more than she normally would, knowing that, in their lives, nothing would ever be the same again.

Toork, looking around, could see how distraught the others were, all silently steeped in their own grief. Walking over, he lifted Rayna from the chair at her father's side. With a nod he motioned to Kelda. She came to join him and they left the longhouse together. As they walked in silence back to Kelda's dwelling, Toork suddenly felt a deep, searing anger. This anger, accompanied by his grief, overwhelmed him. It coursed through every vein in his body. He wanted to scream and rage and lash out. At that moment, he had to fight hard to contain it. He held on to Rayna as he tried to bring his feelings under control. He questioned why this child had to suffer even more by being cursed with the same silence as he himself endured. Why had the Gods allowed this to happen? He thought angrily. Of one thing he was certain, his retribution when the time came, to those who did this, would be fierce, swift and final.

CHAPTER TEN

In the weeks following the burials, everyone awaited the arrival of the winter snow: but it did not come. Instead, the heavens opened and the rain came thundering down. It was wet, stormy and miserable, reflecting the mood of those living within the settlement. The men were angry and restless; forced to now wait until spring before being avenged for these atrocious acts. However, with the absence of snow, people were still able to move about. They found themselves drifting from house to house, in an effort to gain solace in the company of each other.

Leif was finding it hard to stay in his dwelling, where everything reminded him of what he had lost. He spent most of his time in the longhouse, in the company of Ragnar and his loyal men. Here, he began to drink heavily, in an effort to relieve himself of the ever present anguish and pain. He drank so much, that at times, his body just shut down; allowing him the respite he so greatly desired in the realms of his dreams. There, he could pretend everything was as before, hold Fraida and Olaf in his arms, feel their warmth, be comforted by Fraida's words and laughter.

However, in the first few minutes of awakening, reality would set in. The great weight he bore would instantly return. This caused him to reach again for his horn, to seek what solace there was in drink. Relief came in the knowledge it would take him back to the fantasy of that shadowy world, where the process could begin all over again.

Toork watched this pattern slowly unfold. It caused him concern. Leif was beginning to lose weight; he looked pale, haggard and drawn. It seemed to Toork the only thing to heal in the settlement this winter would be Eric's wounds, which the boy still proudly sported.

Toork, unlike Leif, preferred, of all places, to be in Leif's dwelling, where he could still feel strongly the presence of Fraida. He was in there now. He sat hunched forward in the chair, and for the first time in a long time, he felt so alone. He rubbed his hand over his face wearily, then sat back and thought of Olaf. His friend was a broken man. Still being very weak from his illness, he spent his days in bed, mourning, refusing to get up. Toork did not like this turn of events. It could not carry on. He himself felt that his heart had been torn out. He mourned Fraida as much as anyone, but this is not what she would have wanted. Instead of gaining comfort from each other, they had isolated themselves, trying to deal with their grief individually, in their own way. It was not working. Fraida would expect him to do something, so he would have to think of some way to alter their situation.

He thought for a while, then decided the only solution would be to bring Rayna and Volga back to their home. It was all he could think of doing at this moment in time. Rayna being here, running about the place, might help pull both men back to the present. Besides, he thought wryly, Rayna would have to come down soon anyway, because the snow could come at any time. He wanted her here, not isolated with Kelda up on the hill. He would go and find Vaila he thought, stretching as he stood up. He hoped she was sober, because she too had taken to drifting aimlessly about the settlement the worse for wear. This would give Vaila something to occupy her time, he thought, because she was the one who would have to take care of Rayna.

The situation down in the settlement had not escaped Kelda's notice either. She was, at that moment, while Rayna was busy playing, stirring the contents of a small pot placed over her fire. She had noticed Leif seemed to have lost all purpose in life. He needed to be reminded there was still Rayna. She, herself, had thought it was time for the child to return to her home. Rayna was well now, although it bothered Kelda that she still did not speak. Kelda had left things as they were, hoping the child's voice would return, given time, but that was not happening. She knew she herself would now have to intervene, before the coming of the snow. It would be intolerable for Leif to have to spend the winter enclosed in his dwelling in silence, with no sound either from the dark one or from Rayna.

Kelda continued stirring the pot while looking round at Volga. She was pleased at the dog's progress. The wound on her shoulder was healing as it should. Although she still walked slowly, she was eating well and moving about. A knock came at her door. Rayna looked over as Kelda set aside her pot, leaving the fire to go and open it. Toork and Vaila stood outside. Vaila looked pale and drawn, Kelda thought, noting the darkness of the shadows under her eyes. Vaila entered, saying to Rayna as she ran towards her, "We have come to take you home." Rayna smiled and nodded, then motioned was Kelda coming too. "No," Kelda said to Rayna smiling, "this is my home and I must stay here," but I will come down as usual to see you every day, until the snow comes. Papa needs you now, and you have to be back in your home before the weather changes." Rayna nodded and agreed. The rest of the day was spent moving her small bed and clothes back down to her room.

When Rayna was just about ready to go, Kelda sat down and drew her onto her knee. She hugged her and kissed her. Then removing her bone bracelet, she gave it to Rayna. Rayna looked up at her in question, and Kelda said, "This is to replace the one you so kindly gave to Olaf. I know you miss having it with you, so you can take mine. This winter I will make another and then we can both be the same again." Rayna smiled and brought the bracelet up to her cheek. She closed her eyes, taking comfort from the familiar feel of the smooth bones. She thought of her Mamma, and of her little brother, and tears sprung to her eyes. Turning, she hugged Kelda in thanks.

Toork had ensured the fire was built up and all was in order, before he carried Rayna down. When they arrived, Vaila was already there, cooking food on the fire. He set Rayna down. She stood, Volga at her side, looking about her.

Toork and Vaila smiled at the child, hiding their concern, because both knew the last time she had been in her home her mother and brother had been there too. Vaila had removed the baby's cot and anything else she found she thought might upset the child. She was glad she had, as the first thing Rayna did was to walk over to the bedroom. She wandered around, clutching at her bracelet going from room to room, with Volga walking slowly at her side.

Volga then left Rayna's side and returned to Leif and Fraida's room door, where she stood as if looking for signs of her mistress and Dalgar. She entered the room and went slowly over to the bed. She stood sniffing at the covers, then grabbing one of the furs, she trailed it with her back through to the main room.

Vaila looked at Toork. He walked across the room to take the fur from the dog's mouth. He carried it over and placed it at the side of the fire. Volga walked slowly over and lay wearily down on it. The scent of her mistress and Dalgar was all she had left to comfort her. Rayna then looked at them and mouthed, "Papa." "Your father will be coming soon," Vaila said with a smile to Rayna, not telling her that her father did not yet know she was home. Rayna looked at them both for a minute then she mouthed, "Mamma," and tears filled her eyes. Toork rushed over and grabbed the child, lifting her into his arms. Tears ran from his own eyes as he sat on the chair holding her close, comforting her while she cried. Vaila sobbed silently at the child's distress and hid it from her by bending to stir the pot suspended over the fire.

After they had eaten, the child's mood seemed to lighten. Toork fetched her wooden top and he sat on the floor, spinning it to her. This proved to be a good distraction while Vaila cleared everything away. Then he got up and motioned to Vaila to take his place while he slipped away. He went out in search of Leif, but what he found did not please him. He found him lying drunk, on a bench in the longhouse. Not wanting Rayna to see her father like this, he left him there and went back to the dwelling. He shook his head to Vaila's question when she looked up as he entered. Vaila got Rayna ready for bed and lay down with her until she was asleep. When she returned to the other room, Toork motioned he would stay there for the night, to allow Vaila to return home.

Sometime in the night, Leif woke up on the floor of the longhouse. He lay still for a moment, before struggling to get up, onto his feet. He would return to his dwelling, he thought, swaying unsteadily, and go to bed, their bed, where the scent still remained of his beloved Fraida. He could dream of their nights together and that, he thought wearily, rubbing his hand over his face, might allow him some comfort from this infernal pain.

Leif stood for a moment more, trying to gather himself together, before leaving the longhouse. He managed somehow to stagger all the way back to their home. In the darkness he saw the outline of Toork lying on the bed in the main room, but he failed to notice Volga who lay at the fire. He walked over and stood for a moment swaying at the door of his darkened room. This blackness was familiar he thought wryly, it felt like his soul, dark and empty. He stumbled over and fell onto his bed, remaining on top, lying spread out, unmoving and still. Wanting relief from his pain, he willed himself the oblivion of sleep. However, some time later, the light of dawn filtered in and Leif was still awake. He felt lost, and alone, and physically drained. He had no energy or will to even raise his hand to wipe the tears from his pale and hollowed face. Finally, realising he was not going to be able to sleep, he got up.

Creeping from the room, he went once more out into the cold greyness of another winter morning, leaving behind the bleak loneliness of his unwelcoming, empty, dwelling.

Rayna stirred from her sleep, feeling cold. Still half asleep, she rose and put on her slippers, then padded through to creep in beside Mamma and Papa. She reached the bed, only to find no one there. Suddenly she became fully awake, the feeling that frightened her quickly returning, when she remembered her Mamma was dead and gone forever.

She turned and walked silently into the other room. She stood looking down at the outline of the sleeping Toork. He did not stir. Rayna walked over to where Volga lay. The dog yawned, stretched and stood up. The tears ran silently down her little face as she thought of her Mamma. She wanted the comfort of her Mamma's arms. Rayna walked over and lifted the cloak her Mamma had made for her. Wrapping it around her small body, she opened the door and stepped out in the dim, half light, to the cold driving rain.

Volga, when realising Rayna was about to go out, gave a small whine in warning, then grabbed the cloak in her teeth, trying to pull her back. Rayna tugged and pulled her cloak from the dog's mouth. Freeing herself, she then put her head down into the wind, making her way round to the back of the building. She struggled against the driving rain and set off in the direction of where she knew her mother's grave to be. Volga, being unable to stop her, then followed close behind.

As the wet and bedraggled pair approached the grave, over the sound of the wind, Rayna could hear deep, heart wrenching, sobs. She screwed up her eyes and in the half light, she could just make out the outline of her Papa as he lay slouched over the mound of her Mamma's grave.

Leif had a longing to hold, just once more, his beautiful wife who lay beneath. He could not stand the thought of her, or his baby son, being forever interred in the darkness. He could not accept that neither would ever again see the light of day. Leif, in his anguish, did not hear Rayna coming. She stood looking down at him with her wet cloak plastered to her little body, her hair in straggles from the wind and the driving rain. Rayna dropped to her knees and frantically started to pull away the earth with her small hands. She had to see her Mamma again. She wanted her Mamma.

Leif jerked up with a start when he heard the long, drawn out howl of Volga coming from somewhere behind him. Leif looked over at his daughter in shock. Where had she come from, he questioned of himself? He quickly shook himself in an effort to pull himself together, then reaching over he grabbed her. He shouted out, " No, no!" but Rayna tried to shrug him off, wanting only her Mamma. Her little mouth formed the word but no sound came out. He stood up, lifting her body with him, but she struggled and fought as he brought her tear streaked face close to his.

"Don't you know," Leif shouted over the wind, "that I would give anything in this world, or the next come to that," he said with a sob, "to bring them back to us! I would give my own life, or whatever it takes," he continued with desperation in his voice, "so that your Mamma could hold you again in her arms. But this, I can't fix. I can't make it better," he shouted, while shaking his head. "I could take on the world, fight every person in it, but it would not bring her back to us," he said sobbing brokenly. Rayna's breast heaved as she too sobbed. He clutched his daughter into his shoulder and as he held her tight, he shouted over the wind into the darkness, "I swear Fraida, as long as I have life, I will do everything in my power never to let harm come to this child who is part of us both, and who you loved so much. Where I failed you," he began to sob again, "I will not fail her," and with that, he slowly turned away from the grave. Holding on closely to Rayna, he called Volga to his side. They started to make their way back to the emptiness, and loneliness, of what was once, a happy home.

Neither saw the dark figure of Toork hurriedly turn back to reach the house before them. The cold wind blowing through the open door had woke him. He had jumped up and rushed over to look in Rayna's room, only to find her gone. He had glanced into Leif's room as he ran past and saw that, it too, was empty.

Toork had rushed from the building and from the corner of his eye, spotted Rayna going in the direction of her mother's grave. He gave chase, intending to bring her back, that was, until he saw Leif. The thought then occurred that this might be what Leif needed to shake him up, to bring him back to the world of the living. He had stayed in the shadows watching, sharing their anguish, fighting his own grief when he saw what transpired.

Toork wiped the tears from his face as he reached the dwelling. Going in, he quickly built up the fire. He had milk warming in a pan by the time the pair walked in out of the rain. Leif looked over at him, Toork, with his eyebrows raised, looked back. Leif did not speak, but walked through to the bedroom where he changed the clothes of himself and Rayna. Toork gently rubbed Volga dry, then settled her in front of the fire.

Leif and Rayna came back into the room and Toork poured them all some hot milk, cooling some down to give to the dog. Rayna sat on her father's lap drinking the milk. Suddenly, she jumped down and ran over to fetch some bread. Rayna dipped the bread into the hot milk and holding it to her father's lips, she forced him to eat. For the first time since Fraida's death, Leif smiled. Then everyone laughed as she forced Toork and Volga to eat some too. This was the sight that met Vaila's eyes when she arrived that morning and her heartache began to ease when she saw them all smile at each other as they sat huddled together around the fire.

Kelda was up and around early that morning too, because the cold Norse wind was blowing in earnest. She knew there was not much time before the coming of the snow that always followed. She had made a potion she hoped would bring back Rayna's voice, but she wanted to test it out to ensure it worked, before she gave it to the child. There was no good in giving Rayna any false hope. So after wrapping up well, she struggled through the wind to make her way down to the longhouse, in the hope that some of the men would still be there.

It was dark, being the early hours of the morning. But she saw, as she entered, that a few of the men were beginning to surface from their drunken sleep. Some of the lamps were lit, but their flames were now low. Kelda slipped unseen, over to the table, and she put some of her potion into the ewers of ale left from the night before. She had sweetened her potion with honey this time, so the men would not detect what their ale contained. Keeping her cloak wrapped around her, to disguise that she was there, she then pretended to be one of the servant woman. Walking over, she kept her back to them as she stocked up the fire.

A few of the men managed to struggle to their feet. They staggered over to sit around the table. Without further ado, they grabbed at the leftover bread and cheese from platters placed there the night before, and began to eat. She waited patiently, pottering around, until she saw them lift their horns and fill them with ale; then she watched as they took a swig to swill the dry food down. They were talking quietly among themselves, but suddenly one of the men shouted as he asked the others a question. The men looked at his startled face and one of them said, "No need to shout, we are only sitting next to you," but before he finished the sentence his voice too, had become loud. Both men put their hands to their throats in puzzlement. Another started to ask, "What was their game?" when his voice also increased in volume. Kelda smiled and slipped out through the door. She heard them all behind her begin to shout, "What foolery was this?" Yes, she thought with satisfaction, hurrying through the rain to return to her dwelling. Her potion did, in fact, work.

Kelda sat by her fire keeping warm, waiting until it was time for her to go down and see Rayna. Kelda knew as she sat contemplating, that the others would not willingly allow her to give any potions to Rayna, so she would need to find a way to get the child on her own. She had not yet thought of how to achieve this, but hoped she would find a way when she reached Leif's dwelling.

However, Kelda need not have worried, because when she reached Rayna's, no one took much notice. They were all busy with the process of moving beds and furniture. Leif had decided for this coming winter, Toork and Olaf should move in with him, not be isolated over in Toork's dwelling. Olaf, he knew, would be too weak to struggle through the snow to reach them. He was afraid, that being the case, he would just remain in his bed, pining away. Rayna, Leif thought wryly, had already lost enough of her family. He himself did not want to see another death, so he took the only solution left open to him.

He had also asked Vaila to move in for the winter, knowing his daughter needed her there. Vaila had agreed and Leif instructed a bed for Vaila be put in the child's room. Vaila herself had gone back to her own dwelling in order to gather clothes and personal belongings she would need to see her through the winter. Toork was at that moment over in his dwelling doing the same for Olaf and himself. Vaila, on the previous day, had taken all of Fraida's possessions and placed them carefully in trunks, so when Rayna was of age, she could have all her mother's belongings, to do with as she wished.

Everyone was so busy they did not take much heed of Kelda. All that was, except Rayna, who gladly ran into her open arms. Kelda pulled Rayna to the side and they sat on their stools close to the fire. Kelda said secretly to Rayna that she had made a potion she hoped would make her talk again. Rayna smiled and became excited. Kelda looked around at the men who were carrying in the beds. She saw Leif's back was towards them as he directed the men on where to go. She hushed the child and told her to fetch a cup of milk. Rayna went over and fetched one for them both. She smiled as Kelda put in her cup a few drops of the potion. Kelda then told her quietly, to just relax and drink her milk.

The two of them sat closely together, waiting for something to happen, when Rayna started to say, "Do you think it will work Kelda?, when she realised she had in fact, spoken the words. She jumped up into Kelda's arms to kiss her. Smiling broadly, she ran over and called, "Papa!" Leif turned in shock. Grabbing Rayna he swung her up into his arms. Tears sprung to his eyes and he looked at her in wonderment when she said, "I can speak again." Just hearing his child's voice made Leif feel, half normal. Nothing would ever be the same again in his life, he knew, but this was a step in the right direction. Hugging Rayna close to him, he wondered how this had come about. He looked over at Kelda. He had his suspicions, but whatever Kelda had done he was grateful for it, he thought. Not only had she returned Rayna and Volga to him, but now, she had in some way, returned his child's voice to her.

Vaila and Toork, when they came back with arms full, had tears in their eyes when they heard Rayna's exited chatter as she tried to make up for the weeks of silence she had been forced to endure. Vaila said this was a cause for celebration and insisted Kelda stay and eat with them. She told her one of the men could take her back home later that evening. This pleased Kelda greatly. She was enjoying the family atmosphere in Leif's that day. After the loss of her own family, this was something she sorely missed.

Toork decided to carry Rayna over to see her grandfather, in the hope that on hearing the child's voice, it would somewhat ease his pain. Toork put Rayna down. She ran over to the bed, calling to out to her grandfather. Olaf, surprised, pushed himself up onto his elbows. He looked down at this miniature of Fraida who called out to him. He smiled then, tears springing to his eyes as he listened to the excited chatter of the child. Toork then returned Rayna to Leif. Going over, he washed Olaf and dressed him. Then got him up on to his feet and over to, what would now be, his new home for the coming winter.

They all, in the company of each other, felt happier that day. All the pain and anguish each had suffered, eased slightly for the first time since Fraida's death. Before Kelda left that night, Rayna took her to the side to whisper secretly to her. Rayna had an idea. If the potion had worked on her, might it not also work on Toork? Kelda looked in surprise at Rayna, as the thought had not even entered her head. Kelda, not knowing the reason for Toork's silence, became excited. The child could be right. She slipped the potion to Rayna, explaining to the child how she was to use it. But she told her to be careful and to use it only as she had instructed. They smiled secretly at each other as Kelda left to return to her home.

That night was the first where everyone slept soundly. The following morning at breakfast, Rayna managed to slip a few drops of the potion, unseen, into Toork's goblet. She ate her breakfast and waited with excitement for something to happen. Everyone looked up in surprise as strange noises suddenly burst forth from Toork. Rayna watched closely, waiting for him to say a word. Toork put his hand to his throat and looked over at Olaf with a frown. Everyone sat staring, with the food halfway to their mouths, as they listened to the involuntary deep groans and grunts emitting from Toork. He shook his head and gripped his throat, but still the noises persisted. He stood up and Leif stood up with him, because he could see something was wrong. Toork waved for Leif to sit back down. Turning, he strode across the room to the door and quickly left the dwelling.

Rayna was at a loss. She couldn't understand why it hadn't worked. The sound was there, but no words. Maybe she had not put enough of the potion in his drink, she thought. Or it might be that it would take longer to work on him as he had not spoken for a long time. She decided then to leave it for today, to see if his words would return, then if not, she would try again tomorrow.

The next day, when seeing Toork was silent and not attempting to speak to anyone, Rayna, once more, slipped some of the potion into his drink. Again, strange noises began emitting from a reluctant Toork's mouth. The adults at the table looked over at him with concern. Toork became angry, lifting the bread, then the cheese, looking at them with a frown on his face, as he tried to figure out what was the cause. He threw them down. Rising, grunting involuntarily all the while, he once again left the dwelling. Olaf and Leif looked at each other, but said nothing. Olaf just shrugged his shoulders at the question in Leif's eyes.

Leif carried on eating, then happened to look across at his daughters thoughtful face, as she tried to figure it out. Then it dawned on him. Something was afoot. Rayna's voice, for some unknown reason, recovers two days previously and then strange noises begin to come from Toork. This could not be coincidence he thought. Saying nothing to the others, he vowed he would take his daughter aside at the first available opportunity and ask what she was about.

Later, while Vaila was clearing up, Leif took Rayna aside. He asked if she had given any kind of potion to Toork. Rayna shook her head in denial, but Leif knew his daughter, he knew she protested too much. Leif sat down and drew Rayna onto his knee. He explained to her he knew she would not harm Toork and anything she did, would, in her eyes, be to help him. Rayna grew quiet. Leif then asked if she had given any of the potion to Toork, that Kelda had given to her? Rayna, before she thought, blurted out , how had her father known Kelda had given her a potion? Leif smiled and tried not to laugh. Leif then began to explain to Rayna, without giving her any of the gory details, the reason for Toork's silence. He told her, years ago, because of an unfortunate incident, Toork had lost his tongue. He then went on to say because of this, although Toork still had sound in his throat, he could not speak because your tongue formed the words. Rayna suddenly began to understand. "So then," she said to her father sadly, "no matter how much of the potion I gave to him, it would not work." "Unfortunately, no," Leif replied. " So you can return the potion to Kelda and explain to her what I have just explained to you, and we will say no more about it." Leif then stood up and kissed and hugged his daughter before setting her down.

Later that night, when Rayna was in bed, they gathered round the fire. Leif smiled when he thought of what had transpired earlier that day. The others looked at him in question, so he told them what had been ailing Toork. Olaf burst out with laughter and then they all joined in. Toork's shoulders shook as he laughed, relieved now that he had found the reason for his problem. He should have known, he thought, still smiling to himself, that it was something to do with Kelda. They had his best interest at heart, he knew. Rising from the chair, he went through and gently kissed the sleeping child, pleased that she had thought of him and of a way in which she thought she could make him better.

The following day, the wind was bitterly cold. The younger men in the settlement visited all the dwellings in a last minute check to ensure everyone was settled and ready for the snow. Leif had a large stone slab brought into his dwelling, and he told the men to put it against the wall. He intended to spend the long, dark days carving a stone to put on the grave of Fraida, Dalgar and baby Olaf. He fetched his tools from his work shed and put them beside the stone. His heart ached with longing for his wife and son. He missed them so much, and although he still had Rayna, his life felt empty and meaningless without Fraida by his side.

Leif became lost in thought as he stood staring at the stone, wishing he could turn back time. His eyes misted over and without being aware, a tear spilled out to run down his face. At that moment, Toork's arm gripped him unexpectedly around his shoulder. He pulled himself together and patted Toork on the back. The two men, when they looked at each other, could see in the eyes of the other, the pain they suffered from the loss of Fraida. Both knew in their hearts, it was a wound that would never heal.

At that moment Vaila returned with a basket of vegetables for the following day. She said with a shiver the snow had come, so they all stood at the door for a few minutes to watch it fall. Leif held Rayna in his arms and his thoughts drifted back to that first winter with Fraida. He had visions of her and the dogs as they played, carefree, in the falling snow. If only he had known then they had but a few years together ahead of them. What could he have done differently, he thought in despair? then turning away, he followed everyone back to the fire.

Vaila walked across the room and threw more logs on the fire. They all pulled their seats nearer to share in the warmth from its glow. Olaf decided to fetch Rayna's spinning top. Bending down he set it in motion. It spun over towards Toork, he bent to retrieve it and Leif had a glimpse of something strange hanging on a thin strip of leather underneath Toork's tunic. Leif waited until Olaf and Rayna were once more distracted by the toy before asking Toork what it was. Toork hesitated for a moment, then turning his back to the others, he quietly withdrew it, raising his eyebrows as he held up the withered ear.

Leif looked at it in puzzlement. His thoughts suddenly flashed back to Dalgar, when he had knelt by his side, and to the conversation he had with Vaila about what had befallen Fraida. Suddenly realisation dawned. "That one is mine when the time comes!" Leif said quietly, but forcefully, to Toork, a look of anger spreading across his face. Toork hesitated for a moment, then with a long, studied look at Leif, he finally gave in and nodded.

Silence again descended upon the settlement as the snow came down thick and fast. Over the following days, everyone in Leif's dwelling began to settle into a routine. Leif and Toork were satisfied at the progress of Volga, who seemed to be walking better. The dog's spirits had been low. It was obvious she was pinning for her mistress and Dalgar, Leif had remarked. But she had now perked up a bit. They were pleased to see she was putting on weight. She had become a little fatter, probably caused, they thought, by the lack of exercise due to her wound.

Vaila sat by the fire sewing. She was making new tunics for Rayna, the child was growing and she wanted to have clothes for her to wear in the spring. The left over scraps, she decided, would make Rayna a new doll, so she put them carefully to the side. The doll Vaila had made her when she was a baby, Rayna had put in her mother's grave. Vaila knew she missed having it. It gave Vaila some satisfaction to know a little part of her had gone with her friend to the afterlife. She hoped wherever Fraida was, she would think of her and know she would always see to the needs of Rayna.

Leif had made a start to carving out the stone. Toork decided to teach Rayna some of his markings. He drew them on a piece of slate he carried with him, and Olaf translated them to Rayna. This held the child's interest and helped to amuse her in the long days that followed.

One particular night, after they had eaten, Toork walked over and stood looking at the partially carved stone. Leif joined him and Toork motioned to Leif, could he carve something on it too? Leif was surprised, because the thought had never crossed his mind. He told Toork he would welcome it, knowing it would please Fraida. He gave Toork his tools and left him to it. Leif went over to sit by the fire and lifting Rayna onto his knee, he began to amuse her, by telling her tales of battles that had taken place in the time of their ancestors.

A few nights later they all stood looking down at what Toork had carved. A lump came into Leif's throat as he looked at the carving of Dalgar. "Good thinking," he said, patting Toork on the shoulder. Olaf piped in he would like to carve something on it too. They all laughed as carving was not one of Olaf's talents. However Leif asked him what he would like on the stone and Olaf drew one of Toork's signs. It was a simple marking, so Leif sat with Olaf, guiding his hand as they carved in the sign. Then Rayna wanted to do one too, and Vaila. So they all took turns, with Leif's guidance each night, until the stone was complete. Leif had worked to absorb their markings into his design and everyone was very pleased at the end result. It was a fine stone they all thought. One they all had a part in.

The days turned into weeks and Toork was growing restless. He had risen from his bed after lying awake for what seemed like hours. Everyone else was asleep, but his heart was heavy because his thoughts kept returning to Fraida. He could almost sense her presence. Tonight he was missing her badly.

Toork wiped the tears from his face as he leaned forward to throw some small logs onto the fire; to catch at the embers which still had a faint glow. He sat hunched forwards with his arms on his thighs and he watched Volga as she again padded across the room. She, like himself, was restless. The dog walked over and stood in front of him, looking up at his face. You miss them too, he thought to himself, fondling the dogs head. But Volga walked away again, wandering from corner to corner.

Toork began to wonder if she wanted a drink. Rising he went quietly over to fetch her some milk. When he turned back, he saw she was dragging her fur over to a corner, away from the fire. The heat from the fire must be too much for her, he thought, placing down her drink. Volga however, took only a few laps of the milk before plonking herself down on the fur. Toork watched her for a moment then shrugged. At least she had now settled, he thought with a sigh. Turning he went back to the fire, to let his thoughts return to his memories of Fraida.

A few minutes later, his reverie was again disturbed when he heard a small moan coming from Volga. Turning to see what was wrong with the dog, he saw she was now lying on her side with her leg in the air. He looked closely at her and for the first time he saw the milk which leaked from her teats. By the gods!, he thought, she couldn't be!

He walked quietly over and knelt as she gave birth to her first pup. They had all been so absorbed in their grief, they had missed the signs that Volga was pregnant. Volga and Dalgar had never mated before. He could not understand why this was happening now. Had Dalgar had some sort of premonition of what was to come? he thought to himself, because he was finding this very hard to comprehend. He lifted the puppy with hope in his heart, only to find it was dead. He rushed over and grabbed some cloths and he wrapped the dead puppy in one. The next to be born was dead too. Were none to be born alive? he thought sadly. Had what she suffered been too much for her litter to survive? The third one he thought, was also dead, until he detected the slightest of movements. He rubbed at it gently with a cloth. It's small body began to squirm. He placed the puppy up at Volga's face and she began to lick it. She gave birth to four more, but only one other survived. Toork sat quietly back on his haunches watching Volga, to make sure there were no others to come. Then, standing, he went to dispose of the dead pups. He fetched another fur. Lifting Volga and the pups gently, he moved them so he could dispose of the fur she had used to give birth. He still could not believe what was in front of his eyes. How pleased Fraida would have been at this, he thought with a smile. When he had brought her the pups, Dalgar and Volga, from one of their trading trips some years ago, she had been ecstatically happy. The dogs had given her much pleasure, this he knew. She would have been thrilled at having two more.

Toork yawned and rubbed his hand over his face. He was now beginning to tire, but he did not want to sleep because he wanted to see everyone's face when they emerged in the morning to find Volga had two pups. The thought then crossed Toork's mind that, in his haste, he had not looked to see if the pups were male or female. He leaned over, then hesitated. Better not disturb Volga any more for the moment he thought, seeing her busy cleaning the pups. He would leave her in peace and look again later that day.

Toork did go back to bed, and being a little happier, he did sleep. When he arose the next morning, everyone else was already up, but they were just beginning to move around. No one had yet noticed Volga and her pups as they still lay in a darkened corner of the room. Toork sat down, a big grin spread over his face as he looked at them all in question. Leif looked at him with a slight frown, wondering why, this early in the morning, Toork was so happy. Olaf grunted as he looked over, then back at his grinning friend. Vaila also looked over and raised her eyebrows, but she too was none the wiser to the cause of Toork's good demeanour this morning.

Toork waited patiently until Rayna came into the room. Then taking her by the hand, he walked her over to Volga, pointing to the two little bodies half hidden in their mother's fur. Rayna gasped, then shouted, "Papa, Papa, Volga has got two babies!" Leif jumped up with a start, and said, "What the?" and trailed off as he quickly crossed the room. "What?, how has this happened?, Leif said with astonishment. He was astounded as he looked down at the newborn pups. Olaf and Vaila came rushing over. They all stood looking down with shock at Volga and the pups. Leif glanced at Toork and said, "Were you up through the night?" Toork nodded with a grin. "Did you know she was pregnant?" Leif went on to say. Toork raised his eyebrows and shook his head. "How could this be?," Leif said with puzzlement. Toork shrugged his shoulders, spreading his arms as he shook his head, showing it was as big a puzzle to him as it was to everyone else. "How many pups did she give birth to? he asked Toork quietly. Toork held up his fingers, "and the others? Leif questioned. Toork drew his hand across his throat to tell Leif the rest had been dead. Leif knelt down to look closely at Volga. "I can't believe this," he said, over his shoulder, to the others who stood behind, "especially after what she has been through." He clapped Volga gently on the head, making soothing noises as he did so.

Then Rayna bent and made a move to lift one of the pups. Leif stopped her saying, "No, they are too young yet for you to handle, we must not touch them. We will leave Volga to care for them in these first few days, to ensure they have the best possible chance to survive." Everyone however, still stood staring for ages at Volga and the pups. It took a long time for this unexpected turn of events to sink in.

In the days following, they all found they now had something to focus on. The boredom of seclusion began to diminish. Volga became the centre of attention. They constantly watched the progress of her and the pups. Rayna was very excited. She told her father, everyday, that she could not wait to tell Kelda. Leif told Rayna when the pups were a bit older, he and Toork would take her up on the sledge to tell Kelda, then they would bring Kelda back down with them, to see the pups. After all, if it had not been for Kelda, he said, Volga and her pups would not be here today. Rayna clapped her hands excitedly at the thought of seeing Kelda again; then she jumped up and hugged her father in thanks.

When a week had passed, Leif, one morning, lifted the pups gently to see if they were male or female. He said with surprise to Rayna, "One is a boy and one is a girl." Rayna jumped up clapping and saying, "Oh good, we can call them Dalgar and Fraida." Then she noticed her father's face, because Leif's smile faded when a painful jolt struck at his heart. She said hesitatingly, "That would be alright wouldn't it Papa?." Leif turned to look up at his daughters crestfallen face. He smiled and hugged her as he said, "Those names would suit very well." Leif however, as he walked away, thought of Dalgar. The dog had always competed with Leif to come first in his mistress's affections, always trying to ensure he was the one to walk closest to Fraida's side. He had won, Leif thought with an inward smile. Dalgar had been the one who got to cross over with Fraida, into the afterlife, and now the pair were linked together in the form of dogs. Dalgar would be very pleased at this turn of events, he thought, laughing somewhat wryly to himself.

When the pups were three weeks old, Vaila dressed Rayna in her furs, ready to go out in the snow. Toork and Leif had already donned their snow slats and had gone to fetch the sledge. The two men returned and Leif lifted Rayna onto the sleigh. They set off through the deep snow, pulling Rayna behind them. She was so excited to have this outing. More so at the thought of Kelda's surprise when she saw them at her door. She giggled and laughed all the way. When they reached Kelda's door, Leif brushed away the built up snow before giving a loud knock. He lifted Rayna into his arms, then, as a wary Kelda opened the door, Rayna shouted excitedly, "We have a surprise for you Kelda but you have to come with us to see it!" Kelda was stunned to see them standing at her door. "It can't be a bigger surprise than this!" Kelda said with a wide grin, taking the child into her arms to give her a big hug.

Leif told Kelda to wrap up warmly. While they waited for her to change, Leif and Toork knocked away the snow from the stack of logs outside. They carried a pile into the dwelling to replace the ones Kelda had used. Leif then built up the fire so it would keep the room warm while she was out. The two men put Rayna and Kelda onto the sledge. Ensuring they were secure, they started back down to the settlement. Kelda and Rayna hugged each other in excitement, all the way back to Leif's dwelling.

Kelda was really enjoying this new experience. She had been growing weary of her solitary existence, and lately, she had begun to feel very lonely. This was the very tonic she needed she thought, to lift her spirits.

Vaila had baked fresh bread and had meat cooking on the fire by the time they got back. She welcomed Kelda warmly and was quick to take all their cloaks and boots, which she would later place round the fire to dry. Rayna, impatient to see the look on Kelda's face, took her by the hand and straight away walked her over to see the pups. Kelda was just as shocked as they themselves had been when she saw the pups. How had they managed to survive? she thought to herself, given what Volga had been through. She was very glad they had though, she thought, smiling down at the two small writhing bodies. Rayna lifted one gently to place into Kelda's hands. Lifting the other she held it close to herself.

"Isn't it wonderful Kelda," Rayna said with a big smile. Then she told Kelda what she had called them. Kelda said, as she looked down with sadness at the child, "It truly is Rayna. Those are names that suit them very well, because they are beautiful, just like your Mamma and Dalgar." Then she bent and kissed Rayna affectionately on the cheek.

There was a lightened atmosphere as they sat down to eat. Vaila had prepared lots of good food for them all to enjoy, even Olaf's spirits lifted somewhat. He turned to Kelda and said he understood he owed his recovery to her, and he had to thank her for that. Kelda shrugged in embarrassment and they all laughed.

The rest of the day was spent enjoying the company of each other. Then it was time for Kelda to leave. Vaila made up a basket of food for Kelda to take with her. Leif told her sternly, but with a smile, to eat more, as she was looking too thin. Kelda, being on her own, sometimes felt that preparing food for one was too much bother, but she knew she would enjoy the food Vaila had packed for her to take home. Rayna, sad to see her go, hugged Kelda. She held on to her tight before she left. Leif said it would not be long until the first day of spring, when they would all gather together in the longhouse to celebrate. They would see each other then.

Rayna Vaila and Olaf, all stood and waved from the door. They watched Toork and Leif pull the sled away. Kelda grinned and waved back, before turning to settle down to enjoy her ride in the snow. She was now feeling very pleased and content, after experiencing such a lovely surprise. She had really enjoyed her unexpected day out. The companionship of the others had given her a much welcomed break, from what she was beginning to find, a very lonely existence.

The time now seemed quicker in passing. It was not long before Ragnar struggled through the snow to tell Leif and Toork, it was time for the annual hunt. The first day of spring was only a week away. No one had been in the mood for hunting that year and this would be the first hunt of the season. However, it was an important feast day and they all knew the spring rituals would have to be observed.

Ragnar, like the rest, was very surprised to see the pups. But watching them all laugh at the antics of the two furry bundles, he thought to himself, what a gift from the Gods it had been. Ragnar had been worried about what Leif and Rayna's state of mind would be. Confined all those long, dark days with nothing to do but think about what had passed, but the pups he could see, had proved to be a diversion from those dark and sombre thoughts.

After some preparation, the younger, fitter men, left to go on the hunt. The others, who stayed behind, helped the women to trudge through the snow to reach the longhouse. This would be cleaned and prepared for the feast days ahead. Vaila took Rayna with her. Rayna was very pleased to be allowed to assist the women. Vaila tried to keep Rayna occupied whenever she could. The child still had spells when she wept for her mother and brother who, understandably, she missed very much. With her father and Toork also absent, this would help take the child's mind off the dark times, Vaila thought, watching her chatter to the women.

The next few days flew by as they finalised all the preparations. The men returned triumphant, trailing the carcasses of animals they would cook and eat in the many days of feasting. Vaila and the women began baking fresh bread, as much would be needed in the week ahead. Rayna was only too pleased to help. When that task was finished, on the following day they laid out what clothes they would wear to the feast. In a few weeks the snow would thankfully start to melt, Vaila thought, then the child could start to go outdoors again; for a short while with Kelda. Vaila knew this would cheer Rayna up, as well as Kelda. It would at the same time help divert her thoughts and occupy some of her time.

The men went through the usual motions of the rituals, but this year with all that had happened, their hearts lacked hope in the ceremony. It was a feeling shared by all. No one felt like celebrating and the people in the settlement who looked on, were somewhat subdued. That being over, the feasting began, and everyone tried to lift their spirits. Everyone smiled and put on a face as they sat eating. But the atmosphere within the longhouse was muted and strained. It was obvious to the women, the men were restless. Their heads being full of thoughts of the battle which still lay ahead.

Leif, as he sat in silence eating his meat, could not help but compare the changes in this year's feast with that of the previous year. Last year they had so much to celebrate. He had a new son, a beautiful wife, as well as Rayna. It was almost too much to comprehend that so much could happen in such a short time. In the course of just a few months, everything that had meaning in his life had been destroyed, changing his life forever

Eventually, the entertainers began to perform, to amuse the children. But they kept away from the men, who, in order to dampen down their rage and anger, had now taken to drinking heavily. The day had also brought back all the grief of the previous year to Vaila. She was finding it hard to stay strong. Knowing Rayna was safe in the hands of Kelda, she eventually gave in and joined the men in the drinking session. Olaf's health had improved and he sat with Leif. He too abandoned all thought as he downed the wine and ale. Toork however, sat back and just watched. He was in no mood for drink. He preferred to stay sober, in case he was needed to calm things down.

Normally, the spring celebrations would carry on for a week, but this year, on the second day, people began drifting back to their homes. Vaila sobered up that second day. As evening drew in, after filling a basket of food for Kelda, she got one of the older men to take her back to her home. Then she took Rayna home to bed, leaving the feasting, as she had no mood for it this year. Olaf and Leif stayed on with the rest of the men, drowning their sorrows with the fill of a horn, and Toork stayed to watch.

On the third night, Vaila opened the door to Hakon, who stood holding up a very drunk Leif. Trying to keep quiet, so as not to wake Rayna, the two of them managed to lay Leif on his bed. Vaila thanked Hakon for bringing Leif home. Hakon told her Toork was staying to watch Olaf, who was still drinking and refusing to come home. Vaila nodded and walked with Hakon to the door. She then went back to check on Leif, who was lying unconscious, face down, on the bed. She stood looking down at him with sadness in her heart. How could she blame him, she thought, as tears fell silently from her eyes. At least this way he would get some sleep that would, hopefully, be free from pain. Vaila left him to his slumber and quietly crept from the room. Going through, she stocked up the fire to keep the place warm. Then blowing out the lights she too went to bed.

The noise of a loud thud woke Vaila some hours later. She lay listening, but no other noise was forthcoming, so she thought she had better rise to check on Leif. She crept through to see he had moved. He now lay on his back, one of his boots lay on the floor. She quietly picked up a blanket to throw over him. But as she turned back, his eyes opened. All Leif saw as he looked up was a silhouette of someone with long hair. "Fraida," he said slurring, grabbing at her arm to draw her down."Where have you been? I have missed you so." Vaila started to draw back, saying urgently to Leif, "It's me, Vaila," but Leif wasn't listening; lost as he was in his drunken world. She struggled, but Leif pulled her down on top of him, then he rolled over, trapping her beneath. Vaila was frightened Rayna would wake and see her father like this. So she quietly, but urgently, told Leif to think, to remember that it was her, Vaila, not Fraida! Leif however, was too far gone to listen. As his mouth came down on hers, it silenced all talk.

Vaila struggled to free herself, but as his lovemaking began, her heart melted. She made one last desperate effort to push him off, but it only made him more determined. He laughed, thinking Fraida was playing with him. Vaila's love for Leif had never died, but she didn't want him this way. She had long since accepted he belonged to Fraida, but her feelings for him made her weak. She was not strong enough to stop this now, she thought in despair. She stopped struggling and let it happen.

Afterwards, she waited for a while to make sure Leif had again sunk into a deep sleep. The silent tears flowed from her eyes at the feeling of being held in his arms once more, something she had always missed. Vaila rose quietly from the bed, wrapped a blanket around herself, and picking up her tunic she left the room. Through her tears, she failed to notice Toork, who had decided to return home after seeing Olaf fall asleep over one of the tables. He stood silent, deep in thought, as he watched her go hurriedly to her room.

The following morning, Toork watched the pair closely. But Leif was as normal. Leif, Vaila could see, thankfully had no recollection of what had happened the night before. She herself was not going to remind him, and carried on as usual with the routine of her daily chores. Toork, watching the behaviour of them both, thought maybe all was not as it had seemed. That he must have been wrong about what he thought had happened the previous night. He decided to put it from his mind.

The men, their thoughts having only one purpose, soon sobered up. They began to move about in the melting snow. Going to the sheds, they began preparing their weapons. In other years they would wait a few more weeks before venturing out, but they were restless. Eager for the weather to break, so they could at last have their revenge.

The weather grew calmer in the week that followed. The height of the waves reduced when the gusty wind began to ease. Some of the men suggested to Leif they should now sail to Olaf's to bring back their people who had wintered there. Leif put his hands to his head, as with all that had happened, he had completely forgotten about those who were on Olaf's Island. He then realised they would still be unaware of what had happened to the people they left behind.

He quickly called Ragnar and asked him to put a crew together. "Choose men who can sail without delay to the Islands," he stated urgently, "our people must be informed of the attack on the settlement and be told to return home now, to prepare for war." Olaf, hearing of Leif's instructions, then met with Ragnar. He told Ragnar to tell the crew to relate his orders to his people. Every able bodied man, along with all his ships, were to accompany Leif's people and sail with them to the settlement. They would join with Leif in this war, to avenge the killing of his daughter Fraida and his grandson Olaf.

Vaila, when hearing that very soon there would be an influx of people arriving at the settlement, took matters into her own hands. She met with some of the older men and told them the settlement would need a lot of food to feed the visiting crews. They had plenty of grain with which to make bread and the women would start now, to make more butter and cheese. But they themselves, would have the responsibility of organising the supply of meat. They told Vaila they would gladly see to that. While the younger men saw to the weapons and the ships, they themselves would go out to hunt game. In the week the boats were due to arrive they would also fish, to ensure there was plenty of food for all. Vaila then asked Leif to send a boat down to the township with a request for some of the women to come to the settlement to help, as more hands would be needed for the work that now lay ahead.

CHAPTER ELEVEN

A boat from the township arrived with women who had volunteered to help out at the settlement. Accompanying them were the elders. They wanted to meet with Leif to receive their instructions. They, themselves, they told him, had sent out word throughout his land, for all ships and men to prepare for war. They said "even as we speak," more longships were arriving at the township, crewed by men who were armed, ready and awaiting his instructions. Leif told the elders Ragnar's son, and a few of the men, had spent the winter in the lands to the south. Their task was to track his father's ship and to find out where it berthed. He was awaiting information of the area where the ship would be, before they sailed. Sweyn would send word with the first of the trading ships. Leif said he wanted all longships prepared and ready to sail as soon as word reached him. He then told the elders a crew had set sail for Olaf's Islands, to carry the news to his people. Olaf's men and ships would also join with them to war against this enemy who lived in the land to the south. Leif pointed to the unmanned longships berthed at the palisade and he told the elders he had spare ships he needed to fill with crews of fighting men. The Elders said they would see to all that and ensure everyone at the township was prepared and ready for when the time came.

Over the following week, the settlement became a hive of activity. More men were drafted in to fill Leif's empty ships. Each ship was brought over in turn; checked and made ready before being returned to its berth at the palisade. All the women were kept busy feeding and seeing to the men. Even Rayna and Kelda, sensing the air of excitement and anticipation now within the settlement, lent a helping hand. They spent each morning making lots of bread, while some of the woman took turns to make butter and cheese, which they stored in a shed; because all these men would need food to take on their voyage. Hakon and some of the others went to the forest to bring in more wood, as extra fires had to be lit. The fires burned constantly because of the amount of food having to be cooked, and with the weather still being cold, everyone had to keep warm. The older men, seeing the number of people who were now arriving, fished daily. Although they had already been out to hunt, all the game they had caught was now being cooked over the fires, so they went out again. Casks of ale and wine, along with more bags of grain, were brought up in small boats from the township, along with word that whatever else the settlement needed, it would be supplied.

Leif stood on the headland watching the ships on the horizon returning from Olaf's. He counted ten ships in all, two of which would be his own. He turned to go in search of Ragnar because they would need to discuss where these ships would berth. His own two ships pulled into berth at the dock. The men who had been absent all winter, jumped off and came hurrying towards Leif. They gathered around him. Having only recently been told of what had befallen Fraida and Olaf, their anger and rage at such a villainous deed was still fresh in their minds. They hugged Leif in sympathy, while telling him they would do whatever was needed to send these murderers straight to hell. At their words of support, Leif struggled to contain himself. Again he felt the pain from the grief he bore, weighing him down. He clapped his men on the back and thanked them, but inside he despaired, because no matter what they did, it could not bring back the meaning of his existence. That which was the very substance of his life, Fraida and baby Olaf.

It was decided Olaf's ships would remain in the bay. Small boats were sent out to ferry the men in. Olaf's people were distraught at the death of Fraida, who was much loved in her homeland. Their anger and rage matched that of those who lived within the settlement. They knew what effect this would have on her father and they rushed to their leader to offer him their comfort and support.

In the settlement everyone was glad they had the foresight to think ahead. There was now many more mouths to feed, but they were well prepared and had carcasses of boar, deer, and cow, roasting over various fires. They had plenty of fish and shellfish, and Vaila had previously sent for more vegetables from the township. Both longhouses were now full, along with many of the dwellings. The settlement began to resemble a township, because of the number of people moving about. The forges were in use, constantly, as the men honed their many weapons. Over the following days more ships arrived and soon the bay was full. Leif had to send word down to the township for more people to help. He sent instructions that all other incoming ships were to remain there, at the township, and they would come together when they sailed.

Leif, as he looked out from the headland, was bewildered at the number of ships now anchored in the bay. He hoped news would come soon from Sweyn and the others. The first trading ships were due at the township any time now, that's if they could get into dock Leif thought wryly, if the townships waters were anything like his. He and Ragnar were satisfied that all preparations were complete, and were content in the knowledge they were now ready to sail at a moment's notice. The women had prepared the men's boxes. All that was left to be stored onboard was the food and drink. That too was in hand, as the fires had been kept burning to cook meat in large quantities, so there would be sufficient food for each ship to store aboard when the time came to sail. Leif looked up at the sky. It was grey, but there was no wind. Leif hoped the weather would hold to allow them to sail without further ado.

Leif did not have long to wait, as the following day, news arrived from the township. Sweyn had sent word for Leif to sail. The messenger told of where the five men were to be picked up. Everyone began to rush about. Lines were formed, as the men queued up with their boxes for the women to fill with food. Each ship was then given, in turn, further large boxes, filled with plenty of meat, bread, cheese, and butter as spare. Casks of ale and milk were ferried out to each ship and stored onboard. Then after, what was only a few hours, the men were ready to sail.

Vaila stood on the dock with Rayna and Kelda at her side. Leif looked over at her as he boarded his ship. When Fraida had been killed, the light had gone from his eyes and they appeared now to be dull and lifeless. She could see by his manner, his thoughts were similar to hers. The last time the boats had left these shores, Fraida had been standing here with baby Olaf wrapped in her arms. Leif, when he sailed then, had not known it would be the last time he would see his wife and son alive. Tears sprung to Vaila's eyes as she visualised that day, when Fraida and the baby stood here by her side. Why oh why did all this have to happen, and happen to them? she thought with a heavy heart. She herself would give anything to turn back time. She often questioned of herself, if only she had woke up sooner. She might have then been able to reach their killer in time to stop the axe from being thrown.

Unknown to Vaila, the same axe that had delivered the fatal blow, was now honed and sharp and tucked in Ragnar's belt. He had purposely kept the weapon to use to kill the owner. These were the people who had killed his lifelong friend and also his son Jon. Leif, Ragnar knew, wanted to be the one to kill the earless man, but if Ragnar got his chance, he in his anger would take any opportunity given, to strike the axe home.

Toork's thoughts, unknown to Ragnar, were along the same lines, when he walked forward to step aboard Leif's ship. He put his hand up to feel the withered ear that still hung round his neck. He thought angrily, if he got to the barbarian first, the killer of women and children would soon be missing more than an ear. Toork then turned to look over towards Leif, while at the same time he felt at his pouch to see he had the phial Kelda had given him of the potion to take, in case of bad weather. That's when he noticed Fraida's small sword tucked in Leif's belt. This was the weapon Leif himself had decided to use for the final act on the earless man. He would drive it straight into the evil, black heart, he thought to himself angrily. Just as Fraida would have done, had she been given the chance. Toork then turned away to help Olaf on board, because they would be travelling with Leif on his ship, which would sail out in front, leading the fleet. Ragnar's boat would follow close behind.

Vaila, as she watched them cast off, knew it was time for the women to sit back, because they had carried out their task. It was now up to the men to carry out theirs. She, as much as the others, wanted revenge for Fraida and Olaf's deaths and poor Dalgar too. She found she missed him just as much as she did her friend. She wanted those responsible for their loss, to pay. She knew Leif would not give up this time until they had.

Leif's longship sailed out through the centre of the bay and Ragnar's ship followed close behind. The others raised their anchors and waited until the two ships had a clear path ahead. Then raising their sails and keeping grouped together, they proceeded to sail in their wake. The people stood watching this spectacle from the shore. The sun, emerging from behind a cloud, cast its bright rays, which reflected and bounced off the helmets and glistening shields lining the sides of the ships, creating a myriad of stars in the choppy waters of the surrounding sea. The people were proud of their fleet. They smiled as they watched the multitude of figureheads slice effortlessly through the waves. The figureheads resembled silent hunters from the depths, rising to seek and destroy any who dare stand in their way. Everyone continued to watch until the ships were but a dark cloud in the distance, before they dispersed to go back to their homes.

The distance at the start of their journey was short. Leif drew in his breath when they were nearing the township. He looked over towards Ragnar, whose ship was almost abreast. Ragnar just smiled wryly as he nodded back. This is exactly what Ragnar would have expected. Vikings could command an army when needed and of this their enemy would soon be aware.

An area had been cleared to allow Leif's ships passage. When they sailed through the gauntlet of waiting ships, a tremendous cheer erupted at the arrival of their leader. Leif stood at the helm, he smiled, raising his axe high. The air began to vibrate with the echo of shouts of support from the many warriors, now ready for battle, and hungry for war.

Nigh on a hundred Viking ships left their shores that day. The crews of the trading ships watched in awe this large fleet as it sailed on, while thanking the Gods they themselves, and their people, would not be the ones to face such a forceful army.

The weather remained reasonably calm, with just enough wind to billow the sails. With the longest part of their journey completed, Leif was pleased at their progress. He looked back at the fleet of ships sailing close behind. He knew by their position it would not be long before they had sight of land. So at this point he pulled at the steering oar to change direction.

There would be no hugging the coast on this trip, he thought. He knew this number of ships could easily be spotted from land. What he didn't want, was for the enemy to be warned of his approaching army. So for as long as they were able, they would sail in deep waters, well out to sea. Leif was aware the further down the coast they travelled, the harder this would be to achieve. But by that time, any warning given would come too late for their enemy to amass a large force in defence. Above all things, he wanted his father's ship and the crew who now sailed in her. To achieve this, he was determined nothing be allowed to stand in his way.

Leaving the shallower water behind, Leif steered the fleet well out to sea. The further out they sailed, the rougher the water became. The boats began to pitch and toss on the ever increasing swell of the waves. Leif looked over with some concern at Toork. The rough weather would not affect the Vikings he knew, they were all hardy sailors, the sea was in their blood, but what he did not need was an ailing Toork. Toork looked back at Leif, knowing what he was thinking. Smiling, he lifted the phial from his pouch and took a swig. Another of Kelda's potions, Leif thought, as he smiled back. He could only hope that it worked.

Leif however was soon assured of the potions properties, when sometime later, he looked across to see Toork curled up with his cloak wrapped around him. He smiled to himself when he saw Toork was sound asleep. Leif hoped he would stay that way for some time, and be able to cope until they reached the shelter of land where the water would be much calmer.

The boats covered the distance swiftly, aided by gusting winds billowing at the sails, keeping them taut. The crews took turns and worked in shifts. The days soon passed, and before long, they were making their way down the east coast to the place where Leif would pick up Sweyn and the men. The weather had indeed improved the further down the coast they sailed, much to Toork's relief. He had been glad of Kelda's potion, which had made him sleep for most of the journey, but now, as the boat sailed in calmer waters, he felt better. He had joined Olaf to sit with him at the stern of the ship. He had just finished eating when he saw Leif raise his arms to signal the boats to anchor. Leif's boat, accompanied by Ragnar's, then turned their sails to head towards land.

The trip inland was short and not too far. Before long, the crews were lowering the sails and taking to the oars to row the boats ashore. As they approached, they could see Sweyn and the others waving from the beach. They could also see a small gathering of people, but they stood further back.

Both boats ground to a halt on the shingle. Leif, Ragnar and some of the men jumped ashore. Sweyn smiled as he looked at his father and Leif, but he saw they were not looking at him, but studying the people who stood behind. Leif nodded to his men, and suddenly, raising their shields, they began to advance. The smile quickly left Sweyn's face. He swung round and spread out his arms as he shouted to the men, "What are you doing?" The men halted. Sweyn then swung back to look at Leif in question.

Leif's face remained impassive. It was absent of any emotion as he said flatly to Sweyn, "They wear the cross." Sweyn drew in his breath, then said with a nod of agreement, "Yes, that they do, but nevertheless, these are good people." Sweyn then began to speak urgently, trying to get his message through to Leif. "These people have explained to us the wearing of the cross in itself does not make you a Christian, just the same as donning a pair of fur boots and a helmet," he said forcefully, "would not make them Vikings. A Christian," he carried on saying, "to them, is someone who treats his fellow man with kindness and respect. This has been proved by their treatment of us in the months we have lived among them. They have been shocked at the acts of murder carried out, by others, in the name of their faith. That is why they have helped us gain information on the whereabouts of our ship. These people," he went on to say, "have fed us and sheltered us, for the whole of the winter. I will not have their hospitality repaid in this way."

Leif turned his head slowly to look at Ragnar. Ragnar just raised his eyebrows and stayed silent. Sweyn, Leif knew, was not a fool. He had always been a good judge of character and Leif had no reason to doubt him now. If Sweyn felt protective towards these Christians who had sheltered them, so be it, Leif thought. He motioned to his men to stand down. Leif himself then approached the small crowd. He took from his waist a pouch, and pouring some gold coins into his hand, he offered them to an elder. "Take this in payment for helping my men," he said holding out his hand. The old man shook his head, while saying there was no payment necessary, but Leif insisted. "Take it and give it to any of your people who need it, and let it be known that Vikings always pay their debts."

Leif then turned away to walk back to the ship. Sweyn and two of the men followed, but the other pair ran back to say goodbye to two young women who stood to the side of the group. Leif looked over and noticed the women were pretty young things. Their actions were very demure, he thought wryly, but they were pretty young things nonetheless. Sweyn boarded with Leif so he could direct him to where his father's ship was berthed. The two men with him jumped aboard Ragnar's ship. Sweyn then called out to the others to make haste and they left the women to run back to board with Leif.

The crews on the ships waiting out at sea had taken this time to rest and eat. Some had cast lines over the side in order to catch fish. When they saw the two ships returning, they began drawing in their lines. They hurriedly prepared for sail.

Sweyn, on the journey back, explained to Leif all what he had managed to find out about their missing ship and about the men who had taken her. Their ship was at that moment berthed at the head of a river. To reach her they would have to sail its length. There was a bastion filled with men at this port he stated with some concern. They would probably have to attack their defences in order to retake their ship. He had also learned these men were in the employ of a lord who had lands further down the coast. He had forces and a fortification there too, which they would have to face if they wanted to attack. Leif nodded thoughtfully and told Sweyn this would not be a problem. Sweyn was puzzled at Leif's lack of concern, but when they neared the flotilla of ships, Sweyn stood up for a better view. He drew in his breath and grinned, now understanding, when seeing the number of ships waiting at sea.

Most of the ships had roped themselves together while waiting for Leif and Ragnar to return. Leif was able to spread word they would continue to sail down the east coast, to where they were going to rout out their enemies. He told them what they would probably find when they reached their destination. A resounding cheer went up from all the men aboard the many ships. Being weary of days spent at sea on cramped ships, they were eager to stretch their legs and for the battle to begin. Leif then told them to follow his lead. On the journey down, he would work out how and when they would carry out their attack. A further cheer went up. Leif grinned, waiting until all the ropes were cast before giving the signal for the ships to sail on.

It was mid afternoon the following day when Leif called out to Ragnar to issue the order for all ships to drop anchor. They would wait until dusk before heading for land, he stated. It would be nightfall before they reached the mouth of the river and they could proceed upriver unseen, cloaked by the darkness the night would bring. Ragnar was to relate to the crews that once there, they would rope the ships together, to allow the men to move ashore. However, he told Ragnar urgently, he wanted some of the boats to surround his father's ship. He told him to pick men who could go aboard to capture alive any crew remaining on the ship. These men were not, he stressed not, to be killed, but were to be taken ashore and kept captive until he himself returned from battle.

Ragnar then waved for all the ships to stop. Leif's orders were relayed and passed on from ship to ship. Ragnar appointed the boats and crews to deal with Leif's father's ship, and word was spread the rest of the ships were to rope together, so the men could follow the leaders ashore. With everyone aware of the plan now in force, all the crews anchored.

To pass the time they settled down for a few hours sleep.

In the silence that ensued, Olaf found sleep to be evasive. He lay stretched out, his thoughts focused on Fraida. He could picture her smiling face. His heart was heavy, because all he wanted to do was hold her close in the safety of his arms. However, that was something he would never again be able to do, he thought with despair. He sighed deeply, he missed her so much. Tears from the deep grief he carried, sprung to his eyes. He hoped wherever she was she could look down to see the revenge they would wreak against those who had robbed her, and the baby, of their young lives. It would not bring his daughter and grandson back, he knew, but on the other hand, he thought angrily; he would have the satisfaction of knowing by putting paid to these murdering savages, it would prevent them from carrying out the same crime against others.

At the setting of the sun the ships prepared to sail. It was nightfall when the boats, with the men at the oars, reached the mouth of the river. Cloaked by darkness, they slipped unseen into the river mouth. They rowed steadily, in unison, not rushing, preferring to conserve their energy for the battle ahead.

Everyone took a turn at the oars until the leading ships reached the head of the river. Leif, as he looked over at the outline of his father's ship, felt a jolt in his heart as he gazed upon it for the first time since it had left their shores all those years ago. As they silently rowed passed, he could visualise his father standing at the helm. Anger rose up to overwhelm him. He had a strong urge to jump aboard and put paid to those who slept within her, right now. But he had to overcome that urge, because he knew he had a battle to lead before he could be afforded that pleasure.

The first boats moored wherever they could find space. Everyone worked in silence, roping together the boats now gliding in to berth at either side. Vikings were the masters of stealth. All the men stepped carefully from boat to boat until they managed to reach the shore. No one stirred within this place; they all slept on, unaware as they were of the size of the invading force now standing in darkness on their very shores.

Leif waited with Ragnar, then he raised his sword in signal. Both watched the appointed men swarm onto his father's ship. They remained watching until they could see the silhouettes of the crew onboard being captured, and with knives held close to their throats, they remained silent. Leif watched until they were led ashore. Then, being satisfied his orders had been carried out, Leif turned and waved for the rest of the men to follow on.

Leif, Toork, Ragnar, and Olaf led the men forward. On Ragnar's direction, some slipped ahead to deal with the guards that would be at the gates. They entered the open courtyard unhindered. After looking around, checking their way was clear, they crept quietly forward towards two large, wooden doors, which barred them entry to the bastion.

Men formed in a line to position themselves to ram the doors, when suddenly, a shout came from the turrets. The guards who were inside, at the sound of the alarm, threw open the doors. They stood for a minute, stunned, looking straight into the faces of the Viking force standing right at their door. Leif grinned wryly, the smile never reaching his eyes. Their shock turned to horror and they immediately pushed at the doors, trying to close them, but it was too late. Leif and the men pushed forward, sweeping the guards out of their way, swiftly striking them down.

All hell broke loose when the guards in the turrets began shouting out in alarm. The Vikings looked to each other and smiled when men, armed and half dressed, came rushing from rooms to run down the staircases. Leif and Ragnar grinned at each other, then raising their swords, they went forward into battle. In that second, Toork remembered his promise to Fraida, to protect Leif. Turning to Hakon, he pointed to Leif, then he pointed to himself then Olaf; motioning he would protect Olaf if Hakon protected Leif. Hakon grunted and nodded, showing he understood. Hakon then pushed Leif out of the way so he could stand before him. Leif frowned and gritted his teeth in anger. He looked over at Ragnar in consternation, but Ragnar just shrugged and laughed back. Leif tried to push Hakon out of his way, but Hakon was having none of it. So Leif began to strike out at the enemy who were advancing from the side. The room soon filled with the sound of clashing swords and grinding axes. Men swarmed in from all directions. This enemy however, soon found no one fought fiercer than those who were not afraid to die. Some who fought in this battle, through grief, would at this moment in time, welcome death.

Toork's moves, long practiced, were precise and accurate. Both swords swung continuously, quicker than the eye could see. His body swung round, at times he extended his leg, bringing his opponents down, then using his swords he finished them off. Olaf, who was not a small man, blinded by anger at the loss of his daughter, used all his brute strength to bring his sword crashing down, putting paid to all who stood in his path. The enemy were further frustrated by Hakon, when they found no way of advancing from that part of the room. They were hemmed in, because this giant of a man, with his large swinging axe, took down anyone who tried to break through.

The battle between the opposing forces went into full swing. But each Viking, eager to show his prowess in battle, fought fiercely, easily outwitting their enemy. Leif had his sword in one hand and his axe in the other. With all the force he could muster, he struck men down, for his father, for Jon, for Fraida, and for his son Olaf, who had been robbed of the opportunity to grow into manhood; where he could have stood proudly at his father's side in any future battle.

Leif fought on. Suddenly, over the noise of the mayhem, he began to hear a voice calling his name. This puzzled him. While keeping his eye on the enemy before him, he took whatever chance there was to look around. He tried to locate where the voice was coming from, but he couldn't quite locate the area. Then the one voice turned to two, they were urgently calling his name. He swung his head round to look down behind him, at the top part of a wooden grid. He saw a face staring up at him and an arm waving urgently through the slats. The man was calling his name, but Leif did not recognise him and wondered how this could be so.

Leif then called out to Ragnar. He signalled for him to work his way over and to bring some men as a defence, so he could stop fighting long enough to investigate who this person was. Leif brought his axe down on the neck of the man before him, and as he sank to his knees and toppled over, Leif took the opportunity to again glance round. That was when he saw not one face, but two. The two faces were identical. As Leif looked into familiar eyes, he gasped in shock and said to himself, this could not be!

Ragnar reached Leif's side. Leif told him urgently to tell the men to form a defence around them both. Ragnar looked in puzzlement at Leif, but did what he asked nonetheless. When the men were in place, Leif grabbed Ragnar's arm and he swung him round and pointed down. Ragnar looked down at the two faces for some seconds before exclaiming, "By the gods, this cannot be!" He was stunned. He too now recognised Kelda's twins. "We thought you were dead!" he called out to the two, now smiling, faces. Leif shouted urgently to, "stand well back!" Grabbing Hakon's arm, Leif told him to swing his axe at the wooden grid. Hakon, not knowing what was down there, did not falter in his swing. He smashed the grid into bits, before immediately turning to swing back at the enemy.

Leif and Ragnar both put their arms down to grip the twins, hauling them up. Leif looked in wonder at the two boys, who had now grown to be men. Shadows were present under their sunken eyes. Their lovely golden hair was dank and unkempt, but their smiles were the same as always. Tears came to Leif's eyes. In the middle of all the mayhem surrounding them, he gripped them both in a tight hug. "We have waited a long time for your father to come and get us," they said to Leif as they looked around, "and our father too. Where are they?" they said as their eyes searched the room.

Leif looked over at Ragnar. For the first time it dawned on them, the twins did not know. "My father is dead," said Leif reluctantly, not wanting to be the bearer of this bad news. "And ours?" the twins questioned. Leif hesitated for a moment before saying, "He, unfortunately, is also dead," and he saw tears spring to the twins eyes as they questioned, "Jon?"

"Everyone who sailed on the ship was ambushed and slaughtered" Leif said with a lump in his throat. The twins looked at each other and shook their heads in denial. They were hardly able to believe what they were hearing. "We thought you were dead too," Leif said to them, but the twins then explained they had been left aboard the ship to keep watch. Then, that very night, the ship had been overrun with men and they themselves had been taken captive and brought here as slaves.

Rage suddenly swept through Leif. It overwhelmed him when he thought of the years the twins had suffered at the hands of these men. "Our poor mother, what of her?" the twins questioned. "Your mother is fine, heartbroken but fine. We have looked after her," said Leif in reply. "Give us a weapon," one of the twins said urgently to Leif, "so we can avenge our father!" Leif looked over at Ragnar, he hesitated before saying, "I don't want to risk your lives now that we have found you. Your mother would never forgive me, if after having found you, I then let you die in battle." "We still know how to fight, and you cannot deny us the chance we now have to take our revenge" they said staunchly. Leif could see they were determined to brook no argument. Leif thought for a moment. He knew how important it was for the twins to feel they would, in part, avenge the death of their father. So giving in, he said, "Only if you stay close to Ragnar and myself." He then handed one of them his axe. Ragnar gave the other his sword. Swinging round, all four, now eager to make this enemy pay, pushed through the line of defence in order to join in the battle.

The twins did indeed remember how to fight, Leif thought, as they battled on. Their work as slaves had strengthened their muscles and they had grown to be strong men. Ragnar, while still keeping one eye out for the twins who were fighting fiercely at their side, smiled over at Leif and said, above the noise, "Kelda was right. We were wrong, they were still alive!"

All the men, as they continued to fight on, looked out for any sign of the earless man, because they had been warned he belonged to Leif. However, it was now clear, as the battle drew to a close and many began lowering their weapons, that the man had not been in the midst of this lot. Leif looked around despondently. He could now only hope he was one of the men who had been taken captive from his father's ship, he thought grimly.

A group of his men left to search the fortification, to ensure it was now clear of the enemy. Those who had known the twins, exclaimed in disbelief at their sudden appearance. They gathered round to hug and heartily clap them on the back. Leif smiled to himself and thought from all this carnage had come some good; the unexpected recovery of the much loved twins. He was elated to discover they were still alive. It was something of worth to carry away from this evil place.

The routing men then returned, herding a group of captives, but the twins piped up they were all slaves, so Leif strolled over and looking them up and down he said, "We need food, lots of food. If you go to the kitchens to cook all you can find, then after I will allow you to be free, to go wherever you will." The group, not being able to believe their luck, all nodded eagerly. They quickly returned to the kitchens to do this small task in return for their, much longed for, freedom. Leif then told his men to search the fortification for loot, room to room, and to bring back all they could unearth. Turning, he asked Ragnar to fetch the men they had taken from his father's ship. He could wait no longer, he said to Ragnar impatiently, because he was eager to see if the earless man was among them.

Leif laughed, along with his men, as they stood looking down at various chests filled with gold coins. At jewellery studied with precious gems, and at the mound of gold and silver goblets they had easily unearthed in their search. The enemy had not had time to hide these treasures, the men said, while laughing heartily, because of the suddenness of their surprise attack.

At that point, Ragnar returned with a big grin on his face. Leif's heart lightened, knowing it could only mean one thing. He walked out into the courtyard, to where the captives now stood surrounded by his men. Olaf and Toork followed at his back. Leif looked over at the large, ugly man, who had been singled out, who now stood apart from the rest. At the sight of the earless man, all the rage and anger Toork had struggled to suppress, now erupted. He was unable to stop himself from rushing over. Olaf was close behind. Grabbing the man by the neck, Toork forcefully thrust the withered ear into his face. Toork moved to draw his sword and at the same time Olaf angrily raised his, but Ragnar and some of the men quickly leapt forward, pulling Toork and Olaf back. Leif looked at both their enraged faces before telling them he was sorry, but this was one man who was definitely his.

Leif walked slowly over. Remaining silent, it was with disdain, he looked him up and down. This, at last, he thought, was the man who had robbed him of his wife and son. Anger raged within Leif. He had to breathe deeply in order to remain in control. Taking his axe and his sword from his belt, he turned to Ragnar and told him to give this killer of women and children weapons. Ragnar frowned, looking at Leif in question. Leif's reply was quiet but menacing. "I don't want to just kill him; I want to defeat him and to bring him to his knees!" Ragnar slowly shook his head, looking at the size of the man before turning his back and saying quietly to Leif, "Are you sure about this?" "I have never been more sure of anything in my life" Leif said grittily in reply. "Give the dog weapons and lets see what he is like when faced with a man," he repeated forcefully.

Toork, Olaf and Ragnar, surrounded by the men, stood to the side watching, as Leif and the earless man circled each other. A wry smile slowly spread across Leif's face. The earless man began to feel on edge. Leif calmly flexed his wrist, playing with his axe. Then suddenly, without warning, he lunged forward; quick as a flash, using his sword, he cut the man's leg. The earless man had not seen the move coming, so he lunged back at Leif. This time, Leif swung round behind him to slash at his back. The large man grunted and turned. As he was turning, Leif slashed at his arm. Now enraged, the man came at Leif. Both swords met with a clang. They began fighting fiercely and it was with tremendous force the two swords clashed.

Eventually they became entangled; as both bodies met, the earless man tried to bear hug Leif. But Leif, using one of the techniques Fraida had shown him, brought his leg round and the man toppled to the ground. The man lay looking up from the floor, but still Leif did not go in for the kill. He circled, allowing the bleeding man time to get to his feet. Leif carried on for some time, playing with the man, using every given opportunity to inflict more wounds. The earless man, in one last desperate bid, came running angrily towards Leif. At this point, Leif dropped his own sword and quickly grabbed Fraida's from his belt. Leif brought his axe down on the man's neck, to pull him forward, at the same time he thrust Fraida's sword, with all the force he could muster, home. The man then staggered back. Leif's axe was left in his hand, but this was the moment Toork and Ragnar had been waiting for. Ragnar threw the axe that had killed Fraida and it embedded itself deep in the man's back. As he fell to his knees, Toork rushed forward and raising both swords, he brought them down with all the force his strength would allow. The man's head immediately detached from his body and as the onlookers gasped, it fell to the floor and rolled on the ground.

Leif stood, breathing heavily. He felt no remorse as he looked down at the body on the floor. All the men cheered when Leif bent to remove Fraida's sword, but although he was satisfied he had now killed this man, and his body would no longer walk on this earth, it did not ease his pain. It would not bring Fraida and Olaf back. Nothing he did, he knew, could ever bring his Fraida back to him. "Let your God help you now," he said in disgust, to the body, before turning to slowly walk away. Ragnar then nodded to the rest of the men to dispose of the other crew members, who were also killers of women and children. Then putting his arms around Toork and Olaf's shoulders, he led them to follow Leif.

This stronghold held plenty of food and drink. The men feasted well that night, celebrating their victory. Leif, as they all sat drinking, told his merry warriors they would rest here for a couple of days, then sail further down the coast to confront the Lord under whose pay these men had been employed; along with what was left of his army. This would give them time to reorganise, to work out some sort of strategy, before entering into yet another battle. "It could also though," Leif said wryly with a smile, "give this Lord time to amass more troops." But one of the men shouted, "The more the merrier," and Leif laughed heartily when all the men raised their horns to cheer in agreement.

The following day, the grey sky turned to blue. It felt warmer in the filtering heat from the rising sun. Leif had the men swill down his father's ship. They scrubbed the decks to rid it of the build up of filth caused by the barbarians. Vikings, unlike those who had taken her, always looked after their ships. They prided themselves in keeping them in pristine condition. Leif took from one of the other ships a sail, in his father's colours, and the old sail was taken down and the new one hoisted. Leif, as he and Ragnar looked around the drying ship, then ordered the loot they had taken be stored aboard, along with the men who were wounded. He insisted the twins, who argued fervently against it, also stayed aboard this ship. He would not risk them again, he said. Their mother had suffered enough. He wanted to be able to, at the very least, bring a smile back to her face. His fathers boat, Leif had decided, would remain at the back of the fleet. It would not go into battle. It was a knorr ship with plenty of room for storage, and Leif told the men to take all the furniture in the stronghold, and to put it aboard the ship. The strong tables, chairs, and benches, would be put to good use at home. Ragnar then picked some of the older men as crew. Although the twins were not pleased, and tried to plead with Ragnar, he would not go against Leif's orders.

Early next morning, all the remaining food and drink was distributed between the ships. After ensuring everyone was safely aboard, the ropes were cast and the sails hoisted. Once again they put to sea. The men's spirits were high from their victory. They were eager for battle. But even with the wind in their sails, it was the morning of the following day before they reached the mouth of the second river.

It was at this point, Olaf told Leif he himself wanted to be the one to take the lead in this forthcoming battle. He put forward his argument to Leif that he had allowed him to take his revenge, single-handedly, against the killer of Fraida and the baby. But now he wanted his revenge, against the Lord who had been responsible for all that had gone before. Leif looked over at Toork, who, on hearing Olaf state this, now sat with a slight frown on his face. Leif thought of Fraida. He knew she would not wish for her father to be put in any danger, but he did not know how he could possibly refuse this request. Leif thought for a moment, then looking first at Toork, then at Olaf, he said, "I will only agree to this on one condition and that is if you will allow us to stand and fight at your side." Olaf hesitated, then nodded, and said he would find that acceptable.

The river was wide enough for a number of the boats to sail abreast. Leif sat back to allow Olaf the honour of standing at the prow, to lead the fleet in. The ships drew into the estuary and they stopped and anchored at a small Island. Leif slowly stood to look at the army, who were ready and waiting, lined along the opposite shore. This came as no surprise: he had half expected this, knowing full well their delay would inevitably allow time for a warning of their presence to reach the area. Leif looked over at Toork and then across at Ragnar. Both just raised their eyebrows at the sight of the waiting army. Olaf stood at the prow. Taking out his sword, he held it high, so the enemy could see him. Ragnar and Toork grinned over at Leif. Heartened by Olaf's courage, they were now ready for war.

Ragnar's boat moved closer to Leif's, so Ragnar could jump aboard. He, as well as the rest of the men, could see they had a problem. Leading from this Island was a small causeway, which would allow only two men abreast, at the most, to cross. This would give the opposing army a great advantage. They would be able to pick the men off, one by one, before they even had a chance to reach land. However, the army who stood on the other side had not taken into account the Vikings shallow bottomed boats.

The men on Leif's ship huddled together while discussing their battle plan. They would wait until the water was at its highest point, then would move as many of their ships abreast as they could. The first ships would move forward in a line, closely followed by the others. The men on the ships out in front would hold up their shields as a barrier to any arrows and spears that were likely to be thrown. The ships that were behind, would at the same time, launch arrows and spears, allowing time for the first ships to make it to the shore. The first men to jump ashore would engage with the enemy. This would allow time for the second wave of ships to reach land.

Everyone was in agreement this would be the best way forward, so

Leif then turned to tell Hakon to fetch his spear. It was customary for Vikings, before a large battle, to throw a spear. If the spear landed behind enemy lines, then that enemy was claimed for Odin and they would be the victors. It was a good distance, Leif thought, while looking over, but if the Gods were with them, it would reach its mark.

Leif watched as Hakon removed the pins that attached the head of the spear to the shaft. This was to stop the spear being thrown back, as any attempt to remove it from the ground would result in the head separating from the shaft. Everyone watched as Hakon stood at the prow to take aim, then he threw the spear with all the strength he could muster. The spear flew through the air, covering the distance with ease. As it landed behind enemy lines, all the men cheered when they saw the troops jump in order to avoid it. This tradition however, was unknown to the men standing on the other side. They, seeing this as the first weapon to be deployed, launched their own spears in retaliation. None of which came anywhere near Leif's ships.

It was another hour before Leif and Ragnar deemed the water to be deep enough for the ships to proceed. Ragnar directed the boats into position, pulling forward the ships he had chosen for the front line. He had his best fighting men on these ships. They would need to be strong to hold back the enemy until the others reached the shore. The ships began moving forward. The men crouched down, but they raised their shields to form a protection for the men at the oars. Ragnar had joined Leif on his ship, because he too wanted to protect Olaf. Being the leader in this battle, it would take all of them to form a barrier around him, so they could keep him safe.

The men who crouched in the first line of ships felt their shields vibrate from the barrage of arrows and spears now raining down. They held on tight with both hands. The distance was short, and when the boats ground to a halt the men, keeping their shields up, all jumped ashore. Olaf went rushing in with his sword raised and almost immediately began striking men down. He fought hard, but at the same time, he continuously cast his eyes around, trying to locate the area of this infamous Lord.

It took little time for all the ships to cross. As they ground to a halt on the shore, the Vikings pushed forward, in formation, to break through the enemy lines. It was only then Olaf managed to catch sight of what he knew must be the Lord, by the manner of his dress, and all his rage and anger rose up to overwhelm him. Olaf, without hesitation, turned to grab a spear from the nearest man. He took time to aim, then threw the spear with all his might. The Gods were with him, Olaf thought, when he saw his spear hit its mark. It lodged in the battling Lords throat. Olaf watched with satisfaction, the leader of the enemy sink slowly to the ground. The men nearest to Olaf were astounded at his marksmanship, they all cheered him. The enemy force however, were shocked and devastated at the loss of their leader so early in the battle. But being surrounded by Vikings, they could do nothing but put their heads down and fight on.

The battling continued. Leif, as he fearlessly advanced, could see some of this enemy force were highly trained fighting men, but then, he thought with a smile, so were the Vikings. He found he was enjoying the challenge of coming up against men who knew how to fight. He brought forth all his own fighting skills in order to defeat them.

Some of the men on the opposing side, seeing the disarray within their own troops, could now sense defeat. They took to their heels and ran, soon there was no one left for Leif's men to fight. The men then rushed over to aid Leif, but he motioned for them to stay back. Ragnar, himself, Toork, Olaf and Hakon, and a few of Ragnar's right hand men, were enjoying battling with this band of highly trained men. The band of men continued to fight valiantly, but it was to no avail, Leif and the others were more than a match for them. At this point, neither side were willing to give an inch.

However, soon the battle was over. As the last man fell, only the Vikings were left standing to celebrate a victory. Leif, as he lowered his sword, stood back for a few minutes to catch his breath. He patted Ragnar and the others on the back, while saying breathlessly, "they had fought well."

Leif then led everyone to the stronghold, where they proceeded to loot; taking everything within sight. They did not tarry at this place, preferring instead to carry it back to the ships. They took all the food, ale, and wine they could find. They rowed back to the island. Leif had all the food and drink quickly distributed among the ships, but he told them they would eat as they sailed and leave this place, in case any reinforcements were advancing from other areas. They had battled enough for this day, he told them with a smile. All the men cheered at their victory. Then grinning and talking to each other of the battle they had fought, they set about raising the sails.

The weather in the few days that followed, was calm and warm. As the ships sailed up the coast, the two men who had remained for the winter with Sweyn in this land, now approached Leif. They explained to him they wanted to be dropped off at the place where he had picked them up. They had fallen in love with the two Christian girls and they wanted to wed. As the girls had refused to leave their home, they had both decided to remain here, with the girls and their families.

Leif was not sure if it was safe for them to remain in this land, he told them this, but they assured him they would be safe with these people. Leif thought about it. He thought of Fraida and of the time when they had first met. It would not have mattered to him, he had to admit to himself, if she had been of a different culture or religion, because he would have wanted her, regardless.

Giving in, he nodded to the two young men. "So be it," he said to them both, and they started to smile. Taking two pouches of gold from his belt, Leif handed one to each man. "This will help in your new life here. Buy yourselves some land, build yourselves houses," he said with a smile, "and always remember if things don't work out, you can always return to your home."

All the ships waited at sea while Leif's ship sailed to shore, to the place where he would drop the men off. The place was deserted, but they assured Leif, as they jumped from the boat, they would soon make their way back in safety, to where their girls and these people lived. Leif shook them by the hand. He wished them well, and as his boat sailed away, he waved back at the two solitary figures. He was saddened to be leaving his men behind. But they were happy, this was what they wanted. That was what mattered most, Leif thought to himself. Shrugging, he turned away.

Leif's ship soon joined with the others. As they set sail, Leif began to think of the next time they would drop anchor. That would not be until they reached home. For the first time in his life though, this thought gave him no pleasure. Although he missed Rayna, this was overtaken by the painful realisation there would be no smiling Fraida, with the baby in her arms, and Dalgar by her side, waiting to greet him. He drew his hand over his face tiredly. Wondering to himself how he was going to face the future without her. He had to think of Rayna, he told himself, because she was also suffering from the loss of her mother and brother. But he was finding it very hard at this moment, to go beyond his own grief and pain. He looked up then, over at Toork and Olaf, only to see they too seemed, by the looks on their faces, to be steeped in thoughts of what they had all lost. Knowing they had many long days of their journey still ahead, he decided what they needed was something to take them from their reverie. Standing up, he said loudly with a smile, "Let's all have a drink!"

A fishing boat, with some of the older men from the settlement on board, had been casting their nets in the bay, when suddenly, their eyes were drawn to a large, dark shape far away on the horizon. They studied it for some minutes in puzzlement. Then, realising what this dark shape would be, smiling at each other, they began rushing about hauling in their nets. Turning the boat they made their way quickly back to shore. They didn't wait to dock before shouting to everyone, "Our ships are coming, they are still far out at sea, but nearing home."

Everyone who heard, started to cheer. They themselves ran quickly about spreading word throughout the settlement. The fishermen left their catch where it was, and made their way to the large outdoor fires to set them alight. They had carcasses of boar, cow and deer already hanging to drain, intending to butcher them to steep in brine, so the meat could be used in the winter months. Now they would put them on spits over the open fires, and there would be freshly roasted meat to feed the returning army.

Everyone began rushing about in excitement. The older men sent some of the children down to their boat with baskets. Telling them to fill the baskets with their catch and carry the fish to the longhouses so the women could cook them on the fires there. The servant women quickly built up the fires in the dwellings and pots of vegetables were put on to boil. The other women began to bake fresh bread. There was a plentiful supply of butter and cheese stored in the cool of the sheds, away from the warmth of the sun. Everyone moved about quickly, setting things in place, because by the time the boats reached the shores, they wanted a feast almost prepared for the returning men.

When land was in sight, Leif halted the boats. Signalling to his father's ship to sail up front. He wanted this ship to be the first his people would see. With that, they would know they had wreaked their revenge on the enemy and recovered their missing ship. When the ship drew abreast, Leif boarded her and stood at the helm with a twin at each side. Tears started to spill from the eyes of the twins when they looked, at last, on the shores of their home. Their years in captivity had been long in passing. Both had almost given up hope this day would ever come. They watched from the ship as people gathered on the shore. Their tears flowed faster, knowing their mother, who they had missed so much, would be one of the people who stood waiting for the ships to berth.

Kelda had been out with Rayna when they spotted the ships out at sea. Rayna had shouted excitedly and jumped up and down," Papa is coming, Papa is coming," then grabbing Kelda's hand, they both, as quickly as they could, rushed home. Vaila had changed and brushed her own hair before they reached the dwelling. Grabbing them both, she rushed them indoors. She quickly changed Rayna, putting on a clean tunic, then brushed Rayna's hair, which had now grown longer. As she looked down at the child, it felt like she was looking at a miniature of Fraida. A lump came into her throat, then she smiled as she hugged the excited child before turning to a grinning Kelda. Vaila sat Kelda down so she could wash her face and brush her tangled hair. Then standing her up, she straightened her tunic, fixing the brooches at her shoulders. Looking them both over and being satisfied, Vaila then said, "Right, let us now go down to the dock to wait for the ships."

As the boats drew near, tears sprung to the eyes of both Vaila and Kelda when they saw out in the lead, Leif's father's ship. Through the mist of her tears, Kelda gasped when she thought she saw her twins at Leif's side. She rubbed her eyes and shook her head. But when she looked back, she could see they were still there. Kelda thought she was the only one who could see them. As she studied them she could see, although they were taller and older, they were, nevertheless, her sons. They had returned to her, be it only in spirit, she thought, to be forever at her side. Kelda now began to cry in earnest, deep wrenching sobs. Her heart ached for the loving sons she had lost. Rayna, unable to understand Kelda's sudden distress, put her arms comfortingly around the sobbing Kelda's hips. She said urgently, trying to placate her, "Don't cry Kelda, Papa is back, everything will be alright. Papa won't let anything bad happen Kelda," Rayna said in a reassuring way. Vaila, understanding in part the reason for Kelda's tears, also turned to put her arms around her.

All three being huddled together, did not see the twins jump from the docking ship. They ran towards their weeping mother, calling out to her, tears of joy streaming down their faces. Kelda looked up at the sound of their voices. She began to feel faint at the sight of them before her very eyes. She sunk to her knees just as the boys reached her. They scooped her up and held her tight. They cried out at the pain etched in her much aged face. They spoke to her tenderly, while touching her hair and face, saying, "It's all right now Mamma, we are back, we will take care of you, we know Papa is gone, but we are both here now and we will look after you always."

Kelda looked back dazedly, unsmiling, into both their faces and she hoped this was not a dream. She looked over at Leif who now stood before her. "We found them Kelda," Leif said quietly and with a smile. "We found your boys and we brought them back to you." Kelda then came out of her trance. Running over to Leif, she hugged him. A lump came into his throat as he watched her smile radiantly through her tears, before turning to clutch at both her sons. "I knew you were not dead," she exclaimed. "I never gave up hope that you would return to me," she said, kissing and hugging them both. Everyone who had been watching had been puzzled and very surprised at the sudden appearance of the missing twins, and they cried with happiness at the scene before them. Now however, they all cheered and surged forward, wanting to welcome the boys back home.

Vaila looked over to where Leif stood. She could see, although he was smiling, the smile did not reach his eyes. She watched him as he looked forlornly around. Her heart ached for him, knowing only too well the great sadness he still carried within. Then Rayna, who had been standing looking with much puzzlement at these two men who had called Kelda Mamma, turned to look at her father. She rushed across, calling out his name. He swooped her up and held her high in his arms, before bringing her down and hugging her tight. Her little arms clung to his neck as she kissed his cheeks. Looking at her, Leif's heart missed a beat, because he could see his Fraida in her little face. He still had part of her here, he thought, and he struggled to hold back the tears.

Then the moment was gone as Olaf bellowed, "Where is my granddaughter!" and Rayna looked over to see her grandfather and Toork beckoning to her. Leif put her down and watched as she eagerly ran towards them. Leif then turned to look over at Vaila, who was standing on her own. She looked quite pale he thought, smiling at her. He walked over and kissed her on the cheek, then asked if everything had been alright in their absence. She nodded as she smiled back. Then both turned together to walk back to Leif's dwelling. Leif told her on the way about how they had found the twins.

All the crews on board the ships came ashore to eat. Some however, did not want to stay on for the feasting, because they knew they had fallen behind with the work waiting for them at home, so they said, somewhat reluctantly, they had better be on their way. Leif insisted they waited until all the spoils had been unloaded from the ships, then he divided it equally. He gave each group, some gold and furniture, to take back with them as presents for their people. Then everyone stood waving as they sailed away.

Over the next few days, some of the other boats left to go home. By the end of the week, they stood at the docks to wave the last one goodbye. Leif, Olaf and Toork turned to look at the settlement which now seemed empty. Only Olaf's ships now remained in the bay and he said after a few days rest, he too, would have to return to his people, to get things back in order, as he had stayed away far too long.

The settlement over the following days grew quiet. Everyone just sat talking, and resting, while absorbing the warmth of the early summer sun. Kelda was like a different person, now having her sons always at her side. But she still came down to take Rayna, Volga and the pups out with her each day, even if only for a little while. Leif had explained to Rayna about Kelda's sons. Rayna smiled as she told her father she was happy Kelda now had a family too. It would mean Kelda need not be lonely in the long winter months when she could not get out and about. Leif had smiled at his daughter's enthusiasm for this turn of events and he had hugged her close.

Kelda's twins were very taken with this little girl, who they could see had brought much happiness to their mother when she had been so grief-stricken and alone. On some of the days they accompanied Kelda, and would play with the pups as they all walked along. The twins were saddened the child and Leif had also suffered so much grief. Losing a wife, mother, son and brother, they themselves had not even had the chance to meet. With the loss of so many loved ones, the settlement was very different to what it had been when they were last at home. There was a sadness throughout, they thought, that would take many years to heal.

After Olaf's departure, Leif began to find it difficult to get through the days. The weather was warm and calm, but he wandered about aimlessly and without purpose, feeling lost and alone. Everywhere reminded him of Fraida. His pain, which he thought would now ease, in fact increased. On one of the days, he tried to shake himself out of this heart wrenching grief that was pulling him down. He went to his work shed, with the intention of making a start on carving a new figurehead. However, as he chipped at the first piece of wood, the face of Dalgar came into his mind. He put his head down onto the hand that clasped the tool. His thoughts flew back to the day when Fraida had first caught sight of his carved figurehead of Dalgar. He thought of how pleased she had been. The vision he had of her smiling face wrenched at his heart. Dropping his tools despondently, he put his head in his hands and wept.

In the weeks that followed, Toork watched Leif with more than a little concern. Dark shadows had begun to appear under Leif's eyes. He seemed to have lost all the spirit with which he used to live. Toork watched him as he wandered aimlessly about. Lately he had noticed Leif had taken to standing up on the headland, for hours, just looking vacantly out to sea.

Toork knew Leif was not sleeping because most nights he would wake and hear Leif moving quietly about the dwelling. On one of those nights, Toork rose and went silently into Leif's room. Leif was sitting in front of Fraida's chair. Toork crossed the room, crouching down at Leif's side, he put his arm around Leif's shaking shoulders. Leif's face was wet from tears which streamed from his welled up eyes. "I can't stay here Toork," Leif said, shaking his head. "The pain is eating away at my very soul. I miss her so much," he said with a sob. "I have tried to stay because of Rayna, but what good am I to her like this? She senses my sadness and she too becomes sad, and that cannot go on. I have to go away," he carried on to say, "if only for a while."

Leif hesitated for a moment, then rubbing his hand roughly over his face he said, "I want to sail to new places, to go where the wind will take me. I need time away to allow the hurt to heal. My life will be forever dimmed with the pain of losing her. But I need to go away from here, where everything I see reminds me of her and of what I have lost." Leif then looked up at Toork and said, "If I was to go, I would have to ask you to stay, so you could look after and protect Rayna while I am gone. Would you be willing to do that for me?" Leif quietly questioned of Toork. Toork, with tears in his own eyes, nodded, then putting his big, dark arms round Leif, he hugged him tight. Toork then motioned for Leif to go to bed. He stood there until he saw him settled. Leif having got what he intended to do, off his chest, now managed to close his eyes. For the first time in a long time, he sunk slowly into a deep sleep.

The following day, Leif went to see Ragnar, to tell him of what he intended to do. Ragnar remained silent as Leif explained to him what he had told Toork. "I will only need one ship, with enough men for crew," Leif began to say, when Ragnar interrupted him. "No, you will need two ships," said Ragnar with a smile, "because where you go, I go, and where I go, my men go too." Leif smiled and protested that Ragnar had already spent too much time away from his home, but Ragnar shook his head. "I would be bored within a month if you were not here, and besides, I would have no peace as I would always be wondering where you were, and if you were unharmed." Then he said to Leif with a smile, clapping him on the back, "We will sail together on this new venture, or you don't go at all."

That afternoon they called for a meeting and gathered together all the men. Leif told them of his intended trip and asked for any man to step forward who would want to go with him. Hakon stood up before he had finished speaking, then all the men stood up. Leif looked at Ragnar, who was looking back at him with a grin. Leif then explained that, because he did not know how long he would be away, they would need some good men to stay behind to look after the settlement. A groan then went up as he carried on to say they would only choose for the most, the men who were single and unattached to make up the numbers required for a crew. Many of the married men complained, in a jocular manner, about being left behind. But in the hours that followed, they all came to a decision on who was best to sail with Leif on his forthcoming venture.

That evening, Leif then explained to Vaila what he intended to do, and the reasons why. Her heart began to sink. A lump came into her throat at the thought of him leaving once more, but she could understand why. This, she thought, as she held her stomach and thought of the life growing within, could be one way out of her predicament. She would not have to explain to Leif how she had managed to become pregnant. Avoiding for the moment, having to tell him of the night it happened.

The following day, the men began to prepare the ships. Leif took Rayna aside to tell her he was going away for a while. He told her Toork would stay with her, and Vaila, to look after her. She would see her Grandfather often as he would also come to visit. Rayna became tearful and Leif felt guilty at having to leave her. He explained how unhappy he was at not having her Mamma here. He said he was going away for a while, so he could become happy again. He would try to make it not too long, but when he returned things would hopefully be better for them both. This she then accepted with a nod of, somewhat, resignation.

A week later, Vaila stood again with Rayna at her side, watching the two ships as they prepared to sail. Toork stood to the side looking over at Vaila. He had noticed she had gained a little weight.

He watched her reactions closely, to see if what he suspected could be right. Leif then walked over to Toork and thanked him for what he was doing and he shook him by the hand. Toork pressed into Leif's hand a talisman made of silver. As Leif looked down at it he said, "I will keep it with me always." Then turning he went over to lift Rayna. Hugging her close, he kissed her goodbye. Kelda and the twins then joined Vaila and Rayna, and approaching Leif, Kelda handed him some potions and explained to him what they were for. Some were medicines in case they were wounded, one would make fire flare up whenever needed. Leif kissed her on the cheek as he thanked her. Then going over he also kissed Vaila on her cheek, while saying to her, "Look after Rayna for me."

Tears streamed from Vaila's eyes as she watched the boats sail away from their shores. Her heart ached and she wondered how long it would be before she would have sight of Leif again, but then her hands moved over her stomach. She gained some comfort from knowing what Leif did not, that part of him would still remain here, and it was growing strong within her.

THE END